JEFFREY ARCHER

THE CLIFTON CHRONICLES

VOLUME FOUR

BE CAREFUL WHAT YOU WISH FOR

PAN BOOKS

First published 2014 by Macmillan

This edition published 2014 by Pan Books
an imprint of Pan Macmillan, a division of Macmillan Publishers Limited
Pan Macmillan, 20 New Wharf Road, London N1 9RR
Basingstoke and Oxford
Associated companies throughout the world
www.panmacmillan.com

ISBN 978-1-4472-6509-2

1 3 5 7 9 8 6 4 2

A CIP catalogue record for this book is available from the British Library.

Typeset by Ellipsis Digital Limited, Glasgow
Printed and bound by Gopsons Papers Ltd

Visit www.panmacmillan.com to read more about all our books
and to buy them. You will also find features, author interviews and
news of any author events, and you can sign up for e-newsletters
so that you're always first to hear about our new releases.

TO

GWYNETH

My thanks go to the following
for their invaluable advice and research:

Simon Bainbridge, Eleanor Dryden,
Professor Ken Howard RA, Cormac Kinsella,
National Railway Museum, Bryan Organ,
Alison Prince, Mari Roberts, Dr Nick Robins,
Shu Ueyama, Susan Watt and Peter Watts.

THE BARRINGTONS

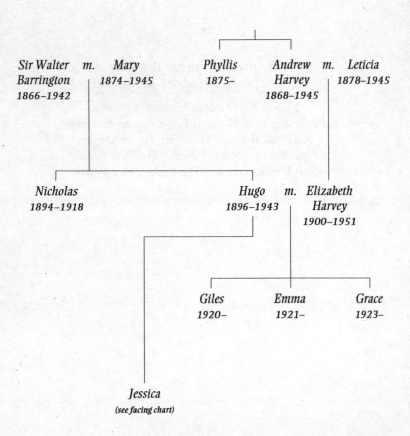

Sir Walter Barrington 1866–1942   m.   Mary 1874–1945

Phyllis 1875–

Andrew Harvey 1868–1945   m.   Leticia 1878–1945

Nicholas 1894–1918

Hugo 1896–1943   m.   Elizabeth Harvey 1900–1951

Giles 1920–

Emma 1921–

Grace 1923–

Jessica
(see facing chart)

THE CLIFTONS

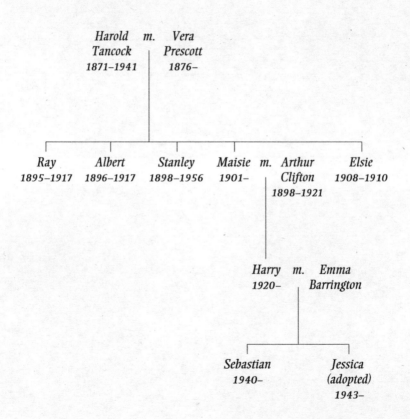

Harold Tancock *m.* Vera Prescott
1871–1941   1876–

Ray 1895–1917   Albert 1896–1917   Stanley 1898–1956   Maisie 1901– *m.* Arthur Clifton 1898–1921   Elsie 1908–1910

Harry 1920– *m.* Emma Barrington

Sebastian 1940–   Jessica (adopted) 1943–

PROLOGUE

SEBASTIAN tightened his grip on the steering wheel of the little MG. The lorry behind him touched his rear bumper and jolted the car forward, sending its number plate flying high into the air. Sebastian tried to advance a couple more feet, but he couldn't go any faster without running into the lorry in front of him and being squeezed between the two of them like a concertina.

A few seconds later they were nudged forward a second time as the lorry behind them drove into the back of the MG with considerably more force, pushing it to within a foot of the lorry in front. It was only when the rear lorry hit them a third time that Bruno's words *Are you certain you're making the right decision?* flashed into Sebastian's mind. He glanced across at his friend Bruno who was white with fear, clinging on to the dashboard with both hands.

'They're trying to kill us,' he screamed. 'For God's sake, Seb, do something!'

Sebastian looked helplessly across at the southbound traffic to see a steady stream of vehicles heading in the opposite direction.

When the lorry in front began to slow down, he knew that if they were to have any hope of surviving, he had to make a decision, and make it quickly. He glanced across to the other side of the road, desperately searching for a gap in the traffic. When the lorry behind hit him for a fourth time, he knew he'd been left with no choice.

He yanked the steering wheel firmly to the right, careered

across the grass verge and straight into the face of the oncoming vehicles. Sebastian pressed his foot hard down on the accelerator and prayed they would reach the safety of the wide open fields that stretched in front of him before a car could hit them.

A van and a car threw on their brakes and swerved to avoid the little MG as it shot across the road in front of them. Just for a moment, Sebastian thought he might make it, until he saw the tree looming up in front of him. He took his foot off the accelerator and swung the steering wheel to the left, but it was too late. The last thing Sebastian heard was Bruno screaming.

HARRY AND EMMA

1957–1958

1

HARRY CLIFTON was woken by the sound of a phone ringing.

He was in the middle of a dream, but couldn't remember what it was about. Perhaps the insistent metallic sound was just part of his dream. He reluctantly turned over and blinked at the little phosphorescent green hands on the bedside clock: 6.43 a.m. He smiled. Only one person would consider calling him at that time in the morning. He picked up the phone and murmured in an exaggeratedly sleepy voice, 'Good morning, my darling.' There was no immediate response, and for a moment Harry wondered if the hotel operator had put the call through to the wrong room. He was about to replace the receiver when he heard sobbing. 'Is that you, Emma?'

'Yes,' came the reply.

'What's the matter?' he asked soothingly.

'Sebastian is dead.'

Harry didn't reply immediately, because he now wanted to believe he was still dreaming. 'How can that be possible?' he eventually said. 'I spoke to him only yesterday.'

'He was killed this morning,' said Emma, clearly only able to manage a few words at a time.

Harry sat bolt upright, suddenly wide awake.

'In a car accident,' continued Emma between sobs.

Harry tried to remain calm as he waited for her to tell him exactly what had happened.

'They were travelling up to Cambridge together.'

'They?' repeated Harry.

5

'Sebastian and Bruno.'

'Is Bruno still alive?'

'Yes. But he's in a hospital in Harlow, and they're not sure if he'll make it through the night.'

Harry threw back the blanket and placed his feet on the carpet. He was freezing, and felt sick. 'I'll take a taxi to the airport immediately and catch the first flight back to London.'

'I'm going straight to the hospital,' said Emma. She didn't add anything else, and Harry wondered for a moment if the line had gone dead. Then he heard her whisper, 'They need someone to identify his body.'

-◦-

Emma replaced the receiver, but it was some time before she could gather enough strength to stand up. She eventually made her way unsteadily across the room, clinging on to several pieces of furniture, like a sailor in a storm. She opened the drawing room door to find Marsden standing in the hall, his head bowed. She had never known their old retainer to show the slightest emotion in front of a member of the family, and hardly recognized the shrunken figure now clutching on to the mantelpiece for support; the usual mask of self-composure had been replaced with the cruel reality of death.

'Mabel has packed an overnight case for you, madam,' he stammered, 'and if you'll allow me, I'll drive you to the hospital.'

'Thank you, Marsden, that's most considerate of you,' Emma said as he opened the front door for her.

Marsden took her arm as they made their way down the steps towards the car; the first time he'd ever touched the mistress. He opened the door, and she climbed in and sank into the leather upholstery, as if she was an old lady. Marsden switched on the ignition, shifted the gear lever into first and set out on the long journey from the Manor House to the Princess Alexandra Hospital in Harlow.

Emma suddenly realized she hadn't rung her brother or sister to let them know what had happened. She would call Grace and Giles this evening, when they were more likely to be alone. This was not something she wanted to share when strangers might be present. And then she felt a piercing pain in her stomach, as if she'd been stabbed. Who was going to tell Jessica that she would never see her brother again? Would she ever be the same cheerful little girl who ran around Seb like an obedient puppy, tail wagging with unbridled adoration? Jessica must not hear the news from someone else's lips, which meant that Emma would have to return to the Manor House as quickly as possible.

Marsden pulled into the forecourt of the local garage, where he usually filled up on a Friday afternoon. When the petrol pump attendant spotted Mrs Clifton sitting in the back seat of the green Austin A30, he touched the rim of his cap. She didn't acknowledge him, and the young man wondered if he'd done something wrong. He filled the tank and then lifted the bonnet to check the oil. Once he'd slammed the bonnet back down he touched the rim of his hat again, but Marsden drove off without a word, not parting with the usual sixpence.

'What's got into them?' murmured the young man as the car disappeared.

Once they were back on the road, Emma tried to recall the exact words the Peterhouse college admissions tutor had used when he haltingly told her the news. *I'm sorry to have to tell you, Mrs Clifton, that your son has been killed in a motor car accident*. Beyond the stark statement, Mr Padgett seemed to know very little – but then, as he explained, he was no more than the messenger.

Questions kept colliding in Emma's mind. Why had her son been travelling to Cambridge by car, when she'd bought him a train ticket only a couple of days before? Who had been driving, Sebastian or Bruno? Were they going too fast? Had a tyre burst? Had another car been involved? So many questions, but she doubted if anyone knew all the answers.

A few minutes after the tutor had called, the police had rung to ask if Mr Clifton would be able to visit the hospital to identify the body. Emma explained that her husband was in New York on a book tour. She might not have agreed to take his place if she'd realized that he would be back in England the following day. Thank God he was coming by plane and wouldn't have to spend five days crossing the Atlantic, mourning alone.

As Marsden drove through unfamiliar towns, Chippenham, Newbury, Slough, Don Pedro Martinez interrupted Emma's thoughts more than once. Was it possible that he could have been seeking revenge for what had taken place in Southampton just a few weeks ago? But if the other person in the car was Martinez's son Bruno, that didn't make any sense. Emma's thoughts returned to Sebastian as Marsden left the Great West Road and turned north in the direction of the A1; the road Sebastian had been travelling on only hours before. Emma had once read that in times of personal tragedy, all anyone wanted to do was turn the clock back. She was no different.

The journey passed quickly, as Sebastian was rarely out of her mind. She recalled his birth, when Harry was in prison on the other side of the world, his first steps at the age of eight months and four days, his first word, 'More', and his first day at school, when he jumped out of the car even before Harry had had time to put on the brakes, then later at Beechcroft Abbey, when the headmaster had wanted to expel him but granted Seb a reprieve when he won a scholarship to Cambridge. So much to look forward to, so much to achieve, all made history in a moment. And finally, her dreadful mistake when she'd allowed the cabinet secretary to persuade her that Seb should become involved with the government's plans to bring Don Pedro Martinez to justice. If she'd refused Sir Alan Redmayne's request, her only son would still be alive. If, if . . .

As they reached the outskirts of Harlow, Emma glanced out of the side window to see a signpost directing them to the Princess Alexandra Hospital. She tried to concentrate on what would be expected of her. A few minutes later Marsden drove through a set of wrought-iron gates that never closed, before drawing up outside the main entrance of the hospital. Emma got out of the car and began walking towards the front door while Marsden went in search of a parking space.

She gave the young receptionist her name, and the cheerful smile on the girl's face was replaced with a look of pity. 'Would you be kind enough to wait for a moment, Mrs Clifton,' she said as she picked up a phone. 'I'll let Mr Owen know you're here.'

'Mr Owen?'

'He was the consultant on duty when your son was admitted this morning.'

Emma nodded and began pacing restlessly up and down the corridor, jumbled thoughts replacing jumbled memories. *Who, why, when* . . . She only stopped pacing when a starched-collared, smartly dressed nurse enquired, 'Are you Mrs Clifton?' Emma nodded. 'Please come with me.'

The nurse led Emma along a green-walled corridor. No words were spoken. But then, what could either of them say? They came to a halt outside a door which displayed the name 'Mr William Owen FRCS'. The nurse knocked, opened the door and stood aside to allow Emma to enter.

A tall, thin, balding man with an undertaker's doleful visage rose from behind his desk. Emma wondered if that face ever smiled. 'Good afternoon, Mrs Clifton,' he said, before ushering her into the only comfortable chair in the room. 'I'm so sorry we have to meet in such sad circumstances,' he added.

Emma felt sorry for the poor man. How many times a day did he have to deliver those same words? From the look on his face, it didn't get any easier.

'I'm afraid there's rather a lot of paperwork to be completed, but I fear the coroner will require a formal identification before we can think about that.'

Emma bowed her head and burst into tears, wishing, as Harry had suggested, that she'd allowed him to carry out the unbearable task. Mr Owen leapt up from behind his desk, crouched down beside her and said, 'I'm so sorry, Mrs Clifton.'

--<o>--

Harold Guinzburg couldn't have been more considerate and helpful.

Harry's publisher had booked him on to the first available flight to London, first class. At least he would be comfortable, Harold thought, although he didn't imagine the poor man would be able to sleep. He decided this was not the time to tell him the good news, but simply asked Harry to pass on his heartfelt condolences to Emma.

When Harry checked out of the Pierre Hotel forty minutes later, he found Harold's chauffeur standing on the sidewalk waiting to drive him to Idlewild airport. Harry climbed into the back of the limousine, as he had no desire to speak to anyone. Instinctively, his thoughts turned to Emma, and what she must be going through. He didn't like the idea of her having to identify their son's body. Perhaps the hospital staff would suggest she waited until he returned.

Harry didn't give a thought to the fact he would be among the first passengers to cross the Atlantic non-stop, as he could only think about his son, and how much he'd been looking forward to going up to Cambridge to begin his first year at university. And after that . . . he'd assumed that with Seb's natural gift for languages, he'd want to join the Foreign Office, or become a translator, or possibly even teach, or . . .

After the Comet had taken off, Harry rejected the glass of champagne offered by a smiling air hostess, but then how could she know he had nothing to smile about? He didn't explain why he wouldn't be eating or sleeping. During the war, when he was behind enemy lines, Harry had trained himself to stay awake for thirty-six hours, only surviving on the adrenalin of fear. He knew he wouldn't be able to sleep until he'd seen his son for the last time, and he suspected not for some considerable time after that: the adrenalin of despair.

◄○►

The consultant led Emma silently down a bleak corridor until they came to a halt outside a hermetically sealed door, with the single word, *Mortuary*, displayed in appropriately black letters on its pebbled glass pane. Mr Owen pushed open the door and stood aside to allow Emma to enter. The door closed behind her with a squelch. The sudden change in temperature made her shiver, and then her eyes settled on a trolley standing in the middle of the room. The faint outline of her son's body was visible under the sheet.

A white-coated assistant stood at the head of the trolley, but didn't speak.

'Are you ready, Mrs Clifton?' asked Mr Owen gently.

'Yes,' said Emma firmly, her fingernails cutting into the palms of her hands.

Owen nodded, and the mortician pulled back the sheet to reveal a scarred and battered face that Emma recognized immediately. She screamed, collapsed on to her knees, and began to sob uncontrollably.

Mr Owen and the mortician were not surprised by this predictable reaction of a mother at the first sight of her dead son, but they were shocked when she said quietly, 'That's not Sebastian.'

2

AS THE TAXI drew up outside the hospital, Harry was surprised to see Emma standing by the entrance, clearly waiting for him. He was even more surprised when she ran towards him, relief etched on her face.

'Seb's alive,' she shouted long before she'd reached him.

'But you told me—' he began as she threw her arms around him.

'The police made a mistake. They assumed it was the owner of the car who was driving, and that therefore Seb must have been in the passenger seat.'

'Then Bruno was the passenger?' said Harry quietly.

'Yes,' said Emma, feeling a little guilty.

'You realize what that means?' said Harry, releasing her.

'No. What are you getting at?'

'The police must have told Martinez that *his* son had survived, only for him to discover later that it was Bruno who'd been killed, not Sebastian.'

Emma bowed her head. 'Poor man,' she said as they entered the hospital.

'Unless . . .' said Harry, not finishing the sentence. 'So how's Seb?' he asked quietly. 'What state is he in?'

'Pretty bad, I'm afraid. Mr Owen told me there weren't many bones left in his body to break. It seems he'll be in hospital for several months, and may end up spending the rest of his life in a wheelchair.'

'Just be thankful he's alive,' said Harry, placing an arm around his wife's shoulder. 'Will they let me see him?'

'Yes, but only for a few minutes. And be warned, darling, he's covered in plaster and bandages, so you might not even recognize him.' Emma took his hand and led him up to the first floor, where they came across a woman dressed in a dark blue uniform who was bustling around, keeping a close eye on the patients while giving the occasional order to her staff.

'I'm Miss Puddicombe,' she announced, thrusting out her hand.

'Matron to you,' whispered Emma. Harry shook her hand and said, 'Good day, Matron.'

Without another word, the diminutive figure led them through to the Bevan Ward to find two neat rows of beds, every one of them occupied. Miss Puddicombe sailed on until she reached a patient at the far end of the room. She drew a curtain around Sebastian Arthur Clifton, and then withdrew. Harry stared down at his son. His left leg was held up by a pulley, while the other one, also encased in plaster, lay flat on the bed. His head was swathed in bandages, leaving one eye to focus on his parents, but his lips didn't move.

As Harry bent down to kiss him on the forehead, the first words Sebastian uttered were, 'How's Bruno?'

—◦—

'I'm sorry to have to question you both after all you've been through,' said Chief Inspector Miles. 'I wouldn't unless it was absolutely necessary.'

'And why is it necessary?' asked Harry, who was no stranger to detectives or their methods of extracting information.

'I'm yet to be convinced that what happened on the A1 was an accident.'

'What are you suggesting?' asked Harry, looking directly at the detective.

'I'm not suggesting anything, sir, but our back-room johnnies have carried out a thorough inspection of the vehicle, and they think one or two things just don't add up.'

'Like what?' asked Emma.

'For a start, Mrs Clifton,' said Miles, 'we can't work out why your son crossed the central reservation when he so obviously risked being hit by an oncoming vehicle.'

'Perhaps the car had a mechanical fault?' suggested Harry.

'That was our first thought,' replied Miles. 'But although the car was badly damaged, none of the tyres had burst, and the steering-wheel shaft was intact, which is almost unknown in an accident of this kind.'

'That's hardly proof of a crime being committed,' said Harry.

'No, sir,' said Miles, 'and on its own, it wouldn't have been enough for me to ask the coroner to refer the case to the DPP. But a witness has come forward with some rather disturbing evidence.'

'What did he have to say?'

'She,' said Miles, referring to his notebook. 'A Mrs Challis told us she was overtaken by an open-top MG which was just about to pass three lorries that were in convoy on the inside lane, when the front lorry moved into the outside lane, although there was no other vehicle in front of him. This meant that the driver of the MG had to brake suddenly. The third lorry then also moved across into the outside lane, again for no apparent reason, while the middle lorry maintained its speed, leaving the MG with no way to overtake or move to the safety of the inside lane. Mrs Challis went on to say that the three lorries kept the MG boxed in this position for some considerable time,' continued the detective, 'until its driver, without rhyme or reason, careered across the central reservation straight into the face of the oncoming traffic.'

'Have you been able to question any of the three lorry drivers?' asked Emma.

'No. We've been unable to track down any of them, Mrs Clifton. And don't think we haven't tried.'

'But what you're suggesting is unthinkable,' said Harry. 'Who would want to kill two innocent boys?'

'I would have agreed with you, Mr Clifton, if we hadn't

recently discovered that Bruno Martinez didn't originally intend to accompany your son on the journey to Cambridge.'

'How could you possibly know that?'

'Because his girlfriend, a Miss Thornton, has come forward and informed us that she had planned to go to the cinema with Bruno that day, but she had to cancel at the last moment because she'd caught a cold.' The chief inspector took a pen out of his pocket, turned a page of his notebook and looked directly at Sebastian's parents before asking, 'Do either of you have any reason to believe that someone might have wanted to harm your son?'

'No,' said Harry.

'Yes,' said Emma.

3

'JUST MAKE SURE you finish the job this time,' Don Pedro Martinez almost shouted. 'It shouldn't prove too difficult,' he added as he sat forward in his chair. 'I was able to stroll into the hospital unchallenged yesterday morning, and at night it ought to be a whole lot easier.'

'How do you want him disposed of?' asked Karl, matter-of-factly.

'Cut his throat,' said Martinez. 'All you'll need is a white coat, a stethoscope and a surgeon's knife. Just make sure it's sharp.'

'Might not be wise to slit the boy's throat,' suggested Karl. 'Better to suffocate him with a pillow and let them assume he died as a result of his injuries.'

'No. I want the Clifton boy to suffer a slow and painful death. In fact, the slower the better.'

'I understand how you feel, boss, but we don't need to give that detective any more reason to reopen his inquiries.'

Martinez looked disappointed. 'All right then, suffocate him,' he said reluctantly. 'But make sure it lasts for as long as possible.'

'Do you want me to involve Diego and Luis?'

'No. But I want them to attend the funeral, as Sebastian's friends, so they can report back. I want to hear that they suffered every bit as much as I did when I first realized it wasn't Bruno who'd survived.'

'But what about—'

The phone on Don Pedro's desk began to ring. He grabbed it. 'Yes?'

'There's a Colonel Scott-Hopkins on the line,' said his secretary. 'He wants to discuss a personal matter with you. Says it's urgent.'

⊷◦⊶

All four of them had rearranged their diaries so they could be at the Cabinet office in Downing Street by nine the following morning.

Sir Alan Redmayne, the cabinet secretary, had cancelled his meeting with M. Chauvel, the French Ambassador, with whom he'd planned to discuss the implications of Charles de Gaulle's possible return to the Elysée Palace.

Sir Giles Barrington MP would not be attending the weekly shadow cabinet meeting because, as he explained to Mr Gaitskell, the Leader of the Opposition, an urgent family problem had arisen.

Harry Clifton wouldn't be signing copies of his latest book, *Blood is Thicker than Water*, at Hatchards in Piccadilly. He'd signed a hundred copies in advance to try to placate the manager, who couldn't hide his disappointment, especially after he'd learnt that Harry would top the bestseller list on Sunday.

Emma Barrington had postponed a meeting with Ross Buchanan to discuss the chairman's ideas for the building of a new luxury liner that, if the board backed him, would become part of the Barrington shipping line.

The four of them took their seats around an oval table in the cabinet secretary's office.

'It was good of you to see us at such short notice,' said Giles from the far end of the table. Sir Alan nodded. 'But I'm sure you can appreciate that Mr and Mrs Clifton are worried that their son's life might still be in danger.'

'I share their anxiety,' said Redmayne, 'and allow me to say how sorry I was to learn of your son's accident, Mrs Clifton. Not least because I feel partly to blame for what happened. However, let me assure you that I have not been idle. Over the weekend I spoke to Mr Owen, Chief Inspector Miles, and the local coroner. They couldn't have been more cooperative. And I have to agree with Miles, there just isn't enough evidence to prove that Don Pedro Martinez was in any way involved in the accident.' Emma's look of exasperation caused Sir Alan to quickly add, 'Nevertheless, proof and not being in any doubt are often two very different animals, and after learning that Martinez wasn't aware that his son was in the car at the time, I concluded that he just might consider striking again, however irrational that might seem.'

'An eye for an eye,' said Harry.

'You could be right,' said the cabinet secretary. 'He clearly hasn't forgiven us for what he sees as stealing eight million pounds of his money, even if it was all counterfeit, and although he may not yet have worked out that the government was behind the operation, there's no doubt that he believes your son was personally responsible for what took place in Southampton and I am only sorry that, at the time, I did not take your understandable concern seriously enough.'

'I'm at least grateful for that,' said Emma. 'But it's not you who is continually wondering when and where Martinez will strike next. And anyone can stroll in and out of that hospital as easily as if it were a bus station.'

'I can't disagree,' said Redmayne. 'I did so myself yesterday afternoon.' This revelation caused a momentary silence that allowed him to continue. 'However, you can be assured, Mrs Clifton, that this time I've taken the necessary steps to make sure that your son is no longer in any danger.'

'Can you share with Mr and Mrs Clifton the reason for your confidence?' asked Giles.

'No, Sir Giles, I cannot.'

'Why not?' demanded Emma.

'Because on this occasion I had to involve the home secretary as well as the secretary of state for defence, so I am therefore bound by Privy Council confidentiality.'

'What sort of mumbo jumbo is that?' demanded Emma. 'Try not to forget that we're talking about my son's life.'

'Should any of this ever become public,' said Giles, turning to his sister, 'even in fifty years' time, it will be important to show that neither you nor Harry was aware that ministers of the Crown were involved.'

'I am grateful, Sir Giles,' said the cabinet secretary.

'I can just about stomach these pompous coded messages you two keep passing to each other,' said Harry, 'as long as I can be assured that my son's life is no longer in danger, because if anything else were to happen to Sebastian, Sir Alan, there would only be one person to blame.'

'I accept your admonition, Mr Clifton. However, I am able to confirm that Martinez no longer poses a threat to Sebastian or any other member of your family. Frankly, I've bent the rules to breaking point to make sure that it's literally more than Martinez's life is worth.'

Harry still looked sceptical, and although Giles seemed to accept Sir Alan's word, he realized that he would have to become prime minister before the cabinet secretary would reveal the reason for his confidence, and perhaps not even then.

'However,' continued Sir Alan, 'one mustn't forget that Martinez is an unscrupulous and treacherous man, and I have no doubt he will still want to seek some form of revenge. And as long as he abides by the letter of the law, there's not much any of us can do about it.'

'At least we'll be prepared this time,' said Emma, only too aware what the cabinet secretary was getting at.

◄○►

Colonel Scott-Hopkins knocked on the door of number 44 Eaton Square at one minute to ten. A few moments later, the front door was opened by a giant of a man who dwarfed the commanding officer of the SAS.

'My name is Scott-Hopkins. I have an appointment with Mr Martinez.'

Karl gave a slight bow, and opened the door just enough to allow Mr Martinez's guest to enter. He accompanied the colonel across the hall and knocked on the study door.

'Come in.'

When the colonel entered the room, Don Pedro rose from

behind his desk and looked at his guest suspiciously. He had no idea why the SAS man needed to see him so urgently.

'Will you have a coffee, colonel?' asked Don Pedro after the two men had shaken hands. 'Or perhaps something a little stronger?'

'No, thank you, sir. It's a little early in the morning for me.'

'Then have a seat, and tell me why you wanted to see me urgently.' He paused. 'I feel sure you'll appreciate that I'm a busy man.'

'I am only too aware how busy you've been recently, Mr Martinez, so I'll come straight to the point.'

Don Pedro tried not to show any reaction as he settled back into his chair and continued to stare at the colonel.

'My simple purpose is to make sure that Sebastian Clifton has a long and peaceful life.'

The mask of arrogant confidence slipped from Martinez's face. He quickly recovered and sat bolt upright. 'What are you suggesting?' he shouted, as he gripped the arm of his chair.

'I think you know only too well, Mr Martinez. However, allow me to make the position clear. I'm here to ensure that no further harm comes to any member of the Clifton family.'

Don Pedro leapt out of his seat and jabbed a finger at the colonel. 'Sebastian Clifton was my son's closest friend.'

'I have no doubt he was, Mr Martinez. But my instructions could not be clearer, and they are quite simply to warn you that if Sebastian or any other member of his family were to be involved in another *accident*, then your sons, Diego and Luis, will be on the next plane back to Argentina, and they won't be travelling first class, but in the hold, in two wooden boxes.'

'Who do you think you're threatening?' bellowed Martinez, his fists clenched.

'A two-bit South American gangster, who, because he's got some money and lives in Eaton Square, thinks he can pass himself off as a gentleman.'

Don Pedro pressed a button underneath his desk. A moment later the door burst open and Karl came charging in. 'Throw this man out,' he said, pointing at the colonel, 'while I get my lawyer on the line.'

'Good morning, Lieutenant Lunsdorf,' said the colonel as Karl began to advance towards him. 'As a former member of the SS, you'll appreciate the weak position your master is in.' Karl stopped in his tracks. 'So allow me to also give you a word of advice. Should Mr Martinez fail to abide by my terms, our plans for you do not include a deportation order to Buenos Aires, where so many of your former colleagues are currently languishing; no, we have another destination in mind, where you'll find several citizens who will be only too happy to give evidence concerning the role you played as one of Dr Goebbels' trusted lieutenants, and the lengths you went to in order to extract information from them.'

'You're bluffing,' said Martinez. 'You'd never get away with it.'

'How little you really know about the British, Mr Martinez,' said the colonel as he rose from his chair and walked across to the window. 'Allow me to introduce you to a few typical specimens of our island race.'

Martinez and Karl joined him and stared out of the window. On the far side of the road stood three men you wouldn't want as enemies.

'Three of my most trusted colleagues,' explained the colonel. 'One of them will be watching you night and day, just hoping you'll make a false move. On the left is Captain Hartley, who was unfortunately cashiered from the Dragoon Guards for pouring petrol over his wife and her lover, who were sleeping peacefully at the time, until he lit a match. Understandably, after leaving prison he found it difficult to secure employment. That was until I picked him up off the streets and put some purpose back in his life.'

Hartley gave them a warm smile, as if he knew they were talking about him.

'In the middle is Corporal Crann, a carpenter by trade. He so enjoys sawing things up, wood or bone, it doesn't seem to make any difference to him.' Crann stared blankly through them. 'But I confess,' continued the colonel, 'my favourite is Sergeant Roberts, a registered sociopath. Harmless most of the time, but I'm afraid he never really settled back into civvy street after the war.' The colonel turned to Martinez. 'Perhaps I shouldn't have told him that you made your fortune collaborating with the Nazis, but of course that's how you met Lieutenant Lunsdorf. A titbit I don't think I'll share with Roberts unless you really annoy me, because, you see, Sergeant Roberts's mother was Jewish.'

Don Pedro turned away from the window to see Karl staring at the colonel as if he would have been happy to strangle him, but accepted that now was not the time or place.

'I'm so glad to have caught your attention,' said Scott-Hopkins, 'because I now feel even more confident that you'll have worked out what is in your best interests. Good day, gentlemen. I'll show myself out.'

4

'THERE'S A GREAT DEAL for us to cover on today's agenda,' said the chairman. 'So I would appreciate it if my fellow directors would keep their contributions short and to the point.'

Emma had come to admire Ross Buchanan's business-like approach when chairing the Barrington Shipping Company board meetings. He never showed favour to any particular director, and always listened carefully to anybody who offered a view contrary to his own. Occasionally, just occasionally, he could even be persuaded to change his mind. He also possessed the ability to sum up a complex discussion while making sure that everyone's particular view was well represented. Emma knew that some board members found his Scottish manner a little brusque, but she considered it no more than practical, and sometimes wondered how her approach might differ from his, if she were ever to become chairman. She quickly dismissed the thought and began to concentrate on the most important item on the agenda. Emma had rehearsed what she was going to say the night before, with Harry acting as chairman.

Once Philip Webster, the company secretary, had read the minutes of the last meeting and dealt with any questions arising, the chairman moved on to the first item on the agenda: a proposal that the board should put out to tender the building of the MV *Buckingham*, a luxury liner that would be added to the Barrington fleet.

Buchanan left the board in no doubt that he felt this was the only way forward if Barrington's hoped to continue as one of the premier shipping companies in the land. Several members of the board nodded in agreement.

Once the chairman had put his case, he called upon Emma to present the contrary view. She began by suggesting that while the bank rate was at an all-time high, the company should be consolidating its position, and not risking such a large financial outlay on something that, in her opinion, had at best a 50/50 chance of succeeding.

Mr Anscott, a non-executive director who had been appointed to the board by Sir Hugo Barrington, her late father, suggested it was time to push the boat out. No one laughed. Rear Admiral Summers felt they shouldn't go ahead with such a radical decision without the shareholders' approval.

'It is we who are on the bridge,' Buchanan reminded the admiral, 'and therefore we who should be making the decisions.' The admiral scowled, but offered no further comment. After all, his vote would speak for itself.

Emma listened carefully as each member of the board gave his opinion, and quickly realized that the directors were evenly divided. One or two hadn't yet made up their minds, but she suspected that if it came to a vote, the chairman would prevail.

An hour later, the board were no nearer to making a decision, with some of the directors simply repeating their earlier arguments, which clearly irritated Buchanan. But Emma knew he would eventually have to move on, as there was other important business that needed to be discussed.

'I am bound to say,' said the chairman in his summing up, 'that we can't put off making a decision for much longer, and therefore I suggest we all go away and think carefully about where we stand on this particular issue. Frankly, the future of the company is at stake. I propose that when we meet again next month, we take a vote on whether to put the job out to tender, or to drop the whole idea.'

'Or at least wait until calmer waters prevail,' suggested Emma.

The chairman reluctantly moved on, and as the remaining items on the agenda were far less contentious, by the time

Buchanan asked if there was any other business a more relaxed atmosphere had replaced the earlier heated debate.

'I have one piece of information that it is my duty to report to the board,' said the company secretary. 'You cannot have failed to notice that our share price has been rising steadily over the past few weeks, and you may well have wondered why, as we have made no significant announcements or issued any profit forecasts recently. Well, yesterday that mystery was solved when I received a letter from the manager of the Midland Bank in St James's, Mayfair, informing me that one of his clients was in possession of seven and a half per cent of the company's stock, and therefore would be appointing a director to represent them on the board.'

'Let me guess,' said Emma. 'None other than Major Alex Fisher.'

'I fear so,' said the chairman, uncharacteristically lowering his guard.

'And are there any prizes for guessing who the good major will be representing?' asked the admiral.

'None,' replied Buchanan, 'because you'd be wrong. Although I must confess that when I first heard the news, like you, I assumed it would be our old friend, Lady Virginia Fenwick. However, the manager of the Midland assures me that her ladyship is not one of the bank's clients. When I pressed him on the subject of who owned the shares, he said politely that he was unable to disclose that information, which is banking parlance for mind your own business.'

'I can't wait to discover how the major will cast his vote on the proposed building of the *Buckingham*,' said Emma with a wry smile, 'because of one thing we can be sure. Whoever he represents certainly won't have Barrington's interests at heart.'

'Be assured, Emma, I wouldn't want that little shit to be the person who tipped the balance either way,' said Buchanan.

Emma was speechless.

Another of the chairman's admirable qualities was his ability to put any disagreements, however strongly felt, to one side once a board meeting was over.

'So what's the latest news on Sebastian?' he asked as he joined Emma for a pre-lunch drink.

'Matron declares herself well satisfied with his progress. I'm delighted to say that I can see a visible improvement every time I visit the hospital. The cast on his left leg has been removed, and he now has two eyes and an opinion on everything, from why his uncle Giles is the right man to replace Gaitskell as leader of the Labour Party, to why parking meters are nothing more than another government ploy to extract more of our hard-earned money.'

'I agree with him on both counts,' said Ross. 'Let's hope his exuberance is the prelude to a full recovery.'

'His surgeon seems to think so. Mr Owen told me that modern surgery made rapid advances during the war because so many soldiers needed to be operated on without the time to seek second and third opinions. Thirty years ago, Seb would have ended up in a wheelchair for the rest of his life, but not today.'

'Is he still hoping to go up to Cambridge next Michaelmas?'

'I think so. He recently had a visit from his supervisor, who told him that he could take up his place at Peterhouse in September. He even gave him some books to read.'

'Well, he can't pretend there's a whole lot to distract him.'

'Funny you should mention that,' said Emma, 'because he's recently begun to take a great deal of interest in the company's fortunes, which comes as something of a surprise. In fact, he reads the minutes of every board meeting from cover to cover. He's even bought ten shares, which gives him the legal right to follow our every move, and I can tell you, Ross, he's not shy in expressing his views, not least on the proposed building of the *Buckingham*.'

'No doubt influenced by his mother's well-known opinion on the subject,' said Buchanan, smiling.

'No, that's the strange thing,' said Emma. 'Someone else seems to be advising him on that particular subject.'

◄◦►

Emma burst out laughing.

Harry looked up from the other end of the breakfast table and put down his newspaper. 'As I can't find anything even remotely amusing in *The Times* this morning, do share the joke with me.'

Emma took a sip of coffee before returning to the *Daily Express*.

'It seems that Lady Virginia Fenwick, only daughter of the ninth Earl of Fenwick, has issued divorce proceedings against the Count of Milan. William Hickey is suggesting that Virginia will receive a settlement of around £250,000, plus their flat in Lowndes Square, as well as the country estate in Berkshire.'

'Not a bad return for two years' work.'

'And of course Giles gets a mention.'

'That's always going to be the case whenever Virginia makes the headlines.'

'Yes, but it's quite flattering for a change,' she said, returning to the newspaper. '"Lady Virginia's first husband, Sir Giles Barrington, Member of Parliament for Bristol Docklands, is widely tipped to be a cabinet minister should Labour win the next election."'

'I think that's unlikely.'

'That Giles will be a cabinet minister?'

'No, that Labour will win the next election.'

'"He has proved to be a formidable front bench spokesman,"' Emma continued, '"and has recently become engaged to Dr Gwyneth Hughes, a lecturer at King's College, London." Great picture of Gwyneth, ghastly photo of Virginia.'

'Virginia won't like that,' said Harry, returning to *The Times*. 'But there's not a lot she can do about it now.'

'Don't be so sure of that,' said Emma. 'I have a feeling the sting has not yet been fully extracted from that particular scorpion.'

—◦—

Harry and Emma drove up from Gloucestershire to Harlow every Sunday to visit Sebastian, with Jessica always in tow, as she never missed an opportunity to see her big brother. Every time Emma turned left out of the Manor House gates to begin the long drive to the Princess Alexandra Hospital, she could never shake off the memory of the first time she'd made that journey, when she'd thought her son had been killed in a car crash. Emma was only thankful that she hadn't phoned Grace or Giles to tell them the news, and that Jessica had been camping in the Quantocks with the Girl Guides when the tutor rang. Only poor Harry had spent twenty-four hours believing he would never see his son again.

Jessica considered the visits to Sebastian to be the highlight of her week. On arriving at the hospital, she would present him with her latest work of art, and after having covered every inch of his plaster casts with images of the Manor House, family and friends, she moved on to the hospital walls. Matron hung every new picture in the corridor outside the ward, but admitted that it wouldn't be too long before they would have to migrate down the staircase to the floor below. Emma could only hope that Sebastian would be released before Jessica's offerings reached the reception area. She always felt a little embarrassed whenever her daughter presented Matron with her latest effort.

'No need to feel embarrassed, Mrs Clifton,' said Miss Puddicombe. 'You should see some of the daubs I'm presented with by doting parents, who expect them to be hung in my office. In any case, when Jessica becomes an RA, I shall sell them all and build a new ward with the proceeds.'

Emma didn't need to be reminded how talented her daughter was, as she knew Miss Fielding, her art mistress at Red Maids', had plans to enter her for a scholarship to the Slade School of Fine Art, and seemed confident of the outcome.

'It's quite a challenge, Mrs Clifton, to have to teach someone who you know is far more talented than you are,' Miss Fielding had once told her.

'Don't ever let her know that,' said Emma.

'Everyone knows it,' replied Miss Fielding, 'and we're all looking forward to greater things in the future. No one will be surprised when she's offered a place at the Royal Academy Schools, a first for Red Maids'.'

Jessica appeared blissfully unaware of her rare talent, as she was of so many other things, thought Emma. She had repeatedly warned Harry that it could only be a matter of time before their adopted daughter stumbled upon the truth about who her father was, and suggested that it would be better if she heard it from a member of the family first, rather than a stranger. Harry seemed strangely reluctant to burden her with the real reason they had plucked her out of the Dr Barnardo's home all those years ago, ignoring several more obvious candidates. Giles and Grace had both volunteered to explain to Jessica how they all came to share the same father, Sir Hugo Barrington, and why her mother had been responsible for his untimely death.

The moment Emma parked her Austin A30 in the hospital car park Jessica would jump out, her latest picture under one arm, a bar of Cadbury's milk chocolate in her other hand, and run all the way to Sebastian's bedside. Emma didn't believe that anyone could love her son more than she did, but if anyone did, it was Jessica.

When Emma entered the ward a few minutes later, she was surprised and delighted to find Sebastian out of bed for the first time, and sitting in an armchair. The moment he saw his mother, he pushed himself up, steadied himself, and kissed her on both cheeks; another first. When does that moment come, Emma wondered, when mothers stop kissing their children, and young men start kissing their mothers?

Jessica was telling her brother in great detail what she'd been up to during the week, so Emma perched herself on the end of the bed and happily listened to her exploits for a second time. Once she'd stopped talking long enough for Sebastian to get a word in, he turned to his mother and said, 'I reread the minutes of the latest board meeting this morning. You do realize that the chairman will call for a vote at the next meeting, and this time you won't be able to avoid making a decision on whether to go ahead with building the *Buckingham*.'

Emma didn't comment as Jessica turned round and began to draw the old man who was sleeping in the next bed.

'I would do the same if I were in his position,' continued Sebastian. 'So who do you think will win?'

'No one will win,' said Emma, 'because whatever the outcome, the board will remain divided until it can be shown who was right.'

'Let's hope not, because I think you've got a far bigger problem staring you right in the face, and one that will need you and the chairman to be working in harmony.'

'Fisher?'

Sebastian nodded. 'And God knows how he'll vote when it comes to whether or not you should build the *Buckingham*.'

'Fisher will vote whichever way Don Pedro Martinez instructs him to.'

'How can you be sure that it was Martinez, and not Lady Virginia, who bought those shares?' asked Sebastian.

'According to William Hickey in the *Daily Express*, Virginia is going through another messy divorce at the moment, so you can be sure she'll be concentrating on how much maintenance she can extract from the Count of Milan before she decides how to spend it. In any case, I have my own reasons for believing that Martinez is behind the latest round of share buying.'

'I'd already come to that conclusion myself,' said Sebastian, 'because one of the last things Bruno told me, when we were in the car on the way to Cambridge, was that his father had had a meeting with a major, and he overheard the name "Barrington" come up during their conversation.'

'If that's true,' said Emma, 'Fisher will support the chairman, if for no other reason than to get back at Giles for preventing him becoming a Member of Parliament.'

'Even if he does, don't assume he'll want the building of the *Buckingham* to progress smoothly. Far from it. He'll switch sides whenever he thinks he has an opportunity to harm the company's short-term finances or long-term reputation. Forgive the cliché, but leopards don't change their spots. Just remember that his overall aim is exactly the opposite of yours. You want the company to succeed, he wants it to fail.'

'Why would he want that?'

'I suspect you know the answer to that question only too well, Mama.' Sebastian waited to see how she would respond, but Emma simply changed the subject. 'How come you're suddenly so full of wisdom?'

'I have daily lessons at the foot of an expert. And what's more, I'm his only pupil,' Sebastian added without explanation.

'And what does your expert advise that I should do, if I want the board to back me and vote against building the *Buckingham*?'

'He's come up with a plan that would ensure you win the vote at the next board meeting.'

'That's not possible while the board is so evenly divided.'

'Oh, it's possible,' said Sebastian, 'but only if you're willing to play Martinez at his own game.'

'What do you have in mind?'

'As long as the family are in possession of twenty-two per cent of the company's stock,' continued Sebastian, 'you have the right to appoint two more directors to the board. So all you have to do is co-opt Uncle Giles and Aunt Grace, and they can support you when it comes to the crucial vote. That way you can't lose.'

'I could never do that,' said Emma.

'Why not, when so much is at stake?'

'Because it would undermine Ross Buchanan's position as chairman. If he lost such an important vote because the family had ganged up against him, he would be left with no choice but to resign. And I suspect other directors would follow him.'

'But that might be the best outcome for the company in the long run.'

'Possibly, but I must be seen to win the argument on the day, and not have to rely on fixing the vote. That's the sort of cheap trick Fisher would stoop to.'

'My dear Mama, no one could admire you more than I do for always taking the moral high road, but when you're dealing with the Martinezes of this world, you have to understand that they have no morals, and will always be happy to take the low road. In fact, he'd crawl into the nearest gutter if he thought it would ensure he'd win the vote.'

A long silence followed, until Sebastian said, very quietly, 'Mama, when I woke for the first time after the accident, I found Don Pedro standing at the end of the bed.' Emma shuddered. 'He was smiling, and said, "How are you my boy?" I shook my head, and it was only then that he realized I wasn't Bruno. The look he gave me before he marched off was something I will never forget for the rest of my life.' Still Emma said nothing. 'Mama, don't you think the time has come to tell me why Martinez is so determined to bring our family to its knees? Because it wasn't too difficult to work out that he meant to kill me on the A1, and not his own son.'

5

*You're always so impatient, Sergeant Warwick, said the pathol-
ogist as he studied the body more closely.*

*But are you at least able to tell me just how long the body has
been in the water? asked the detective.*

Harry was crossing out the word *just* and changing *has* to
had, when the phone rang. He put down his pen and picked up
the receiver.

'Yes,' he said somewhat abruptly.

'Harry, it's Harold Guinzburg. Congratulations, you're
number eight this week.' Harold rang every Thursday afternoon
to let Harry know where he would feature on the bestseller list
that Sunday. 'That's nine weeks in a row in the top fifteen.'

Harry had been at number 4 a month ago, the highest
position he'd ever managed, and although he didn't admit it even
to Emma, he still hoped to join that select group of British
writers who'd made it to the top on both sides of the Atlantic.
The last two William Warwick mysteries had been number 1 in
Britain, but the top spot in the States still eluded him.

'Sales figures are all that really matter,' said Guinzburg,
almost as if he was reading Harry's thoughts. 'And in any case,
I'm confident that you'll climb even higher when the softback
comes out in March.' Harry didn't miss the words *even higher*
and not *to number one*. 'How's Emma?'

'Preparing a speech on why the company shouldn't be building a new luxury liner at the present time.'

'Doesn't sound like a bestseller to me,' said Harold. 'So tell me, how's Sebastian coming along?'

'He's in a wheelchair. But his surgeon assures me not for much longer, and they're allowing him out for the first time next week.'

'Bravo. Does that mean he'll be going home?'

'No, Matron won't allow him to travel that far yet; perhaps a trip to Cambridge to visit his tutor, and have tea with his aunt.'

'Sounds worse than school to me. Still, it can't be too long before he finally escapes.'

'Or is thrown out. I'm not sure which will come first.'

'Why would they want to throw him out?'

'One or two of the nurses have begun taking a greater interest in Seb as each bandage comes off, and I'm afraid he isn't discouraging them.'

'The dance of the seven veils,' said Harold. Harry laughed. 'Is he still hoping to go up to Cambridge in September?'

'As far as I can tell, yes. But he's changed so much since the accident, nothing would surprise me.'

'How has he changed?'

'Nothing I can put a finger on. It's just that he's matured in a way I wouldn't have thought possible a year ago. And I think I've discovered why.'

'Sounds intriguing.'

'It certainly is. I'll fill you in on the details when I next come to New York.'

'Do I have to wait that long?'

'Yes, because it's like my writing, I have no idea what will happen when I turn the page.'

'So tell me about our one girl in a million.'

'Not you as well,' said Harry.

'Please tell Jessica that I've hung her drawing of the Manor House in autumn in my study, next to a Roy Lichtenstein.'

'Who's Roy Lichtenstein?'

'He's the latest fad in New York, but I can't see him lasting too long. In my opinion Jessica's a far better draughtsman. Please tell her that if she'll paint me a picture of New York in the fall, I'll give her a Lichtenstein for Christmas.'

'I wonder if she's heard of him.'

'Before I ring off, dare I ask how the latest William Warwick novel is progressing?'

'It would be progressing a damn sight faster if I wasn't continually interrupted.'

'Sorry,' said Harold. 'They didn't tell me you were writing.'

'Truth is, Warwick has come up against an insurmountable problem. Or to be more accurate, I have.'

'Anything I can help you with?'

'No. That's why you're the publisher and I'm the author.'

'What sort of problem?' persisted Harold.

'Warwick's found the ex-wife's body at the bottom of a lake, but he's fairly sure that she was killed before being dumped in the water.'

'So what's the problem?'

'Mine, or William Warwick's?'

'Warwick's first.'

'He's being made to wait for at least twenty-four hours before he can get his hands on the pathologist's report.'

'And your problem?'

'I've got twenty-four hours before I have to decide what needs to be in that report.'

'Does Warwick know who killed the ex-wife?'

'He can't be sure. There are five suspects at the moment, and every one of them has a motive . . . and an alibi.'

'But I presume you know who did it?'

'No I don't,' Harry admitted. 'Because if I don't know, then neither can the reader.'

'Isn't that a bit of a risk?'

'Sure is. But it also makes it a damn sight more challenging, both for me and the reader.'

'I can't wait to read the first draft.'

'Neither can I.'

'Sorry. I'll let you get back to your ex-wife's body in the lake. I'll call again in a week's time to see if you've worked out who dumped her there.'

When Guinzburg hung up, Harry replaced the receiver and looked down at the blank sheet of paper in front of him. He tried to concentrate.

So what's your opinion, Percy?

Too early to make an accurate assessment. I'll need to get her back to the lab and carry out some more tests before I can give you a considered judgement.

When can I expect to get your preliminary report? asked Warwick.

You're always so impatient, William . . .

Harry looked up. He suddenly realized who'd committed the murder.

◄o►

Although Emma hadn't been willing to accept Sebastian's suggestion that she should co-opt Giles and Grace on to the board to ensure she couldn't lose the crucial vote, she still considered it her duty to keep her brother and sister up-to-date on what was going on. Emma was proud to represent the family on the board, although she knew only too well that neither of her siblings was particularly interested in what went on behind closed doors at Barrington's, as long as they received their quarterly dividends.

Giles was preoccupied with his responsibilities at the House of Commons, which had become even more demanding after Hugh Gaitskell had invited him to join the Shadow Cabinet, to cover the European portfolio. This meant that he was rarely seen in his constituency, despite being expected to nurse a marginal seat while at the same time regularly visiting those countries that had a vote on whether Britain should be allowed to join the EEC. However, Labour had been ahead in the opinion polls for several months, and it was looking increasingly likely that Giles would become a Cabinet minister after the next election. So the last thing he needed was to be distracted by 'trouble at t'mill'.

Harry and Emma were delighted when Giles had finally

announced his engagement to Gwyneth Hughes, not in *The Times*' social column, but at the Ostrich public house in the heart of his constituency.

'I want to see you married before the next election,' declared Griff Haskins, his constituency agent. 'And if Gwyneth could be pregnant by the first week of the campaign, that would be even better.'

'How romantic,' Giles sighed.

'I'm not interested in romance,' said Griff. 'I'm here to make sure you're still sitting in the House of Commons after the next election, because if you're not, you sure as hell won't be in the Cabinet.'

Giles wanted to laugh, but he knew Griff was right.

'Has a date been fixed?' asked Emma, who had strolled across to join them.

'For the wedding, or the general election?'

'For the wedding, idiot.'

'May the seventeenth at Chelsea Register Office,' said Giles.

'Bit of a contrast from St Margaret's, Westminster, but at least this time Harry and I can hope to receive an invitation.'

'I've asked Harry to be my best man,' said Giles. 'But I'm not so sure about you,' he added with a grin.

◄○►

The timing could have been better, but the only chance Emma had to see her sister was on the evening before the crucial board meeting. She had already been in touch with those directors who she was confident supported her position, as well as one or two she felt might be wavering. But she wanted to let Grace know that she still couldn't predict which way the vote would fall.

Grace took even less interest in the company's fortunes than Giles, and on one or two occasions had even forgotten to cash her quarterly dividend cheque. She had recently been appointed Senior Tutor at Newnham, so she rarely ventured beyond the outskirts of Cambridge. Emma was occasionally able to tempt her sister up to London for a visit to the Royal Opera House, but only for a matinee, with just enough time for supper before catching the train back to Cambridge. As Grace explained, she didn't care to sleep in a strange bed. So sophisticated at one level, so parochial at another, their dear mother had once remarked.

Luchino Visconti's production of Verdi's *Don Carlo* had proved irresistible, and Grace even lingered over supper, listening intently as Emma spelt out the consequences of investing such a large amount of the company's capital reserve on a single project. Grace nibbled away at her green salad in silence, only making the occasional comment, but not offering an opinion until Major Fisher's name entered the conversation.

'He's also getting married in a few weeks' time, I'm reliably informed,' said Grace, taking her sister by surprise.

'Who in God's name would want to marry that vile creature?'

'Susie Lampton, it seems.'

'Why do I know that name?'

'She was at Red Maids' when you were head girl, but she was two years below you, so it's unlikely you'd remember her.'

'Only the name,' said Emma. 'So it's your turn to brief me.'

'Susie was already a beauty by the age of sixteen, and she knew it. Boys just stopped and stared as she passed by, their mouths open. After Red Maids', she took the first available train to London and got herself on the books of a leading model agency. Once she'd stepped on to the catwalk, Susie made no secret of the fact that she was on the lookout for a rich husband.'

'If that's the case, Fisher isn't much of a catch.'

'Perhaps he wouldn't have been back then, but now that she's thirty-something, and her modelling days are over, a director of the Barrington Shipping Line, with an Argentinian millionaire as his backer, may well prove to be her last chance.'

'Can she be that desperate?'

'Oh yes,' replied Grace. 'She's been jilted twice, once at the altar, and I'm told she's already spent the money that the court awarded her following a successful breach of promise suit. She even pawned the engagement ring. Mr Micawber is not a name she's familiar with.'

'Poor woman,' said Emma quietly.

'You needn't lose any sleep over Susie,' Grace assured her. 'That girl possesses a degree of native cunning that you won't find on the curriculum of any university,' she added before finishing her coffee. 'Mind you, I don't know which one I feel more sorry for, because I can't believe it will last that long.' Grace glanced at her watch. 'Must dash. Can't afford to miss the last train.' And without another word, she gave her sister a perfunctory kiss on both cheeks, left the restaurant and hailed a taxi.

Emma smiled as she watched her sister disappear into the back of a black cab. The social graces may not have been among her greatest strengths, but there wasn't a woman Emma admired more. Several past and present generations of Cambridge students could only have benefited from being taught by the Senior Tutor at Newnham.

When Emma asked for the bill, she noticed that her sister had left a pound note on her side plate; not a woman who cared to be beholden to anyone.

—o—

The best man handed the bridegroom a simple gold band. Giles in turn placed the ring on the third finger of Miss Hughes's left hand.

'I now pronounce you husband and wife,' declared the registrar. 'You may kiss the bride.'

A ripple of applause greeted Sir Giles and Lady Barrington. The reception that followed was held at the Cadogan Arms in King's Road. Giles seemed determined to make the complete contrast to his first wedding obvious to everyone.

When Emma entered the pub, she spotted Harry chatting to Giles's agent, who had a broad grin on his face. 'A married candidate gets far more votes than a divorced one,' Griff was explaining to Harry before he downed his third glass of champagne.

Grace was chatting to the bride, who had, not so long ago, been one of her PhD students. Gwyneth reminded her that she had first met Giles at a party Grace had thrown to celebrate her birthday.

'My birthday was only an excuse for that particular party,' said Grace without explanation.

Emma turned her attention back to Harry, who had just been joined by Deakins, no doubt swapping stories about their different experiences of being Giles's best man. Emma couldn't remember if Algernon was now a professor at Oxford. He certainly looked like one, but then, he had since the age of sixteen, and even if he hadn't sported that unkempt beard at the time, it would have been the same suit.

Emma smiled when she spotted Jessica sitting cross-legged on the floor, drawing a picture on the back of the service sheet, of Sebastian – who had been allowed out of the hospital to attend the occasion, on the strict understanding that he would be back before 6 p.m. – talking to his uncle. Giles was bending down and listening attentively to what his nephew had to say. She didn't have to guess what the subject must be.

'But if Emma were to lose the vote,' said Giles.

'Barrington's is unlikely to declare a profit for the foreseeable future, so you can no longer assume that you'll always be receiving a quarterly dividend.'

'Is there any good news?'

'Yes, if Ross Buchanan turns out to be right about the luxury liner business, and he's a shrewd operator, then Barrington's can look forward to a bright future. And you can take your place at the Cabinet table without having to worry about surviving on a minister's salary.'

'I must say, I'm delighted that you're taking such a keen interest in the family business, and can only hope you'll continue to do so once you've gone up to Cambridge.'

'You can be sure of that,' said Sebastian, 'because it's the future of the company I'm most concerned about. I'm rather hoping there'll still be a family business by the time I'm ready to take over as chairman.'

'Do you really think it's possible that Barrington's could go under?' asked Giles, sounding anxious for the first time.

'Seems unlikely, but it doesn't help that Major Fisher has been reappointed to the board, because I'm convinced his interest in the company is diametrically opposed to ours. In fact, if Don Pedro Martinez does turn out to be his backer, I'm not actually sure that the survival of Barrington's is part of their long-term plan.'

'I'm confident that Ross Buchanan and Emma will prove more than a match for Fisher, and even for Martinez.'

'Possibly. But remember that they don't always sing in unison, and Fisher will be sure to take advantage of that. And even if they do foil Fisher in the short term, all he has to do is wait a couple of years for everything to fall into his lap.'

'What are you getting at?' asked Giles.

'It's no secret that Ross Buchanan plans to retire in the not-too-distant future, and I'm told he's recently bought an estate in Perthshire that's conveniently situated near three golf courses and two rivers, which will allow him to indulge in his favourite pastimes. So it won't be too long before the company will be looking for a new chairman.'

'But if Buchanan were to retire, surely your mother would be the obvious choice to take his place? After all, she's a member of the family, and we still control twenty-two per cent of the stock.'

'But by then, Martinez might also have acquired twenty-two per cent, or possibly even more, because we know for a fact that he's still purchasing Barrington's shares as and when they come on the market. And I think we can assume, when it comes to chairman, he'll have another candidate in mind.'

6

WHEN EMMA walked into the boardroom that Friday morning, she was not surprised to find the majority of her fellow directors were already present. Only death would have been an acceptable excuse for non-attendance at this particular meeting; what Giles would have called a three-line whip.

The chairman was chatting to Rear Admiral Summers. Clive Anscott, no surprise, was deep in conversation with his golfing partner, Jim Knowles, who had already informed Emma that they would both be supporting the chairman when it came to the vote. Emma joined Andy Dobbs and David Dixon, both of whom had made it clear that they would be backing her.

Philip Webster, the company secretary, and Michael Carrick, the finance director, were studying the naval architect's plans for the proposed luxury liner, which had been laid out on the boardroom table alongside something Emma had never seen before, a scale model of the MV *Buckingham*. She had to admit, it looked very seductive, and boys do like toys.

'It's going to be a close-run thing,' Andy Dobbs was saying to Emma when the boardroom door opened and the tenth director made his entrance.

Alex Fisher remained by the door. He looked a little nervous, like a new bug on his first day of term who wonders if any of the other boys will talk to him. The chairman immediately broke away from his group and crossed the room to greet him. Emma watched as Ross shook hands with the major formally, and not as if he was greeting a respected colleague. When it came to Fisher, they shared the same opinion of the man.

When the grandfather clock in the corner of the room began to chime ten, conversations immediately ceased, and the directors took their allocated places around the boardroom table. Fisher, like a wallflower at a church dance, remained standing until there was only one empty seat left, as if they were playing Musical Chairs. He slipped into the vacant chair opposite Emma, but didn't look in her direction.

'Good morning,' said the chairman once everyone had settled. 'Can I open this meeting by welcoming back Major Fisher to our ranks as a director?'

Only one person managed a muffled, 'Hear, hear,' but then, he hadn't been on the board when Fisher had first served as a director.

'This will of course be the major's second stint on the board, so he will be accustomed to our ways, and to the loyalty we all expect from any board member when representing this great company.'

'Thank you, Mr Chairman,' responded Fisher. 'And I'd like to say how delighted I am to be back on the board. Let me assure you that I will always do what I consider to be in Barrington's best interests.'

'I'm glad to hear it,' said the chairman. 'However, it is my duty to remind you, as I do every new board member, that it is against the law for a director to buy or sell any of the company's shares without first informing the Stock Exchange, as well as the company secretary.'

If Fisher felt this barbed arrow had been aimed at him, it failed to hit the target, because he simply nodded and smiled, even though Mr Webster assiduously recorded the chairman's words in the minutes. Emma was, at least, glad it was on the record this time.

Once the minutes of the last meeting had been read and approved, the chairman said, 'Members of the board cannot have failed to notice that there is only one item on the agenda for today's meeting. As you all know, I feel the time has come to make a decision that will, and I believe I do not exaggerate, decide the future of Barrington's, and perhaps the future of one or two of us who presently serve the company.'

It was clear that several directors were taken by surprise by Buchanan's opening remarks, and they began to whisper among themselves. Ross had tossed a hand grenade into the middle of the boardroom table, with the implicit threat that if he didn't win the vote, he would resign as chairman.

Emma's problem was that she didn't have a hand grenade to lob back. She couldn't threaten to resign herself, for several reasons, not least because no other member of the family had any desire to take her place on the board. Sebastian had already advised her that if she didn't win the vote, she could always step down from the board and she and Giles could sell their shares, which would have the double advantage of making the family a handsome profit, while at the same time out-manoeuvring Martinez.

Emma looked up at the portrait of Sir Walter Barrington. She could hear Gramps saying, 'Don't do anything you'll live to regret, child.'

'By all means, let us have a robust and no-holds-barred discussion,' continued Ross Buchanan. 'One in which I hope all directors will express their opinions without fear or favour.' He then lobbed his second grenade. 'With that in mind, I suggest that Mrs Clifton should open the debate, not only because she is opposed to my plan of building a new liner at the present time, but we must not forget she represents twenty-two per cent of the company's stock, and it was her illustrious forebear, Sir Joshua Barrington, who founded this company over a hundred years ago.'

Emma had rather hoped to be among the last to contribute to the discussion, as she was well aware that the chairman would be summing up, and her words might have lost some of their impact by the time he spoke. Nevertheless, she was determined to put her arguments as forcefully as she could.

'Thank you, Mr Chairman,' she said, looking down at her notes. 'May I begin by saying that whatever the outcome of today's discussion, I know we all hope that you will continue to lead this company for many years to come.'

Loud 'Hear, hears' followed this statement, and Emma felt she had at least placed the pin back into one of the grenades.

'As the chairman reminded us, my great-grandfather founded this company more than a hundred years ago. He was a man who had the uncanny knack of spotting an opportunity while at the same time being able to side-step a pothole, both with equal skill. I only wish I had Sir Joshua's vision, because then I would be able tell you,' she said, pointing at the architect's plan, 'whether this is an opportunity or a pothole. My serious reservation about this project is the all-your-eggs-in-one-basket issue. To risk such a large percentage of the company's reserves on a single venture could well turn out to be a decision we will all live to regret. After all, the very future of the luxury liner business appears to be in a state of flux. Two major shipping companies have already declared a loss this year, citing the boom in the passenger aircraft industry as the reason for their difficulties. And it is no coincidence that the drop in the numbers of our own transatlantic passengers correlates almost exactly with the rise in the number of air passengers during the same period. The facts are simple. Businessmen want to get to their meetings as quickly as possible, and then return home just as quickly. That is perfectly understandable. We might not like the public's change of allegiance, but we would be foolish to ignore its long-term consequences. I believe we should stick to the business which has rightly given Barrington's a worldwide reputation: the transport of coal, cars, heavy service vehicles, steel, food and other commodities, and leave others to be dependent on passengers. I'm confident that if we continue with our core business of cargo vessels that have cabins for only a dozen or so passengers, the company will survive these troubled times, and go on declaring a handsome profit year on year, giving our shareholders an excellent return on their investment. I don't want to gamble all the money this company has husbanded so carefully over the years on the whim of a fickle public.'

Time for my hand grenade, thought Emma as she turned the page.

'My father, Sir Hugo Barrington – you'll find no oil painting on the walls of this boardroom to remind us of his stewardship – managed, in the space of a couple of years, to bring this company to its knees, and it has taken all of Ross Buchanan's considerable skill and ingenuity to restore our fortunes, for which we should all be eternally grateful. However, for me, this latest proposal is a step too far, and therefore I hope the board will reject it, in favour of continuing with our core business, which has served us so well in the past. I therefore invite the board to vote against this resolution.'

Emma was delighted to see that one or two older members of the board, who had previously been wavering, were now nodding. Buchanan invited the other directors to make their contributions, and an hour later, every one of them had offered an opinion, except for Alex Fisher, who had remained silent.

'Major, now that you've heard the views of your colleagues, perhaps you would care to share your thoughts with the board.'

'Mr Chairman,' said Fisher, 'during the past month, I've studied the detailed minutes of previous board meetings on this particular subject, and I am certain of only one thing: we cannot afford to procrastinate any longer, and must make a decision one way or the other today.'

Fisher waited for the 'Hear, hears' to die down before he continued.

'I have listened with interest to my fellow directors, particularly Mrs Clifton, who I felt presented a reasoned and well-argued case with considerable passion, remembering her family's long association with the company. But before I decide how to cast my vote, I would like to hear why the chairman feels so strongly that we should go ahead with the building of the *Buckingham* at the present time, as I still need to be convinced that it's a risk worth taking, and not a step too far, as Mrs Clifton has suggested.'

'Wise man,' said the admiral.

Emma wondered, just for a moment, if she might have misjudged Fisher, and he really did have the best interests of the company at heart. Then she recalled Sebastian's reminder that leopards don't change their spots.

'Thank you, major,' said Buchanan.

Emma didn't doubt that despite his well-prepared and well-delivered words, Fisher's mind had already been made up for him, and he would carry out Martinez's instructions to the letter. However, she still had no idea what those instructions were.

'Members of the board are well aware of my strongly held views on this subject,' began the chairman as he glanced down at seven headings on a single sheet of paper. 'I believe the decision we will make today is an obvious one. Is this company willing to take a step forward, or should we be satisfied with simply treading water? I don't have to remind you that Cunard has recently launched two new passenger ships, P&O has the *Canberra* under construction in Belfast, and Union-Castle is adding the *Windsor Castle* and the *Transvaal Castle* to their South African fleet, while we seem content to sit and watch, as our rivals, like marauding pirates, take control of the high seas. There will never be a better time for Barrington's to enter the passenger business, transatlantic in the summer, cruising in the winter. Mrs Clifton points out that our passenger numbers are falling, and she is right. But that is only because our fleet is out of date, and we no longer offer a service that our customers cannot find elsewhere at a more competitive price. And if we were to decide today to do nothing, but simply wait for the right moment, as Mrs Clifton suggests, others will surely take advantage of our absence and leave us standing on the quayside, no more than waving spectators. Yes, of course, as Major Fisher has pointed out, we would be taking a risk, but that's what great entrepreneurs like Sir Joshua Barrington were always willing to do. And let me remind you, this project is not the financial risk that Mrs Clifton has suggested,' he added, pointing to the model of the liner in the centre of the table, 'because we can cover a great deal of the expense of constructing this magnificent vessel from our present reserves, and won't need to borrow large amounts from the bank to finance it. I have a feeling Joshua

Barrington would also have approved of that.' Buchanan paused, and looked around the table at his fellow directors. 'I believe we are faced today with a stark choice: to do nothing, and be satisfied with standing still at best, or to cast a vote for the future, and give this company a chance of continuing to take the lead in the world of shipping, as it has done for the past century. I therefore ask the board to support my proposal, and make an investment in that future.'

Despite the chairman's stirring words, Emma still wasn't sure which way the vote would go. Then came the moment Buchanan chose to remove the pin from his third grenade.

'I will now call upon the company secretary to invite each director to state whether they are for or against the proposal.'

Emma had assumed that in line with the company's normal procedure it would be a secret ballot, which she believed would give her a better chance of securing a majority. However, she realized that if she were to raise an objection at this late stage, it would be seen as a sign of weakness, which would play into Buchanan's hands.

Mr Webster extracted a single sheet of paper from a file in front of him, and read out the resolution. 'Members of the board are invited to vote on a resolution proposed by the chairman and seconded by the managing director, namely that the company should proceed with the building of a new luxury liner, the MV *Buckingham*, at the present time.'

Emma had requested that the last four words should be added to the resolution, as she hoped they would persuade some of the more conservative members of the board to bide their time.

The company secretary opened the minute book and read out the names of the directors one by one.

'Mr Buchanan.'

'In favour of the proposition,' the chairman replied, without hesitation.

'Mr Knowles.'

'In favour.'

'Mr Dixon.'

'Against.'

'Mr Anscott.'

'In favour.'

Emma placed a tick or a cross by each name on her list. So far there were no surprises.

'Admiral Summers.'

'Against,' he declared, equally firmly.

Emma couldn't believe it. The admiral had changed his mind, which meant that if everyone else stuck to their position, she couldn't lose.

'Mrs Clifton.'

'Against.'

'Mr Dobbs.'

'Against.'

'Mr Carrick.'

The finance director hesitated. He had told Emma that he was opposed to the whole concept, as he was certain the costs would spiral and, despite Buchanan's assurances, the company would end up having to borrow large sums from the bank.

'In favour,' Mr Carrick whispered.

Emma swore under her breath. She put a cross next to Carrick's name, and re-checked her list. Five votes each. Every head turned to face the newest member of the board, who now held the casting vote.

Emma and Ross Buchanan were about to discover how Don Pedro Martinez would have voted, but not why.

DON PEDRO MARTINEZ

1958–1959

7

'By one vote?'

'Yes,' said the major.

'Then buying those shares has already proved a worthwhile investment.'

'What do you want me to do next?'

'Go on backing the chairman for the time being, because it won't be too long before he'll be needing your support again.'

'I'm not sure I understand.'

'You don't need to understand, major.'

Don Pedro rose from behind his desk and walked towards the door. The meeting was over. Fisher quickly followed him out into the hall.

'How's married life treating you, major?'

'Couldn't be better,' lied Fisher, who had quickly been made aware that two people cannot live as cheaply as one.

'I'm glad to hear that,' said Martinez, as he handed the major a thick envelope.

'What's this?' asked Fisher.

'A little bonus for pulling off the coup,' replied Martinez as Karl opened the front door.

'But I'm already in your debt,' said Fisher, slipping the envelope into an inside pocket.

'And I'm confident you'll pay me back in kind,' Martinez said, noticing a man sitting on a bench on the opposite side of the road, pretending to read the *Daily Mail*.

'Do you still want me to come up to London before the next board meeting?'

'No, but the moment you hear who's been awarded the contract to build the *Buckingham*, phone me.'

'You'll be the first to know,' said Fisher. He gave his new boss a mock salute before marching off in the direction of Sloane Square. The man on the opposite side of the road didn't follow him, but then, Captain Hartley knew exactly where the major was going. Don Pedro smiled as he strolled back into the house.

'Karl, tell Diego and Luis that I want to see them immediately, and I'll need you as well.'

The butler bowed as he closed the front door, making sure he remained in character whenever someone was watching. Don Pedro returned to his office, sat down at his desk, smiled, and thought about the meeting that had just taken place. This time they wouldn't foil him. Everything was in place, to finish off not one, but the entire family. He didn't intend to tell the major what his next move would be. He had a feeling that despite his regular bonuses, the man might prove squeamish under fire, and there could be a limit to how far he was willing to go. Don Pedro didn't have to wait long before there was a tap on the door and he was joined by the only three men he trusted. His two sons took their seats on the other side of the desk, which only reminded him that his youngest son couldn't be present. It made him even more resolute. Karl remained standing.

'The board meeting could not have gone better. They agreed by one vote to go ahead with the commissioning of the *Buckingham*, and it was the major's vote that swung it. The next thing we need to find out is which shipyard will be awarded the contract to build it. Until we know that, we can't go ahead with the second part of my plan.'

'And as that might prove rather expensive,' chipped in Diego, 'do you have any ideas as to how we're going to bankroll this whole operation?'

'Yes,' said Don Pedro. 'I intend to rob a bank.'

―◇―

Colonel Scott-Hopkins slipped into the Clarence just before midday. The pub was only a couple of hundred yards from Downing Street, and was well known for being frequented by tourists. He walked up to the bar and ordered a half pint of bitter and a double gin and tonic.

'That'll be three and six, sir,' said the barman.

The colonel put two florins on the counter, picked up the drinks and made his way over to an alcove in the far corner, where they would be well hidden from prying eyes. He placed the drinks down on a small wooden table covered in rings from beer glasses and cigarette butts. He checked his watch. His boss was rarely late, even though in his job problems did have a habit of arising at the last minute. But not today, because the cabinet secretary walked into the pub a few moments later and headed straight for the alcove.

The colonel rose from his place. 'Good morning, sir.' He would never have considered addressing him as Sir Alan; far too familiar.

'Good morning, Brian. As I only have a few minutes to spare, perhaps you could bring me up to date.'

'Martinez, his sons Diego and Luis, as well as Karl Lunsdorf, are clearly working as a team. However, since my meeting with Martinez, not one of them has been anywhere near the Princess Alexandra Hospital in Harlow, or paid a visit to Bristol.'

'That's good to know,' said Sir Alan as he picked up his glass. 'But it doesn't mean Martinez isn't working on something else. He's not a man to back off quite that easily.'

'I'm sure you're right, sir. Although he may not be going to Bristol, it doesn't mean Bristol isn't coming to him.'

The cabinet secretary raised an eyebrow.

'Alex Fisher is now working full time for Martinez. He's back on the board of Barrington's, and reports directly to his new boss in London once, sometimes twice a week.'

The cabinet secretary sipped his double gin while he considered the implications of the colonel's words. The first thing he would have to do was purchase a few shares in Barrington Shipping so he could be sent a copy of the minutes following every board meeting.

'Anything else?'

'Yes. Martinez has made an appointment to see the governor of the Bank of England next Thursday morning at eleven.'

'So we're about to find out just how many counterfeit five-pound notes the damn man still has in his possession.'

'But I thought we destroyed them all in Southampton last June?'

'Only those he'd hidden in the base of the Rodin statue. But he's been smuggling smaller amounts out of Buenos Aires for the past ten years, long before any of us realized what he was up to.'

'Why doesn't the governor simply refuse to deal with the man, when we all know they're counterfeits?'

'Because the governor is a pompous ass, and refuses to believe that anyone is capable of reproducing a perfect copy of one of his precious five-pound notes. So Martinez is about to swap all his old lamps for new, and there's nothing I can do about it.'

'I could always kill him, sir.'

'The governor, or Martinez?' said Sir Alan, not quite sure if Scott-Hopkins was joking.

The colonel smiled. He wouldn't have minded which one.

'No, Brian, I can't sanction killing Martinez until I have a lawful excuse, and when I last checked, counterfeiting was not a hanging offence.'

◄○►

Don Pedro sat at his desk, impatiently drumming his fingers on a blotting pad as he waited for the phone to ring.

The board meeting had been scheduled for ten o'clock, and usually finished around midday. It was already 12.20 p.m., and he hadn't heard a word from Fisher, despite giving him clear instructions to call the moment the meeting was over. However, he recalled that Karl had recommended that Fisher shouldn't attempt to contact the boss until he was far enough away from Barrington House to be sure that no other board member witnessed him making the call.

Karl had also advised the major to select a venue that none

of his fellow directors would consider frequenting. Fisher had chosen the Lord Nelson, not only because it was less than a mile from Barrington's shipyard, but because it was situated on the lower dockside: a pub that specialized in pints of bitter, the occasional cider, and didn't need to stock Harvey's Bristol Cream. Even more important, there was a phone box outside the front door.

The phone rang on Don Pedro's desk. He grabbed the receiver before the second ring. Karl had also advised Fisher not to identify himself when calling from a public phone box, or to waste any time on small talk, and to make sure he delivered his message in under a minute.

'Harland and Wolff, Belfast.'

'There is a God in heaven,' said Don Pedro.

The line went dead. Clearly nothing else had been discussed at the board meeting that Fisher felt couldn't wait until he travelled up to London the following day. Don Pedro replaced the receiver and looked across at the three men on the other side of the desk. Each of them already knew what their next job would be.

–◦–

'Come.'

The chief teller opened the door and stood aside to allow the banker from Argentina to enter the governor's office. Martinez entered the room, dressed in a pinstriped double-breasted suit, white shirt and silk tie, all purchased from a tailor in Savile Row. He was followed by two uniformed guards who carried a large, battered school trunk displaying the initials *BM*. Bringing up the rear was a tall, thin gentleman dressed in a smart black jacket, grey waistcoat, pinstriped trousers and a dark tie with pale blue stripes, to remind lesser mortals that he and the governor had been educated at the same school.

The guards placed the trunk in the centre of the room as the governor slipped out from behind his desk and shook hands with Don Pedro. He looked fixedly at the trunk as his guest unlocked its clasps and opened the lid. The five men stared down at row upon row of neatly stacked five-pound notes. Not an unusual sight for any of them.

The governor turned to the chief teller and said, 'Somerville, these notes are to be counted and then double-checked, and if Mr Martinez is in agreement with your figure, you will then shred them.'

The chief teller nodded, and one of the guards lowered the trunk's lid and flicked the clasps back into place. The guards then slowly lifted the heavy trunk and followed the chief teller out of the room. The governor didn't speak again until he heard the door close.

'Perhaps you'd care to join me for a glass of Bristol Cream, old man, while we wait to confirm that our figures tally?'

It had taken Don Pedro some time to accept that 'old man' was a term of endearment, even a recognition that you were a member of the club, despite being a foreigner.

The governor filled two glasses and passed one across to his guest. 'Good health, old fellow.'

'Good health, old fellow,' mimicked Don Pedro.

'I'm surprised,' said the governor after taking a sip, 'that you kept such a large amount in cash.'

'The money's been stored in a vault in Geneva for the past five years, and it would have remained there if your government hadn't decided to print new bank notes.'

'Not my decision, old man. In fact I counselled against it, but that fool of a cabinet secretary – wrong school and wrong university,' he mumbled between sips, 'insisted that the Germans had been counterfeiting our five-pound notes during the war. I told him that simply wasn't possible, but he wouldn't listen. Seemed to think he knew better than the Bank of England. I also told him that as long as my signature was on an English bank note, the amount would be honoured in full.'

'I wouldn't have expected less,' said Don Pedro, risking a smile.

After that, the two men found it difficult to settle on a subject with which they both felt at ease. Only polo (not water), Wimbledon, and looking forward to the twelfth of August kept them going long enough for the governor to pour a second sherry, and he couldn't hide his relief when the phone on his desk finally rang. He put down his glass, picked up the phone and listened intently. The governor removed a Parker pen from an inside pocket and wrote down a figure. He then asked the chief teller to repeat it.

'Thank you, Somerville,' he said before putting the receiver down. 'I'm happy to say that our figures tally, old fellow. Not that I ever doubted they would,' he added quickly.

He opened the top drawer of his desk, took out a cheque book and wrote *Two million, one hundred and forty-three thousand, one hundred and thirty-five pounds,* in a neat, bold, copperplate hand. He couldn't resist adding the word *only* before appending his signature. He smiled as he handed the cheque to Don Pedro, who checked the figure before returning his smile.

Don Pedro would have preferred a banker's draft, but a cheque signed by the governor of the Bank of England was the next best thing. After all, like the five-pound note, it had his signature on it.

8

THE THREE OF THEM left 44 Eaton Square at different times during the morning, but they all ended up at the same destination.

Luis was the first to appear. He walked to Sloane Square underground station and boarded a Circle line train to Hammersmith, where he crossed platforms to the Piccadilly line. Corporal Crann was never far behind.

Diego took a cab to Victoria coach station, and climbed on board a bus for the airport; a moment later he was joined by his shadow.

Luis made it easy for Captain Hartley to follow his every move, but then, he was doing no more than his father had ordered. At Hounslow West he exited the underground and took a taxi to London Airport, where he checked the departures board to confirm that his flight would be leaving in just over an hour. He purchased the latest copy of *Playboy* from W.H. Smith and, as he had no bag to check in, made his way slowly towards gate 5.

Diego's bus dropped him outside the terminal a few minutes before ten. He also checked the departure board, to find that his flight to Madrid had been delayed by forty minutes. It was of no consequence. He strolled across to Forte's Grill, bought a coffee and a ham sandwich, and took a seat near the entrance so that no one could miss him.

Karl opened the front door of number 44 a few minutes after Luis's flight had taken off for Nice. He headed in the direction of Sloane Street, carrying a Harrods bag that was already full. He paused to window-shop on the way, not to admire the goods on display, but to look at the reflections in the glass; an old ruse to check if you're being followed. He was, by the same shabbily dressed little man who'd been shadowing him for the past month. By the time he reached Harrods, he was well aware that his pursuer was only a few strides behind him.

A doorman in a long green overcoat and wearing a top hat opened the door for Karl and saluted. He took pride in recognizing his regular customers.

The moment Karl stepped inside the store he began to walk quickly through haberdashery, speeding up as he passed leather goods, and he was almost running by the time he reached the bank of six lifts. Only one of them had its gate open. It was already packed, but he squeezed in. His shadow almost caught up with him, but the lift attendant pulled the grille shut before he could jump in. The pursued couldn't resist smiling at the pursuer as the lift disappeared out of sight.

Karl didn't get out until the lift reached the top floor. He then walked quickly through electrical goods, furniture, the bookshop and the art gallery, before reaching the rarely used stone staircase at the north end of the store. He took the steps in twos, and only stopped running once he was back at the ground floor. He then cut through menswear, perfume, pens and stationery until he reached a side door that led out on to Hans Road. Once he was on the pavement, he hailed the first available cab, climbed in and crouched down, out of sight.

'London Airport,' he said.

He waited until the cab had passed through two sets of traffic lights before he risked glancing out of the back window. No sign of his pursuer, unless Sergeant Roberts was on a bicycle or driving a London bus.

Karl had visited Harrods every morning during the past fortnight, going straight to the food hall on the ground floor and purchasing a few items before returning to Eaton Square. But not today. Although he had shaken off the SAS man this time, he knew that he wouldn't be able to pull off the Harrods stunt a second time. And as he might have to travel to today's destination fairly often, it wasn't going to be difficult for them to work out where he was heading, so in future they would be waiting for him as he got off the plane.

When the taxi dropped him off outside the Europa terminal, Karl didn't buy a copy of *Playboy* or have a coffee, he just headed straight for gate number 18.

—◦—

Luis's plane touched down in Nice a few minutes after Karl's took off. Luis had a wad of new five-pound notes secreted in his washbag, and instructions that could not have been clearer: enjoy yourself, and don't come back for at least a week. Hardly a taxing assignment, but all part of Don Pedro's overall plan.

Diego's plane entered Spanish airspace an hour behind schedule, but as his appointment with one of the nation's leading beef importers wasn't until four that afternoon, he had time to spare. Whenever he travelled to Madrid, he always stayed at the same hotel, dined in the same restaurant and visited the same brothel. His shadow also booked himself into the same hotel and ate in the same restaurant, but he sat alone in a coffee shop on the opposite side of the road whenever Diego spent a couple of hours at La Buena Noche. Not an expense claim he felt Colonel Scott-Hopkins would be amused by.

—◦—

Karl Lunsdorf had never visited Belfast, but after several 'drinks on me' evenings at Ward's Irish House in Piccadilly, he left the pub for the last time with almost all of his questions answered. He also vowed never to drink another pint of Guinness in his life.

On leaving the airport, he took a taxi to the Royal Windsor Hotel in the city centre, where he booked himself in for three nights. He told the receptionist that he might have to stay longer, depending on how his business worked out. Once he was in his room, he locked the door, unpacked his Harrods carrier bag and ran a bath. Afterwards he lay on his bed thinking about what he planned to do that evening. He didn't move until he saw the street lights go on. He then checked the city road map once more, so that by the time he left the hotel he would not need to refer to it again.

He left his room just after six, and took the stairs to the ground floor. He never used the hotel lift – a tiny, exposed, over-lit space that would make it far too easy for other guests to remember him. He walked quickly, but not too quickly, across the foyer and out on to Donegall Road. After a hundred yards of window-shopping, he was confident no one was following him. He was, once again, on his own behind enemy lines.

He didn't take the direct route to his destination, but doub-led back down side streets so that a walk that normally would have taken him twenty minutes took just under an hour. But then, he wasn't in a hurry. When he finally reached the Falls Road, he could feel the beads of sweat on his forehead. He knew that fear would be a constant companion while he remained in the fourteen blocks occupied only by Roman Catholics. Not for the first time in his life he found himself somewhere where he wasn't quite certain he would get out alive.

At six foot three, with a mane of thick blond hair and weigh-ing 208lbs, mostly muscle, it wasn't going to be easy for Karl to melt into the background. What had been an advantage when he was a young SS officer was going to be the exact opposite for the next few hours. He only had one thing going for him, his German accent. Many of the Catholics who lived on the Falls Road hated the English even more than the Germans, although sometimes it was a close-run thing. After all, Hitler had promised to reunite the north and the south once he'd won the war. Karl often wondered what post Himmler would have given him if, as he'd recommended, Germany had invaded Britain and not made the disastrous mistake of turning east and heading for Russia. Pity the Führer hadn't read more history. However, Karl didn't doubt that many of those who espoused the cause of Irish unity were no more than thugs and criminals who regarded patriotism as a thinly disguised opportunity to make money. Something the Irish Republican Army had in common with the SS.

He saw the sign swinging in the evening breeze. If he was going to turn back, it would have to be now. But he didn't hesitate. He would never forget that it was Martinez who had made it possible for him to escape from his homeland when the Russian tanks were within firing distance of the Reichstag.

He pushed through the peeling green-painted door that led into the bar, feeling about as inconspicuous as a nun in a betting shop. But he'd already accepted that there was no subtle way of letting the IRA know he was in town. It wasn't a question of who you know . . . he didn't know anyone.

When he ordered a Jameson's whiskey, Karl exaggerated his German accent. He then took out his wallet, removed a crisp five-pound note, and placed it on the counter. The barman eyed the money suspiciously, not even sure there was enough change in the till to cover it.

Karl downed the whiskey and immediately ordered another. He had at least to try and show he had something in common with them. It always amused him how many people imagined big men must be big drinkers. After his second whiskey he glanced around the room, but no one was willing to make eye contact. There must have been about twenty people in the bar, chatting, playing dominoes, sipping their pints, all of them pretending they hadn't noticed the elephant in the room.

At 9.30 p.m. the barman rang a bell and hollered last orders, which caused several customers to rush up to the counter and order another drink. Still no one gave Karl a second look, let alone spoke to him. He hung around for a few more minutes, but nothing changed, so he decided to return to his hotel and try again tomorrow. He knew it would take years before they would treat him like a native, if ever, and he only had a few days to meet someone who would never have considered entering that bar, but who would have been told by midnight that Karl had been there.

As he walked back out on to the Falls Road, he became aware of several pairs of eyes watching his every move. A moment later, two men, more drunk than sober, swayed across the road whenever he did. He slowed down to make sure his pursuers couldn't fail to see where he was spending the night, so they could pass the information on to a higher authority. He strolled into the hotel, turned around and spotted them hanging about in the shadows on the far side of the road. He climbed the stairs to the third floor and let himself into his room, feeling that he probably couldn't have done much more on his first day in the city than make them aware of his presence.

Karl devoured all the complimentary biscuits that had been left on the sideboard, as well as an orange, an apple and a banana from the fruit bowl; quite enough. When he'd escaped from Berlin in April 1945, he'd survived on water from muddy rivers recently disturbed by tanks and heavy vehicles, and the luxury of an uncooked rabbit; he'd even eaten its skin by the time he crossed the border into Switzerland. He never slept under a roof, never walked on a road, and never entered a town or village during the long, circuitous route to the Mediterranean coast, where he was smuggled aboard a tramp steamer like a sack of coal. It would be another five months before he stepped off the boat and set foot in Buenos Aires. He immediately went in search of Don Pedro Martinez, carrying out the last order Himmler had given him before committing suicide. Martinez was now his commanding officer.

9

KARL ROSE LATE the following morning. He knew he couldn't afford to be seen in a hotel breakfast room full of Protestants, so he grabbed a bacon butty at a café on the corner of Leeson Street, before he made his way slowly back to the Falls Road, which was now packed with shoppers, mothers with prams, children with dummies in their mouths, and black-frocked priests.

He was back outside the Volunteer moments after the land-lord had opened the front door. He recognized Karl immediately – the five-pound man – but didn't acknowledge him. Karl ordered a pint of lager and paid for it with the change from the bacon butty. He remained propping up the bar until closing time, with only two short breaks to relieve himself. A packet of Smith's crisps with salt in a little blue sachet was his lunch. He had munched his way through three packets by the early evening, which only made him want to drink more. Locals came and went, and Karl noticed that one or two of them didn't stop for a drink, which made him feel a little more hopeful. They looked without looking. But as the hours slipped by, still no one spoke to him or even glanced in his direction.

Fifteen minutes after calling last orders, the barman shouted, 'Time, gentlemen please,' and Karl felt he'd spent another wasted day. As he headed towards the door, he even thought about plan B, which would involve changing sides and making contact with the Protestants.

The moment he stepped out on to the pavement, a black

Hillman drew up beside him. The back door swung open and, before he could react, two men grabbed him, hurled him on to the back seat and slammed the door shut. The car sped off.

Karl looked up to see a young man who certainly wasn't old enough to vote, holding a gun to his forehead. The only thing that worried him was that the youth was clearly more frightened than he was, and was shaking so much that the gun was more likely to go off by accident than by design. He could have disarmed the boy in a moment, but as that wouldn't have served his purpose, he didn't resist when the older man seated on his other side tied his hands behind his back, then placed a scarf over his eyes. The same man checked to see if he was carrying a gun, and deftly removed his wallet. Karl heard him whistle as he counted the five-pound notes.

'There's a lot more where that came from,' said Karl.

A heated argument followed, in a language Karl assumed must be their native tongue. He got the sense that one of them wanted to kill him, but he hoped the older man would be tempted by the possibility of more money. Money must have won, because he could no longer feel the gun touching his forehead.

The car swerved to the right, and moments later to the left. Who were they trying to fool? Karl knew they were simply going back over the same route, because they wouldn't risk leaving their Catholic stronghold.

Suddenly, the car came to a halt, a door opened and Karl was thrown out on to the street. If he was still alive in five minutes' time, he thought, he might live to collect his old-age pension. Someone grabbed him by the hair and yanked him to his feet. A shove in the middle of his back propelled him through an open door. A smell of burnt meat wafted from a back room, but he suspected that feeding him wasn't on their agenda.

He was dragged up a flight of stairs into a room that had a bedroom smell, and pushed down on to a hard wooden chair. The door slammed, and he was left alone. Or was he? He assumed he must be in a safe house, and that someone senior, possibly even an area commander, would now be deciding what should be done with him.

He couldn't be sure how long they kept him waiting. It felt like hours, each minute longer than the last. Then suddenly the door was thrown open, and he heard at least three men enter the room. One of them began to circle the chair.

'What do you want, Englishman?' said the gruff circling voice.

'I'm not English,' said Karl. 'I'm German.'

A long silence followed. 'So what do you want, Kraut?'

'I have a proposition to put to you.'

'Do you support the IRA?' another voice, younger, passionate, but with no authority.

'I don't give a fuck about the IRA.'

'Then why risk your life trying to find us?'

'Because, as I said, I have a proposition you might find worthwhile. So why don't you bugger off and get someone in here who can make decisions. Because I suspect, young man, that your mother is still teaching you your potty drill.'

A fist smashed into his mouth, followed by a loud angry exchange of opinions, several voices speaking at the same time. Karl felt blood trickle down his chin, and braced himself for the second blow, but it never came. The older man must have prevailed. A moment later three of them left the room, and the door slammed. But this time Karl knew he wasn't alone. Having his eyes covered for so long had made him more sensitive to sound and smell. At least an hour passed before the door opened again, and a man wearing shoes, not boots, entered the room. Karl could sense that he was just inches away.

'What is your name?' asked a man with a cultured voice and almost no accent.

Karl guessed the voice belonged to someone aged between thirty-five and forty. He smiled. Although he couldn't see him, this was the man he'd come to negotiate with.

'Karl Lunsdorf.'

'And what brings you to Belfast, Mr Lunsdorf?'

'I need your help.'

'What do you have in mind?'

'I need someone who believes in your cause and works at Harland and Wolff.'

'I am sure you already know that very few Catholics can find work at Harland and Wolff. It's a closed shop. I fear you may have made a wasted journey.'

'There are a handful of Catholics, carefully vetted I admit, who work there in specialized areas, electrical, plumbing and welding, but only when the management can't find a Protestant with the necessary skills.'

'You're well informed, Mr Lunsdorf. But even if we could find such a man who supported our cause, what would you expect him to do?'

'Harland and Wolff have just been awarded a contract by Barrington Shipping—'

'To build a luxury liner called the *Buckingham*.'

'Now it's you who's well informed,' said Karl.

'Hardly,' said the cultured voice. 'An architect's drawing of the proposed ship was printed on the front page of both our local papers the day after the contract was signed. So, Mr Lunsdorf, tell me something I don't know.'

'Work on the liner begins some time next month, with a delivery date to Barrington's of March fifteenth, 1962.'

'And what are you hoping we will be able to do? Speed the process up, or slow it down?'

'Bring it to a halt.'

'Not an easy task, when so many suspicious eyes will always be watching.'

'We would make it worth your while.'

'Why?' said the gruff voice.

'Let's just say I represent a rival company who would like to see Barrington Shipping in financial difficulty.'

'And how will we earn our money?' asked the cultured voice.

'By results. The contract stipulates that the construction of the ship is to be carried out in eight stages, with specific dates attached to each stage. For example, stage one has to be signed off by both sides on December the first this year at the latest. I propose that we pay you a thousand pounds for every day any stage is delayed. So, if it was held up for a year, we would pay you three hundred and sixty-five thousand.'

'I know how many days there are in a year, Mr Lunsdorf. If we were to agree to your proposition, we would expect a "good-will" payment in advance.'

'How much?' demanded Karl, feeling like an equal for the first time.

The two men whispered to each other. 'I think a down payment of twenty thousand would help to convince us that you are serious,' said the cultured voice.

'Give me the details of your bank account, and I'll transfer the full amount tomorrow morning.'

'We'll be in touch,' said the cultured voice. 'But not before we've given your proposition further consideration.'

'But you don't know where I live.'

'Forty-four Eaton Square, Chelsea, Mr Lunsdorf.' It was Karl's turn to fall silent. 'And should we agree to assist you, Mr Lunsdorf, be sure you don't make the common mistake of underestimating the Irish, as the English have done for almost a thousand years.'

<o>

'So how did you manage to lose Lunsdorf?'

'He got away from Sergeant Roberts in Harrods.'

'I sometimes wish I could do that when I'm shopping with my wife,' said the cabinet secretary. 'And what about Luis and Diego Martinez? Did they also get away?'

'No, but they turned out to be nothing more than a couple of smokescreens to keep us occupied while Lunsdorf made good his escape.'

'How long was Lunsdorf away?'

'Three days. He was back in Eaton Square by Friday afternoon.'

'He couldn't have travelled too far during that time. If I was a betting man, I doubt I'd get very long odds on Belfast, remembering he's spent several evenings during the past month drinking Guinness at Ward's Irish House in Piccadilly.'

'And Belfast is where they're building the *Buckingham*. But

I still haven't worked out exactly what Martinez is up to,' said Scott-Hopkins.

'Neither have I, but I can tell you that he recently deposited just over two million pounds at the St James's branch of the Midland Bank, and immediately starting buying more Barrington's shares. It won't be long before he'll be able to place a second director on the board.'

'Perhaps he's planning to take over the company.'

'And for Mrs Clifton, the idea of Martinez running the family business would be humiliating enough. *Take away my good name . . .*'

'But Martinez could lose a fortune if he tried to do that.'

'I doubt it. That man will already have a contingency plan in place, but like you I'm damned if I can work out what it is.'

'Is there anything we can do?'

'Not a lot, except sit and wait, and hope one of them makes a mistake.' The cabinet secretary finished his drink before adding, 'It's at times like this I wish I'd been born in Russia. By now I'd be head of the KGB, and I wouldn't have to waste time playing by the rules.'

10

'NO ONE'S to blame,' said the chairman.

'Perhaps, but we seem to be lurching from one inexplicable disaster to another,' said Emma. She began to read aloud from the long list in front of her. 'A fire in a loading bay that holds up construction for several days; a boiler breaks its straps as it's being unloaded and ends up at the bottom of the harbour; a bout of food poisoning that results in seventy-three electricians, plumbers and welders being sent home; a wildcat strike—'

'What's the bottom line, chairman?' asked Major Fisher.

'We're falling quite badly behind schedule,' replied Buchanan. 'There's no chance of stage one being completed by the end of the year. If things go on like this, we have little hope of keeping to our original timetable.'

'And the financial consequences of failing to make the dates?' enquired the admiral.

Michael Carrick, the company's finance director, checked his figures. 'So far, the over-run is around £312,000.'

'Can we cover the extra expense out of our reserves, or will we have to resort to some short-term borrowing?' asked Dobbs.

'We have more than enough to cover the initial shortfall in our capital account,' said Carrick. 'But we'll have to do everything in our power to make up for the lost time over the coming months.'

In our power Emma wrote on the pad in front of her.

'Perhaps it might be wise in the circumstances,' said the chairman, 'to postpone any announcement on the proposed launch date, as it's beginning to look as if we'll have to revise our original predictions, both on timing and financial outlay.'

'When you were deputy chairman of P&O,' said Knowles, 'did you ever come across a series of problems like this? Or is what we're experiencing unusual?'

'It's exceptional, in fact I've never come across anything like it before,' admitted Buchanan. 'Every build has its setbacks and surprises, but things usually even out in the long run.'

'Does our insurance policy cover any of these problems?'

'We've been able to make a few claims,' said Dixon, 'but insurance companies always impose limits, and in one or two cases we've already exceeded them.'

'But surely some of these hold-ups are the direct responsibility of Harland and Wolff,' said Emma, 'so we can invoke the relevant penalty clauses in the contract.'

'I wish it was that easy, Mrs Clifton,' said the chairman, 'but Harland and Wolff are contesting almost every one of our claims, arguing that they haven't been directly responsible for any of the hold-ups. It's become a battlefield for the lawyers, which is costing us even more money.'

'Do you see a pattern emerging, chairman?'

'I'm not sure I know what you're suggesting, admiral.'

'Faulty electrical equipment from a normally reliable company in Liverpool, a boiler ending up in the harbour that was being unloaded from a Glaswegian coaster, our gang gets food poisoning but it doesn't spread to any other part of the yard although the food was supplied by the same Belfast caterer?'

'What are you implying, admiral?'

'There are too many coincidences for my liking, which just happen to all be taking place at the same time as the IRA are beginning to flex their muscles.'

'That's one hell of a leap you're making,' suggested Knowles.

'I may well be reading too much into it,' admitted the admiral, 'but then I was born in County Mayo to a Protestant father and a Roman Catholic mother, so perhaps it goes with the territory.'

Emma glanced across the table to see Fisher furiously

scribbling notes, but he put his pen down the moment he noticed her taking an interest. She knew that Fisher wasn't a Catholic, and for that matter neither was Don Pedro Martinez, whose only creed was self-interest. After all, he'd been willing to sell arms to the Germans during the war, so why wouldn't he deal with the IRA if it served his purpose?

'Let's hope I'll be able to make a more positive report when we meet again next month,' said the chairman, not looking altogether convinced.

After the meeting broke up, Emma was surprised to see Fisher quickly leave the room without speaking to anyone; another of the admiral's coincidences?

'Can I have a word with you, Emma?' asked Buchanan.

'I'll be back in a moment, chairman,' said Emma, before following Fisher out into the corridor, to glimpse him vanishing down the stairs. Why didn't he just take the waiting lift? She stepped into it and pressed the button marked G. When the doors slid open on the ground floor, she didn't get out immediately, but watched as Fisher pushed through the revolving door and made his way out of the building. By the time she reached the door, Fisher was already climbing into his car. She remained inside the building and watched as he drove towards the front gate. To her surprise he turned left towards the lower docks, and not right in the direction of Bristol.

Emma pushed open the door and ran to her car. When she reached the front gate, she looked left and spotted the major's car in the distance. She was just about to follow him when a lorry passed in front of her. She cursed, turned left and tucked in behind it. A stream of vehicles coming in the opposite direction made it impossible for her to overtake. She had only gone about half a mile, when she spotted Fisher's car parked in front of the Lord Nelson. As she drew nearer, she saw the major standing in the phone box outside the pub, dialling a number.

She remained in the slipstream of the lorry, and kept on driving until she could no longer see the phone box in her rearview mirror. She then swung round and headed slowly back, until the phone box came into sight. She pulled over to the side of the road, but left the engine running. It wasn't long before the major stepped out of the phone box, got back into his car and drove away. She didn't pursue him until he was out of sight. After all, she knew exactly where he was going.

As Emma drove back through the gates of the shipyard a few minutes later, she wasn't surprised to see the major's car parked in its usual place. She took the lift up to the fourth floor and went straight to the dining room. Several of the directors, including Fisher, were standing at a long side table, serving themselves from the buffet. Emma grabbed a plate and joined them, before sitting down next to the chairman. 'You wanted a word, Ross?'

'Yes. There's something we need to discuss rather urgently.'

'Not now,' said Emma, as Fisher took his place opposite her.

‑‑◅◦▻‑‑

'This had better be important, colonel, because I've just come out of a meeting with the Leader of the House.'

'Martinez has a new chauffeur.'

'And?' said the cabinet secretary.

'He used to be Liam Doherty's bag man.'

'The IRA commander in Belfast?'

'No less.'

'What's his name?' said Sir Alan, picking up a pencil.

'In Northern Ireland, Kevin Rafferty.'

'And in England?'

'Jim Croft.'

'You'll be needing another man on your team.'

‑‑◅◦▻‑‑

'I've never had tea in the Palm Court room before,' said Buchanan.

'My mother-in-law, Maisie Holcombe, used to work at the Royal Hotel,' explained Emma. 'But in those days, she wouldn't let Harry or me on the premises. "Most unprofessional", she used to say.'

'Another woman clearly years ahead of her time,' said Ross.

'And you only know the half of it,' said Emma, 'but I'll save Maisie for another time. First, I must apologize for having been unwilling to talk to you during lunch, or at least not while Fisher could eavesdrop.'

'Surely you don't suspect him of having anything to do with our present problems?'

'Not directly. In fact I was even beginning to think he might have turned over a new leaf, until this morning.'

'But he couldn't be more supportive at board meetings.'

'I agree. It wasn't until this morning that I found out where his true loyalties lie.'

'I'm lost,' said Ross.

'Do you remember at the end of the meeting you asked to speak to me, but I had to slip away?'

'Yes, but what's that got to do with Fisher?'

'I followed him, and discovered he'd left to make a phone call.'

'As, no doubt, did one or two of the other directors.'

'No doubt, but they will have made their calls on the premises. Fisher left the building, drove off in the direction of the docks, and made his call from a telephone box outside a pub called the Lord Nelson.'

'Can't say I know it.'

'That's probably why he chose it. The call took less than a couple of minutes, and he was back at Barrington's in time for lunch, before anyone would have noticed his absence.'

'I wonder why he felt it necessary to be so secretive about who he was calling?'

'Because of something the admiral said, which meant Fisher had to report to his backer immediately, and couldn't risk being overheard.'

'Surely you don't believe Fisher is involved in any way with the IRA?'

'Fisher no, but Don Pedro Martinez, yes.'

'Don Pedro who?'

'I think the time has come to tell you about the man Major Fisher represents, how my son Sebastian came across him, and the significance of a Rodin statue called *The Thinker*. Then you'll begin to understand what we're up against.'

◄o►

Three men boarded the Heysham ferry for Belfast later that evening. One carried a kitbag, one a briefcase and the other carried nothing. They were not friends, or even acquaintances. In fact, it was only their particular skills and beliefs that brought them together.

The voyage to Belfast usually took about eight hours, and during that time, most passengers try to grab some sleep; but not these three men. They made their way to the bar, purchased three pints of Guinness, one of the few things they had in common, and found seats on the top deck.

They agreed that the best time to carry out the job would be at around three in the morning, when most of the other passengers would be asleep, drunk or too exhausted to give a damn. At the appointed hour, one of them left the group, climbed over a chain with a sign warning CREW ONLY, and noiselessly descended the companionway to the cargo deck. He found himself surrounded by large wooden crates, but it wasn't difficult for him to locate the four he was looking for. After all, they were clearly stamped Harland and Wolff. With the aid of a claw hammer, he loosened all the nails on the blindside of the four crates, 116 of them. Forty minutes later, he rejoined his companions and told them everything was ready. Without another word, his two colleagues made their way down to the cargo deck.

The larger of the two men, who with cauliflower ears and a broken nose looked like a retired heavyweight boxer, possibly because he was, extracted the nails from the first box, then ripped off its wooden slats to reveal an electrical panel consisting of hundreds of red-, green- and blue-coated wires. It was destined for the bridge of the MV *Buckingham*, and was designed to allow the captain to keep in touch with every section of the ship, from the engine room to the galley. It had taken a group of specialist electrical engineers five months to construct this remarkable piece of machinery. It took a young postgraduate from Queen's University Belfast, with a PhD in Physics and a pair of pliers, twenty-seven minutes to dismantle it. He stood back to admire his handiwork, but only for a moment, before the pugilist shoved the slats from the side of the crate back into place. After checking that they were still alone, he got to work on the second crate.

It contained two bronze propellers that had been lovingly forged by a team of craftsmen in Durham. The workmanship had taken them six weeks, and they were rightly proud of the finished articles. The postgrad opened his briefcase, removed a bottle of nitric acid, unscrewed the top and poured the contents slowly into the grooves of the propellers. When the crate was opened later that morning, the propellers would look as if they were ready for the scrapyard, not for installation.

The contents of the third crate were what the young PhD had been most looking forward to seeing, and when his muscle-bound colleague levered off its side to reveal the prize, he was not disappointed. The Rolex navigational computer was the first of its kind, and would feature in all of Barrington's promotional material, explaining to potential passengers why, when it came to safety, they should forsake all others in favour of the *Buckingham*. It only took him twelve minutes to transform the masterpiece from unique to obsolete.

The final crate contained a magnificent oak and brass ship's wheel built in Dorset, which any captain would have been proud to stand behind on his bridge. The young man smiled. As time was running out and the wheel no longer served any purpose, he left it in its full glory.

Once his colleague had replaced the last of the wooden slats, the two of them returned to the top deck. If anyone had been unfortunate enough to disturb them during the past hour, they would have discovered why the former boxer had been nicknamed the 'Destroyer'.

As soon as they reappeared, their colleague made his way back down the spiral staircase. Time was no longer on his side. With the aid of a handkerchief and a hammer, he carefully knocked every one of the 116 nails back into place. He was working on the final crate when he heard two blasts on the ship's horn.

When the ferry docked alongside Donegall Quay in Belfast, the three men disembarked at fifteen-minute intervals, still unaware of each other's names and destined never to meet again.

11

'LET ME ASSURE YOU, major, there are no circumstances in which I would ever consider doing business with the IRA,' said Don Pedro. 'They're nothing more than a bunch of murderous thugs, and the sooner they're all locked up in Crumlin Road jail, the better it will be for all of us.'

'I'm glad to hear that,' said Fisher, 'because if I thought you were making deals with those criminals behind my back, I'd have to resign immediately.'

'And that's the last thing I want you to do,' protested Martinez. 'Don't forget, I see you as the next chairman of Barrington's, and perhaps in the not-too-distant future.'

'But Buchanan isn't expected to retire for some time.'

'It could be sooner if he felt he had to resign.'

'Why would he do that, when he's just signed up for the biggest investment programme in the company's history?'

'Or the biggest turkey. Because if that investment proves to be an unwise one, after he put his reputation on the line to make sure the board backed him, there will be no one to blame but the man who proposed it, remembering that the Barrington family were against the whole idea in the first place.'

'Possibly. But the situation would have to get a lot worse before he'd consider resigning.'

'How much worse can it get?' said Martinez, pushing a copy of the *Daily Telegraph* across his desk. Fisher stared at the head-line: *Police believe IRA behind Heysham Ferry sabotage.* 'That's put the building of the *Buckingham* back another six months, and don't forget, this is all happening on Buchanan's watch. What else has to go wrong before he begins to consider his position? I can tell you, if the share price falls any further, he'll be sacked before he's given the chance to resign. So you ought to be thinking seriously about taking his place. You may not get an opportunity like this again.'

'Even if Buchanan were to go, the obvious choice to replace him would be Mrs Clifton. Her family founded the firm, they still own twenty-two per cent of the stock, and she's well liked by her fellow directors.'

'I've no doubt she's the favourite, but favourites have been known to fall at the first fence. So I suggest you go on loyally supporting the present chairman, because he may end up with the casting vote.' Martinez rose from his place. 'Sorry to leave you, but I have an appointment with my bank to discuss this very subject. Ring me this evening. By then I may have an interesting piece of news for you.'

◄○►

Once Martinez had climbed into the back of his Rolls-Royce and the driver had eased out into the morning traffic, he said, 'Good morning, Kevin. Your lads did a fine job on the Heysham ferry. I only wish I could have seen the faces when the crates were opened at Harland and Wolff. So what have you got planned next?'

'Nothing, until you pay the hundred grand you still owe us.'

'I will be dealing with that this morning. In fact, it's one of the reasons I'm visiting my bank.'

'I'm glad to hear that,' said Rafferty. 'It would be a pity if you were to lose another of your sons so soon after the unfortunate death of Bruno.'

'Don't threaten me!' shouted Martinez.

'It wasn't a threat,' said Rafferty, coming to a halt at the next light. 'And it's only because I like you that I'd let you choose which of your sons would be allowed to survive.'

Martinez fell back in his seat and didn't open his mouth again as the car continued on its journey, before finally coming to a halt outside the Midland Bank in St James's.

Whenever Martinez walked up the steps of the bank, he felt he was entering another world, one in which he was made to feel he didn't belong. He was just about to grasp the door handle, when it swung open and a young man stepped forward.

'Good morning, Mr Martinez. Mr Ledbury is looking forward to seeing you.' Without another word, he led one of the bank's most valued customers straight to the manager's office.

'Good morning, Martinez,' said the manager as Don Pedro entered the room. 'Mild weather we're having for this time of year.'

It had taken Martinez some time to accept that when an Englishman drops the Mr and refers to you only by your surname, it is in fact a compliment, because they are treating you as an equal. But not until they call you by your first name can you be considered a friend.

'Good morning, Ledbury,' said Martinez, but he still wasn't sure how to respond to the English obsession with the weather.

'Can I get you some coffee?'

'No, thank you. I have another appointment at twelve.'

'Of course. We have, as you instructed, continued to purchase Barrington's shares as and when they come on the market. As you are aware, now that you are in possession of twenty-two point five per cent of the company's stock, you are entitled to nominate two more directors to join Major Fisher on the board. However, I must stress that were your shareholding to increase to twenty-five per cent, it would be a legal requirement for the bank to inform the Stock Exchange that you intend to make a takeover bid for the entire company.'

'That's the last thing I want to do,' said Martinez. 'Twenty-two point five per cent is quite enough to serve my purpose.'

'Excellent, then all I require is the names of the two new directors you have chosen to represent you on the board of Barrington's.'

Martinez removed an envelope from an inside pocket and handed it to the bank manager. Ledbury opened it, extracted the nomination form, and studied the names. Although he was surprised, he didn't comment. All he said was, 'As your banker,

I must add that I hope the unfortunate setbacks Barrington's has experienced recently will not prove a problem for you in the long term.'

'I have never been more confident about the company's future.'

'I'm delighted to hear that, because the purchase of such a large number of shares has made considerable inroads into your capital. We must hope that the price will not fall any lower.'

'I think you'll find that the company will shortly be making an announcement that should please both the shareholders and the City.'

'That is indeed good news. Is there anything else I can do for you at the present time?'

'Yes,' said Martinez. 'I would like you to transfer one hundred thousand pounds to an account in Zurich.'

⊸◦⊷

'I'm sorry to have to inform the board that I have decided to resign as chairman.'

The immediate reaction of Ross Buchanan's colleagues was shock and disbelief, quickly followed by almost universal protest. One director remained silent: the only one who wasn't surprised by the announcement. It quickly became clear that almost every member of the board didn't want Buchanan to stand down. The chairman waited for everyone to settle, before he continued.

'I'm touched by your loyalty, but it's my duty to inform you that a major shareholder has made it clear that I no longer enjoy his confidence,' he said, stressing the word *his*. 'He reminded me, and quite rightly, that I put my full authority behind the building of the *Buckingham*, which in his opinion has proved to be ill-judged at best, and irresponsible at worst. We have already missed the first two of our completion dates, and our expenditure is currently running at eighteen per cent over budget.'

'All the more reason for you to stay on the bridge,' said the admiral. 'The skipper should be the last person to abandon ship when there's a storm brewing.'

'In this case I think our only hope is for me to abandon ship, admiral,' said Buchanan. One or two heads bowed, and Emma feared that nothing she could say would make Buchanan change his mind. 'In my experience,' he continued, 'whenever circumstances such as those we are now facing arise, the City looks for fresh leadership to resolve the problem, and resolve it quickly.' Ross looked up at his colleagues, and added, 'I am bound to say that I don't think you'll have to look beyond the current directors to find the right person to take my place.'

'Perhaps if we were to appoint Mrs Clifton and Major Fisher as joint deputy chairmen,' suggested Anscott, 'that might calm the nerves of our masters who occupy the Square Mile.'

'I'm afraid they would see that for what it is, Anscott, a short-term compromise. If at some time in the future Barrington's needs to borrow even more cash, your new chairman must go to the banks not cap in hand, but with confidence, the most important word in the City's dictionary.'

'Would it help, Ross' – the first time Emma had called the chairman by his Christian name during a board meeting – 'if I made it clear that my family has full confidence in your stewardship and wishes you to remain as chairman?'

'I'd be touched, of course, but the City would be unmoved, and would regard it as nothing more than a gesture. Although at a personal level, Emma, I am most grateful for your support.'

'And you can always rely on my support,' Fisher chipped in. 'I'll back you to the end.'

'That's the problem, major. If I don't go, it may well turn out to be the end, the end of this great company as we know it, and that isn't something I could live with.' The chairman looked around the table in case anyone else wanted to offer an opinion, but they all now appeared to accept that the die had been cast.

'At five o'clock this afternoon, after the Stock Exchange has closed, I shall announce that for personal reasons, I have tendered my resignation as chairman of the board of Barrington Shipping. However, with your agreement, I will remain in charge of the day-to-day affairs of the company until a new chairman has been appointed.'

No one raised any objection. The meeting broke up a few

minutes later, and Emma was not surprised to see Fisher quickly leave the boardroom. He returned twenty minutes later to join his colleagues for lunch.

<o>

'You'll need to play your one trump card,' said Martinez after Fisher had told him the details of what had happened at the board meeting.

'And what might that be?'

'You're a man, and there isn't a publicly listed company in the country that has a female chairman. In fact, few even have a woman on the board.'

'Emma Clifton makes a habit of breaking the mould,' Fisher reminded him.

'Maybe so, but can you think of any of your fellow directors who might not be able to stomach the idea of a woman chairman?'

'No, but—'

'But?'

'I do know that Knowles and Anscott voted against women being allowed inside the club house of the Royal Wyvern Golf Club on match days.'

'Then let them know how much you admire their principled stand, and that you would have done the same had you been a member of the club.'

'I did, and I am,' said the major.

'Then that's two votes in the bag. What about the admiral? After all, he's a bachelor.'

'A possibility. I remember he abstained when her name was first put up as a board member.'

'A possible third.'

'But even if they did back me, that's still only three votes, and I'm fairly certain the other four directors would support Mrs Clifton.'

'Don't forget, I'll be appointing two more directors the day before the meeting is due to take place. That will give you six votes, more than enough to tip the balance in your favour.'

'Not if the Barringtons were to take up all the other places on the board. Then I'd still need another vote to be certain of victory, because if the result was a tie, I'm fairly sure Buchanan would give his casting vote to Mrs Clifton.'

'Then we'll need to have another director in place by next Thursday.'

Both men fell silent, until Martinez said, 'Can you think of anyone who has a little spare cash, remembering how cheap the shares are at the moment, and who wouldn't, under any circumstances, want Mrs Clifton to be the next chairman of Barrington's?'

'Yes,' said Fisher without hesitation. 'I know someone who detests Emma Clifton even more than you do, and she's recently been awarded a large divorce settlement.'

12

'GOOD MORNING,' said Ross Buchanan, 'and welcome to this extraordinary general meeting. There is only one item on today's agenda, namely to appoint a new chairman of the Barrington Shipping Company. I would like to open by saying what a privilege it's been to serve as your chairman for the past five years, and how sad I am to relinquish that post. However, for reasons I do not need to rake over again, I feel this is an appropriate time to stand down and allow someone else to take my place.

'My first responsibility,' he continued, 'is to introduce those shareholders who have joined us today and who are entitled to vote at an EGM, as set out in the statutes of the company's constitution. One or two of those seated around this table will be familiar to the board, while others may not be quite as well known. On my right is Mr David Dixon, the company's chief executive, and on my left is Mr Philip Webster, the company secretary. To his left is our finance director, Mr Michael Carrick. Seated next to him is Rear Admiral Summers, then Mrs Clifton, Mr Anscott, Mr Knowles, Major Fisher and Mr Dobbs, all of whom are non-executive directors. They are joined today by individuals or representatives of companies who have a large shareholding in Barrington's, including Mr Peter Maynard and Mrs Alex Fisher, both of whom are Major Fisher's nominees, as he now represents twenty-two point five per cent of the company.' Maynard beamed, while Susan Fisher bowed her head and blushed when everyone turned to look at her.

'Representing the Barrington family and their twenty-two

per cent holding are Sir Giles Barrington MC MP and his sister, Dr Grace Barrington. The other two individuals present who have also met the legal requirement to vote on this occasion are the Lady Virginia Fenwick' – Virginia patted Fisher on the back, leaving no one in any doubt where her support lay, 'and –' the chairman checked his notes – 'Mr Cedric Hardcastle, who represents Farthings Bank, which currently holds seven point five per cent of the company's stock.'

Everyone around the table turned to look at the one person none of them had come across before. He was dressed in a three-piece grey suit, white shirt and well-worn blue silk tie. He couldn't have been more than an inch over five foot, and he was almost completely bald except for a thin semi-circle of grey hair that barely reached his ears. Because he wore thick, horn-rimmed glasses, it was almost impossible to guess his age. Fifty? Sixty? Possibly even seventy? Mr Hardcastle removed his glasses to reveal steel-grey eyes, and Emma felt certain that she had seen him before, but couldn't remember where.

'Good morning, Mr Chairman,' was all he said, although those four words revealed which county he hailed from.

'Let us move on to the business at hand,' said Buchanan. 'By the deadline of six o'clock yesterday evening, two candidates had allowed their names to be put forward as prospective chairmen: Mrs Emma Clifton, who is proposed by Sir Giles Barrington MC MP, and seconded by Dr Grace Barrington, and Major Alex Fisher, proposed by Mr Anscott and seconded by Mr Knowles. Both candidates will now address the board on how they see the future of the company. I call upon Major Fisher to open proceedings.'

Fisher didn't move from his place. 'I feel it would be courteous to allow the lady to speak first,' he said, giving Emma a warm smile.

'How kind of you, major,' replied Emma, 'but I'm quite happy to abide by the chairman's decision and allow you to go first.'

Fisher appeared to be a little flustered, but quickly recovered. He shuffled his notes, rose from his place and took a long look around the table, before he began to speak.

'Mr Chairman, members of the board. I consider it a great privilege even to be considered as a candidate for chairman of the Barrington Shipping Company. As a Bristol man born and bred, I have been aware of this great company all my life, its history, its tradition, as well as its reputation, which has become part of Bristol's great sea-going heritage. Sir Joshua Barrington was a legendary figure, and Sir Walter, whom I had the privilege of knowing' – Emma looked surprised, unless 'knowing' her grandfather meant bumping into him at a school speech day some thirty years ago – 'was responsible for taking this company public and building its reputation as one of the leading shipping institutions, not only in this country, but around the world. But sadly that is no longer the case, partly because Sir Walter's son, Sir Hugo, was simply not up to the job, and although our present chairman has done a great deal to restore the firm's reputation, a series of recent events, not of his making, have led to a lack of confidence among some of our shareholders. What you, my fellow directors, have to decide today,' said Fisher, once again looking around the table, 'is who is best equipped to deal with that crisis of confidence. Given the circumstances, I feel I should mention my credentials when it comes to fighting battles. I served my country as a young lieutenant at Tobruk, described by Montgomery as one of the bloodiest battles in history. I was lucky enough to survive that onslaught, when I was decorated in the field.'

Giles put his head in his hands. He would have liked to tell the board what had really happened when the enemy had appeared over the North African horizon, but he knew it wouldn't help his sister's cause.

'My next battle was when I stood against Sir Giles Barrington as the Conservative candidate at the last general election,' said Fisher, emphasizing the word *Conservative*, as he felt it was unlikely that, with the exception of Giles, anyone else around that table had ever voted Labour, 'for the safe Labour seat of Bristol Docklands, losing by a mere handful of votes, and then only after three recounts.' This time he graced Giles with a smile.

Giles wanted to leap up and wipe the smile off Fisher's face, but somehow managed to restrain himself.

'So I think I can say with some conviction that I have experienced both triumph and disaster, and, to quote Kipling, have treated those two imposters just the same.

'And now,' he continued, 'allow me to touch on some of the problems facing our distinguished company at the present time. And I stress at the present time. Just over a year ago we made an important decision, and may I remind the board that at that time I fully supported the chairman's proposal to build the MV *Buckingham*. However, since then, there has been a succession of calamities, some unexpected, others that we should have foreseen, which have caused us to fall behind on our timetable. As a result, for the first time in the company's history, we have had to consider going to the banks for a loan to assist us through these troubled times.

'If I were elected chairman, allow me to tell you the three changes I would instigate immediately. First, I would invite Mrs Clifton to be my deputy chairman, so that the City would be in no doubt that the Barrington family remains fully committed to the company's future, as it has been for over a century.'

Several 'Hear, hears' emanated from around the table, and Fisher smiled at Emma for the second time since he'd joined the board. Giles had to admire the man's gall, because he must have known that Emma wouldn't consider returning the compliment, as she believed that Fisher was responsible for the company's present troubles, and she certainly would never agree to serve as his deputy.

'Secondly,' continued Fisher, 'I would fly to Belfast tomorrow morning, sit down with Sir Frederick Rebbeck, chairman of Harland and Wolff, and set about re-negotiating our contract, pointing out that his company has persistently declined to take responsibility for any of the unfortunate setbacks that have taken place during the construction of the *Buckingham*. And thirdly, I would employ a top security company to guard any equipment that is sent to Belfast on Barrington's behalf, so that an act of sabotage like the one that took place on the Heysham ferry could never happen again. At the same time, I would take out new insurance policies that didn't have pages of penalty clauses in very small print. Finally, I would add that if I am fortunate enough to become your chairman, I will start work this afternoon and not rest until the MV *Buckingham* has been launched on the high seas, and is showing the company a profitable return on its investment.'

Fisher sat down to warm applause, smiles and nods of approval. Even before the clapping had died away, Emma realized she'd made a tactical mistake by allowing her opponent to go first. He had covered most of the points she had intended to make, and it would now look as if she was, at best, agreeing with him and, at worst, as if she had no ideas of her own. How well she recalled Giles humiliating the same man at Colston Hall during the recent election campaign. But it was a different man who had turned up at Barrington House that morning, and one look at her brother confirmed that he also had been taken by surprise.

'Mrs Clifton,' said the chairman. 'Perhaps you'd like to share your ideas with the board?'

Emma rose unsteadily to her feet as Grace gave her a thumbs-up sign, making her feel like a Christian slave about to be thrown to the lions.

'Mr Chairman, let me begin by saying that you see a reluctant candidate standing before you today, because if I had a choice you would remain as chairman of this company. It was only when you decided that you had no alternative but to stand down that I even considered taking your place and continuing the tradition of my family's long association with this company. Let me begin by confronting what some board members may well consider my biggest disadvantage, my sex.'

This remark caused an outburst of laughter, some of it nervous, although Susan Fisher looked sympathetic.

'I suffer,' Emma continued, 'from being a woman in a man's world, and frankly there is nothing I can do about it. I appreciate that it will take a brave board to appoint a woman as chairman of Barrington's, especially in the difficult circumstances we are currently facing. But then, courage and innovation are precisely what this company needs at the present time. Barrington's stands at a crossroads, and whoever you select today will have to choose which signpost to follow. As you know, when the board decided last year that we should go ahead with the building of the *Buckingham*, I opposed the idea, and voted accordingly. So it is only fair that I should let the board know where I currently stand on that issue. In my opinion, we cannot consider turning back, because that would spell humiliation, and possibly even oblivion, for the company. The board took its decision in good faith, and we owe it to our shareholders not to walk away and blame others, but instead to do everything in our power to make up any lost time, and to ensure that we succeed in the long term.'

Emma looked down at a page of notes that repeated almost everything her rival had already said. She ploughed on, hoping her natural enthusiasm and energy would overcome the fact that her colleagues were hearing the same ideas and opinions voiced for a second time.

But by the time she reached the last line of her speech, she could feel the board's interest slipping away. Giles had warned her that something unexpected would happen on the day, and it had. Fisher had raised his game.

'May I close my remarks, Mr Chairman, by saying that it would be a great privilege for this Barrington to be allowed to join her illustrious forebears and chair the board, especially at a time when the company faces such real difficulties. I know that with your help I can overcome those difficulties and win back Barrington's good name, and its reputation for excellence and financial probity.'

Emma sat down with a feeling that her report card would have read *Could have done better*. She just hoped that Giles was right about another of his pronouncements. Almost all of the people around that table would have already decided how they were going to vote long before the meeting had been called to order.

Once the two candidates had pleaded their case, it was the

board members' turn to offer their opinion. Most of them wanted to have their say, but not a great deal of insight or originality was evident during the next hour, and despite refusing to answer the question 'Would you appoint Major Fisher as your deputy', Emma still felt the outcome was in the balance. That was until Lady Virginia spoke.

'I only want to make one observation, chairman,' she cooed, accompanied by the fluttering of eyelashes. 'I don't believe that women were put on earth to chair boards, take on trade union leaders, build luxury liners or have to raise vast sums of money from bankers in the City of London. Much as I admire Mrs Clifton and all she has achieved, I shall be supporting Major Fisher, and I only hope that she will accept the major's generous offer to serve as his deputy. I came here with an open mind, willing to give her the benefit of the doubt, but sadly she has not lived up to my expectations.'

Emma had to admire Virginia's nerve. She had clearly memorized every word of her script long before she'd entered the room, rehearsing even the dramatic pauses, yet somehow she managed to give the impression that she'd never intended to intervene until the last moment when she had been left with no choice but to deliver a few off-the-cuff remarks. Emma could only wonder how many of those seated around the boardroom table had been fooled. Certainly not Giles, who looked as if he could have strangled his former wife.

Only two people had not offered an opinion by the time Lady Virginia resumed her seat. The chairman, courteous as ever, said, 'Before I call for a vote, I wonder if Mrs Fisher or Mr Hardcastle would like to make a contribution?'

'No, thank you, Mr Chairman,' Susan Fisher blurted out, before once again bowing her head. The chairman glanced towards Mr Hardcastle.

'It's kind of you to ask, chairman,' Hardcastle replied, 'but I only wish to say that I have listened with great interest to all the contributions, and in particular to those of the two candidates, and that, like Lady Virginia, I have made up my mind who I shall be supporting.'

Fisher smiled at the Yorkshireman.

'Thank you, Mr Hardcastle,' said the chairman. 'Unless anyone else wishes to make a further contribution, the time has come for the members of the board to cast their votes.' He paused for a moment, but no one spoke. 'The company secretary will now call out each name in turn. Please let him know which candidate you support.'

'I will begin with the executive directors,' said Webster, 'before I invite the rest of the board to cast their votes. Mr Buchanan?'

'I will not be supporting either candidate,' Buchanan said. 'However, should the vote result in a tie, I will, as is the chairman's prerogative, cast my vote in favour of the person I believe should be the next chairman.'

Ross had spent several sleepless nights wrestling with the question of who should succeed him, and had finally come down in favour of Emma. But Fisher's resounding speech, and Emma's rather feeble response, had caused him to reconsider. He still couldn't bring himself to vote for Fisher, so he had decided to abstain, and allow his colleagues to make the decision. Nevertheless, if the vote resulted in a tie, he would have to reluctantly support Fisher.

Emma couldn't hide her surprise and disappointment at Ross's decision not to vote. Fisher smiled, and drew a line through the chairman's name, which had, until then, been in the Clifton column.

'Mr Dixon?'

'Mrs Clifton,' said the chief executive without hesitation.

'Mr Carrick?'

'Major Fisher,' said the finance director.

'Mr Anscott?'

'Major Fisher.' Emma was disappointed, but not surprised, because she knew that meant Knowles would also vote against her.

'Sir Giles Barrington?'

'Mrs Clifton.'

'Dr Grace Barrington?'

'Mrs Clifton.'

'Mrs Emma Clifton?'

'I shall not be voting, chairman,' said Emma, 'and will abstain.' Fisher nodded his approval.

'Mr Dobbs?'

'Mrs Clifton.'

'Lady Virginia Fenwick?'

'Major Fisher.'

'Major Fisher?'

'I shall vote for myself, as is my right,' said Fisher, smiling across the table at Emma.

How many times had Sebastian begged his mother not to abstain, as he had been certain that there was absolutely no chance that Fisher would behave like a gentleman.

'Mrs Fisher?'

Susan looked up at the chairman, hesitated a moment then whispered nervously, 'Mrs Clifton.'

Alex swung round and stared at his wife in disbelief. But this time Susan didn't bow her head. Instead, she glanced across at Emma and smiled. Emma, looking equally surprised, put a tick by Susan's name.

'Mr Knowles?'

'Major Fisher,' he said without hesitation.

'Mr Maynard?'

'Major Fisher.'

Emma checked the ticks and crosses on her pad. Fisher led by six to five.

'Admiral Summers?' said the company secretary. There was a silence that felt interminable to Emma, but was in fact only a few seconds.

'Mrs Clifton,' he eventually said. Emma gasped. The old man leant across and whispered, 'I've never been sure about Fisher, and when he voted for himself, I knew I'd been right all along.'

Emma wasn't sure whether to laugh or to kiss him, but the company secretary interrupted her thoughts. 'Mr Hardcastle?' Once again, everyone in the room turned their attention to the one man no one knew anything about. 'Would you be kind enough to let us know your decision, sir?' Fisher scowled. Six all. If Susan had voted for him, Hardcastle's vote would have been irrelevant, but he still felt confident the Yorkshireman would back him.

Cedric Hardcastle took a handkerchief out of his top pocket, removed his glasses and polished them before he spoke. 'I shall abstain, and allow the chairman, who knows both candidates far better than I do, to decide who is the right person to succeed him.'

–◦–

Susan Fisher pushed back her chair and slipped quietly out of the boardroom as the newly elected chairman took her place at the top of the table.

Everything had gone well so far. However, Susan knew that the next hour would be vital if she hoped to complete the rest of her plan. Alex hadn't even commented when she'd offered to drive him to the board meeting that morning so he could concentrate on his speech. What she hadn't told him was that she wouldn't be driving him back.

For some time, Susan had accepted that their marriage was a sham, and she couldn't even remember when they'd last made love. She often wondered why she'd agreed to marry him in the first place. Her mother's constant reminder, 'If you're not careful, my girl, you'll be left on the shelf,' hadn't helped. Still, she now intended to clear everything off the shelves.

–◦–

Alex Fisher was unable to concentrate on Emma's acceptance speech, as he was still trying to work out how he would explain to Don Pedro that his wife had voted against him.

Martinez had originally proposed that Diego and Luis represent him on the board, but Alex had persuaded him that if there was one thing that would frighten the directors more than the thought of a female chairman, it would be the thought of a foreigner taking over the company.

He decided that he would simply tell Don Pedro that Emma

had won the vote, and not mention the fact that his wife hadn't supported him. He didn't care to think about what would happen if Don Pedro ever read the minutes.

—◄○►—

Susan Fisher parked the car outside Arcadia Mansions, opened the front door with her latch key, took the lift to the third floor and let herself into the flat. She walked quickly through to the bedroom, dropped on her knees and pulled two suitcases out from under the bed. She then began to empty one of the wardrobes of six dresses, two suits, several skirts and a ball gown, which she wondered if she'd ever wear again. Next she pulled open the chest of drawers one drawer at a time, and took out her stockings, underwear, blouses and jumpers, which almost filled the first suitcase.

When she got off her knees, her eyes settled on a watercolour of the Lake District that Alex had paid a little too much for when they were on their honeymoon. She was delighted to find that it fitted neatly into the bottom of the second case. She then walked through to the bathroom and gathered up all her toiletries, a dressing gown and several towels, cramming them into every available space left in the second suitcase.

There wasn't a lot she wanted in the kitchen, other than the Wedgwood dinner service, a wedding present from Alex's mother. She wrapped each piece carefully in pages from the *Daily Telegraph*, and placed them in two shopping bags she found under the sink.

She left the plain green tea set that she'd never really liked, not least because it had so many chips, and there was no room left in the second case. 'Help,' she said out loud, once she realized there was still a lot more she intended to remove but both suitcases were already full.

Susan walked back into the bedroom, stood on a chair and pulled down Alex's old school trunk from the top of the wardrobe. She dragged it out into the corridor, undid its straps and continued with her mission. The drawing-room mantelpiece yielded a carriage clock which Alex claimed was a family heirloom and three photographs in silver frames. She removed the photographs and tore them up, only packing the frames. She would have liked to take the television, but it was far too large and, in any case, her mother wouldn't have approved.

--◦--

Once the company secretary had closed the meeting, Alex didn't join his fellow directors for lunch. He quickly left the boardroom without speaking to anyone, Peter Maynard following in his wake. Alex had been given two envelopes by Don Pedro, each containing a thousand pounds. His wife certainly wouldn't be getting the five hundred he'd promised her. Once they were in the lift, Alex took one of the envelopes out of his pocket.

'At least you kept your side of the bargain,' he said, handing it across to Peter.

'Thank you,' said Maynard gratefully, pocketing the money. 'But what came over Susan?' he added as the lift door opened on the ground floor. Alex didn't reply.

As the two men left Barrington House, Alex wasn't surprised to see that his car was no longer in its usual place, but he was puzzled to find another car he didn't recognize occupying his parking space.

A young man carrying a Gladstone bag was standing by the front door of the car. The moment he spotted Alex, he began walking towards him.

--◦--

Finally, exhausted by her efforts, Susan entered Alex's study without knocking, not expecting to find anything worthwhile to add to her spoils: two more picture frames, one silver, one leather, and a silver letter opener she'd given him for Christmas. But as it was only silver plated, she decided he could keep it.

Time was running out and she didn't think it would be long before Alex returned, but just as she was about to leave, she spotted a thick envelope with her name scribbled across it. She ripped it open and couldn't believe her eyes. It contained the five hundred pounds Alex had promised her if she attended the board meeting and voted for him. She'd kept her side of the bargain, well, half of it, so she slipped the money into her handbag, and smiled for the first time that day.

Susan closed the study door and quickly checked through the flat one more time. She'd forgotten something, but what was it? Oh yes, of course. She rushed back to the bedroom, opened the smaller cupboard and smiled a second time when she saw the rows and rows of shoes left over from her modelling days. She took her time placing them all in the trunk. Just as she was about to close the cupboard door, her eyes settled on a neat row of black leather shoes and brown brogues, all polished as if they were about to go on parade. She knew they were Alex's pride and joy. All hand made by Lobb of St James's and, as he so often reminded her, they would last a lifetime.

Susan took the left shoe of each pair and dropped them into Alex's old school trunk. She also took one right slipper, one right Wellington boot and one right gym shoe, before sitting on the lid of the trunk and fastening the straps.

Finally she dragged the trunk, two suitcases and two shopping bags out on to the landing, and closed the door of a home she would never return to.

—◦—

'Major Alex Fisher?'

'Yes.'

The young man handed him a long, buff-coloured envelope and said, 'I've been instructed to give you this, sir.' Without another word, he turned, walked back to his car and drove off. The whole encounter was over in less than a minute.

A bemused Alex nervously ripped open the envelope and extracted a document of several pages. When he saw the words on the cover sheet, *Petition for divorce: Mrs Susan Fisher v. Major Alex Fisher*, he felt his legs give way, and grasped Maynard's arm for support.

'What's the problem, old chap?'

CEDRIC HARDCASTLE

1959

13

ON THE TRAIN journey back to London, Cedric Hardcastle thought once again about how he'd ended up attending the board meeting of a shipping company in Bristol. It had all begun when he'd broken his leg.

For nearly forty-five years, Cedric had led what even his local vicar would have described as a blameless life. During that time, he'd built a reputation for probity, integrity and sound judgement.

After leaving Huddersfield Grammar School at the age of fifteen, Cedric had joined his father at Farthings Bank, on the corner of the high street, where you couldn't open an account unless you were a Yorkshire man, born and bred. Every employee had drilled into them from their first day as a trainee the bank's overriding philosophy: *Take care of the pennies, and the pounds will take care of themselves.*

At the age of thirty-two, Cedric was appointed the youngest branch manager in the bank's history, and his father, still a counter clerk, retired only just in time not to have to call his son 'sir'.

Cedric was invited to join the board of Farthings a few weeks before his fortieth birthday, and everyone assumed it would not be long before he would outgrow the little county bank and, like Dick Whittington, head for the City of London; but not Cedric. He was, after all, first and foremost a Yorkshireman. He'd married Beryl, a lass from Batley, and their son, Arnold, was conceived on holiday in Scarborough and born in Keighley.

Being born in the county was a necessity if you wanted your son to join the bank.

When Bert Entwistle, the chairman of Farthings, died of a heart attack at the age of sixty-three, a vote wasn't required to decide who should replace him.

After the war, Farthings became one of those banks that were often referred to in the financial pages of national newspapers as 'ripe for takeover'. However, Cedric had other plans, and despite several approaches from larger institutions, all of which were rebuffed without discussion, the new chairman set about building up the bank and opening new branches, so that within a few years it was Farthings that was making the takeovers. For three decades, Cedric had spent any spare cash, bonuses or dividends, purchasing shares in the bank, so that by his sixtieth birthday, he was not only chairman, but the majority shareholder with 51 per cent of Farthings.

At the age of sixty, when most men start thinking about retirement, Cedric was in charge of eleven branches in Yorkshire and a presence in the City of London, and certainly wasn't looking for anyone to replace him as chairman.

If he had one disappointment in life, it was his son Arnold. The lad had done well at Leeds Grammar School, but had then rebelled, accepting a place at Oxford rather than the scholarship he'd been offered at Leeds University. And worse, the boy didn't want to join his father at Farthings, preferring to train as a barrister – in London. This meant Cedric had no one to hand the bank on to.

For the first time in his life, he considered a takeover bid, from the Midland. They offered him a sum of money that would have allowed him to spend the rest of his life playing golf on the Costa del Sol, donning slippers, drinking Horlicks and being tucked up in bed by ten. But what no one except Beryl seemed to understand about Cedric Hardcastle was that banking was not only his job, it was his hobby, and as long as he had a majority shareholding in Farthings, the golf, the slippers and the Horlicks could wait for a few more years. He told his wife he'd prefer to pop his clogs sitting at his desk rather than on the eighteenth tee.

As it turned out, he nearly popped his clogs on the way back to Yorkshire one evening. But even Cedric could not have anticipated just how much his life would change when he became involved in a car accident on the A1 late on a Friday night. He was exhausted following a series of lengthy meetings at the bank's head office in the City and should have stayed at his flat in London overnight. But he always preferred to travel up to Huddersfield and spend the weekend with Beryl. He fell asleep at the wheel, and the next thing he remembered was waking up in hospital with both his legs in plaster; the only thing he had in common with the young man in the next bed.

Sebastian Clifton was everything Cedric disapproved of. He was a stuck-up southerner, disrespectful, lacked discipline, had opinions on everything, and, worse, seemed to assume that the world owed him a living. Cedric immediately asked Matron if he could be moved to another ward. Miss Puddicombe refused his request, but pointed out that there were two private rooms available. Cedric stayed put; he didn't waste brass.

During the weeks that followed his imprisonment, Cedric couldn't be sure which of them became the greater influence on the other. To begin with, the boy's endless questions about banking got on his nerves, until he eventually gave in and reluctantly became his surrogate tutor. When Matron asked, he was forced to admit that not only was the boy extremely bright, but you never had to tell him anything twice.

'Aren't you glad I didn't move you?' she teased.

'Well, I wouldn't go that far,' said Cedric.

There were two added bonuses to being Sebastian's tutor. Cedric much enjoyed the weekly visits of his mother and sister; two formidable ladies, both with problems of their own. It didn't take him long to work out that Jessica couldn't possibly be Mrs Clifton's daughter, and when Sebastian eventually told him the whole story, all he said was, 'It's time someone told her.'

It also became clear to Cedric that Mrs Clifton was facing some sort of crisis in her family business. Every time she visited her son in hospital, Cedric would turn over and pretend to be asleep, while, with Sebastian's blessing, he listened to every word that passed between them.

Jessica would often come round to his side of the bed so she could sketch her new model, which meant that Cedric had to keep his eyes closed.

Occasional visits from Sebastian's father, Harry Clifton, his uncle Giles and his aunt Grace helped Cedric to put more pieces into a colourful jigsaw that was slowly coming together. It wasn't difficult to work out what Martinez and Fisher were up to, even if he wasn't sure what motivated them, partly because even Sebastian didn't seem to know the answer to that question. However, when it came to the vote on whether they should go ahead and build the *Buckingham*, Cedric felt that Mrs Clifton's gut instinct, or what women call intuition, might well turn out to be right. So after checking the company's by-laws, he advised Sebastian that as his mother controlled 22 per cent of the company's stock, she was entitled to have three representatives on the board, which should be more than enough to stop the proposal going ahead. Mrs Clifton didn't take his advice, and lost the motion by one vote.

The following day, Cedric purchased ten shares in Barrington Shipping, so they could follow the regular deliberations of the board. It only took Cedric a few weeks to work out that Fisher was setting himself up to be the next chairman. If Ross Buchanan and Mrs Clifton shared a common weakness, it was their naïve belief that everyone would abide by their own moral standards. It was just a pity that Major Fisher had no standards, and Don Pedro Martinez no morals.

Cedric regularly scoured the *Financial Times* and the *Economist* in search of any information on why Barrington's shares were in free-fall. If, as one article in the *Daily Express* suggested, the IRA was involved, then Martinez had to be the link. What Cedric couldn't understand was why Fisher was so willing to fall in line. Did he need the money that badly? He prepared a list of questions for Sebastian to ask his mother on her weekly visits, and it wasn't long before he was as well informed about the daily workings of Barrington's Shipping Company as any member of the board.

By the time Cedric had fully recovered, and was fit enough to be discharged from hospital and return to work, he had made two decisions. The bank would purchase 7.5 per cent of Barrington Shipping, the minimum shareholding that would allow him to take a place on the board and vote to decide who should be the next chairman of the company. When he called his broker the following day, he was surprised to discover how many other people were also buying Barrington's shares, clearly with the same purpose in mind. This meant that Cedric ended up having to pay a little more than he'd bargained for and, although this was contrary to his usual practice, he had to agree with Beryl, he was thoroughly enjoying himself.

After several months as an onlooker, he couldn't wait to be introduced to Ross Buchanan, Mrs Clifton, Major Fisher, Admiral Summers et al. However, a second decision he made turned out to be more far-reaching.

Just before Cedric was discharged from hospital, Sebastian had a visit from his supervisor at Cambridge. Mr Padgett made it clear that if he wished to, he could take up his place at Peterhouse the following September.

One of the first letters Cedric wrote on returning to his desk in the City was to offer Sebastian a holiday job at Farthings Bank before he went up to Cambridge.

—◦—

Ross Buchanan stepped out of the cab a few minutes before his appointment with the chairman of Farthings. Waiting for him in the front hall of 127 Threadneedle Street was Mr Hardcastle's personal assistant, who escorted him to the chairman's office on the fifth floor.

Cedric rose from behind his desk as Buchanan entered the room. He shook his guest warmly by the hand, and ushered him to one of the two comfortable chairs by the fireplace. The Yorkshireman and the Scotsman quickly discovered that they shared many common interests, not least their mutual concern for the future of Barrington Shipping.

'I see the share price has picked up a little recently,' said Cedric. 'So perhaps things are beginning to settle down.'

'Certainly the IRA seems to have lost interest in harassing the company at every possible turn, which must be a great relief to Emma.'

'Could it simply be that their payments have dried up? After all, Martinez must have invested a considerable sum of money purchasing twenty-two point five per cent of the company's stock, only to fail in his attempt to elect the next chairman.'

'If that's the case, why doesn't he cash in his chips and call it a day?'

'Because Martinez is clearly an obstinate man who refuses to admit when he's beaten, and I certainly don't think he's the type to curl up in a corner and lick his wounds. We have to accept that he must be simply biding his time. But biding his time to do what?'

'I don't know,' said Ross. 'The man's an enigma, and almost impossible to fathom. All I do know is that when it comes to the Barringtons and the Cliftons, it's personal.'

'That doesn't come as a surprise, but it might prove to be his downfall in the end. He should remember the mafia's dictum: when it comes to killing a rival, it must only ever be business, never personal.'

'I hadn't thought of you as a mafia man.'

'Don't kid yourself, Ross, Yorkshire was operating a mafia long before the Italians sailed for New York. We don't kill our rivals, we just don't allow them to cross the county border.' Ross smiled. 'Whenever I come across someone as slippery as Martinez,' continued Cedric, sounding serious again, 'I try to put myself in their shoes and work out exactly what they're trying to achieve. But in Martinez's case, I'm still missing something. I'd hoped you might be able to fill in the missing pieces.'

'I don't know the full story myself,' admitted Ross, 'but what Emma Clifton told me is worthy of a Harry Clifton novel.'

'That many twists?' said Cedric, who sat back in his chair and didn't interrupt again until Ross had told him everything he knew about an auction at Sotheby's, a Rodin statue that had contained eight million pounds of counterfeit money, and a car crash on the A1 that had never been satisfactorily explained. 'Martinez may well have beaten a tactical retreat,' Ross concluded, 'but I'm not convinced he's left the battlefield.'

'Perhaps if you and I were to work together,' suggested Cedric, 'we might be able to cover Mrs Clifton's back and allow her to get on with restoring the company's fortunes as well as its reputation.'

'What do you have in mind?' asked Buchanan.

'Well, to start with, I was hoping you might agree to join the board of Farthings as a non-executive director.'

'I'm flattered.'

'You shouldn't be. You'd bring the bank considerable experience and expertise in many fields, not least shipping, and there's certainly no one better qualified to keep an eye on our investment in Barrington's. Why don't you give it some thought, and let me know when you've come to a decision?'

'I don't have to think about it,' said Buchanan. 'I'd be honoured to join your board. I've always had a great deal of respect for Farthings. "Take care of the pennies and the pounds will take care of themselves" is a philosophy several other establishments I won't name could benefit from.' Cedric smiled. 'And in any case,' added Buchanan, 'I consider Barrington's unfinished business.'

'So do I,' said Cedric as he stood up, walked across the room and pressed a button under his desk. 'Would you care to join me for lunch at Rules? Then you can explain why you changed your mind at the last moment and gave Mrs Clifton your casting vote, when you had clearly originally intended to back Fisher.'

Buchanan was stunned into a silence that was interrupted by a knock on the door. He looked up to see the young man who had met him in the front hall.

'Ross, I don't think you've met my personal assistant.'

14

EVERYONE STOOD when Mr Hardcastle entered the room. It had taken Sebastian some time to get used to the esteem in which those who worked at Farthings clearly held their chairman. But when you've slept in the next bed to a man for months on end, and seen him unshaven, in his pyjamas, peeing into a bottle and snoring, it's quite difficult to be in awe of him, although within days of their first meeting, Sebastian had come to respect the banker from Huddersfield.

Mr Hardcastle waved them down and took his seat at the head of the table.

'Good morning, gentlemen,' he began, looking around at his colleagues. 'I've called this meeting because the bank has been offered an extraordinary opportunity that, if handled correctly, might open up a whole new stream of income that could benefit Farthings for many years to come.'

He had caught the team's attention.

'The bank has recently been approached by the founder and chairman of the Japanese engineering company Sony International, who are hoping to arrange a short-term, pre-fixed coupon loan of ten million pounds.'

Cedric paused so he could study the expressions on the faces of the fourteen top executives seated around the table. They ranged from unconcealed disgust to what an exciting opportunity and almost everything in between. However, Cedric had prepared the next section of his presentation most carefully.

'The war has been over for fourteen years. Nevertheless,

some of you may still feel, as expressed so vividly by the *Daily Mirror*'s leader this morning, that we should never consider dealing with that *"war-mongering bunch of Nip bastards"*. However, one or two of you may also have noticed the success the Westminster had when they signed a partnership deal with Deutsche Bank to build a new Mercedes plant in Dortmund. We are being offered a similar opportunity. I want to pause for a moment, and ask every one of you to consider what business will be like in fifteen years' time. Not today, and certainly not fifteen years ago. Will we continue to display the same old prejudices, or will we have moved on and embraced a new order that accepts that there is a new generation of Japanese who should not be condemned by the past. If anyone in this room feels unable to deal with even the idea of doing business with the Japanese because it will reopen painful wounds, now is the time to make your position clear, because without your wholehearted support, this venture cannot hope to succeed. The last time I uttered those words, through clenched teeth, was in 1947, when I finally allowed a Lancastrian to open an account at Farthings.'

The ripple of laughter that followed helped to break the tension, although Cedric didn't doubt that he would still face opposition from some of his senior staff, and that a few of his more conservative customers might even consider moving their accounts to another bank.

'Now, all I am able to tell you,' he continued, 'is that the chairman of Sony International and two of his company directors plan to visit London in about six weeks. They have made it clear that we are not the only bank they are approaching, but at the same time they have let me know that we are at present their favoured choice.'

'Why would Sony even consider us, chairman, when there are several larger banks which specialize in this field?' asked Adrian Sloane, head of the currency exchange desk.

'You may not believe it, Adrian, but last year I was interviewed by the *Economist*, and in the photograph taken at my home in Huddersfield, a Sony transistor radio is visible in the background. On such whims are fortunes made.'

'John Kenneth Galbraith,' said Sebastian.

A ripple of applause followed from one or two staff who would not normally have considered interrupting the chairman, which caused Sebastian to do something he rarely did, blush.

'It's good to know we have at least one educated person in the room,' said the chairman. 'On that note, let's get back to work. If anyone wants to discuss this matter privately, you don't have to make an appointment, just come and see me.'

When Cedric returned to his office, Sebastian quickly followed him, and immediately apologized for his off-the-cuff remark.

'No need, Seb. In fact, you helped clear the air, at the same time as raising your status among the senior staff. Let's hope it will encourage one or two others to stand up to me in the future. But on to more important matters. I have a job I need you to do.'

'At last,' said Sebastian, who was sick of escorting valued customers up and down in the lift, only to see the door closed in his face the moment they entered the chairman's office.

'How many languages do you speak?'

'Five, if you include English. But my Hebrew is a little rusty.'

'Then you've got six weeks to learn passable Japanese.'

'Who will decide if I pass?'

'The chairman of Sony International.'

'Ah, so no pressure then.'

'Jessica told me that when you were on holiday in the family villa in Tuscany, you picked up Italian in three weeks.'

'Picked up is not mastering,' said Sebastian. 'In any case, my sister does have a tendency to exaggerate,' he added, looking at a drawing of Cedric in bed at the Princess Alexandra Hospital, entitled, *Portrait of a Dying Man*.

'I don't have another candidate in mind,' said Cedric, handing him a prospectus. 'London University is currently offering three courses in Japanese – beginners, intermediate and advanced. So you'll be able to spend two weeks on each.' Cedric at least had the grace to laugh.

The phone on the chairman's desk began to ring. He picked

it up, listened for a few moments and said, 'Jacob, it's good of you to return my call. I needed to have a word with you about the Bolivian mine project, because I know you're the lead financier . . .'

Sebastian left the room, closing the door quietly behind him.

-◄o►-

'Protocol is the key to understanding the Japanese psyche,' said Professor Marsh as he looked up at the tiered ranks of expectant faces. 'It's every bit as important as mastering the language.'

Sebastian had quickly discovered that the beginners, intermediate and advanced classes were held at different times of the day, which made it possible for him to attend fifteen classes each week. This, combined with the hours he had to devote to countless books, a tape recorder and a dozen tapes, meant he had hardly a moment left to eat or sleep.

Professor Marsh had become used to seeing the same young man sitting in the front row of his lectures, furiously scribbling notes.

'Let us begin with the bow,' said the professor. 'It is important to understand that the bow in Japanese circles reveals far more than shaking hands does for the British. There are no different degrees of handshake, other than firm or weak, and as a result the handshake does not reveal either participant's social standing. For the Japanese, however, there is an entire code when it comes to bowing. Starting at the top, only the emperor bows to no one. If you are meeting someone of your own rank, you both nod –' the professor gave a measured jerk of the head. 'But if, for example, the chairman of a company had a meeting with his managing director, the chairman would merely nod while the managing director would bow thus, bending from the waist. Should a worker come across the chairman, he would bow very low, so their eyes did not meet, and the chairman might not even acknowledge him, just pass by.'

'So,' said Sebastian after he'd returned to the bank later that afternoon, 'if I was Japanese and you were chairman, I would bow very low to show I knew my place.'

'Some hope,' said Cedric.

'And you,' said Sebastian, ignoring the comment, 'would either nod, or simply walk by. So when you see Mr Morita for the first time, as the meeting is taking place in your country, you must allow him to nod first, return the compliment, and then exchange business cards. If you really want to impress him, your business card will be in English on one side and Japanese on the reverse. When Mr Morita presents his managing director, he will bow low, but you will just nod again. And when he introduces the third person in his party, he will bow even lower, while once again you will just nod.'

'So I just go on nodding. Is there anyone I should bow to?'

'Only the emperor, and I don't think he's looking for a short-term loan at the present time. Mr Morita will see that you are placing him above his colleagues and, equally important, his colleagues will appreciate the respect you have shown for their chairman.'

'I think this whole philosophy should be put into practice at Farthings immediately,' said Cedric.

'And then there is the tricky etiquette when you dine together,' continued Sebastian. 'At a restaurant, Mr Morita must order first and be served first, but he cannot begin his meal before you do. His colleagues cannot start before he does, but they must finish just before him.'

'Imagine if you were at a dinner party for sixteen, and you were the most junior person present . . .'

'You'd get indigestion,' said Sebastian. 'However, at the end of the meal, Mr Morita will not leave the table until you rise and ask him to join you.'

'What about women?'

'A minefield,' said Sebastian. 'The Japanese cannot understand why an Englishman stands when a woman enters the room, allows them to be served first, and won't lift their knife and fork until their wives do.'

'Are you suggesting it would be better to leave Beryl in Huddersfield?'

'That might be wise given the circumstances.'

'And what if you were to join us for dinner, Seb?'

'I would have to order last, be served last, begin my meal last and leave the table last.'

'Another first,' said Cedric. 'By the way, when did you learn all this?'

'This morning,' said Sebastian.

—◦—

Sebastian would have given up the beginners' class by the end of the first week if he hadn't become distracted. He tried to concentrate on what Professor Marsh was saying, but all too often he found himself glancing back in her direction. Although she was a lot older than Sebastian, thirty, perhaps even thirty-five, she was very attractive, and the boys at the bank had assured him that women who worked in the City often preferred younger men.

Sebastian turned and looked in her direction again, but she was concentrating on every word the professor had to say. Or was she just playing hard to get? There was only one way he was going to find out.

When the lecture finally came to an end, he followed her out of the hall, and decided she was just as attractive from behind. A pencil skirt revealed a slim pair of legs he was happy to follow into the student bar. His confidence grew when she walked straight up to the counter, and the barman immediately reached for a bottle of white wine. Sebastian sat down on the stool next to her.

'Let me guess, a glass of chardonnay for the lady, and I'll have a beer.'

She smiled.

'Coming up,' said the barman.

'My name's Seb.'

'I'm Amy,' she replied. The American accent took him by surprise. Was he about to find out if American girls were as easy as the guys at the bank claimed?

'So what do you do when you're not studying Japanese?' asked Sebastian as the barman placed two drinks on the counter.

'That'll be four shillings.'

Sebastian handed over two half-crowns and said, 'Keep the change.'

'I've just retired as an air hostess,' she said.

Could this get any better, thought Sebastian. 'What made you pack it in?'

'They're always on the lookout for younger recruits.'

'But you can't be a day over twenty-five.'

'I wish,' she said, before taking a sip of her wine. 'And what do you do?'

'I'm a merchant banker.'

'That sounds exciting.'

'Sure is,' said Sebastian. 'Earlier today I closed a deal with Jacob Rothschild to buy a tin mine in Bolivia.'

'Wow, that makes my world look pretty mundane. So why are you learning Japanese?'

'The head of the Far East desk has just been promoted, and I'm on the shortlist for his job.'

'Aren't you a little young for such a responsible position?'

'Banking is a young man's game,' said Sebastian, as she finished her wine. 'Can I get you another?'

'No, but thank you. I've got a lot of revision to do, so I'd better go home if the professor isn't going to find me out tomorrow.'

'Why don't I come with you, and we can revise together?'

'Sounds tempting,' she said, 'but it's raining, so we'll need a taxi.'

'Leave it to me,' he said, giving her a warm smile. Sebastian almost ran out of the bar, and straight into the pouring rain. It took him some time to find a taxi, and when he eventually flagged one down he could only hope she didn't live too far away, because he was down to loose change. He spotted her standing behind the glass door and gave her a wave.

'Where to, guv?'

'Can't be sure, don't know where the lady lives,' said Sebastian, giving the cabbie a wink. He turned to see Amy running towards the cab, and quickly opened the back door so she wouldn't get soaked. She slid into the seat, and he was just about to join her when a voice behind him said, 'Thank you, Clifton. Good of you to find my wife a taxi in this dreadful weather.

'See you tomorrow,' added the professor as he pulled the cab door closed.

15

'Good morning, Mr Morita. What a pleasure to meet you,' said Cedric, giving a smart nod.

'And it's a pleasure to meet you, Mr Hardcastle,' he ventured, returning the compliment. 'May I introduce my managing director, Mr Ueyama?' He in turn stepped forward and bowed respectfully. Cedric nodded again. 'And my private secretary, Mr Ono,' who bowed even lower, but, once again, Cedric only gave a curt nod.

'Please have a seat, Mr Morita,' said Cedric, and then waited for his guest to sit down before he took his place behind his desk. 'I hope you had a pleasant flight?'

'Yes, thank you. I was able to catch a few hours' sleep between Hong Kong and London, and it was most considerate of you to send a car and your personal assistant to meet us at the airport.'

'My pleasure. And is your hotel comfortable?'

'Very satisfactory, thank you, and most convenient for the City.'

'I'm delighted to hear that. So, shall we get down to business?'

'No, no, no!' said Sebastian, jumping up. 'No Japanese gentleman would consider discussing business until he has been offered tea. In Tokyo, the tea ceremony would be conducted by a geisha and can last for thirty minutes or more, depending on how senior you are. Of course, he may turn the offer down, but he will still expect you to make it.'

'I forgot,' said Cedric. 'A foolish mistake and I won't make it on the day. Thank heavens you'll be there to rescue me if I do.'

'But I won't be able to,' said Sebastian. 'I'll be sitting at the back of the room with Mr Ono. We'll be making notes of your conversation, and neither of us would ever consider interrupting our masters.'

'So when am I allowed to talk to him about business?'

'Not until Mr Morita has taken the first sip of his second cup of tea.'

'But during the pre-business chat, should I mention my wife and family?'

'Not unless he raises the subject first. He's been married to Yoshiko for eleven years, and she occasionally accompanies him on his trips abroad.'

'Do they have any children?'

'He has three young children: two sons, Hideo, aged six, and Masao, four, and a daughter, Naoko, who's only two.'

'Am I allowed to tell him that my son is a barrister and has recently become a QC?'

'Only if he raises the subject of his own children first, which is most unlikely.'

'I understand,' said Cedric. 'Or at least I think I do. Do you think the chairmen of the other banks will be taking this much trouble?'

'They'd better be, if they want the contract as much as you do.'

'I'm very grateful, Seb. So how's your Japanese coming along?'

'It was going well until I made a complete fool of myself and tried to pick up the professor's wife.'

Cedric couldn't stop laughing when Sebastian gave him a blow-by-blow account of what had happened the previous evening. 'Soaked, you say?'

'To the skin. I don't know what it is with me and women, because I don't seem to have the same pulling power as the other lads in the bank.'

'I'll tell you about the other lads,' said Cedric. 'Once they've got a couple of pints in them, they'd have you believe they give James Bond lessons. And I can tell you, with most of them, it's all talk.'

'Did you have the same problem when you were my age?'

'Certainly not,' said Cedric. 'But then I met Beryl when I was six, and I haven't looked at another woman since.'

'Six?' said Sebastian. 'You're worse than my mother. She fell for my dad when she was ten, and after that the poor man never had a chance.'

'Neither did I,' admitted Cedric. 'You see, Beryl was the milk monitor at Huddersfield primary, and if I wanted an extra third of a pint . . . bossy little thing. Still is, come to think of it. But I've never wanted anyone else.'

'And you've never even looked at another woman?'

'Looked, yes, but that's as far as it goes. If you've struck gold, why go in search of brass?'

Sebastian smiled. 'So how will I know when I've struck gold?'

'You'll know, my boy. Believe me, you'll know.'

◄o►

Sebastian spent the last two weeks before Mr Morita's plane was due to touch down at London Airport attending every lecture Professor Marsh had on offer, never once so much as glancing back at his wife. In the evening, he returned to his uncle Giles's home in Smith Square, and after a light supper, when he abandoned his knife and fork in favour of chopsticks, he would return to his room, read, listen to tapes and regularly bow in front of a full-length mirror.

The night before the curtain was due to go up, he felt he was ready. Well, half ready.

◄o►

Giles was becoming accustomed to Sebastian bowing every morning when he entered the breakfast room.

'And you must acknowledge me with a nod, otherwise I can't sit down,' said Sebastian.

'I'm beginning to enjoy this,' said Giles, as Gwyneth walked in to join them. 'Good morning, my darling,' he said, as both men rose from their places.

'There's a smart Daimler parked outside the front door,' said Gwyneth, taking a seat opposite Giles.

'Yes, it's taking me to London Airport to pick up Mr Morita.'

'Ah, of course, today's the big day.'

'That's for sure,' said Sebastian. He drained his orange juice, jumped up, ran out into the corridor and took one more look in the mirror.

'I like the shirt,' said Gwyneth, buttering a piece of toast, 'but the tie's a little . . . old school. I think the blue silk one you wore at our wedding would be more appropriate.'

'You're right,' said Sebastian, and immediately dashed upstairs and disappeared into his bedroom.

'Good luck,' said Giles as he came bounding back down the stairs.

'Thank you,' Sebastian shouted over his shoulder as he headed out of the house.

Mr Hardcastle's chauffeur was standing by the back door of the Daimler.

'I think I'll join you in the front, Tom, as that's where I'll be sitting on the way back.'

'Suit yourself,' said Tom, climbing in behind the wheel.

'Tell me,' said Sebastian as the car turned right out of Smith Square and on to the Embankment, 'when you were a young man—'

'Steady on, my lad. I'm only thirty-four.'

'Sorry. I'll try again. When you were single, how many women did you, you know, before you were married?'

'Fuck?' said Tom.

Sebastian turned bright red, but managed, 'Yes.'

'Having trouble with the birds, are we?'

'In a word, yes.'

'Well, I've no intention of answering that question, m'lud, on account of the fact that it would undoubtedly incriminate me.' Sebastian laughed. 'But not as many as I'd have liked, and not as many as I told my mates I had.'

Sebastian laughed again. 'And what's married life like?'

'Up and down like Tower Bridge. What's brought all this on, Seb?' asked Tom as they passed Earl's Court. 'Found someone you fancy, have you?'

'If only. No, it's just that I'm useless when it comes to women. I seem to blow it whenever I meet a girl I like. I somehow manage to send out all the wrong signals.'

'Which isn't that clever when you've got everythin' goin' for you, is it?'

'What do you mean?'

'You're a good-lookin' lad, in a toffee-nosed sort of way, well-educated, talk proper, come from a good family, so what more do you want?'

'But I'm penniless.'

'Possibly. But you've got potential, and girls like potential. Always think they can harness it, turn it to their advantage. So believe me, you won't have any problems in that department. Once you get goin', you'll never look back.'

'You're wasted, Tom, you should have been a philosopher.'

'None of your cheek, lad. It's not me what's got a place booked at Cambridge. 'Cause I tell you what, given half a chance, I'd swap places with you.'

A thought that had never crossed Sebastian's mind.

'Mind you, I'm not complainin'. Got a good job, Mr Hard-castle's a diamond, and Linda's all right. But if I'd had your start in life, I wouldn't be a chauffeur, that's for sure.'

'What would you be?'

'I'd own a fleet of cars, by now, and you'd be callin' me sir.'

Sebastian suddenly felt guilty. He took so much for granted, never giving a thought to what was going on in other people's lives, or how privileged they might think he was. He remained silent for the rest of the journey, having been made painfully aware that birth is life's first lottery ticket.

Tom broke the silence as he turned off the Great West Road. 'Is it right we're picking up three Nips?'

'Behave yourself, Tom. We're picking up three Japanese gentlemen.'

'Now don't get me wrong, I've got nothin' against the little yellow bastards. Stands to reason doesn't it, they only went to war 'cause they were told to.'

'You're a historian as well,' said Sebastian as the car came to a halt outside the airport terminal. 'Have the back door open and the engine running when you next see me, Tom, because these three gentlemen are very important to Mr Hardcastle.'

'I'll be right 'ere, standin' to attention,' said Tom. 'Even practised my bow, 'aven't I?'

'Very low, in your case,' said Sebastian, grinning.

—◦—

Although the arrivals board showed that the aircraft was on time, Sebastian was an hour early. He bought a lukewarm coffee from a small, overcrowded café, picked up a copy of the *Daily Mail*, and read about two monkeys the Americans had sent into space that had just returned safely to Earth. He went to the lavatory, twice, checked his tie in the mirror, three times – Gwyneth had been right – and walked up and down the concourse countless times rehearsing 'Good morning, Mr Morita, welcome to England', in Japanese, followed by a low bow.

'Japan Airlines flight number 1027 from Tokyo has just landed,' announced a prim voice over the loudspeaker.

Sebastian immediately selected a place outside the arrivals gate from where he would have a good view of the passengers as they came out of customs. What he hadn't anticipated was that there would be a large number of Japanese businessmen disembarking from flight 1027, and he had no idea what Mr Morita or his colleagues looked like.

Every time three passengers came through the gate together, he immediately stepped forward, bowed low and introduced himself. He managed to get it right the fourth time, but he had become so flustered that he delivered his little speech in English.

'Good morning, Mr Morita, welcome to England,' he said before bowing low. 'I am Mr Hardcastle's personal assistant, and I have a car waiting to take you to the Savoy.'

'Thank you,' said Mr Morita, immediately revealing that his English was far superior to Sebastian's Japanese. 'It was most considerate of Mr Hardcastle to go to so much trouble.'

As Morita made no attempt to introduce his two colleagues, Sebastian immediately led them out of the terminal. He was relieved to find Tom standing to attention by the open back door of the car.

'Good morning, sir,' said Tom, bowing low, but Mr Morita and his colleagues climbed into the car without acknowledging him.

Sebastian jumped into the front seat, and the car joined the slow-moving traffic into London. He remained silent during the journey to the Savoy, while Mr Morita chatted quietly to his colleagues in their native tongue. Forty minutes later, the Daimler came to a halt outside the hotel. Three porters rushed to the back of the car and began unloading the luggage.

When Mr Morita stepped out on to the pavement, Sebastian bowed low. 'I will return at eleven thirty, sir,' he said in English, 'so that you will be in time for your meeting with Mr Hard-castle at twelve o'clock.'

Mr Morita managed a nod as the manager of the hotel stepped forward and said, 'Welcome back to the Savoy, Morita San.' He bowed low.

Sebastian didn't get back into the car until Mr Morita had disappeared through the hotel's revolving doors. 'We need to get back to the office, and as quickly as possible.'

'But my instructions are to stay put,' said Tom, not budging, 'in case Mr Morita needs to use the car.'

'I don't give a damn what your instructions were,' said Sebastian. 'We're going back to the office, and right now, so step on it.'

'On your head be it,' said Tom, before shooting down the wrong side of the road and out on to the Strand.

Twenty-two minutes later, they drew up outside Farthings. 'Turn the car round and keep the engine running,' said Sebastian. 'I'll be back as quickly as I can.' He leapt out of the car, ran into the building, headed for the nearest lift and, on arriving on the fifth floor, charged down the corridor and marched into the chairman's office without knocking. Adrian Sloane turned round, and made no attempt to hide his disapproval at having his meeting with the chairman interrupted so abruptly.

'I thought I gave you instructions to remain at the Savoy,' said Cedric.

'Something's come up, chairman, and I've only got a few minutes to brief you.'

Sloane looked even less pleased when Hardcastle asked him to leave them and to come back in a few minutes. 'So what's the problem?' he asked Sebastian once the door was closed.

'Mr Morita has an appointment with the Westminster Bank at three this afternoon, and another with Barclays at ten tomorrow morning. He and his advisers are concerned that Farthings hasn't done many company loans before, and you'll have to convince them that you're capable of handling such a large deal. And by the way, they know everything about you, including the fact that you left school at fifteen.'

'So he can read English,' said Cedric. 'But how did you come across the rest of the information, because I can't believe they volunteered it.'

'They didn't. But then, they have no idea that I speak Japanese.'

'Let's keep it that way,' said Cedric. 'It might come in useful later. But for now, you'd better get back to the Savoy, and sharpish.'

'One more thing,' said Sebastian as he headed towards the door. 'It's not the first time Mr Morita has stayed at the Savoy. In fact, the hotel manager greeted him as if he was a regular guest. And I've just remembered, they're hoping to get three tickets for *My Fair Lady*, but they've been told it's sold out.'

The chairman picked up the phone and said, 'Find out which theatre *My Fair Lady* is playing at, and get the box office on the line.'

Sebastian ran out of the room and down the corridor, willing the lift to be on the top floor. It wasn't, and it seemed to take forever to return. When it finally appeared, it stopped at every floor on the way down. He ran out of the building, jumped into the car, checked his watch and said, 'We've got twenty-six minutes to be back at the Savoy.'

Sebastian could never remember the traffic moving so slowly. Every light seemed to turn red just as they approached it. And why were the zebra crossings so packed with pedestrians at this time in the morning?

Tom turned into Savoy Place at twenty-seven minutes past eleven, to face a fleet of stationary limousines disgorging their passengers outside the hotel. Sebastian couldn't afford to wait, so, with Professor Marsh's words ringing in his ears, *The Japanese are never late for a meeting and consider it an insult if you fail to be on time,* he jumped out and began running down the street towards the hotel.

Why didn't I use the hotel phone, he was asking himself long before he'd reached the front entrance. But it was too late to worry about that. He ran past the doorman, and pushed through the revolving doors propelling a lady out on to the street far more quickly than she had intended.

He looked up at the foyer clock: 11.29. He walked quickly across to the lifts, checked his tie in the mirror and took a deep breath. The clock struck twice, the lift doors opened and out stepped Mr Morita and his two colleagues. He graced Sebastian with a smile, but then, he assumed the young man had been standing there for the past hour.

16

SEBASTIAN OPENED the door to allow Mr Morita and his two colleagues to enter the chairman's office.

As he walked across to greet them, Cedric felt tall for the first time in his life. He was just about to bow when Mr Morita thrust out his hand.

'I'm delighted to meet you,' said Cedric, shaking hands while preparing to bow a second time, but Morita turned and said, 'May I introduce my managing director, Mr Ueyama.' He stepped forward and also shook hands with Cedric. The chairman would have shaken hands with Mr Ono too, if he hadn't been clutching a large box in both hands.

'Do have a seat,' said Cedric, trying to get back on script.

'Thank you,' said Morita. 'But first, it is an honourable Japanese tradition to exchange gifts with a new friend.' The private secretary stepped forward and handed the box to Mr Morita, who passed it to Cedric.

'How very kind of you,' said Cedric, looking faintly embarrassed as all three of his visitors remained standing, clearly waiting for him to open the gift.

He took his time, first removing the blue ribbon, so carefully tied in a bow, and then the gold paper, as he tried to think of something he could give Morita in return. Would he have to sacrifice his Henry Moore? He glanced at Sebastian, more in hope than expectation, but he was looking equally embarrassed. The traditional exchange of gifts must have been covered in one of the few lessons he'd missed.

Cedric removed the lid from the box, and gasped as he gently lifted out a beautiful, delicate vase of turquoise and black. Sebastian, standing at the back of the room, took a pace forward, but said nothing.

'Magnificent,' said Cedric. He removed a bowl of flowers from his desk and put the exquisite oval vase in its place. 'Whenever you come to my office in future, Mr Morita, you will always find your vase on my desk.'

'I am greatly honoured,' said Morita, bowing for the first time.

Sebastian took another step forward, until he was only a foot away from Mr Morita. He turned to face the chairman.

'Do I have your permission to ask our honoured guest a question, sir?'

'Of course,' said Cedric, hoping he was about to be rescued.

'May I be allowed to know the name of the potter, Morita San?'

Mr Morita smiled. 'Shoji Hamada,' he replied.

'It is a great honour to receive a gift crafted by one of your nation's living national treasures. Had the chairman known, he would have offered a similar gift by one of our finest English potters, who has written a book on Mr Hamada's work.' All the endless hours of chatter with Jessica were finally proving useful.

'Mr Bernard Leach,' said Morita. 'I am fortunate enough to have three of his pieces in my collection.'

'However, our gift, selected by my chairman, although not as worthy, is nevertheless given in the same spirit of friendship.'

Cedric smiled. He couldn't wait to find out what his gift was.

'The chairman has obtained three tickets for tonight's performance of *My Fair Lady* at the Theatre Royal, Drury Lane. With your permission, I will collect you from your hotel at seven o'clock, and escort you to the theatre, where the curtain rises at seven thirty.'

'One cannot think of a more agreeable gift,' said Mr Morita. Turning to Cedric, he added, 'I am humbled by your thoughtful generosity.'

Cedric bowed, but realized this wasn't the time to let Sebastian know that he'd already called the theatre, only to be told it was sold out for the next fortnight. A languid voice had informed him, 'You can always join the queue for returns,' which was exactly what Sebastian would be doing for the rest of the day.

'Do have a seat, Mr Morita,' said Cedric, trying to recover. 'Perhaps you would like some tea?'

'No, thank you, but, if possible, a cup of coffee.'

Cedric thought ruefully about the six different blends of tea from India, Ceylon and Malaya he'd selected at Carwardine's earlier in the week, which had all been rejected in a sentence. He pressed a button on his phone, and prayed that his secretary drank coffee.

'Some coffee, please, Miss Clough. I do hope you had a pleasant flight,' he said after he'd put the phone back down.

'Too many stopovers, I fear. I look forward to the day when you can fly from Tokyo to London non-stop.'

'What a thought,' said Cedric. 'And I hope your hotel is comfortable?'

'I only ever stay at the Savoy. So convenient for the City.'

'Yes, of course,' said Cedric. Wrong-footed again.

Mr Morita leant forward, looked at the photograph on Cedric's desk and said, 'Your wife and son?'

'Yes,' said Cedric, unsure if he should elaborate.

'Wife a milk monitor, son a QC.'

'Yes,' said Cedric helplessly.

'My sons,' said Morita, removing a wallet from an inside pocket and taking out two photographs, which he placed on the desk in front of Cedric. 'Hideo and Masao are at school in Tokyo.'

Cedric studied the photographs, and realized the time had come to tear up the script. 'And your wife?'

'Mrs Morita was unable to visit England this time, because our young daughter, Naoko, has chicken pox.'

'I'm sorry,' said Cedric, as there was a gentle tap on the door and Miss Clough entered carrying a tray of coffee and short-bread biscuits. Cedric was about to take his first sip, and was wondering what he could possibly talk about next, when Morita suggested, 'Perhaps the time has come to discuss business?'

'Yes, of course,' said Cedric, putting his cup down. He opened a file on his desk and reminded himself of the salient points he'd highlighted the night before. 'I'd like to say from the outset, Mr Morita, that coupon loans is not the field in which Farthings has made its reputation. However, as we wish to build a long-term relationship with your distinguished company, I hope you will allow us the opportunity to prove ourselves.' Morita nodded. 'Remembering that the amount you require is ten million pounds, with a short-term payback coupon of five years, and having studied your most recent cash-flow figures, while assessing the current exchange rate of the yen, we consider a realistic percentage . . .'

Now that he was back on familiar ground, Cedric relaxed for the first time. Forty minutes later, he had presented his ideas and answered every one of Mr Morita's questions. Sebastian felt his boss couldn't have done much better.

'May I suggest you draw up a contract, Mr Hardcastle? I was in no doubt that you were the right man for this job long before I left Tokyo. After your presentation, I am even more convinced. I do have appointments with two other banks, but that is simply to assure my shareholders that I am considering alternatives. Take care of the rin, and the yen will take care of themselves.'

Both men laughed.

'If you are free,' said Cedric, 'perhaps you would care to join me for lunch? A Japanese restaurant has recently opened in the City, and has received excellent reviews, so I thought—'

'And you can think again, Mr Hardcastle, because I didn't travel six thousand miles in search of a Japanese restaurant. No, I will take you to Rules, and we will enjoy roast beef and Yorkshire pudding, appropriate for a man from Huddersfield, I think.' Both men burst out laughing again.

When they left the office a few minutes later, Cedric held back and whispered in Sebastian's ear, 'Good thinking, but as there are no tickets available for tonight's performance of *My Fair Lady*, you're going to have to spend the rest of the day in the returns queue. Just let's hope it doesn't rain, or you'll be soaked again,' he added before joining Mr Morita in the corridor.

Sebastian bowed low as Cedric and his guests stepped into the lift and disappeared down to the ground floor. He hung around on the fifth floor for a few more minutes but didn't call for the lift until he felt certain they would be well on their way to the restaurant.

Once Sebastian had left the bank, he hailed a taxi. 'Theatre Royal, Drury Lane,' he said, and when they pulled up outside the theatre twenty minutes later, the first thing he noticed was just how long the queue for returns was. He paid the cabbie, strolled into the theatre and went straight up to the box office.

'I don't suppose you have three tickets for tonight?' he pleaded.

'You suppose correctly, my dear,' said the woman sitting in the booth. 'You could of course join the returns queue, but frankly not many of them will get in before Christmas. Someone has to die before this show gets returns.'

'I don't care what it costs.'

'That's what they all say, dear. We've got people in the queue who claim it's their twenty-first birthday, their fiftieth wedding anniversary . . . one of them was so desperate he proposed to me.'

Sebastian walked out of the theatre and stood on the pavement. He took one more look at the queue, which seemed to have grown even longer in the past few minutes, and tried to work out what he could possibly do next. He then recalled something he'd once read in one of his father's novels. He decided he would try to find out if it would work for him as well as it had for William Warwick.

He jogged down the hill towards the Strand, dodging in and out of the afternoon traffic, arriving back in Savoy Place a few minutes later. He went straight to the front desk and asked the receptionist for the name of the head porter.

'Albert Southgate,' she replied.

Sebastian thanked her and strolled across to the concierge's desk, as if he were a guest.

'Is Albert around?' he asked the porter.

'I think he's gone to lunch, sir, but I'll just check.' The man disappeared into a back room.

'Bert, there's a gentleman asking for you.'

Sebastian didn't have long to wait before an older man appeared in a long blue coat adorned with gold braid on the cuffs, shiny gold buttons and two rows of campaign medals, one of which he recognized. He gave Sebastian a wary look, and asked, 'How can I help you?'

'I have a problem,' said Sebastian, still wondering if he could risk it. 'My uncle, Sir Giles Barrington, once told me that if I was ever staying at the Savoy and needed anything, to have a word with Albert.'

'The gentleman what won the MC at Tobruk?'

'Yes,' said Sebastian, taken by surprise.

'Not many survived that one. Nasty business. How can I help?'

'Sir Giles needs three tickets for *My Fair Lady*.'

'When?'

'Tonight.'

'You must be joking.'

'And he doesn't care what it costs.'

'Hang about. I'll see what I can do.'

Sebastian watched as Albert marched out of the hotel, crossed the road and disappeared in the direction of the Theatre Royal. He paced up and down the foyer, occasionally looking anxiously out on to the Strand, but it was another half an hour before the head porter reappeared, clutching an envelope. He walked back into the hotel and handed the envelope to Sebastian.

'Three house seats, row F, centre stalls.'

'Fantastic. How much do I owe you?'

'Nothing.'

'I don't understand,' said Sebastian.

'Box office manager asked to be remembered to Sir Giles – his brother, Sergeant Harris, was killed at Tobruk.'

Sebastian felt ashamed.

◄◦►

'Well done, Seb, you saved the day. Now the only task you have left today is to make sure the Daimler remains outside the Savoy until we know Mr Morita and his colleagues are safely tucked up in bed.'

'But it's only a couple of hundred yards from the hotel to the theatre.'

'That can be a long way if it's raining, as your brief encounter with Professor Marsh's wife should have taught you. Besides, if we don't make the effort, you can be sure someone else will.'

-<o>-

Sebastian got out of the car and entered the Savoy at 6.30 p.m. He walked across to the lift and waited patiently. Just after seven, Mr Morita and his two colleagues appeared. Sebastian bowed low and handed them an envelope containing three tickets.

'Thank you, young man,' said Mr Morita. They made their way across the foyer, through the swing doors and out of the hotel.

'The chairman's car will take you to the Theatre Royal,' said Sebastian as Tom opened the back door of the Daimler.

'No, thank you,' said Morita, 'the walk will do us good.' Without another word, the three men set off in the direction of the theatre. Sebastian bowed low once again, before joining Tom in the front of the car.

'Why don't you go home?' said Tom. 'No need to hang about, and if it starts to rain, I'll drive up to the theatre and pick them up.'

'But they might want to go to dinner after the show, or to a nightclub. Do you know any nightclubs?'

'Depends what they're lookin' for.'

'Not *that*, I suspect. But either way, I'm staying put until, to quote Mr Hardcastle, they're safely tucked up in bed.'

It didn't rain, not a drop, and by ten o'clock Sebastian knew everything there was to know about Tom's life, including where he'd been to school, where he'd been billeted during the war and where he'd worked before becoming Mr Hardcastle's chauffeur. Tom was chatting about his wife wanting to go to Marbella on their next holiday, when Sebastian said, 'Oh my God,' and slithered down the seat and out of sight as two smartly dressed men walked past the front of the car and strode into the hotel.

'What are you doing?'

'Avoiding someone I'd hoped never to see again.'

'Looks as if the curtain's come down,' said Tom, as hordes of chattering theatregoers began to pour out on to the Strand. A few minutes later, Sebastian spotted his three charges making their way back to the hotel. Just before Mr Morita reached the entrance, Sebastian got out of the car and bowed low.

'I hope you enjoyed the show, Morita San.'

'Couldn't have been better,' Morita responded. 'I haven't laughed so much in years, and the music was wonderful. I will thank Mr Hardcastle personally when I see him tomorrow morning. Please go home, Mr Clifton, because I won't need the car again tonight. Sorry to have kept you up.'

'My pleasure, Morita San,' said Sebastian. He remained on the pavement, and watched the three of them enter the hotel, cross the foyer and head towards the bank of lifts. His heart began to beat faster when he saw two men step forward, bow and then shake hands with Mr Morita. Sebastian remained rooted to the spot. The two men spoke to Morita for a few moments. He then dismissed his colleagues and accompanied the two men into the American Bar. Sebastian wanted desperately to go into the hotel and take a closer look, but he knew he couldn't risk it. Instead, he reluctantly slipped back into the car.

'Are you all right?' asked Tom. 'You're as white as a sheet.'

'What time does Mr Hardcastle go to bed?'

'Eleven, eleven thirty, depends. But you can always tell if he's still up, because his study light will be on.'

Sebastian checked his watch. 10.43 p.m. 'Then let's go and find out if he's still awake.'

Tom drove out on to the Strand, crossed Trafalgar Square, continued on down the Mall to Hyde Park Corner, and arrived outside 37 Cadogan Place just after eleven. The study light was still burning. No doubt the chairman was triple-checking the contract he was anticipating the Japanese would be signing in the morning.

Sebastian got slowly out of the car, climbed the steps and rang the front door bell. A few moments later the hall light went on and Cedric opened the door.

'I'm sorry to disturb you at this late hour, chairman, but we've got a problem.'

17

'THE FIRST THING you must do is tell your uncle the truth,' said Cedric. 'And I mean the whole truth.'

'I'll tell him everything as soon as I get back this evening.'

'It's important that Sir Giles knows what you did in his name, because he'll want to write and thank Mr Harris at the Theatre Royal, as well as the head porter of the Savoy.'

'Albert Southgate.'

'And *you* must write and thank them both as well.'

'Yes, of course. And I apologize again, sir. I feel I've let you down, because the whole exercise has turned out to be a waste of your time.'

'These experiences are rarely a complete waste of time. Whenever you bid for a new contract, even if you are unsuccessful, you almost always learn something that will stand you in good stead for the next one.'

'What did I learn?'

'Japanese for a start, not to mention one or two other things about yourself that I'm sure you'll benefit from at some later date.'

'But the amount of time you and your senior staff have spent on this project . . . along with a great deal of the bank's money.'

'It won't have been any different for Barclays or the Westminster. If you manage a success rate of one in five with projects like this, that's considered par for the course,' he added as the phone on his desk rang. He picked it up and, after a moment, said, 'Yes, send him in.'

'Shall I leave, sir?'

'No, stay put. I'd rather like you to meet my son.' The door opened, and in walked a man who could only have been of Cedric Hardcastle's lineage: an inch taller perhaps, but the same warm smile, broad shoulders and almost bald dome, although with a slightly thicker semi-circle of hair sprouting from ear to ear, making him look like a seventeenth-century friar. And, as Sebastian was about to discover, the same incisive mind.

'Good morning, Pop, good to see you.' And the same Yorkshire accent.

'Arnold, this is Sebastian Clifton, who's been assisting me with the Sony negotiations.'

'I'm glad to meet you, sir,' said Sebastian as they shook hands.

'I'm a huge admirer of your—'

'– my father's books?'

'No, can't say I've ever read one. Have quite enough of detectives during the day without reading about them at night.'

'My mother, then, the first woman chairman of a public company?'

'No, it's your sister Jessica that I'm in awe of. What a talent,' he added, nodding towards the drawing of his father on the wall. 'So what's she up to now?'

'She's just enrolled at the Slade in Bloomsbury, and is about to begin her first year.'

'Then I feel sorry for the other poor sods in her year.'

'Why?'

'They'll either love her or hate her, because they're about to discover they're just not in her class. But back to more mundane matters,' Arnold said, turning to his father. 'I've prepared three copies of the contract, as agreed by both parties, and once you've signed them, you'll have ninety days to raise the ten million loan for a five-year period at a rate of two and a quarter per cent. The quarter being your fee on the transaction. I should also mention—'

'Don't bother,' said Cedric, 'because I have a feeling we're no longer in the running for this one.'

'But when I spoke to you last night, Pop, you sounded quite bullish.'

'Let's just say that circumstances have changed since then, and leave it at that,' said Cedric.

'I'm sorry to hear it,' said Arnold. He gathered up the contracts, and was just about to put them back in his briefcase, when he saw it for the first time.

'I've never thought of you as an aesthete, Pop, but this is quite superb,' he said, carefully picking up the Japanese vase from his father's desk. He studied the piece more closely before checking the bottom. 'And by one of Japan's national treasures, no less.'

'Not you as well,' said Cedric.

'Shoji Hamada,' said Sebastian.

'Where did you find it?'

'I didn't,' said Cedric. 'It was a gift from Mr Morita.'

'Well, you didn't end up completely empty-handed on this deal,' said Arnold, as they heard a tap on the door.

'Come in,' said Cedric, wondering if it just might be . . . the door swung open and Tom marched in. 'I thought I told you to stay at the Savoy,' said the chairman.

'Not much point, sir. I was waiting outside the hotel at nine thirty, as instructed, but Mr Morita never showed up. And him being a gentleman what's never late, I decided to have a word with the doorman, who tipped me off that the three Japanese guests had checked out and left the hotel in a taxi just after nine.'

'I never would have thought it possible,' said Cedric. 'I must be losing my touch.'

'You can't win 'em all, Pop, as you so often remind me,' said Arnold.

'Lawyers seem to win even when they lose,' replied his father.

'Tell you what I'll do,' said Arnold. 'I'll forgo my vast, unearned fee, in exchange for this small, insignificant bauble.'

'Get lost.'

'Then I'll be on my way, as there's clearly not much more I can do here.'

Arnold was placing the contracts in his Gladstone bag when the door swung open, and Mr Morita and his two colleagues walked in, just as several church bells in the Square Mile began to chime eleven times.

'I hope I'm not late,' were Mr Morita's first words as he shook hands with Cedric.

'Bang on time,' said Cedric.

'And you,' said Morita, looking at Arnold, 'can only be the unworthy son of a great father.'

'That's me, sir,' said Arnold as they shook hands.

'Have you prepared the contracts?'

'I have indeed, sir.'

'Then all you'll need is my signature, and then Father can get on with his work.' Arnold took the contracts back out of his Gladstone bag and laid them out on the desk. 'But before I sign, I have a gift for my new friend, Sebastian Clifton, which is why I had to leave the hotel so early this morning.'

Mr Ono stepped forward and handed a small box to Mr Morita, who in turn gave it to Sebastian.

'Not always a good boy but, as the British say, his heart is in the right place.'

Sebastian said nothing as he untied the red ribbon and removed the silver paper before lifting the box's lid. He took out a tiny vase glazed in crimson and yellow. He couldn't take his eyes off it.

'You're not looking for a lawyer, by any chance?' asked Arnold.

'Only if you can name the potter without looking at the base.'

Sebastian handed the vase to Arnold, who took his time admiring how the red ran into the yellow, creating orange streaks, before he ventured an opinion. 'Bernard Leach?'

'This son is of some use after all,' said Morita.

Both men laughed, as Arnold handed the exquisite piece back to Sebastian, who said, 'I don't know how to thank you, sir.'

'But when you do, be sure to deliver your speech in my native tongue.'

Sebastian was so taken by surprise, he nearly dropped the vase. 'I'm not sure I understand, sir.'

'Of course you do, and should you fail to respond in Japanese, I will be left with no choice but to present this vase to the son of Cedric.'

Everyone waited for Sebastian to speak. 'Arigatou gozaimasu. Taihenni kouei desu. Isshou taisetsuni itashimasu.'

'Most impressive. Needs a little attention to the finer brush strokes, unlike your sister's work, but impressive all the same.'

'But how, Morita San, did you work out that I could speak your language when I've never said a word of Japanese in your presence?'

'Three tickets for *My Fair Lady* would be my bet,' said Cedric.

'Mr Hardcastle is a shrewd man, which was why I selected him to represent me in the first place.'

'But how?' repeated Sebastian.

'The tickets were too much of a coincidence,' said Morita. 'Think about it, Sebastian, while I get on with signing the contract.' He removed a fountain pen from his top pocket and handed it to Cedric. 'You must sign first, otherwise the gods will not bless our union.'

Morita watched as Cedric signed all three contracts, before adding his own signature. Both men bowed and then shook hands.

'I have to rush to the airport and take a plane to Paris. The French are causing me many problems.'

'What kind of problems?' asked Arnold.

'Nothing you can help me with, sadly. I have forty thousand transistor radios sitting in a bonded warehouse. The French customs are refusing to allow me to distribute them to my suppliers until every box has been opened and inspected. At the moment, they are managing two a day. The idea is to hold me up as long as possible, so that French manufacturers will be able to sell their inferior product to impatient customers. But I have a plan to defeat them.'

'I can't wait to hear it,' said Arnold.

'Simple really. I shall build a factory in France, employ locals and then distribute my superior product without having to bother with customs officials.'

'The French will work out what you're up to.'

'I'm sure they will, but by then everyone will be like Cedric and want a Sony radio in their front room. I can't afford to miss my plane, but first I'd like a word in private with my new partner.' Arnold shook hands with Morita before he and Sebastian left the room. 'Cedric,' Morita said, taking the seat on the other side of the chairman's desk. 'Have you ever come across a man called Don Pedro Martinez? He came to see me after the show last night, along with a Major Fisher.'

'I only know Martinez by reputation. However, I have met Major Fisher, who represents him on the board of the Barrington Shipping Company, where I also serve as a director.'

'My view is that Martinez is a thoroughly nasty piece of work, while Fisher is weak, and I suspect dependent on Martinez's money to keep afloat.'

'You worked that out after only one meeting?'

'No, after twenty years of dealing with such men. But this one is clever and devious, and you should not underestimate him. I suspect that for Martinez, even life is a cheap commodity.'

'I am grateful for your insight, Akio, but even more for your concern.'

'May I beg a small favour in return before I leave for Paris?'

'Anything.'

'I would like Sebastian to remain the link between our two companies. It will save us both a lot of time and trouble.'

'I only wish I could grant you that favour,' said Cedric, 'but the boy's going up to Cambridge in September.'

'Did you go to university, Cedric?'

'No, I left school at fifteen and, after a couple of weeks' holiday, joined my father at the bank.'

Morita nodded. 'Not everyone is cut out for university, and some are even held back by the experience. I think Sebastian has found his natural metier, and with you as his mentor, it's even possible you might have found the right person to eventually take your place.'

'He's very young,' said Cedric.

'So is your Queen, and she ascended the throne at the age of twenty-five. Cedric, we are living in a brave new world.'

GILES BARRINGTON

1963

18

'ARE YOU SURE you want to be leader of the opposition?' asked Harry.

'No I don't,' said Giles. 'I want to be prime minister, but I'll have to do a spell in opposition before I can expect to get my hands on the keys to Ten Downing Street.'

'You may have held your seat at the last election,' said Emma, 'but your party lost the general election by a landslide. I'm beginning to wonder if Labour can ever win another election. They seem destined to be the party of opposition.'

'I know it must look like that right now,' said Giles, 'but I'm convinced that by the time the next election comes round, the voters will have had enough of the Tories and think it's time for a change.'

'And certainly the Profumo affair hasn't helped,' said Grace.

'Who gets to decide who'll be the next leader of the party?'

'Good question, Sebastian,' said Giles. 'Only my elected colleagues in the House of Commons, all 258 of them.'

'That's a tiny electorate,' said Harry.

'True, but most of them will take soundings in their constituencies to find out who the rank and file would prefer to lead the party, and when it comes to trade union affiliated members, they'll vote for the man their union supports. So any shipping union members from constituencies like Tyneside, Belfast, Glasgow, Clydesdale and Liverpool ought to back me.'

'The man,' repeated Emma. 'Does that mean that out of 258

Labour Members of Parliament, there's not a single woman who can hope to lead the party?'

'Barbara Castle may decide to enter the lists, but frankly she hasn't got a snowball's chance in hell. But let's face it, Emma, there are more women sitting on the Labour benches than on the Conservative side of the House, so if a woman ever does make it to Downing Street, my bet is she'll be a socialist.'

'But why would anyone want to be leader of the Labour Party? It must be one of the most thankless jobs in the country.'

'And at the same time, one of the most exciting,' said Giles. 'How many people get the chance to make a real difference, to improve people's lives, and leave a worthwhile legacy for the next generation? Don't forget, I was born with the proverbial silver spoon in my mouth, so perhaps it's payback time.'

'Wow,' said Emma. 'I'd vote for you.'

'Of course, we'll all support you,' said Harry. 'But I'm not sure there's a lot we can do to influence 257 MPs we've never come across, and are hardly likely to.'

'It's not that kind of support I'm looking for. It's more personal, because I have to warn all of you sitting around this table that once again you can expect the press to start delving into your private lives. You may feel you've had enough of that already, and I couldn't blame you if you did.'

'As long as we all sing from the same hymn sheet,' said Grace, 'and say nothing other than that we're delighted Giles is standing for leader of his party because we know he's the right man for the job and we're confident he'll win, surely they'll soon get bored and move on?'

'That's just when they'll start digging around for something new,' said Giles. 'So if anyone wants to admit to anything more serious than a parking ticket, now's your chance.'

'I'm rather hoping my next book will get to number one on the *New York Times* bestseller list,' said Harry, 'so perhaps I ought to warn you that William Warwick is going to have an affair with the chief constable's wife. If you think that might harm your chances, Giles, I could always hold off publication until after the election.' Everyone laughed.

'Frankly, darling,' said Emma, 'William Warwick ought to have an affair with the mayor of New York's wife, because that would give you a far better chance of making it to number one in the States.'

'Not a bad idea,' said Harry.

'On a more serious note,' said Emma, 'perhaps this is the moment to tell you all that Barrington's is just about holding its head above water, and things aren't going to get any easier during the next twelve months.'

'How bad is it?' asked Giles.

'The building of the *Buckingham* is running more than a year behind schedule, and although we've had no major setbacks recently, the company has had to borrow a large sum of money from the banks. If it could be shown that our overdraft exceeded our asset value, the banks could call in those loans, and we might even go under. That's the worst possible scenario, though it's not impossible.'

'And when could that happen?'

'Not in the foreseeable future,' said Emma, 'unless of course Fisher felt that washing our dirty linen in public could be used to his advantage.'

'Martinez won't let him do that while he has such a large shareholding in the company,' said Sebastian. 'But that doesn't mean he's just going to sit on the sidelines and watch, if you do decide to throw your hat in the ring.'

'I agree,' said Grace. 'And he's not the only person I can think of who'd be only too happy to throw that hat back out of the ring.'

'Who do you have in mind?' asked Giles.

'The Lady Virginia Fenwick, for a start. That woman will be delighted to remind every Member of Parliament she comes across that you're a divorcee, and left her for another woman.'

'Virginia only knows Tories, and they've already had a prime minister who was divorced. And don't forget,' added Giles, taking Gwyneth's hand, 'I'm now happily married to that other woman.'

'Frankly,' said Harry, 'I think you should be more worried

about Martinez than Virginia, because he's clearly still looking for any excuse to harm our family, as Sebastian discovered when he first went to work at Farthings. And, Giles, you're a far bigger prize than Seb, so my bet is that Martinez will do everything in his power to make sure you never become prime minister.'

'If I decide to stand,' said Giles, 'I can't spend my life looking over my shoulder, wondering what Martinez is up to. At the moment, I have to concentrate on some rivals who are far closer to home.'

'Who is your biggest rival?' asked Harry.

'Harold Wilson is the favourite with the bookmakers.'

'Mr Hardcastle wants him to win,' said Sebastian.

'Why, in heaven's name?' asked Giles.

'Nothing to do with heaven,' said Sebastian. 'It's also far closer to home. Both of them were born in Huddersfield.'

'It's often something as seemingly insignificant as that that can sway someone either to support or oppose you,' sighed Giles.

'Perhaps Harold Wilson has some skeletons in his cupboard that the press will take an interest in,' said Emma.

'None that I'm aware of,' said Giles, 'unless you include being awarded a first at Oxford and then coming top in the civil service exam.'

'But he didn't fight in the war,' said Harry. 'So your MC could be an advantage.'

'Denis Healey also won an MC and he might well stand.'

'He's too clever by half to ever lead the Labour Party,' said Harry.

'Well, that certainly won't be your problem, Giles,' said Grace. Giles gave his sister a wry smile, as the family burst out laughing.

'I can think of one problem Giles might have to face up to . . .' They all looked at Gwyneth, who hadn't spoken until then. 'I'm the only outsider in this room,' she said, 'someone who's married into the family, so perhaps I see things from a different perspective.'

'Which makes your opinions all the more relevant,' said

Emma, 'so don't hesitate to let us know what's making you concerned.'

'If I do, I'm afraid it could mean opening a festering wound,' said Gwyneth hesitantly.

'Don't let that stop you telling us what's on your mind,' said Giles, taking her hand.

'There's another member of your family, not in this room, who is, in my opinion, a walking time bomb.'

A long silence followed, before Grace said, 'You're quite right, Gwyneth, because if a journalist were to stumble across the fact that the little girl Harry and Emma adopted is Giles's half-sister and Sebastian's aunt, and that her father was killed by her mother after he had stolen her jewellery and then deserted her, the press would have a field day.'

'And her mother then committed suicide, don't forget,' said Emma quietly.

'The least you can do is tell the poor mite the truth,' said Grace. 'After all, she's now at the Slade, and has a life of her own, so it wouldn't be hard for the press to find her, and if they did before you'd told her . . .'

'It's not that easy,' said Harry. 'As we all know only too well, Jessica suffers from bouts of depression, and despite her un-doubted talent, she often loses confidence in herself. And as she's only a few weeks away from her mid-term exams, now isn't exactly the ideal moment.'

Giles decided not to remind his brother-in-law that he'd first warned him over a decade ago that there was never going to be an ideal moment.

'I could always talk to her,' volunteered Sebastian.

'No,' said Harry firmly. 'If anyone's going to do it, it has to be me.'

'And as soon as possible,' said Grace.

'Please let me know when you have,' said Giles, before adding, 'Are there any other bombshells you think I ought to be prepared for?' A long silence followed before Giles continued. 'Then thank you all for giving up your time. I'll let you know my final decision before the end of the week. I have to leave you

now, as I ought to be getting back to the House. That's where
the voters are. If I do decide to stand, you won't see much of me
during the next few weeks, as I'll be glad-handing, making endless speeches, visiting far-flung constituencies and spending any
free evenings I have buying drinks for Labour members in
Annie's Bar.'

'Annie's Bar?' said Harry.

'The most popular watering hole in the House of Commons,
frequented mainly by Labour members, so that's where I'm off
to now.'

'Good luck,' said Harry.

The family rose as one and applauded him as he left the
room.

—◦—

'Has he got any chance of winning?'

'Oh yes,' said Fisher. 'He's very popular among the rank
and file in the constituencies, although Harold Wilson is the
favourite with the sitting members, and they're the only ones
who have a vote.'

'Then let's send Wilson a large donation towards his campaign fund, cash if necessary.'

'That's the last thing we need to do,' said Fisher.

'Why?' demanded Diego.

'Because he'd send it back.'

'Why would he do that?' asked Don Pedro.

'Because this isn't Argentina, and if the press found out
that a foreigner was backing Wilson's campaign, he would not
only lose, but be forced to withdraw from the contest. In fact,
he'd not only return the money, but make it public that he'd
done so.'

'How can you possibly win an election if you haven't got any
money?'

'You don't need a great deal of money if your electorate is
only 258 Members of Parliament, most of whom spend all their
time in the same building. You might have to buy some stamps,
make a few phone calls, stand the odd round of drinks in Annie's

Bar, and by then you'd have been in touch with almost all your electorate.'

'So if we can't help Wilson win, what can we do to make sure Barrington loses?' asked Luis.

'If there are 258 voters, we must surely be able to bribe some of them,' said Diego.

'Not with money,' said Fisher. 'The only thing that lot care about is preferment.'

'Preferment?' repeated Don Pedro. 'What the hell is that?'

'For younger members, a candidate might hint that they were being considered for a front bench job, and for older members who are retiring at the next general election, a suggestion that their experience and wisdom would be greatly appreciated in the Lords. And for those who have no hope of ever holding office, but will still be around after the next election, a party leader always has jobs that need to be filled. I knew one member who wanted nothing more than to be chairman of the House of Commons Catering Committee because they get to select which wines go on the menu.'

'OK, so if we can't give Wilson any money, or bribe the voters, the least we can do is recycle all the dirt we have on Barrington's family,' suggested Diego.

'Not much point, when the press will be only too happy to do that without any help from us,' said Fisher. 'And they'll get bored after a few days, unless we come up with something fresh for them to get their teeth into. No, we have to think of something that would be certain to make the headlines and, at the same time, knock him out with one blow.'

'You've obviously been giving this considerable thought, major,' said Don Pedro.

'I must admit I have,' said Fisher, looking rather pleased with himself. 'And I think I may have come up with something that will finally sink Barrington.'

'Then spit it out.'

'There's one thing a politician can never recover from. But if I'm to set Barrington up, I'll need to put a small team in place, and the timing will have to be perfect.'

19

GRIFF HASKINS, the Labour Party's agent for Bristol Dock-lands, decided he would have to give up drinking if Giles was to have any chance of becoming leader of the party. Griff always went on the wagon for a month before any election, and on a bender for at least a month after, depending on whether they'd won or lost. And since the Member for Bristol Docklands had been safely returned to the green benches with an increased majority, he'd felt he was entitled to the occasional night off.

It wasn't good timing when Giles called his agent the morning after he'd been on the binge to let him know that he was going to stand for leader. As Griff was nursing a hangover at the time, he called back an hour later to make sure he'd heard the member correctly. He had.

Griff immediately phoned his secretary, Penny, who was on holiday in Cornwall, and Miss Parish, his most experienced party worker, who admitted she was bored out of her mind and only came alive during election campaigns. He told them both to be waiting on platform seven at Temple Meads station at four thirty that afternoon if they wanted to be working for the next prime minister.

At five o'clock, the three of them were seated in a third-class carriage on a train bound for Paddington. By noon the following day, Griff had set up an office in the House of Commons, and another at Giles's home in Smith Square. He still needed to recruit one more volunteer for his team.

Sebastian told Griff that he would be delighted to cancel his fortnight's holiday to help his uncle Giles win the election, and Cedric agreed to make it a month, as the lad could only benefit from the experience, even though Sir Giles was his second choice.

Sebastian's first job was to make a wall chart that listed all 258 Labour Members of Parliament who were entitled to vote, and then place a tick beside each name to show which category they fell into: certain to vote for Giles, red tick; certain to vote for another candidate, blue; and undecided – the most important category of all – green. Although the chart was Sebastian's idea, it was Jessica who produced the finished article.

On the first count, Harold Wilson had 86 certainties, George Brown 57, Giles 54, and James Callaghan 19, with Undecided a crucial 42. Giles could see that his immediate task was to get rid of Callaghan and then overhaul Brown, because if the Member for Belper were to withdraw, Griff calculated that most of his votes would come their way.

After a week of canvassing, it was clear that Giles and Brown were no more than a percentage point apart in second place and, although Wilson was clearly in the lead, the political pundits all agreed that if Brown or Barrington were to withdraw it would be a close-run contest.

Griff never stopped roaming the corridors of power, happy to arrange private meetings with the candidate for any member who claimed they were undecided. Several of them would remain that way until the last moment, as they had never enjoyed so much attention in their lives, and were also keen to end up backing the winner. Miss Parish was never off the phone, and Sebastian became Giles's eyes and ears, continually running between the House of Commons and Smith Square, keeping everyone up to date.

Giles delivered twenty-three speeches during the first week of the campaign, although they rarely made more than a paragraph in the following day's papers, and never the front page. With only two weeks to go, and Wilson beginning to look a dead cert, Giles decided it was time to go off message and take a risk. Even Griff was surprised by the reaction of the press the next morning, when Giles made every front page, including the *Daily Telegraph*.

'There are too many people in this country unwilling to do a day's work,' Giles had told an audience of trade union leaders. 'If someone is fit and healthy and has turned down three jobs in a period of six months, they should automatically lose their unemployment benefit.'

These words were not greeted with rapturous applause, and the initial reaction from his colleagues in the House was unfavourable; *shot himself in the foot* was the expression his rivals kept repeating. But as the days passed, more and more journalists began to suggest that the Labour Party had at last found a potential leader who lived in the real world, and clearly wanted his party to govern, rather than be doomed to perpetual opposition.

All 258 Labour Members of Parliament returned to their constituencies at the weekend, and they quickly discovered a groundswell in favour of the Member for Bristol Docklands. An opinion poll on the following Monday confirmed this, and put Barrington within a couple of points of Wilson, with Brown running a poor third and James Callaghan in fourth place. On Tuesday, Callaghan dropped out of the race, and told his supporters he would be voting for Barrington.

When Sebastian brought the wall chart up to date that evening, Wilson had 122, Giles 107 with 29 still undecided. It only took Griff and Miss Parish another twenty-four hours to identify the 29 MPs who, for one reason or another, were still sitting on the fence. Among them were members of the influential Fabian group, who made up 11 crucial votes. Tony Crosland, the group's chairman, requested a private meeting with both the leading candidates, letting it be known that he was keen to hear their views on Europe.

Giles felt his meeting with Crosland had gone well, but whenever he checked the chart, Wilson still remained in the lead. However, the press were beginning to write the words 'neck and neck' in their headlines as the contest entered its final week. Giles knew that he would need a substantial stroke of luck if he was to overhaul Wilson in the last few days. It came in the form of a telegram delivered to his office on the Monday of the last week of the campaign.

The European Economic Community invited Giles to give the keynote speech at its annual conference in Brussels, just three days before the leadership election. The invitation didn't mention that Charles de Gaulle had dropped out at the last minute.

'This is your chance,' said Griff, 'not only to shine on the international stage, but to capture those eleven Fabian Society votes. It could make all the difference.'

The subject selected for the speech was *Is Britain ready to join the Common Market?* And Giles knew exactly where he stood on that issue.

'But when am I going to find the time to write such an important speech?'

'After the last Labour member has gone to bed, and before the first one gets up the following morning.'

Giles would have laughed, but he knew Griff meant it.

'And when do I sleep?'

'On the plane back from Brussels.'

◆

Griff suggested that Sebastian accompany Giles to Brussels, while he and Miss Parish remained in Westminster, keeping a vigilant eye on the undecided.

'Your flight takes off from London Airport at two twenty,' said Griff, 'but don't forget that Brussels is an hour ahead of us, so you won't touch down until about four ten, which will give you more than enough time to get to the conference.'

'Isn't that cutting it a bit fine?' asked Giles. 'My speech is at six.'

'I know, but I can't afford to have you hanging about in an airport unless it's full of MPs who haven't made up their minds. Now, the session you're addressing should last about an hour, so it will end around seven, well in time for you to catch the eight-forty flight back to London, where the hour time difference will work to your advantage. Grab a taxi as soon as you land, because

I want you back in the House in time for the division on the Pensions Bill at ten.'

'So what do you expect me to do now?'

'Get on with your speech. Everything depends on it.'

—◦—

Giles spent every spare moment honing his speech, showing early drafts to his team and key supporters, and when he delivered it for the first time at his home in Smith Square just after midnight to a one-man audience, Griff declared himself well satisfied. Praise indeed.

'I'll be handing out embargoed copies to be checked against delivery to key members of the press tomorrow morning. That will give them more than enough time to prepare leaders and work on in-depth pieces for the next day's papers. And I think it might be wise to let Tony Crosland see an early draft, so he feels he's being kept in the loop. And for lazy journalists who will only skim the speech, I've highlighted the passage that's most likely to capture the headlines.'

Giles turned a couple of pages of his speech until he came across Griff's marker. *I don't wish to see Britain involved in another European war. The best youth of too many nations have spilt their blood on European soil, and not just in the last fifty years, but for the past thousand. Together we must make it possible for European wars to be found only on the pages of history books, where our children and grandchildren can read about our mistakes, and not repeat them.*

'Why that particular paragraph?' asked Giles.

'Because some of the papers will not only print it word for word, but won't be able to resist pointing out that your rival never saw a shot fired in anger.'

Giles was delighted to receive a handwritten note the following morning from Tony Crosland, saying how much he'd enjoyed the speech, and looked forward to seeing the press reaction the following morning.

When Giles climbed on board the BEA flight to Brussels later that afternoon, he believed for the first time that he just might be the next leader of the Labour Party.

20

WHEN THE PLANE touched down at Brussels airport, Giles was surprised to find Sir John Nicholls, the British Ambassador, standing at the bottom of the steps beside a Rolls-Royce.

'I've read your speech, Sir Giles,' said the ambassador as they were driven out of the airport before any other passenger had even reached passport control, 'and though diplomats are not meant to have an opinion, I'm bound to say that I found it a breath of fresh air. Although I'm not sure what your party will make of it.'

'I'm rather hoping that eleven of them will feel the same way as you do.'

'Ah, that's who it's aimed at,' said Sir John. 'How slow of me.'

Giles's second surprise came when they drew up outside the European Parliament and he was met by a large throng of officials, journalists and photographers, all waiting to greet the keynote speaker. Sebastian leapt out of the front seat and opened the back door for Giles, something he'd never done before.

The President of the European Parliament, Gaetano Martino, stepped forward and shook hands with Giles, before introducing him to his team. On the way to the conference hall, Giles met several other leading European political figures, all of whom wished him luck – and they weren't referring to the speech.

'If you'll be kind enough to wait here,' said the president after they'd climbed up on to the stage, 'I'll make some opening remarks and then hand over to you.'

Giles had gone over his speech one last time on the plane, making only one or two small emendations, and when he finally handed it back to Sebastian he almost knew it by heart. Giles peeped through a chink in the long black curtains to see a thousand leading Europeans waiting to hear his views. His last speech in Bristol during the general election campaign had been attended by an audience of thirty-seven, including Griff, Gwyneth, Penny, Miss Parish and Miss Parish's cocker spaniel.

Giles stood nervously in the wings as he listened to Mr Martino describe him as one of those rare politicians who not only spoke their mind, but didn't allow the latest opinion poll to be their moral compass. He could almost hear Griff saying 'Hear, hear,' in disapproving tones.

'. . . and are we about to be addressed by the next prime minister of Great Britain. Ladies and gentlemen, Sir Giles Barrington.'

Sebastian appeared at Giles's side, handed him his speech and whispered, 'Good luck, sir.'

Giles made his way to the centre of the platform to prolonged applause. Over the years he had become used to the flashbulbs of over-enthusiastic photographers and even the whirr of television cameras, but he'd never experienced anything quite like this. He placed his speech on the lectern, took a step back and waited until the audience had settled.

'There are only a few moments in history,' began Giles, 'that shape the destiny of a nation, and Britain's decision to apply for membership of the Common Market must surely be one of them. Of course, the United Kingdom will continue to play a role on the world stage, but it has to be a realistic role, one that has come to terms with the fact that we no longer rule an Empire on which the sun never sets. I suggest that the time has come for Britain to take on the challenge of that new role alongside new partners, working together as friends, with past animosities consigned to history. I never want to see Britain involved in another European war. The finest youth of too many nations have spilt their blood on European soil, and not just in the last fifty years, but for the past thousand. Together we must make it possible for European wars to be found only on the pages of history books, where our children and grandchildren can read about the mistakes we made, and not repeat them.'

With each new wave of applause, Giles relaxed a little more, so that by the time he came to his peroration, he felt the whole room was under his spell.

'When I was a child, Winston Churchill, a true European, visited my school in Bristol to present the prizes. I didn't win one, about the only thing I have in common with the great man' – this was greeted by loud laughter – 'but it was because of his speech that day that I went into politics, and it was because of my experience in the war that I joined the Labour Party. Sir Winston said these words: "Our nation today faces another of those great moments in history when the British people may once again be asked to decide the fate of the free world." Sir Winston and I may be from different parties, but on that we would undoubtedly agree.'

Giles looked up at the packed gathering, his voice rising with every sentence.

'We in this hall today may be from different nations, but the time has come for us to work together as one, not in our own selfish interests, but in the interests of generations yet unborn. Let me end by saying, whatever the future might hold for me, you can be assured that I will dedicate myself to that cause.' Giles took a pace back as everyone in the room rose, and it was several minutes before he was allowed to leave the stage, and even then he was surrounded by parliamentarians, officials and well-wishers as he made his way out of the chamber.

'We've got about an hour before we have to be back at the airport,' said Sebastian, trying to appear calm. 'Is there anything you need me to do?'

'Find a phone so we can call Griff, and see if there's been any early reaction to the speech back home. I want to be sure this isn't all just a mirage,' Giles said between shaking hands and thanking people for their good wishes. He even signed the occasional autograph; another first.

'The Palace Hotel is on the other side of the road,' said Sebastian. 'We could phone the office from there.'

Giles nodded, as he continued his slow progress. It was another twenty minutes before he was back on the steps of the parliament saying goodbye to the president.

He and Sebastian quickly crossed the wide boulevard and made their way into the relative calm of the Palace Hotel. Sebastian gave the number to a receptionist who dialled London and when she heard a voice on the other end of the line said, 'I'll just put you through, sir.'

Giles picked up the phone to be greeted by Griff's voice. 'I've just been watching the six o'clock news on the BBC,' he said. 'You're the lead story. The phone hasn't stopped ringing with people wanting a piece of you. When you get back to London, there'll be a car waiting at the airport to take you straight to ITV, where Sandy Gall will interview you on the late night news, but don't hang about, because the BBC want you to talk to Richard Dimbleby on *Panorama* at 10.30. The press like nothing more than an outsider making a late run. Where are you now?'

'I'm just about to set off for the airport.'

'Couldn't be better. Phone me the moment you land.'

Giles put the phone down and grinned at Sebastian. 'We'll need a taxi.'

'I don't think so,' said Sebastian. 'The ambassador's car has just arrived, and it's parked outside waiting to take us back to the airport.'

As the two of them made their way through the hotel foyer, a man thrust out his hand and said, 'Congratulations, Sir Giles. A bravura performance. Let's hope it tips the balance.'

'Thank you,' said Giles, who could see the ambassador standing by the car.

'My name is Pierre Bouchard. I am the deputy president of the European Economic Community.'

'Of course,' said Giles, pausing to shake hands. 'I'm aware, Monsieur Bouchard, of all the tireless work you've done to assist

Britain with its application to become a full Member of the EEC.'

'I'm touched,' said Bouchard. 'Can you spare me a moment to discuss a private matter?'

Giles glanced at Sebastian, who checked his watch. 'Ten minutes, no more. I'll go and brief the ambassador.'

'I think you know my good friend Tony Crosland,' Bouchard said as he guided Giles towards the bar.

'Indeed. I gave him an advance copy of my speech yesterday.'

'I'm sure he would have approved. It's everything the Fabian Society believes in. What will you have to drink?' Bouchard asked as they walked into the bar.

'A single malt, lots of water.'

Bouchard nodded to the barman and said, 'I'll have the same.'

Giles climbed on to a stool, glanced around the room and spotted a group of political hacks sitting in the corner, checking over their copy. One of them touched his forehead in a mock salute. Giles smiled.

'What's important to understand,' said Bouchard, 'is that De Gaulle will do anything to stop Britain becoming a member of the Common Market.'

'"Over my dead body", if I remember his exact words,' said Giles, as he picked up his drink.

'Let's hope we don't have to wait that long.'

'It's almost as if the general hasn't forgiven the British for winning the war.'

'Your good health,' said Bouchard before downing his drink.

'Cheers,' said Giles.

'You mustn't forget that De Gaulle has his own problems, not least—'

Suddenly, Giles felt as if he was going to faint. He grabbed at the bar, trying to steady himself, but the room seemed to be going around in circles. He dropped his glass, slid off the stool and collapsed on to the floor.

'My dear fellow,' said Bouchard, kneeling down beside him,

'are you all right?' He looked up as a man who'd been seated in the corner of the room hurried across to join them.

'I'm a doctor,' the man said as he bent down, loosened Giles's tie and undid his collar. He placed two fingers on Giles's neck, then said urgently to the barman, 'Call an ambulance, he's had a heart attack.'

Two or three journalists hurried across to the bar. One of them began taking notes as the barman picked up the phone and hurriedly dialled three numbers.

'Yes,' said a voice.

'We need an ambulance. Quickly, one of our customers has had a heart attack.'

Bouchard stood up. 'Doctor,' he said, addressing the man kneeling beside Giles, 'I'll go outside and wait for the ambulance, and let them know where to come.'

'Do you know the name of that man?' asked one of the journalists, as Bouchard left the room.

'No idea,' said the barman.

The first photographer ran into the bar several minutes before the ambulance arrived, and Giles had to suffer more flashbulbs, not that he was fully aware of what was going on. As the news spread, several other journalists who'd been in the conference centre filing copy about Sir Giles Barrington's well-received speech had dropped their phones and run across to the Palace Hotel.

Sebastian was chatting to the ambassador when he heard the siren, but didn't give it a thought until the ambulance came to a halt outside the hotel and two smartly dressed orderlies jumped out and rushed inside wheeling a stretcher.

'You don't think—' began Sir John, but Sebastian was already running up the steps and into the hotel. He stopped when he saw the orderlies bearing the stretcher towards him. It only took one look at the patient for his worst fears to be confirmed. When they placed the stretcher in the back of the ambulance, Sebastian leapt inside, shouting, 'He's my boss.' One of the orderlies nodded while the other pulled the doors closed.

Sir John followed the ambulance in his Rolls-Royce. When he arrived at the hospital, he introduced himself and asked the receptionist on the front desk if Sir Giles Barrington was being seen by a doctor.

'Yes, sir, he's being checked out in the emergency room by Dr Clairbert. If you'd be kind enough to take a seat, your excellency, I'm sure he'll come and brief you as soon as he's completed his examination.'

◄○►

Griff switched the television back on to catch the seven o'clock news on the BBC, hoping that Giles's speech was still the lead story.

Giles was still the lead story, but it took Griff some time to accept who the man on the stretcher was. He collapsed back into his chair. He'd been in politics too long not to know that Sir Giles Barrington was no longer a candidate to lead the Labour Party.

◄○►

A man who'd spent the night in room 437 of the Palace Hotel handed his key into reception, checked out and paid his bill in cash. He took a taxi to the airport, and an hour later boarded the plane back to London that Sir Giles had been booked on. On arrival at London Airport he queued for a taxi, and when he reached the front of the line he climbed into the back seat and said, 'Forty-four Eaton Square.'

◄○►

'I'm puzzled, ambassador,' said Dr Clairbert after he'd examined his patient for a second time. 'I can't find anything wrong with Sir Giles's heart. In fact, he's in excellent shape for a man of his age. However, I'll only be sure once I've had all the test results back from the lab, which means I'll have to keep him in overnight, just to be absolutely certain.'

◄○►

Giles dominated the front pages of the national press the following morning, just as Griff had hoped he would.

However, the headlines in the first editions, *Neck and Neck* (the *Express*), *All Bets Off* (the *Mirror*), *Birth of a Statesman?* (*The Times*) had quickly been replaced. The *Daily Mail's* new front page summed it up succinctly: *Heart Attack ends Barrington's chances of leading the Labour Party.*

—◦—

The Sunday papers all carried lengthy profiles of the new leader of the opposition.

A photograph of Harold Wilson aged eight, standing outside 10 Downing Street dressed in his Sunday best and wearing a peaked cap, made most of the front pages.

—◦—

Giles flew back to London on the Monday morning, accompanied by Gwyneth and Sebastian.

When the plane touched down at London Airport, there wasn't a single journalist, photographer, or cameraman there to greet him; yesterday's news. Gwyneth drove them back to Smith Square.

'What did the doctor recommend you should do once we'd got you home?' asked Griff.

'He didn't recommend anything,' said Giles. 'He's still trying to work out why I was ever in hospital in the first place.'

—◦—

It was Sebastian who pointed out to his uncle an article on page eleven of *The Times* that had been written by one of the journalists who'd been in the bar of the Palace Hotel when Giles collapsed.

Matthew Castle had decided to stay in Brussels for a few days and make further inquiries, as he wasn't altogether convinced that Sir Giles had suffered a heart attack, even though he'd seen the whole incident unfold in front of his eyes.

He reported: one, Pierre Bouchard, the deputy president of

the EEC, had not been in Brussels to hear Sir Giles's speech that day, as he was attending the funeral of an old friend in Marseille; two, the barman who had phoned for an ambulance dialled only three numbers, and failed to give whoever was on the other end of the line an address to come to; three, the St Jean Hospital had no record of anyone phoning for an ambulance from the Palace Hotel, and was unable to identify the two orderlies who wheeled Sir Giles in on a stretcher; four, the man who left the bar to meet the ambulance never returned, and no one paid for the two drinks; five, the man in the bar who said he was a doctor and claimed Sir Giles had suffered a heart attack hadn't been seen since; and six, the barman didn't report for work the following day.

Perhaps this was nothing more than a string of coincidences, suggested the journalist, but if it wasn't, might the Labour Party now have a different leader?

--◇--

Griff returned to Bristol the following morning, and as there wasn't likely to be an election for at least another year, he spent the next month on a bender.

JESSICA CLIFTON

1964

21

'AM I MEANT to understand what this represents?' said Emma, looking more closely at the painting.

'There's nothing to understand, Mama,' said Seb. 'You've missed the point.'

'Then what is the point, because I can remember when Jessica used to draw people. People I recognized.'

'She's past that phase, Mama; she's now entering her abstract period.'

'I'm afraid they just look like blobs to me.'

'That's because you're not looking at it with an open mind. She no longer wants to be Constable or Turner.'

'Then who does she want to be?'

'Jessica Clifton.'

'Even if you're right, Seb,' said Harry, taking a closer look at *Blob One*, 'all artists, even Picasso, admitted to outside influences. So, who's Jessica influenced by?'

'Peter Blake, Francis Bacon, and she admires an American called Rothko.'

'I haven't heard of any of them,' admitted Emma.

'And they probably haven't heard of Edith Evans, Joan Sutherland or Evelyn Waugh, whom you both admire so much.'

'Harold Guinzburg's got a Rothko in his office,' said Harry. 'He told me it cost him ten thousand dollars, which I reminded him was more than my last advance.'

'You mustn't think like that,' said Sebastian. 'A work of art is worth what someone will pay for it. If it's true for your book, why shouldn't it be equally true for a painting?'

'A banker's attitude,' said Emma. 'I won't remind you what Oscar Wilde said on the subject of price and value, for fear you might accuse me of being old-fashioned.'

'You're not old-fashioned, Mama,' said Sebastian, placing an arm around her. Emma smiled. 'You're positively prehistoric.'

'I admit to forty,' Emma protested, looking up at her son, who couldn't stop laughing. 'But is this really the best Jessica can do?' she asked, turning her attention back to the painting.

'It's her graduation work, which will determine if she's offered a postgraduate place at the Royal Academy Schools this September. And it might even make her a bob or two.'

'These paintings are for sale?' said Harry.

'Oh yes. The graduation exhibition is the first opportunity for a lot of young artists to display their work to the public.'

'I wonder who buys this sort of thing?' said Harry, looking around the room, whose walls were covered with oil paintings, watercolours and drawings.

'Doting parents, I expect,' said Emma. 'So we'll all have to buy one of Jessica's, you included, Seb.'

'You don't have to convince me, Mama. I'll be back here at seven when the show opens, with my cheque book ready. I've already chosen the one I want – *Blob One*.'

'That's very generous of you.'

'You just don't get it, Mama.'

'So where is the next Picasso?' asked Emma, ignoring her son as she looked around the room.

'Probably with her boyfriend.'

'I didn't know Jessica had a boyfriend,' said Harry.

'I think she's hoping to introduce you to him tonight.'

'And what does this boyfriend do?'

'He's also an artist.'

'Is he younger or older than Jessica?' asked Emma.

'Same age. He's in her class, but frankly, he's not in her class.'

'Very droll,' said Harry. 'Does he have a name?'

'Clive Bingham.'

'And have you met him?'

'Yes, they're rarely apart, and I know he proposes to her at least once a week.'

'But she's far too young to be thinking about getting married,' said Emma.

'You don't have to be a wrangler, Mama, to work out that if you're forty-three and I'm twenty-four, you must have been nineteen when I was born.'

'But it was different in those days.'

'I wonder if Grandpa Walter agreed with you at the time.'

'Yes, he did,' said Emma, taking Harry's arm. 'Gramps adored your father.'

'And you'll adore Clive. He's a really nice chap, and it's not his fault that he isn't much of an artist, as you can see for yourself,' said Sebastian, guiding his parents across the room so they could look at Clive's work.

Harry stared at *Self Portrait* for some time before he offered an opinion. 'I can see why you think Jessica is so good, because I can't believe anyone will buy these.'

'Fortunately, he has wealthy parents, so that shouldn't be a problem.'

'But as Jessica's never been interested in money, and he doesn't seem to have any talent, what's the attraction?'

'As almost every female student on the course has painted Clive at some time during the past three years, it's clear that Jessica's not the only person who thinks he's good-looking.'

'Not if he looks like that,' said Emma, taking a closer look at *Self Portrait*.

Sebastian laughed. 'Wait and see before you pass judgement. Though I ought to warn you, Mama, that by your standards you might find him a little disorganized, even vague. But as we all know, Jess always wants to look after any stray she comes across, possibly because she was an orphan herself.'

'Does Clive know she was adopted?'

'Of course,' said Sebastian. 'Jessica never hides the fact. She tells anyone who asks. At art school it's a bonus, almost a badge of honour.'

'And are they living together?' whispered Emma.

'They're both art students, Mama, so I think it's just possible.' Harry laughed, but Emma still looked shocked.

'It may come as a surprise to you, Mama, but Jess is twenty-one, beautiful and talented, and I can tell you Clive's not the only guy who thinks she's a bit special.'

'Well, I look forward to meeting him,' said Emma. 'And if we're not going to be late for the prize-giving, we ought to go and change.'

'While we're on that subject, Mama, please don't turn up this evening looking like the chairman of Barrington's Shipping Company, and as if you're about to preside over a board meeting, because it will embarrass Jessica.'

'But I am the chairman of Barrington's.'

'Not tonight, Mama. Tonight you're Jessica's mother. So if you've got a pair of jeans, preferably old and faded, they'll be just fine.'

'But I don't own a pair of jeans, old or faded.'

'Then wear something you were thinking of giving to the vicar's jumble sale.'

'How about my gardening togs?' said Emma, making no attempt to hide her sarcasm.

'Perfect. And the oldest sweater you can lay your hands on, preferably one with holes in the elbows.'

'And how do you think your father should dress for the occasion?'

'Dad's not a problem,' said Sebastian. 'He always looks like a shambolic, out-of-work writer, so he'll fit in just fine.'

'I would remind you, Sebastian, that your father is one of the most respected authors . . .'

'Mama, I love you both. I admire you both. But tonight belongs to Jessica, so please don't spoil it for her.'

'He's right,' said Harry. 'I used to get more worked up about which hat my mother was going to wear on speech day than whether I might win the Latin prize.'

'But you told me, Papa, that Mr Deakins always won the Latin prize.'

'Quite right,' said Harry. 'Deakins, your uncle Giles and I may all have been in the same class, but just like Jessica, Deakins was in a different class.'

◄○►

'Uncle Giles, I'd like you to meet my boyfriend, Clive Bingham.'

'Hi, Clive,' said Giles, who had taken off his tie and unbuttoned his shirt within moments of entering the room.

'You're that with-it MP, aren't you?' said Clive, as they shook hands.

Giles was lost for words as he looked up at the young man wearing an open-necked yellow polka-dot shirt with a large floppy collar and a pair of drainpipe jeans. But the mop of unruly fair hair, Nordic blue eyes and captivating smile made him understand why Jessica wasn't the only woman in the room who kept glancing in Clive's direction.

'He's the greatest,' said Jessica, giving her uncle a warm hug, 'and he should be the leader of the Labour Party.'

'Now, Jessica,' said Giles, 'before I decide which of your pictures—'

'Too late,' said Clive, 'but you can still get one of mine.'

'But I want an original Jessica Clifton to add to my collection.'

'Then you'll be disappointed. The show opened at seven, and all of Jessica's pictures were snapped up within minutes.'

'I don't know whether to be delighted by your triumph, Jessica, or cross with myself for not turning up earlier,' said Giles, giving his niece a second hug. 'Congratulations.'

'Thank you, but you must take a look at Clive's work, it's really good.'

'Which is why I haven't sold a single one. The truth is, even my own family don't buy them any more,' he added as Emma, Harry and Sebastian walked into the room, and immediately came across to join them.

Giles had never known his sister wear anything that wasn't extremely fashionable, but this evening she looked as if she'd just come out of the potting shed. Harry looked positively smart in

173

comparison. And was it possible there was a hole in her jumper? Clothes are one of a woman's few weapons, Emma had once told him. But not tonight . . . and then he worked it out. 'Good girl,' he whispered.

Sebastian introduced his parents to Clive, and Emma had to admit that he wasn't anything like his self-portrait. Dishy, was the word that came to mind, even if his handshake was a little weak. She turned her attention to Jessica's pictures.

'Do all these red dots mean—?'

'Sold,' said Clive. 'But as I've already explained to Sir Giles, you'll find I don't suffer from the same problem.'

'So is there none of Jessica's work still for sale?'

'None,' said Sebastian. 'I did warn you, Mama.'

Someone was tapping a glass at the far end of the room. They all looked around to see a bearded man in a wheelchair trying to attract everyone's attention. He was scruffily dressed in a brown corduroy jacket and green trousers. He smiled up at the assembled gathering.

'Ladies and gentlemen,' he began, 'if I could just have your attention for a few moments.' Everyone stopped talking and turned to face the speaker. 'Good evening and welcome to the annual Slade School of Fine Art Graduate Exhibition. My name is Ruskin Spear, and, as chairman of the judging panel, my first task is to announce the winners in each category: drawing, watercolours and oil paintings. For the first time in the history of the Slade, the same student has come top in all three categories.'

Emma was fascinated to discover who this remarkable young artist might be, so she could compare their work with Jessica's.

'Frankly, no one will be surprised, other than possibly the winner herself, that the school's star pupil this year is Jessica Clifton.'

Emma beamed with pride as everyone in the room applauded, while Jessica simply bowed her head and clung on to Clive. Only Sebastian really knew what she was going through. Her demons, as she called them. Jessica never stopped chattering whenever they were on their own, but the moment she became the centre of attention, like a tortoise she slipped back into her shell, hoping no one would notice her.

'If Jessica would like to come up, I will present her with a cheque for thirty pounds and the Munnings Cup.'

Clive gave her a little nudge, and everyone applauded as she made her way reluctantly up to the chairman of the judges, her cheeks becoming more flushed with every step she took. When Mr Spear handed over the cheque and the cup, one thing became abundantly clear: there wasn't going to be an acceptance speech. Jessica hurried back to join Clive, who looked so delighted he might have won the prize himself.

'I can also announce that Jessica has been offered a place at the Royal Academy Schools in September to begin her post-graduate work, and I know that my colleagues at the RA are all looking forward to her joining us.'

'I do hope all this adulation doesn't go to her head,' Emma whispered to Sebastian as she turned to see her daughter clutching Clive's hand.

'No fear of that, Mama. She's about the only person in the room who doesn't realize how talented she is.' At that moment an elegant man sporting a red silk bow tie and a fashionable double-breasted suit appeared by Emma's side.

'Allow me to introduce myself, Mrs Clifton.' Emma smiled up at the stranger, wondering if he was Clive's father. 'My name is Julian Agnew. I'm an art dealer and I just wanted to say how much I admire your daughter's work.'

'How kind of you to say so, Mr Agnew. Did you manage to buy any of Jessica's pictures?'

'I bought every one of them, Mrs Clifton. The last time I did that was for a young artist called David Hockney.'

Emma didn't want to admit that she'd never heard of David Hockney, and Sebastian only knew about him because Cedric had half a dozen of his pictures on the wall of his office, but then Hockney was a Yorkshireman. Not that Sebastian was paying much attention to Mr Agnew, as his thoughts were elsewhere.

'So does that mean we'll be given another opportunity to buy one of my daughter's pictures?' asked Harry.

'Most certainly you will,' said Agnew, 'because I'm planning to hold a one-woman exhibition of Jessica's works next spring, by which time I'm rather hoping she'll have painted a few more canvases. Of course, I'll send you and Mrs Clifton an invitation to the opening night.'

'Thank you,' said Harry, 'and we won't be late this time.'

Mr Agnew gave a slight bow, then turned and headed towards the door without another word, clearly not interested in any of the other artists whose work peppered the walls. Emma glanced at Sebastian, to see he was staring at Mr Agnew as he crossed the floor. Then she spotted the young woman by the dealer's side, and understood why her son had been struck dumb.

'Close your mouth, Seb.'

Sebastian looked embarrassed, a rare experience that Emma relished.

'Well, I suppose we'd better go and have a look at Clive's paintings,' suggested Harry, 'which might also give us a chance to meet his parents.'

'They didn't bother to turn up,' said Sebastian. 'Jess told me they never come to see his work.'

'How strange,' said Harry.

'How sad,' said Emma.

22

'I DO LIKE your parents,' said Clive, 'and your uncle Giles is
something else. Even I could vote for him, not that my parents
would approve.'

'Why not?'

'Both of them are dyed-in-the-wool Tories. Mother wouldn't
allow a socialist in the house.'

'I'm sorry they didn't come to the exhibition. They would
have been so proud of you.'

'I don't think so. Mum didn't really approve of me going to
art school in the first place. Wanted me to go to Oxford or Cambridge, and just wouldn't accept that I wasn't good enough.'

'Then they probably won't approve of me.'

'How could they not approve of you?' said Clive, turning over
to face her. 'You're the Slade's most award-winning pupil ever
and, unlike me, you've been offered a place at the RA. Your
father's a bestselling author, your mother is chairman of a public
company, and your uncle's in the shadow cabinet. Whereas my
father's the chairman of a fish paste company, who's hoping to be
appointed the next High Sheriff of Lincolnshire, and that's only
possible because my grandfather made his fortune selling fish
paste.'

'But at least you know who your grandfather is,' said Jessica,
resting her head on his shoulder. 'Harry and Emma aren't my
real parents, although they've always treated me as their daughter, and perhaps because Emma and I even look alike, people
assume she's my mother. And Seb's the best brother a girl could

ever have. But the truth is, I'm an orphan, and have no idea who my real parents are.'

'Have you ever tried to find out?'

'Yes, and I was told that it's Dr Barnardo's strict policy not to release any information about your biological parents without their permission.'

'Why don't you ask your uncle Giles? If anyone knows, he will.'

'Because even if he does, isn't it possible that my family have their reasons for not telling me?'

'Perhaps your father was killed in the war and decorated on the battlefield after carrying out a heroic action, and your mother died of heartache.'

'And you, Clive Bingham, are an unreconstructed romantic, who should stop reading Biggles and try *All Quiet On The Western Front*.'

'When you become a famous artist, will you call yourself Jessica Clifton, or Jessica Bingham?'

'Are you by any chance proposing again, Clive? Because that's the third time this week.'

'You noticed. Yes, I am, and I was hoping you'd come up to Lincolnshire with me at the weekend and meet my parents, so we can make it official.'

'I'd love to,' said Jessica, throwing her arms around him.

'Mind you, there's someone I'll have to visit before you can come to Lincolnshire,' said Clive. 'So don't pack yet.'

—◇—

'It was good of you to see me at such short notice, sir.'

Harry was impressed. He could see that the young man had gone to a lot of trouble. He'd turned up on time, was wearing a jacket and tie, and his shoes shone as if he was on parade. He was clearly very nervous, so Harry tried to put him at ease.

'Your letter said that you wanted to see me about an important matter, so it has to be one of two things.'

'It's quite simple really, sir,' said Clive. 'I'd like permission to ask for your daughter's hand in marriage.'

'How sublimely old-fashioned.'

'It's no more than Jessica would expect of me.'

'Don't you feel you're both a little young to be thinking about getting married? Perhaps you should wait, at least until Jessica graduates from the RA.'

'With respect, sir, Sebastian tells me that I'm older than you were when you proposed to Mrs Clifton.'

'True, but that was at a time of war.'

'I hope I don't have to go to war, sir, just to prove how much I love your daughter.'

Harry laughed. 'Well, I suppose as a prospective father-in-law I ought to ask about your prospects. Jessica tells me you weren't offered a place at the RA schools.'

'I'm pretty sure that didn't come as a surprise to you, sir.'

Harry smiled. 'So what have you been up to since you left the Slade?'

'I've been working at an advertising agency, Curtis Bell and Getty, in their design department.'

'Is that well paid?'

'No, sir. My salary is four hundred pounds a year, but my father tops it up with an allowance of another thousand, and my parents gave me the lease on a flat in Chelsea as a twenty-first birthday present. So we'll have more than enough.'

'You do realize that painting is, and always will be, Jessica's first love, and she'll never allow anything to get in the way of her career, as this family became aware on the day she stepped into our lives.'

'I too am well aware of that, sir, and I'll do everything in my power to make sure she fulfils her ambition. It would be crazy not to, with her talent.'

'I'm glad you feel that way,' said Harry. 'But despite her great talent, there's an insecurity there that you will, at times, have to handle with compassion and understanding.'

'I'm also well aware of that, sir, and it's something I enjoy doing for her. It makes me feel very special.'

'Can I ask how your parents feel about you wanting to marry my daughter?'

'My mother's a great fan of yours, as well as an admirer of your wife.'

'But do they realize we're not Jessica's parents?'

'Oh yes, but, as Dad says, that's hardly her fault.'

'And have you told them you want to marry Jessica?'

'No, sir, but we're going up to Louth this weekend, when I intend to, although I can't imagine it will come as much of a surprise.'

'Then all that's left for me to do is to wish you every happiness together. If there is a kinder, more loving girl in the world, I've yet to meet her. But perhaps every father feels that way.'

'I'm well aware that I'll never be good enough for her, but I swear I won't let her down.'

'I'm sure you won't,' said Harry, 'but I have to warn you there's another side to that coin. She's a sensitive young woman, and if you were ever to lose her trust, you'd lose her.'

'I'd never do anything to let that happen, believe me.'

'I'm sure you mean that. So why don't you ring me if she says yes.'

'I most certainly will, sir,' said Clive as Harry rose from his chair. 'If you don't hear from me by Sunday night, it means she will have turned me down. Again.'

'Again?' said Harry.

'Yes. I've proposed to Jess several times already,' admitted Clive, 'and she's always turned me down. I get the feeling that there's something she's worried about and doesn't want to discuss. Assuming it's not me, I was rather hoping you might be able to throw some light on it.'

Harry hesitated for some time before he said, 'I'm having lunch with Jessica tomorrow, so may I suggest you have a word with her before you travel up to Lincolnshire, and certainly before you break the news to your parents.'

'If you feel that's necessary, sir, of course I will.'

'I think it might be wise in the circumstances,' said Harry as his wife walked into the room.

'Am I to understand that congratulations are in order?'

Emma asked, which made Harry wonder if his wife had been listening to their conversation. 'If so, I couldn't be more pleased.'

'Not quite yet, Mrs Clifton. But let's hope it will be official by the weekend. If it is, I'll try to prove worthy of your and Mr Clifton's confidence.' Turning back to Harry, he added, 'It was kind of you to see me, sir.'

The two men shook hands.

'Drive carefully,' said Harry, as if he was talking to his own son.

He and Emma stood by the window and watched as Clive got into his car.

'So you've finally decided to tell Jessica who her father is?'

'Clive left me with no choice,' said Harry as the car disappeared down the drive and out through the gates of the Manor House. 'And heaven knows how the young man will react when he discovers the truth.'

'I'm much more worried about how Jessica will react,' said Emma.

23

'I HATE THE A1,' said Jessica. 'It always brings back so many unhappy memories.'

'Did they ever get to the bottom of what really happened that day?' asked Clive as he overtook a lorry. Jessica glanced to her left and then looked back. 'What are you doing?'

'Just checking,' she said. 'The coroner's verdict was accidental death. But I know Seb still blames himself for Bruno's death.'

'But that's just not fair, as both of us know.'

'Tell Seb that,' said Jessica.

'Where did your father take you to lunch yesterday?' asked Clive, wanting to change the subject.

'I had to cancel at the last minute. My tutor wanted to discuss which pictures I should enter for the RA summer exhibition. So Dad's taking me to lunch on Monday, although I must admit he sounded disappointed.'

'Perhaps there was something in particular he wanted to talk about.'

'Nothing that can't wait until Monday.'

'So which picture did you and your tutor pick?'

'*Smog Two*.'

'Good choice!'

'Mr Dunstan seems confident the RA will consider it.'

'Was that the painting I saw propped up against the wall in the flat just before we left?'

'Yes. I'd intended to give it to your mother as a present this weekend, but unfortunately all the entries for the exhibition have to be in by next Thursday.'

'She'll be proud to see her future daughter-in-law's painting displayed alongside the RAs.'

'Over ten thousand pictures are submitted to the RA every year, and only a few hundred are chosen, so don't start sending out the invitations yet.' Jessica looked to the left and back again as Clive passed another lorry. 'Do your parents have any idea why we're coming up this weekend?'

'I couldn't have dropped a much bigger hint, like, I want you to meet the girl I'm going to spend the rest of my life with.'

'But what if they don't like me?'

'They'll adore you, and who cares if they don't? I couldn't love you any more than I do now.'

'You're so sweet,' said Jessica, leaning over and kissing him on the cheek. 'But I'd care if your parents weren't sure. After all, you're their only son, so they're bound to be a little protective, nervous even.'

'Nothing makes Mother nervous, and Dad won't need any convincing once he's met you.'

'I wish I had your mother's self-confidence.'

'She can't help herself, dear thing. She went to Roedean, where the only thing they teach you is how to become engaged to a member of the aristocracy, and as she ended up marrying the fish-paste king, she'll be excited by the idea of your family being joined to ours.'

'Does your father care about that sort of thing?'

'Hell no. The factory workers call him Bob, which Mother disapproves of. And they've made him president of everything within a twenty-mile radius of the house, from the Louth Snooker Club to the Cleethorpes Choral Society, and the poor man's colour blind and tone deaf.'

'I can't wait to meet him,' said Jessica as Clive turned off the A1 and began to follow the signs for Mablethorpe.

Although Clive continued to chat away, he could sense that Jessica was becoming more and more nervous as each mile went by, and the moment they drove through the gates of Mable-thorpe Hall she stopped talking altogether.

'Oh my God,' said Jessica eventually, as they continued down a wide drive that boasted tall, elegant elms on either side as far as the eye could see. 'You didn't tell me you lived in a castle.'

'Dad only bought the estate because it was owned by the Earl of Mablethorpe, who tried to put my grandfather out of business at the turn of the century, although I suspect he also wanted to impress my mother.'

'Well, I'm impressed,' said Jessica as a three-storey Palladian mansion loomed up in front of them.

'Yes, I must admit you've got to sell a few jars of fish paste to buy a pile like this.'

Jessica laughed, but stopped laughing when the front door opened and a butler appeared, followed by two footmen who ran down the steps to open the boot and unload their bags.

'I don't have enough luggage for half a footman,' whispered Jessica.

Clive opened the passenger door for her, but she wouldn't budge. He took her hand and coaxed her up the steps and through the front door of the house, to find Mr and Mrs Bing-ham waiting in the hall.

Jessica thought her legs were going to give way when she first saw Clive's mother; so elegant, so sophisticated, so self-assured. Mrs Bingham stepped forward to greet her with a friendly smile.

'It's so wonderful to meet you at last,' she gushed, kissing Jessica on both cheeks. 'Clive's told us so much about you.'

Clive's father shook her warmly by the hand and said, 'I must say, young lady, Clive didn't exaggerate, you're as pretty as a picture.'

Clive burst out laughing. 'I hope not, Dad. Jessica's latest painting is called *Smog Two*.'

Jessica clung on to Clive's hand as their hosts led them into the drawing room, and she only began to relax when she saw a portrait of Clive, which she'd painted for his birthday not long after they met, hanging above the mantelpiece.

'I'm hoping you'll paint a picture of me one day.'

'Jessica doesn't do that sort of thing any longer, Dad.'

'I'd love to, Mr Bingham.'

As Jessica sat down next to Clive on the sofa, the drawing-room door opened and the butler reappeared, followed by a maid carrying a large silver tray, with a silver teapot and two large plates of sandwiches.

'Cucumber, tomato and cheese, madam,' said the butler.

'But, you'll note, no fish paste,' whispered Clive.

Jessica nervously ate everything she was offered, while Mrs Bingham chatted away about her busy life and how she never seemed to have a moment to spare. She didn't seem to notice when Jessica began to draw an outline of Clive's father on the back of a napkin, which she intended to finish off once she was alone in the bedroom.

'We'll have a quiet supper this evening, just the family,' she said, before offering Jessica another sandwich. 'But, tomorrow, I've planned a celebration dinner – just a few friends who can't wait to meet you.'

Clive squeezed Jessica's hand, aware that she hated being the centre of attention.

'It's very kind of you to go to so much trouble, Mrs Bingham.'

'Please call me Priscilla. We don't stand on ceremony in this house.'

'And my friends call me Bob,' said Mr Bingham, as he handed her a slice of Victoria sponge.

By the time Jessica was shown up to her room an hour later, she wondered what she'd been worrying about. It was only when she saw her clothes had been unpacked and hung up in the wardrobe that she began to panic.

'What's the problem, Jess?'

'I can just about survive having to change for supper this evening, but I have nothing to wear for a formal dinner party tomorrow night.'

'I wouldn't worry about that, because I have a feeling Mother plans to take you shopping in the morning.'

'But I couldn't let her buy me anything when I haven't even given her a present.'

'Believe me, she only wants to show you off, and she'll get far more pleasure out of it than you will. Just think of it as a crate of fish paste.'

Jessica laughed, and by the time they went up to bed after supper, she had relaxed so much that she was still chatting happily away.

'Wasn't that bad, was it?' said Clive as he followed her into the bedroom.

'It couldn't have been better,' she said. 'I just adore your father, and your mother went to so much trouble to make me feel at home.'

'Have you ever slept in a four-poster before?' he asked as he took her in his arms.

'No, I haven't,' Jessica replied, pushing him away. 'And where will you be sleeping?'

'In the next room. But as you can see, there's a connecting door, because this is where the earl's mistress used to sleep; so I'll be joining you later.'

'No, you won't,' said Jessica mockingly, 'although I rather like the idea of being an earl's mistress.'

'Not a chance,' said Clive, falling to one knee. 'You're going to have to be satisfied with being Mrs Bingham, the fish-paste princess.'

'You're not proposing again, are you, Clive?'

'Jessica Clifton, I adore you, and I want to spend the rest of my life with you, and I hope you'll do me the honour of becoming my wife.'

'Of course I will,' said Jessica, dropping to her knees and throwing her arms around him.

'You're meant to hesitate and think about it for a moment.'

'I haven't been thinking about much else for the past six months.'

'But I thought—'

'It's never been you, silly. I couldn't love you any more if I wanted to. It's just that . . .'

'Just what?'

'When you're an orphan, you're bound to wonder—'

'You are so silly sometimes, Jess. I fell in love with you, and I don't give a damn who your parents are, or were. Now let go of me, as I have a little surprise for you.'

Jessica released her fiancé, who took out a red leather box from an inside pocket. She opened it, and burst out laughing when she saw the pot of Bingham's Fish Paste. *The paste even the fishermen eat.*

'Perhaps you should look inside,' he suggested.

She unscrewed the lid, and stuck a finger into the paste. 'Yuck,' she said, and then pulled out an exquisite Victorian sapphire and diamond engagement ring. 'Oh. I bet you won't find one of these in every jar. It's so beautiful,' she said after she'd licked it clean.

'It was my grandmother's. Betsy was a local Grimsby girl who Granddad married when he was working on a fishing trawler, long before he made his fortune.'

Jessica was still staring at the ring. 'It's far too good for me.'

'Betsy wouldn't have thought so.'

'But what about your mother? How will she feel when she sees it?'

'It was her idea,' said Clive. 'So let's go down and tell them the news.'

'Not yet,' said Jessica, taking him in her arms.

24

AFTER BREAKFAST the following morning, Clive took his fiancée for a walk around the grounds of Mablethorpe Hall, but they could only manage the garden and the lake, before Clive's mother whisked Jessica off to go shopping in Louth.

'Remember, every time the till rings, just think of it as another crate of fish paste,' said Clive as she climbed into the back of the car next to Priscilla.

By the time they returned to Mablethorpe Hall for a late lunch, Jessica was laden down with bags and boxes, containing two dresses, a cashmere shawl, a pair of shoes and a tiny black evening bag.

'For the dinner tonight,' Priscilla explained.

Jessica could only wonder how many crates of fish paste would have to be sold to cover the bills. In truth, she was very grateful for Priscilla's generosity, but once they were alone in her room, she told Clive firmly, 'This is not a lifestyle I want to indulge in for more than a couple of days.'

After lunch, Clive took her around the rest of the estate, only just getting her back in time for afternoon tea.

'Do your family ever stop eating?' asked Jessica. 'I don't know how your mother manages to stay so slim.'

'She doesn't eat, she just picks at things. Haven't you noticed?'

'Shall we go through the guest list for dinner?' said Priscilla once tea had been served. 'The Bishop of Grimsby and his wife Maureen.' She looked up. 'Of course, we're all hoping that the bishop will perform the ceremony.'

'And what ceremony might that be, my dear?' asked Bob, winking at Jessica.

'I do wish you wouldn't call me "my dear",' said Priscilla. 'It's so common,' she added before continuing with the guest list. 'The Mayor of Louth, Councillor Pat Smith. I do so disapprove of shortening Christian names. When my husband becomes High Sheriff of the county next year, I shall insist on everyone calling him Robert. And finally, my old school friend, Lady Virginia Fenwick, daughter of the Earl of Fenwick. We were debutantes in the same year, you know.'

Jessica grabbed Clive's hand to stop herself shaking. She didn't say another word until they were back in the safety of her room.

'What's the matter, Jess?' asked Clive.

'Doesn't your mother realize that Lady Virginia was Uncle Giles's first wife?'

'Of course she does. But that was all over such a long time ago. Who gives a damn? In fact, I'm surprised you even remember her.'

'I only met her once, on the day of Grandma Elizabeth's funeral, and the one thing I can recall is that she insisted I address her as Lady Virginia.'

'She still does that,' said Clive, trying to make light of it. 'But I think you'll find she's mellowed a little over the years, although, I confess, she does bring out the worst in my dear mother. I know for a fact that Dad can't stand her, so don't be surprised if he finds any excuse to escape whenever the two of them are together.'

'I do like your dad,' said Jessica.

'And he adores you.'

'What makes you say that?'

'Stop fishing. But I have to admit he's already given me the "If I was twenty years younger, my boy, you wouldn't stand a chance" routine.'

'How kind of him.'

'It's not kindness, he meant it.'

'I'd better get changed, otherwise we'll be late for dinner,' said Jessica. 'I'm still not sure which of the two dresses I should wear,' she added as Clive left for his room. She tried them both on, staring in the mirror for some considerable time, but she still hadn't made a decision by the time Clive came back and asked her to help him with his bow tie.

'Which dress should I wear?' she asked helplessly.

'The blue one,' said Clive before returning to his room.

Once again she looked at herself in the mirror and wondered if there would ever be another occasion on which she could wear either one of them. Certainly not the student arts ball.

'You look fantastic,' said Clive when she finally emerged from the bathroom. 'What a dress!'

'Your mother chose it,' said Jessica, twirling around.

'We'd better get a move on. I think I heard a car coming down the drive.'

Jessica picked up the cashmere shawl, draped it around her shoulders and took one more look in the mirror before they walked down the stairs hand in hand. They entered the drawing room just as there was a knock on the front door.

'Oh, you look divine in that dress,' said Priscilla, 'and the shawl is just perfect. Don't you agree, Robert?'

'Yes, just perfect, my dear,' said Bob.

Priscilla frowned as the butler opened the door and announced 'The Bishop of Grimsby and Mrs Hadley.'

'My lord,' said Priscilla, 'how wonderful that you were able to join us. Let me introduce Miss Jessica Clifton, who has just become engaged to my son.'

'Lucky Clive,' said the bishop, but all Jessica could think of was how she would like to draw him in his splendid long black frock coat, purple clerical shirt and brilliant white dog-collar.

A few minutes later, the Mayor of Louth appeared. Priscilla insisted on introducing him as Councillor Patrick Smith. When Priscilla left the room to greet her final guest, the mayor whispered to Jessica, 'Only my mother and Priscilla call me Patrick. I do hope you'll call me Pat.'

And then Jessica heard a voice she could never forget.

'Darling Priscilla, it's been far too long.'

'Far too long, darling,' agreed Priscilla.

'One just doesn't get up to the north as often as one should, and there's so much we have to catch up on,' Virginia said as she accompanied her host into the drawing room.

After she'd introduced Virginia to the bishop and the mayor, Priscilla guided her across the room to meet Jessica. 'And allow me to present Miss Jessica Clifton, who's just become engaged to Clive.'

'Good evening, Lady Virginia. I don't suppose you remember me.'

'How could I forget, although you must have been only seven or eight at the time. Just look at you,' she said, taking a step back. 'Haven't you grown into a beautiful young woman? You know, you remind me so much of your dear mother.' Jessica was lost for words, but it didn't seem to matter. 'And I hear such wonderful reports of your work at the Slade. How proud your parents must be.'

It was only later, much later, that Jessica began to wonder how Lady Virginia could possibly know about her work. But she'd been seduced by *What a stunning dress*, and *Such an exquisite ring* and *Isn't Clive a lucky young man*.

'Another myth exploded,' said Clive as they walked into the dining room arm in arm.

Jessica wasn't completely convinced, and was relieved to find herself seated between the mayor and the bishop, while Lady Virginia sat on Mr Bingham's right, at the other end of the table, far enough away to ensure Jessica would not have to hold a conversation with her. After the main course had been cleared away – there were more servants than guests – Mr Bingham tapped his glass with a spoon and rose from his place at the head of the table.

'Today,' he began, 'we welcome a new member to our family, a very special young lady who has honoured my son by agreeing to be his wife. Dear friends,' he said, raising his glass, 'to Jessica and Clive.'

Everyone rose from their places and echoed the words, 'Jessica and Clive,' and even Virginia raised her glass. Jessica wondered if it was possible to be happier.

After even more champagne had been consumed in the drawing room after dinner, the bishop made his apologies, explaining that he had a service to conduct in the morning and that he needed to go over his sermon one more time. Priscilla accompanied him and his wife to the front door, and then, a few minutes later, the mayor thanked his host and hostess, and once again congratulated the happy couple.

'Good night, Pat,' said Jessica. The mayor rewarded her with a grin before departing.

Once the mayor had left, Mr Bingham returned to the drawing room and said to his wife, 'I'm just going to take the dogs out for their evening canter, so I'll leave you two alone. I suspect you have a lot to catch up on, as you haven't seen each other for such a long time.'

'I think that's a hint that we should also leave,' said Clive, who bade his mother and Lady Virginia goodnight, before accompanying Jessica upstairs to her room.

'What a triumph,' said Clive, once he'd closed the bedroom door. 'Even Lady Virginia appeared to be won over. Mind you, you do look captivating in that dress.'

'Only thanks to your mother's generosity,' said Jessica, taking one more look at herself in the long mirror.

'And don't forget Granddad's fish paste.'

'But where's my beautiful shawl, the one your mother gave me?' Jessica looked around the room. 'I must have left it in the drawing room. I'll just go down and fetch it.'

'Can't it wait until the morning?'

'Certainly not,' said Jessica. 'I should never have let it out of my sight.'

'Just make sure you don't get chatting to those two, because they're probably already planning the finer details of our wedding.'

'I'll only be a moment,' Jessica said as she left the room humming to herself. She skipped down the staircase and was just a few feet from the drawing-room door, which was slightly ajar, when she heard the word *murderer* and froze on the spot.

'The coroner's verdict was death by misadventure, despite Sir

Hugo's body being found in a pool of blood with a letter opener sticking out of his neck.'

'And you say there's reason to believe that Sir Hugo Barrington was her father?'

'No question about it. And frankly, his death came as something of a relief for the family, because he was just about to go on trial for fraud. If he had, the company would undoubtedly have gone under.'

'I had absolutely no idea.'

'And that's not the half of it, my darling, because Jessica's mother then committed suicide to avoid being charged with Sir Hugo's murder.'

'I just can't believe it. She seemed such a respectable girl.'

'I'm afraid it doesn't get any better if you take a closer look at the Clifton side of the family. Harry Clifton's mother was a well-known prostitute, so he's never been quite sure who his father was. In normal circumstances I wouldn't have mentioned any of this,' continued Virginia, 'but you don't need a scandal at this particular time.'

'At this particular time?' queried Priscilla.

'Yes. I have it on good authority that the prime minister is considering putting Robert up for a knighthood, which of course would mean you'd be Lady Bingham.'

Priscilla thought about that for a few moments before she said, 'Do you think Jessica knows the truth about her parents? Clive has never so much as hinted at any suggestion of scandal.'

'Of course she knew, but she never intended to tell you or Clive. The little hussy was hoping to get a gold band on her finger before any of this became public. Haven't you noticed how she's been winding Robert around her little finger? Promising to paint his portrait was nothing less than a masterstroke.'

Jessica stifled a sob, turned and quickly fled back upstairs.

'What on earth's the matter, Jess?' Clive asked as she came running into the bedroom.

'Lady Virginia's been telling your mother that I'm the daughter of a murderer . . . who killed my father,' she said between sobs. 'That . . . that my grandmother used to be a prostitute and that I've only ever been interested in getting my hands on your money.'

Clive took her in his arms and tried to calm her, but she was inconsolable. 'Leave this to me,' he said, letting go of her and pulling on his dressing gown. 'I'm going to tell my mother I don't give a damn what Lady Virginia thinks, because nothing is going to stop me marrying you.' He held her in his arms once again, before walking out of the bedroom and marching downstairs straight into the drawing room.

'What's this pack of lies you've been spreading about my fiancée?' he demanded, looking directly at Lady Virginia.

'It's nothing more than the truth,' replied Virginia calmly. 'I thought it was better that your mother found out before you were married, rather than after, when it would be too late.'

'But to suggest that Jessica's mother was a murderer . . .'

'Not that difficult to check up on.'

'And her grandmother was a prostitute?'

'I'm afraid that's common knowledge in Bristol.'

'Well, I don't give a damn,' said Clive. 'I adore Jess, and to hell with the consequences, because I can tell you, Lady Virginia, you won't stop me marrying her.'

'Clive, darling,' said his mother calmly, 'I would think about it for a moment before you make such a rash decision.'

'I don't need to think about marrying the most perfect creature on earth.'

'But if you were to marry this woman, what would you expect to live on?'

'Fourteen hundred a year will be more than enough.'

'But a thousand pounds of that is an allowance from your father, and when he hears . . .'

'Then we'll have to get by on my salary. Other people seem to manage it.'

'Has it never crossed your mind, Clive, where that four hundred pounds comes from?'

'Yes, Curtis Bell and Getty, and I earn every penny of it.'

'Do you really believe that particular agency would employ you if it didn't have the Bingham's Fish Paste account?'

Clive was silenced for a moment. 'Then I'll have to get another job,' he eventually managed.

'And where do you think you'd live?'

'In my flat, of course.'

'But for how long? You must be aware that the lease on Glebe Place expires in September. I know it was your father's intention to renew it, but given the circumstances . . .'

'You can keep the damned flat, Mother. You won't come between Jess and me.' He turned his back on them both, walked out of the room and closed the door quietly behind him. He then ran upstairs, hoping to reassure Jessica that nothing had changed, and to suggest that they drive back to London immediately. He looked in both bedrooms, but she was nowhere to be seen. On her bed were two dresses, a small evening bag, a pair of shoes, an engagement ring and a drawing of his father. He ran back downstairs to find his father standing in the hall, unable to hide his anger.

'Have you seen Jess?'

'I have. But I'm afraid nothing I could say was going to stop her leaving. She told me what that dreadful woman said, and who can blame the poor girl for not wanting to spend another night under this roof. I asked Burrows to drive her to the station. Get dressed and go after her, Clive. Don't lose her, because you'll never find anyone like that again.'

Clive sprinted back upstairs as his father headed towards the drawing room.

'Have you heard Virginia's news, Robert?' Priscilla asked as he entered the room.

'I most certainly have,' he said, turning to face Virginia. 'Now listen to me carefully, Virginia. You will leave this house immediately.'

'But, Robert, I was only trying to help my dear friend.'

'You were doing nothing of the sort, and you know it. You came here with the sole purpose of ruining that young girl's life.'

'But, Robert darling, Virginia is my oldest friend . . .'

'Only when it suits her. Don't even think about defending the woman, otherwise you can go with her, and then you'll soon find out just how much of a friend she is.'

Virginia rose from her place and walked slowly towards the door. 'I'm so sorry to have to say, Priscilla, I won't be visiting you again.'

'Then at least something good has come out of this,' said Robert.

'No one has ever spoken to me like that before,' Virginia said, turning back to face her adversary.

'Then I suggest you reread Elizabeth Barrington's will, because she certainly had the measure of you. Now get out, before I throw you out.'

The butler only just managed to open the front door in time to allow Lady Virginia to continue on her way.

◄○►

Clive abandoned his car outside the station and ran across the bridge to platform three. He could hear a guard's whistle, and by the time he reached the bottom step, the train was already pulling out. He sprinted after it as if he was in a hundred yard final, and was beginning to make up ground, but the train gathered speed just as Clive ran out of platform. He bent down, placed his hands on his knees and tried to catch his breath. As the last carriage disappeared, he turned and began to walk back along the platform. By the time he reached his car, he'd made a decision.

He climbed in, switched on the ignition and drove to the end of the road. If he turned right, it would take him back to Mablethorpe Hall. He turned left, accelerated, and followed the signs to the A1. He knew that the milk train stopped at almost every station between Louth and London, so with a bit of luck, he would be back at the flat before she arrived.

◄○►

Slipping the front door lock didn't present a problem for the intruder, and although it was a fashionable block of flats, it wasn't grand enough to employ a night porter. He climbed the stairs cautiously, making the occasional creak, but nothing that would wake anyone at two thirty in the morning.

When he reached the second-floor landing, he quickly located flat number 4. He checked up and down the corridor; nothing. This time it took a little longer to slip the two locks. Once he was inside, he quietly closed the door behind him and switched on the light, as he had no fear of being disturbed. After all, he knew where she was spending the weekend.

He walked around the small flat, taking his time to identify all the paintings he was looking for: seven in the front room, three in the bedroom, one in the kitchen, and a bonus, a large oil propped up against the wall by the door with a sticker on it marked *Smog Two, To be delivered to the RA by Thursday*. Once he'd moved them all into the living room, he lined them up in a row. They weren't bad. He hesitated for a moment before taking a flick knife out of his pocket and carrying out his father's instructions.

‑‑◦‑‑

The train pulled into St Pancras just after 2.40 a.m., by which time Jessica had decided exactly what she was going to do. She would take a taxi back to Clive's flat, pack her belongings and phone Seb to ask if she could stay with him for a couple of days while she looked for somewhere to live.

'Are you all right, luv?' asked the driver as she sank into the back of the cab.

'I'm fine. Number twelve Glebe Place, Chelsea,' was all she could manage. There were no more tears left to shed.

When the taxi drew up outside the block of flats, Jessica handed the cabbie a ten-bob note, which was all she had, and said, 'Would you be kind enough to wait? I'll be as quick as I can.'

'Sure thing, luv.'

‑‑◦‑‑

He'd almost completed the job, which he was enjoying, when he thought he heard a car pulling up in the street outside.

He placed the knife on a side table, went across to the window and pulled the curtain back a few inches. He watched as she climbed out of the back of the taxi and had a word with the cabbie. He moved swiftly back across the room, switched off the light and opened the door; another quick check up and down the corridor, again nothing.

He jogged down the stairs and, as he opened the front door, he saw Jessica coming up the path towards him. She was taking a key out of her handbag when he brushed past her. She glanced round, but didn't recognize him, which surprised her, because she thought she knew everyone who lived in the building.

She let herself in and began to climb the stairs. She felt quite exhausted by the time she reached the second floor and opened the door to flat number four. The first thing she must do was phone Seb and let him know what had happened. She switched on the light and headed towards the phone on the far side of the room. That was when she first saw her paintings.

–◦–

Clive turned into Glebe Place twenty minutes later, still hoping he might have got back before her. He looked up, and saw that the bedroom light was on. She must be there, he thought, with overwhelming relief.

He parked his car behind a cab that still had its engine running. Was it waiting for her? He hoped not. He opened the front door and ran up the stairs to find the entrance to the flat wide open and all the lights on. He walked in, and the moment he saw them he fell to his knees and was violently sick. He stared at the wreckage strewn around him. All of Jessica's drawings, watercolours and oils looked as if they'd been stabbed again and again, with the exception of *Smog Two*, in which a large, jagged hole had been cut from the centre of the canvas. What could have driven her to do something so irrational?

'Jess!' he screamed, but there was no reply. He pushed himself up and walked slowly into the bedroom, but there was no sign of her. That was when he heard the sound of a running tap, and swung round to see a trickle of water seeping under the bathroom door. He rushed across, pulled the door open and stared in disbelief at his beloved Jess. Her head was floating above the water, but her wrist, with two deep incisions no longer shedding blood, hung limply over the side of the bath. And then he saw the flick knife on the floor beside her.

He lifted her lifeless body gently out of the water, and collapsed on to the floor, holding her in his arms. He wept uncontrollably. One thought kept running through his mind. If only he hadn't gone back upstairs to get dressed, but had driven straight to the station, Jessica would still be alive.

The last thing he remembered doing was taking the engagement ring out of his pocket and placing it back on her finger.

25

THE BISHOP of Bristol looked down from the pulpit at the packed congregation of St Mary Redcliffe, and was reminded of the impact Jessica Clifton had made on so many different people in her short life. After all, a drawing of him as the Dean of Truro hung proudly in the corridor of the Bishop's Palace. He glanced at his notes.

'When a loved one dies in their seventies or eighties,' he began, 'we gather to mourn them. We recall their long lives with affection, respect and gratitude, exchanging anecdotes and happy memories. We shed a tear, of course we do, but at the same time we accept that it's the natural order of things. When a beautiful young woman, who has displayed such a rare talent that her elders accept without question that they are not her betters, dies, we are bound to shed many more tears because we can only wonder what might have been.'

Emma had shed so many tears since she'd heard the news that she was mentally and physically exhausted. She could only wonder if there was anything she could have done to prevent her beloved daughter suffering such a cruel and unnecessary death. Of course there was. She should have told her the truth. Emma felt she was just as much to blame as anyone.

Harry, who sat beside her in the front pew, had aged a decade in a week, and wasn't in any doubt who was to blame. Jessica's death would continually remind him that he should have told her years ago why they had adopted her. If he had, surely she would be alive today.

Giles sat between his sisters, holding their hands for the first time in years. Or were they holding his? Grace, who disapproved of any public show of emotion, wept throughout the entire service.

Sebastian, who sat on the other side of his father, was not listening to the bishop's oration. He no longer believed in an all-caring, all-understanding compassionate deity, who could give with one hand, then took away with the other. He'd lost his best friend, whom he'd adored, and no one could ever take her place.

Harold Guinzburg sat quietly at the back of the church. When he'd called Harry he was unaware that his life had been shattered in a single moment. He'd just wanted to share with him the triumphant news that his latest novel had gone to number one on the *New York Times* bestseller list.

Harold must have been surprised by his author's lack of response, but then, how could he have known that Harry no longer cared for such baubles, and would have been content not to have sold a single copy if in exchange Jessica could be there standing by his side, and not being laid to rest in an untimely grave.

After the burial ceremony was over and everyone else had departed to continue their lives, Harry fell on his knees and remained by the graveside. His sin would not be expiated quite that easily. He had already accepted that not a day, possibly not an hour, would go by when Jessica wouldn't barge into his thoughts, laughing, chattering, teasing. Like the bishop, he too could only wonder what might have been. Would she have married Clive? What would his grandchildren have been like? Would he have lived long enough to see her become a Royal Academician? How he wished that it was her kneeling by his grave, mourning him.

'Forgive me,' he said aloud.

What made it worse, he knew she would have.

CEDRIC HARDCASTLE

1964

26

'ALL MY LIFE I've been considered by my fellow men to be a cautious, boring, dull sort of fellow. I have often heard myself described as a safe pair of hands. "You won't go far wrong with Hardcastle." It was ever thus. At school, I always fielded at long stop, and I was never asked to open the batting. In the school play, I was always the spear carrier and never the king, and when it came to exams, I passed everything, but never came in the top three. While others might have been hurt, even insulted, by such epithets, I was flattered. If you set yourself up as a fit and proper person to take care of other people's money, then, in my opinion, these are the very qualities that should be expected of you.

'As I approach old age, I have if anything become more cautious, more boring, and, indeed, that is the reputation I would want to take to the grave when I eventually face my maker. So it may come as something of a shock to those seated around this table that I now intend to ignore every tenet on which I have based my whole life, and it may be even more surprising that I am inviting you to do the same.'

The six other people seated around the table may not have interrupted, but they were listening intently to every word Cedric Hardcastle had to say.

'With that in mind, I'm going to ask every one of you to assist me in destroying an evil, corrupt and unscrupulous man, so that when we are finished with him, he will be left so broken that he will never be able to harm anyone else again.

'From a distance, I have been able to observe Don Pedro

Martinez as he systematically went about destroying two decent families with whom I've become associated. And I must tell you that I am no longer willing to stand by and, like Pontius Pilate, wash my hands and leave it to others to do the dirty work.

'On the other side of the cautious, boring, dull coin, is etched a figure with a reputation garnered in the City of London over a lifetime. I now intend to take advantage of that reputation by calling in favours and debts that I have stored up, like a squirrel, for decades. With that in mind, I have recently spent some considerable time devising a plan to destroy Martinez and his family, but I cannot hope for a successful outcome working on my own.'

Still no one seated around that table gave a moment's thought to interrupting the chairman of Farthings.

'During the past few years, I have observed the lengths to which this man is willing to go to destroy the Clifton and Barrington families, who are represented here today. I witnessed at first hand his attempt to influence a potential client of this bank, Mr Morita of Sony International, by having Farthings removed from the bidding list for a major contract, for no other reason than Sebastian Clifton was my personal assistant. We won that contract, but only because Mr Morita had the courage to stand up to Martinez, while I did nothing. Some months ago, I read an article in *The Times* concerning the mysterious Pierre Bouchard and the heart attack that never happened but that nevertheless caused Sir Giles Barrington to withdraw his candidacy for the leadership of the Labour Party, and I still did nothing. More recently, I attended the funeral of an innocent, highly talented young woman who drew the picture of me that you can all see on the wall beside my desk. During her funeral service, I decided I could no longer be a dull and boring man, and if it meant breaking the habits of a lifetime, so be it.

'For the past few weeks, without Don Pedro Martinez being aware of what I was up to, I have spoken in confidence to his bankers, stockbrokers and financial advisors. All of them assumed that they were dealing with that dull fellow from Farthings, who would never consider exceeding his authority, let alone overstep the mark. I discovered that over the years,

Martinez, who is a chancer, has taken several risks, while at the same time showing scant regard for the law. If my plan is to succeed, the trick will be to spot the moment when he takes one risk too many. Even then, if we are to beat him at his own game we may need to take the occasional risk ourselves.

'You will have noticed that I have invited one other person to join us today, whose life has not been tainted by this man. My son Arnold is a barrister,' said Cedric, nodding to the younger imprint of himself seated on his right, 'and, like myself, he is considered a safe pair of hands, which is why I have asked him to act as my conscience and guide. Because if, for the first time in my life, I am going to bend the law to breaking point, I will need someone to represent me who is able to remain detached, dispassionate and uninvolved. Put simply, my son will act as our moral compass.

'I will now ask him to reveal what I have in mind, so you will be in no doubt of the risk you would be taking should you decide to join me in this venture. Arnold.'

'Ladies and gentlemen, my name is Arnold Hardcastle, and much to my father's chagrin, I chose to be a lawyer rather than a banker. When he says that I am, like him, a safe pair of hands, I consider that a compliment, because if this operation is to succeed, one of us will have to be. After studying the government's latest finance bill, I believe I've found a way to make my father's plan work, which, although not breaking the letter of the law, would certainly be ignoring its spirit. Even with that proviso, I have come up against a problem that might possibly prove insurmountable. Namely, we need to identify an individual whom no one around this table has ever met, but who feels just as passionately about bringing Don Pedro Martinez to justice as do all of you.'

Although still no one spoke, the lawyer was greeted with looks of incredulity.

'If such a man or woman cannot be identified,' continued Arnold Hardcastle, 'I have advised my father to drop the whole idea and send you on your separate ways, aware that you may have to spend the rest of your days continually looking over your shoulder, never certain when or where Martinez will strike next.' The lawyer closed his folder. 'If you have any questions, I will try to answer them.'

'I don't have a question,' said Harry, 'but I can't see how it's possible to find such an individual given the circumstances. Everyone I know who has come across Martinez detests the man as much as I do, and I suspect that goes for everyone around this table.'

'I agree,' said Grace. 'In fact, I'd be quite happy for us to draw straws to decide which one of us should kill him. I wouldn't mind spending a few years in jail if it meant we could finally rid ourselves of that dreadful creature.'

'I couldn't help you there,' said Arnold. 'I specialize in company law, not criminal, so you would need to find another advocate. Should you decide to go down that route, however, there are one or two names I could recommend.'

Emma laughed for the first time since Jessica's death, but Arnold Hardcastle didn't.

'I'll bet there are at least a dozen men in Argentina who would meet those requirements,' said Sebastian. 'But how would we go about finding them when we don't even know who they are?'

'And when you did find them,' said Arnold, 'you would have defeated the purpose of my father's plan, because if the action ended up in a court of law, you couldn't claim you didn't know of their existence.'

There followed another long silence, which was finally broken by Giles, who hadn't spoken until then. 'I think I've come across such a man.' He had grabbed the attention of everyone around the table in a single sentence.

'If that's the case, Sir Giles, I will need to ask you a number of questions about this particular gentleman,' said Arnold, 'and the only answer that would be acceptable in law is no. Should your answer to even one of my questions be yes, then the gentleman you have in mind is not eligible to carry out my father's plan. Is that clear?'

Giles nodded as the barrister reopened his file and Emma crossed her fingers.

'Have you ever met this man?'

'No.'

'Have you ever conducted any business transactions with him, either on your own behalf or through a third party?'

'No.'

'Have you ever spoken to him on the telephone?'

'No.'

'Or written to him?'

'No.'

'Would you recognize him if he passed you in the street?'

'No.'

'And finally, Sir Giles, has he ever contacted you in your capacity as a Member of Parliament?'

'No.'

'Thank you, Sir Giles, you have passed the first part of the test with flying colours, but I must now move on to another series of questions that are just as important, but this time, the only acceptable answer is yes.'

'I understand,' said Giles.

'Does this man have good reason to loathe Don Pedro Martinez as much as you do?'

'Yes, I believe he does.'

'Is he as wealthy as Martinez?'

'Most certainly.'

'Does he have a reputation for honesty and probity?'

'As far as I'm aware, yes.'

'Lastly, and perhaps most importantly, do you think he'd be willing to take a serious risk?'

'Undoubtedly.'

'As you have answered all my questions satisfactorily, Sir Giles, perhaps you'd be kind enough to write the gentleman's name on the pad in front of you, without allowing anyone else around the table to see who it is.'

Giles jotted down a name, tore a sheet off the pad, folded it and passed it to the lawyer, who in turn handed it to his father.

Cedric Hardcastle unfolded the slip of paper, praying he'd never come across the man before.

'Do you know this man, Father?'

'Only by reputation,' said Cedric.

'Excellent. Then if he agrees to go along with your plan, no one around this table will be breaking the law. But, Sir Giles,' he said, turning back to the Rt Hon. Member for Bristol Docklands, 'you must not make contact with this man at any time, and you cannot reveal his name to any member of the Barrington or Clifton families, particularly if they are shareholders in Barrington Shipping. Were you to do so, a court might consider that you were in collusion with a third party, and therefore breaking the law. Is that understood?'

'Yes,' said Giles.

'Thank you, sir,' the lawyer said as he gathered up his papers. 'Good luck, Pop,' he whispered, before closing his briefcase and leaving the room without another word.

'How can you be so confident, Giles,' said Emma once the door had closed behind him, 'that a man you've never even met will fall in with Mr Hardcastle's plans?'

'After Jessica had been buried, I asked one of the pall bearers who the man was who had wept throughout the service as if he'd lost a daughter and then hurried away. That was the name he gave me.'

◄○►

'There's no proof Luis Martinez killed the girl,' said Sir Alan, 'only that he desecrated her paintings.'

'But his fingerprints were on the handle of the flick knife,' said the colonel. 'And that's quite enough proof for me.'

'As are Jessica's, so any half-decent lawyer would get him off.'

'But we both know that Martinez was responsible for her death.'

'Perhaps. But that's not the same thing in a court of law.'

'So are you telling me I can't issue the order to kill him?'

'Not yet,' said the cabinet secretary.

The colonel took a swig from his half-pint and changed the subject. 'I see that Martinez has sacked his chauffeur.'

'You don't sack Kevin Rafferty. He leaves when the job is finished, or if he hasn't been paid.'

'So which was it this time?'

'The job must have been finished. Otherwise you wouldn't have to bother about killing Martinez, because Rafferty would already have done the job for you.'

'Could it be possible that Martinez has lost interest in destroying the Barringtons?'

'No. As long as Fisher remains on the board, you can be sure Martinez will still want to get even with every member of that family, believe me.'

'And where does Lady Virginia fit into all this?'

'She still hasn't forgiven Sir Giles for supporting his friend Harry Clifton at the time of the dispute over his mother's will, when Lady Barrington compared her daughter-in-law with her Siamese cat, Cleopatra, describing her as a "beautiful, well-groomed, vain, cunning, manipulative predator". Memorable.'

'Do you want me to keep an eye on her as well?'

'No, Lady Virginia won't break the law. She'll get someone else to do it for her.'

'So what you're saying is that I can't do anything at the moment, other than keep Martinez under close observation and report back to you.'

'Patience, colonel. You can be sure he'll make another mistake, and when he does I'll be happy to take advantage of your colleagues' particular skills.' Sir Alan downed his gin and tonic, rose from his place and slipped out of the pub without shaking hands or saying goodbye. He walked quickly across Whitehall into Downing Street and, five minutes later, was back behind his desk doing the day job.

—◦—

Cedric Hardcastle checked the number before he dialled. He didn't want his secretary to know who he was phoning. He heard a ringing tone and waited.

'Bingham's Fish Paste. How may I help you?'

'Can I speak to Mr Bingham?'

'Who shall I say is calling?'

'Cedric Hardcastle of Farthings Bank.'

'Hold on please.'

He heard a click and a moment later a voice with an accent almost as broad as his said, 'Take care of the pennies and the pounds will take care of themselves.'

'I'm flattered, Mr Bingham,' said Cedric.

'You shouldn't be. You run a damn fine bank. Just a shame you're on the other side of the Humber.'

'Mr Bingham, I need—'

'Bob. No one calls me Mr Bingham except the taxman and head waiters hoping for a larger tip.'

'Bob, I need to see you on a private matter, and I'd be quite happy to travel up to Grimsby.'

'It must be serious, because there aren't many people who are quite happy to travel up to Grimsby,' said Bob. 'As I assume you don't want to open a fish paste account, can I ask what this is all about?'

Dull, boring Cedric would have said that he'd prefer to discuss the matter in person rather than over the telephone, Mr Bingham. Newly minted, risk-taking Cedric said, 'Bob, what would you give to humiliate Lady Virginia Fenwick, and get away with it?'

'Half my fortune.'

MAJOR ALEX FISHER

1964

27

Barclays Bank
Halton Road
Bristol
June 16th, 1964

Dear Major Fisher,

*This morning we honoured two cheques and a standing
order presented on your personal account. The first was
from the West Country Building Society for £12 11s 6d;
the second from Harvey's wine merchants for £3 4s 4d
and the third was by standing order for £1 to the St Bede's
Old Boys' Society.*

*These payments take you just over your overdraft limit
of £500, so we must advise you not to issue any further
cheques until sufficient funds are available.*

Fisher looked at the morning mail on his desk and sighed deeply.
There were more brown envelopes than white, several from
tradesmen reminding him *Must be paid within 30 days*, and one
regretting that the matter had been placed in the hands of
solicitors. And it didn't help that Susan was refusing to return
his precious Jaguar until he was up to date with her monthly
maintenance, not least because he couldn't survive without a car
and had ended up having to buy a second-hand Hillman Minx,
which was another expense.

He placed the slim brown envelopes to one side and began to

open the white ones: an invitation to join his fellow officers of the Royal Wessex for a black tie dinner in the regimental mess, guest speaker Field Marshal Sir Claude Auchinleck – he would accept by return of post; a letter from Peter Maynard, the chairman of the local Conservative Association, asking if he would consider standing as a candidate for the county council elections. Countless hours canvassing and listening to your colleagues make self-serving speeches, expenses that were always queried, and the only accolade was being addressed as 'councillor'. No thanks. He would send a courteous reply explaining he had too many other commitments at the present time. He was slitting open the final envelope when the phone rang.

'Major Fisher.'

'Alex,' purred a voice he could never forget.

'Lady Virginia, what a pleasant surprise.'

'Virginia,' she insisted, which he knew meant that she was after something. 'I was just wondering if you planned to be in London any time during the next couple of weeks?'

'I'm coming up to London on Thursday to see . . . I have an appointment in Eaton Square at ten.'

'Well, as you know, I live just round the corner in Cadogan Gardens, so why don't you pop in for a drink? Shall we say around midday? There's something of mutual interest that I think might appeal to you.'

'Twelve o'clock on Thursday. I look forward to seeing you then . . . Virginia.'

—◆—

'Can you explain why the company's shares have been rising steadily during the past month?' asked Martinez.

'The *Buckingham*'s first booking period is going far better than expected,' said Fisher, 'and I'm told the maiden voyage is almost sold out.'

'That's good news, major, because I don't want there to be an empty cabin on that ship by the time it sails for New York.' Fisher was about to ask why, when Martinez added, 'And is everything in place for the naming ceremony?'

'Yes, once Harland and Wolff have completed the sea trials and the ship is officially handed over, a date will be announced for the naming ceremony. In fact, things couldn't be going much better for the company at the moment.'

'Not for much longer,' Martinez assured him. 'Nevertheless, major, you must go on supporting the chairman loyally, so that when the balloon goes up, no one will be looking in your direction.' Fisher laughed nervously. 'And be sure to phone me the moment the next board meeting breaks up, because I can't make my next move until I know the date of the naming ceremony.'

'Why is the date so important?' asked Fisher.

'All in good time, major. Once I have everything in place, you'll be the first to be informed.' There was a knock on the door and Diego strolled in.

'Shall I come back later?' he asked.

'No, the major was just leaving. Anything else, Alex?'

'Nothing,' said Fisher, wondering if he ought to tell Don Pedro about his appointment with Lady Virginia. He decided against it. After all, it might have nothing to do with the Barringtons or the Cliftons. 'I'll ring you as soon as I know that date.'

'Be sure you do, major.'

'Does he have any idea what you're up to?' asked Diego once Fisher had closed the door behind him.

'Not a clue, and that's the way I intend to keep it. After all, he's unlikely to be very cooperative when he discovers he's about to lose his job. But more important, did you get me the extra money I need?'

'Yes, but at a cost. The bank has agreed to increase your overdraft by another hundred thousand, but they're insisting on more collateral while interest rates are so high.'

'Aren't my shares security enough? After all, they're almost back to what I paid for them.'

'Don't forget, you had to pay off the chauffeur, which turned out to be far more expensive than we'd bargained for.'

'Bastards,' said Martinez, who had never told either of his sons the threat Kevin Rafferty had made if he'd failed to pay up on time. 'But I've still got half a million in the safe in case of emergencies.'

'When I last checked, it was just over three hundred thousand. I'm even beginning to wonder if this vendetta with the Barringtons and the Cliftons is worth pursuing when there's a chance it could end up bankrupting us.'

'There's no fear of that,' said Don Pedro. 'That lot won't have the balls to take me on when it comes to a showdown, and don't forget, we've already struck twice.' He smiled. 'Jessica Clifton turned out to be a bonus, and once I've sold all my shares, I'll be able to sink Mrs Clifton along with the rest of her precious family. It's all just a matter of timing, and I,' said Don Pedro, 'will be holding the stopwatch.'

—◇—

'Alex, how good of you to pop round. It's been far too long. Let me get you a drink,' said Virginia, walking across to the cabinet. 'Your favourite tipple is gin and tonic, if I remember correctly?'

Alex was impressed that she remembered, as they hadn't seen each other since Lady Virginia had caused him to lose his place on the board some nine years ago. What he did remember was the last thing she had said to him before they parted: *And when I say goodbye, I mean goodbye.*

'And how are the Barrington family faring now you're back on the board?'

'The company is just about through the worst of its troubles, and the *Buckingham*'s first booking period is going extremely well.'

'I was thinking of booking a suite for the maiden voyage to New York. That would get them thinking.'

'If you do, I can't imagine they'll invite you to join them at the captain's table,' said Fisher, warming to the idea.

'By the time we dock in New York, darling, mine will be the only table anyone wants to sit at.'

Fisher laughed. 'Is that what you wanted to see me about?'

'No, something far more important,' said Virginia, patting the sofa. 'Come and sit down beside me. I need your help with a little project I've been working on, and you, major, with your military background and business experience, are the ideal person to carry it out.'

Alex sipped his drink and listened in disbelief to what Virginia was proposing. He was about to reject the whole idea when she opened her handbag, extracted a cheque for £250 and handed it to him. All he could see in front of him was a pile of brown envelopes. 'I don't think—'

'And there'll be another two hundred and fifty once the job is done.'

Alex saw a way out. 'No, thank you, Virginia,' he said firmly. 'I would want the full amount up front. Perhaps you've forgotten what happened the last time we made a similar deal.'

Virginia tore up the cheque and, although Alex desperately needed the money, he felt a sense of relief. But to his surprise, she opened her bag again, took out her cheque book and wrote the words, *Pay Major A. Fisher, five hundred pounds*. She signed the cheque and handed it to Alex.

—◦—

On the journey back to Bristol, Alex thought about tearing up the cheque, but his mind kept returning to the unpaid bills, one threatening him with legal action, the outstanding monthly maintenance, and the unopened brown envelopes waiting on his desk.

Once he'd banked the cheque and paid his bills, Alex accepted that there was no turning back. He spent the next two days planning the whole exercise as if it were a military campaign.

Day one, Bath recce.

Day two, Bristol preparation.

Day three, Bath execution.

By Sunday, he was regretting ever agreeing to become involved, but he didn't care to think about the revenge Virginia would inflict if he let her down at the last moment and then failed to return her money.

On Monday morning, he drove the thirteen miles to Bath.

He parked in the municipal car park, made his way across the bridge, past the recreation ground and into the city centre. He didn't need a map as he'd spent most of the weekend memorizing every road until he could have walked the course blindfold. Time spent on preparation is seldom wasted, his old commanding officer used to say.

He began his quest in the high street, only stopping when he came across a grocer's or one of the new supermarkets. Once he was inside, he carefully checked the shelves, and if the product he required was on sale, he purchased half a dozen. After he'd completed the first part of the operation, Alex only needed to visit one other establishment, the Angel Hotel, where he checked the location of the public telephone booths. Satisfied, he walked back across the bridge to the car park, placed the two shopping bags in the boot of his car and drove back to Bristol.

When he arrived home, he parked in the garage, and took the two bags out of the boot. Over supper of a bowl of Heinz tomato soup and a sausage roll, he went over again and again what he needed to do the following day. He woke several times during the night.

After breakfast, Alex sat at his desk and read through the minutes of the last board meeting, continually telling himself that he couldn't go through with it.

At 10.30, he strolled into the kitchen, took an empty milk bottle from the windowsill and washed it out. He wrapped the bottle in a tea towel and put it in the sink before taking a small hammer out of the top drawer. He began to smash the bottle into pieces, which he then broke into smaller and smaller fragments, until he was left with a saucer full of glass powder.

After he'd completed the operation he felt exhausted and, like any self-respecting workman, took a break. He poured himself a beer, made a cheese and tomato sandwich, and sat down to read the morning paper. The Vatican was demanding that the contraceptive pill should be banned.

Forty minutes later, he returned to his task. He placed the two shopping bags on the work surface, took out the thirty-six small jars and stood them neatly in three lines, like soldiers on parade. He unscrewed the lid of the first jar and sprinkled a small amount of the glass powder on top, as if he was adding seasoning. He screwed the lid tightly back on, and repeated the exercise thirty-five times, before placing the jars back in the bags and putting them both in the cupboard under the sink.

Alex spent some time washing what was left of the glass powder down the sink until he was sure it was all gone. He left the house, walked to the end of the road, dropped into his local branch of Barclays, and exchanged a pound note for twenty shilling coins. On the way back to the flat, he picked up a copy of the *Bristol Evening News*. Once he was back home, he made himself a cup of tea. He took it into his study, sat at his desk and dialled directory enquiries. He asked for five London numbers, and one in Bath.

The following day, Alex put the two shopping bags back in the boot and once again set off for Bath. After he'd parked in the far corner of the municipal car park, he took out the shopping bags and returned to the town centre, entering each one of the establishments where he'd purchased the jars and, unlike a shoplifter, he placed them back on the shelves. Once he'd returned the thirty-fifth jar to the last shop, he took the remaining one up to the counter and asked to see the manager.

'What seems to be the problem, sir?'

'I don't want to make a fuss, old chap,' said Alex, 'but I bought this jar of Bingham's Fish Paste the other day – my favourite,' he added, '– and when I got home, I discovered some pieces of glass in it.'

The manager looked shocked when Alex unscrewed the lid and invited him to examine the contents. He was even more horrified when he dipped his finger into the paste and drew blood.

'I'm not the complaining type,' said Alex, 'but perhaps it might be wise to check the rest of your stock and inform the supplier.'

'I'll do that straight away, sir.' He hesitated. 'Do you wish to make an official complaint?' he asked nervously.

'No, no,' said Alex. 'I'm sure this is just a one-off, and I wouldn't want to get you into any trouble.'

He shook hands with a grateful manager, and was about to leave when the man said, 'The least we can do, sir, is give you a refund.'

Alex didn't want to hang around, fearing that someone might remember him, but he realized that if he left without collecting the refund the manager might become suspicious. He turned back as the manager opened the till, took out a shilling and handed it to his customer.

'Thank you,' said Alex, pocketing the money and heading towards the door.

'I'm sorry to bother you again, sir, but would you be kind enough to sign a receipt?'

Alex reluctantly turned back a second time, scribbled 'Samuel Oakshott' on the dotted line, the first name that came into his head, then left quickly. Once he had escaped, he took a more circuitous route than he had originally planned to the Angel Hotel. When he arrived, he looked back to make sure no one had followed him. Satisfied, he entered the hotel, went straight to one of the public phone booths and placed twenty one-shilling pieces on the shelf. He took a sheet of paper out of his back pocket and dialled the first number on the list.

'*Daily Mail*,' said a voice. 'News or advertising?'

'News,' said Alex, who was asked to wait while he was put through to a reporter on the news desk.

He spoke to the lady for several minutes about the unfortunate incident he'd experienced with Bingham's Fish Paste, his favourite brand.

'Will you be suing them?' she asked.

'I haven't decided yet,' said Alex, 'but I'll certainly be consulting my solicitor.'

'And what did you say your name was, sir?'

'Samuel Oakshott,' he repeated, smiling at the thought of how much his late headmaster would have disapproved of what he was up to.

Alex then rang the *Daily Express*, *News Chronicle*, *Daily Telegraph*, *The Times* and, for good measure, the *Bath Echo*. His final call before returning to Bristol was to Lady Virginia, who said, 'I knew I could rely on you, major. We really must get together some time. It's always such fun seeing you.'

He placed the two remaining shillings in his pocket, walked out of the hotel and returned to the car park. On the drive back to Bristol he decided that it might be wise not to visit Bath again in the near future.

⊷⊷

Virginia sent out for all the papers the following morning, except the *Daily Worker*.

She was delighted with the coverage given to the *Bingham's Fish Paste Scandal* (*Daily Mail*). *Mr Robert Bingham, chairman of the company, has issued a statement confirming that all stocks of Bingham's Fish Paste have been removed from the shelves and will not be replaced until a full enquiry has been carried out* (*The Times*).

A junior minister at the Ministry of Agriculture, Fisheries and Food has assured the public that an inspection of the Bingham's factory in Grimsby will be conducted by health and safety officials in the near future (*Daily Express*). *Bingham's shares fall five shillings in early trading* (*Financial Times*).

When Virginia had finished reading all the papers, she only hoped that Robert Bingham might guess who had masterminded the whole operation. How much she would have enjoyed having breakfast at Mablethorpe Hall that morning and hearing Priscilla's views on the unfortunate incident. She checked her watch and, confident that Robert would have left for the factory, picked up the phone and dialled a Lincolnshire number.

'Dearest Priscilla,' she gushed, 'I was just calling to say how dreadfully sorry I was to read about that unpleasant business in Bath. Such bad luck.'

'How kind of you to call, darling,' said Priscilla. 'One realizes who one's friends are at a time like this.'

'Well, you can rest assured that I'm always on the other end of the line should you ever need me, and do please pass on my sympathy and best wishes to Robert. I hope he won't be too disappointed about no longer being in line for a knighthood.'

28

EVERYONE STOOD as Emma took her place at the head of the boardroom table. She had been looking forward to this moment for some time.

'Gentlemen, allow me to open the meeting by reporting to the board that, yesterday, the company's share price returned to its high watermark, and our shareholders will be receiving a dividend for the first time in three years.'

Murmurs of 'Hear, hear,' accompanied by smiles on the faces of all the directors except one.

'Now that we have put the past behind us, let us move on to the future. Yesterday, I received the Department of Transport's preliminary report on the *Buckingham*'s seaworthy status. Subject to a few minor modifications, and following the completion of the navigational trials, the department should be able to grant us a full maritime certificate by the end of the month. Once we are in possession of that certificate, the ship will leave Belfast and sail for Avonmouth. It is my intention, gentlemen, to hold the next board meeting on the bridge of the *Buckingham*, so that we can all be given a tour of the ship, and see at first hand what we have spent our shareholders' money on.

'I know the board will be equally delighted to learn that the company secretary received a call from Clarence House earlier in the week, to say that Her Majesty, Queen Elizabeth the Queen Mother has agreed to conduct the naming ceremony on September twenty-first. It would not be an exaggeration to suggest, gentlemen, that the next three months will be among the most demanding in the company's history because, although the first booking period has been a resounding success, with only a few cabins still available for the maiden voyage, it's the long term that will decide the company's future. And on that subject I am happy to answer any questions. Admiral?'

'Chairman, may I be the first to congratulate you, and to say, although there is still some way to go before we reach calm waters, today is certainly the most satisfying I can remember in the twenty-two years I have served on this board. But allow me to move quickly on to what we used to call in the Navy the points of sail. Have you selected a captain from the shortlist of three candidates approved by the board?'

'Yes, admiral, we have. Our final choice is Captain Nicholas Turnbull RN, who until recently was the first officer on the *Queen Mary*. We are very lucky to have secured the services of such an experienced officer, and it might have helped that he was born and bred in Bristol. We also have a full complement of officers, many of whom served under Captain Turnbull either in the Royal Navy or, more recently, with Cunard.'

'What about the rest of the crew?' asked Anscott. 'After all, this is a cruise ship, not a battle cruiser.'

'Fair point, Mr Anscott. I think you will find that we are well represented, from the engine room to the grill room. There are still a few posts left to fill, but as we are receiving at least ten applications for every position, we are able to be extremely selective.'

'What is the ratio of passengers to crew?' asked Dobbs.

For the first time Emma had to refer to a file of notes in front of her. 'The breakdown of the crew is twenty-five officers, two hundred and fifty ratings, three hundred stewards and catering staff, plus the ship's doctor and his nurse. The ship is divided into three classes: first, cabin and tourist. There is accommodation for one hundred and two first-class passengers, with cabin prices ranging from forty-five pounds to sixty pounds for the penthouse on the maiden New York crossing; two hundred and forty-two in cabin class, who will pay around thirty pounds each, and three hundred and sixty in tourist at ten pounds each, three to a cabin.

If you need more details, Mr Dobbs, you will find everything in section two of your blue folder.'

'As there's bound to be a lot of press interest around the naming ceremony on September twenty-first,' said Fisher, 'and for the maiden voyage to New York the following month, who will be handling our press and public relations?'

'We have appointed J. Walter Thompson, who gave by far the best presentation,' said Emma. 'They have already arranged for a BBC film crew to be on board the ship for one of its sea trials, and for Captain Turnbull to be profiled in the *Sunday Times*.'

'Never did that sort of thing in my day,' snorted the admiral.

'With good reason. We didn't want the enemy to know where you were, whereas we want our passengers not only to know where we are, but also to feel they couldn't be in safer hands.'

'What percentage of cabin occupation will we need to break even?' asked Cedric Hardcastle, clearly not that interested in public relations but, as always, in the bottom line.

'Sixty per cent, only taking running costs into account. But if we are to pay back our capital investment within the ten years as envisaged by Ross Buchanan when he was chairman, we will need an eighty-six per cent occupancy rate during that period. So there's no room for complacency, Mr Hardcastle.'

Alex took notes of any dates or figures he felt would be of interest to Don Pedro, although he still had no idea why they were so important, or what Don Pedro had meant by *'when the balloon goes up'*.

Emma continued to answer questions for another hour, and it pained Alex to have to admit, although he would never have mentioned it in front of Don Pedro, that she was unquestionably on top of her brief.

After she closed the meeting with the words, 'See you all on August twenty-fourth at the AGM,' Alex quickly left the board-room and made his way out of the building. Emma watched from the top-floor window as he drove out of the compound, only reminding her that she could never afford to lower her guard.

Alex parked outside the Lord Nelson and walked across to

the phone box, four pennies ready. 'The ship will be named by the Queen Mother on September twenty-first, and the maiden voyage to New York is still planned for October twenty-ninth.'

'I'll see you in my office at ten tomorrow morning,' was all Don Pedro said before the line went dead.

Alex would like to have told him, just once, 'Sorry, old boy, can't make it. I've got a far more important appointment at that time,' but he knew he would be standing outside 44 Eaton Square at one minute to ten the following morning.

◄○►

24 Arcadia Mansions
Bridge Street
Bristol

Dear Mrs Clifton,

It is with considerable regret that I have to tender my resignation as a non-executive director of the board of Barrington's Shipping. At the time when my fellow directors voted to go ahead with the building of the Buckingham, you were firmly opposed to the idea, and indeed voted against it. I can now see, admittedly with hindsight, that your judgement was sound. As you pointed out at the time, to risk such a large percentage of the company's reserves on a single venture could well turn out to be a decision we will all live to regret.

Since, after several setbacks, Ross Buchanan felt he had to resign – rightly so in my opinion – and you took his place, I must admit you have battled manfully to ensure that the company remains solvent. However, when you informed the board last week that unless the take-up for cabin sales was at 86 per cent for the next ten years, there would be no chance of us returning our original investment, I realized that the project was doomed, and, I fear, the company along with it.

Naturally I hope to be proved wrong, as it would sadden me to see such a fine old company as Barrington's collapse,

*and even, heaven forbid, face bankruptcy. But as I believe
that is a strong possibility, my first responsibility must be to
the shareholders, and I have therefore been left with no
choice but to resign.*

   Yours sincerely
      Alex Fisher (Major Rtd)

'And you expect me to send this letter to Mrs Clifton on
August the twenty-first, just three days before the company's
AGM?'

'Yes, that's exactly what I expect you to do,' said Martinez.

'But if I were to do that, the share price would collapse. It
might even bring the company down.'

'You're catching on fast, major.'

'But you have over two million pounds invested in Barrington's. You'd stand to lose a fortune.'

'Not if I sell all my shares a few days before you release that
letter to the press.' Alex was speechless. 'Ah,' said Martinez, 'the
penny has dropped. Now I can see that at a personal level, major,
this isn't good news, as not only will you lose your only source of
income, but, at your age, you might not find it so easy to get
another job.'

'That's putting it mildly,' said Alex. 'After sending this,' he
added, waving the letter in front of Don Pedro, 'no company
would ever consider asking me to join their board, and I couldn't
blame them.'

'So I felt it was only fair,' continued Don Pedro, ignoring his
outburst, 'that you should be properly compensated for your loyalty, especially after you went through such an expensive divorce.
With that in mind, major, I intend to pay you five thousand
pounds in cash that neither your wife nor the taxman need ever
know about.'

'That's most generous,' said Alex.

'I agree. However, it's dependent on you handing that letter
to the chairman on the Friday before the AGM, as I'm advised
that the Saturday and Sunday papers will be keen to follow up
the story. You must also be available to be interviewed on the

Friday so you can express your anxiety about the future of Barrington's, so that when Mrs Clifton opens the AGM on Monday morning, there will be only one question on every journalist's lips.'

'How long can the company hope to survive?' said Alex. 'But given the circumstances, Don Pedro, I wonder if you'd be prepared to let me have a couple of thousand in advance, and pay the balance after I've sent the letter and dealt with the press interviews?'

'Not a chance, major. You still owe me a thousand for your wife's vote.'

⋘∘⋙

'You do realize, Mr Martinez, the damage this will do to Barrington Shipping?'

'I don't pay you to offer me advice, Mr Ledbury, just to carry out my instructions. If you can't manage to do that, I'll have to find someone who can.'

'But there's a strong possibility that were I to carry out these instructions to the letter, you would lose a great deal of money.'

'It's my money to lose, and in any case, Barrington's shares are currently trading above the price I originally paid for them, so I'm confident of getting most of my money back. At worst, I might lose a few pounds.'

'But if you were to allow me to dispose of the shares over a longer period, say six weeks, even a couple of months, I'd feel more confident that I could claw back your original investment, possibly even make you a small profit.'

'I'll spend my money in any way I please.'

'But it is my fiduciary duty to protect the bank's position, especially remembering you are currently overdrawn by £1,735,000.'

'That is covered by the value of the shares, which at their present price would return me more than two million.'

'Then at least allow me to approach the Barrington family and ask if they—'

'Under no circumstances will you contact any member of the

Barrington or Clifton families!' shouted Don Pedro. 'You will place all my shares on the open market the moment the Stock Exchange opens on Monday, August seventeenth, and accept whatever price is offered at that time. My instructions could not be clearer.'

'Where will you be on that day, Mr Martinez, in case I need to get in touch with you?'

'Exactly where you would expect to find any gentleman: grouse-shooting in Scotland. There will be no way of contacting me, and that's the reason I chose the place. It's so isolated they don't even deliver the morning newspapers.'

'If those are your instructions, Mr Martinez, I shall draw up a letter to that effect, so that there can be no misunderstanding at a later date. I'll send it round to Eaton Square by messenger this afternoon for your signature.'

'I'll be happy to sign it.'

'And once this transaction has been completed, Mr Martinez, perhaps you might consider moving your account to another bank.'

'If you've still got your job, Mr Ledbury, I will.'

29

SUSAN PARKED the car in a side street and waited. She knew the invitation for the regimental dinner was 7.30 for 8 p.m. and, as the guest of honour was a field marshal, she felt confident Alex wouldn't be late.

A taxi drew up outside her former marital home at 7.10 p.m. Alex appeared a few moments later. He was wearing a dinner jacket boasting three campaign medals. Susan noticed that his bow tie was askew, one of his dress-shirt studs was missing, and she couldn't help laughing when she saw the pair of slip-ons that certainly wouldn't last a lifetime. Alex climbed into the back of the taxi, which headed off in the direction of Wellington Road.

Susan waited for a few minutes before she drove the car across the road, got out and opened the garage door. She then parked the Jaguar Mark II inside. Part of the divorce settlement had been that she would return his pride and joy, but she'd refused until he was up to date with his monthly maintenance payments. Susan had cleared his latest cheque that morning, only wondering where the money could possibly have come from. Alex's solicitor had suggested she should return the car while he was at the regimental dinner. One of the few things both sides were able to agree on.

She climbed out of the car, opened the boot and took out a Stanley knife and a pot of paint. After she'd placed the pot of paint on the ground, Susan walked to the front of the car and thrust the knife into one of the tyres. She took a step back and waited for the hissing to stop, before she moved on to the next one. When all four tyres were flat, she turned her attention to the pot of paint.

She prised open the lid, stood on tiptoe, and slowly poured the thick liquid on to the roof of the car. Once she was convinced that not a drop was left, she stood back and enjoyed the sensation of watching the paint slowly trickle down each side as well as over the front and rear windows. It should have dried long before Alex returned from his dinner. Susan had spent some considerable time selecting which colour would blend best with racing green, and had finally settled on lilac. The result was even more pleasing than she'd thought possible.

It was her mother who'd spent hours going over the small print in the divorce settlement and had pointed out to Susan that she had agreed to return the car but without specifying what condition it should be in.

It was some time before Susan dragged herself away from the garage to go up to the third floor where she intended to leave the car keys on his study desk. Her only disappointment was that she wouldn't be able to see the expression on Alex's face when he opened the garage door in the morning.

Susan let herself into the flat with her old latch key, pleased that Alex hadn't changed the lock. She strolled into his study and dropped the car keys on the desk. She was about to leave, when she noticed a letter in his unmistakable hand on the blotting pad. Curiosity got the better of her. She leant over and read the private and confidential letter quickly, and then sat in his chair and read it more slowly a second time. She found it hard to believe that Alex would sacrifice his seat on the board of Barrington's as a matter of principle. After all, Alex didn't have any principles, and as it was his only source of income other than a derisory army pension, what did he expect to live on? More importantly, how would he pay her monthly maintenance without his regular director's fee?

Susan read the letter a third time, wondering if there was something she was missing. She was at a loss to understand why it was dated August 21st. If you were going to resign on a matter of principle, why wait a fortnight before making your position clear?

By the time Susan had arrived back in Burnham-on-Sea, Alex was bending the ear of the field marshal, but she still hadn't fathomed it out.

◄○►

Sebastian walked slowly down Bond Street, admiring the various goods displayed in the shop windows and wondering if he'd ever be able to afford any of them.

Mr Hardcastle had recently given him a raise. He was now earning £20 a week, making him what was known in the City as a 'thousand-pound-a-year man', and he also had a new title, associate director – not that titles mean anything in the banking world, unless you're chairman of the board.

In the distance he spotted a sign flapping in the breeze, *Agnew's Fine Art Dealers, founded 1817*. Sebastian had never entered a private art gallery before, and he wasn't even sure if they were open to the public. He'd been to the Royal Academy, the Tate and the National Gallery with Jessica, and she'd never stopped talking as she dragged him from room to room. It used to drive him mad sometimes. How he wished she was there by his side, driving him mad. Not a day went by, not an hour, when he didn't miss her.

He pushed open the door to the gallery and stepped inside. For a moment he just stood there, gazing around the spacious room, its walls covered with the most magnificent oils, some of which he recognized – Constable, Munnings and a Stubbs. Suddenly, from nowhere, she appeared, looking even more beautiful than she had when he'd first seen her that evening at the Slade, when Jessica had carried off all the prizes on graduation day.

As she walked towards him, his throat went dry. How do you address a goddess? She was wearing a yellow dress, simple but elegant, and her hair was a shade of natural blonde that anyone other than a Swedish woman would pay a fortune to reproduce, and many tried. Today it was pinned up, formal and professional, not falling on her bare shoulders as it had done the last time he'd seen her. He wanted to tell her that he hadn't come to see the pictures, just to meet her. What a feeble pick-up line, and it wasn't even true.

'Can I help you?' she asked.

The first surprise was that she was an American, so obviously she was not Mr Agnew's daughter as he had originally assumed.

'Yes,' he said. 'I was wondering if you had any pictures by an artist called Jessica Clifton?'

She looked surprised, but smiled and said, 'Yes, we do. Would you like to follow me?'

To the ends of the earth. An even more pathetic line, which he was glad he hadn't delivered. Some men think that a woman can be just as beautiful when you walk behind them. He didn't care either way as he followed her downstairs to another large room that displayed equally mesmerizing paintings. Thanks to Jessica, he recognized a Manet, a Tissot and her favourite artist, Berthe Morisot. She wouldn't have been able to stop chattering.

The goddess unlocked a door he hadn't noticed that led into a smaller side room. He joined her to find that the room was filled with row upon row of sliding racks. She selected one and pulled it out to reveal one side that was devoted to Jessica's oils. He stared at all nine of her award-winning works from the graduation show, as well as a dozen drawings and watercolours he'd never seen before, but which were equally seductive. For a moment he felt elation, and then his legs gave way. He grabbed the rack to steady himself.

'Are you all right?' she asked, her professional voice replaced by a gentler, softer tone.

'I'm so sorry.'

'Why don't you sit down?' she suggested, taking a chair and placing it beside him. As he sat, she took his arm as if he was an old man, and all he wanted to do was to hold on to her. Why is it that men fall so quickly, so helplessly, while women are far more cautious and sensible, he wondered. 'Let me get you some water,' she said, and before he could reply, she'd left him.

He looked at Jessica's pictures once again, trying to decide if he had a favourite, and wondered, if he did, if he would be able to afford it. Then she reappeared, carrying a glass of water, accompanied by an older man, whom he remembered from their evening at the Slade.

'Good morning, Mr Agnew,' said Sebastian, as he rose from his chair. The gallery owner looked surprised, clearly unable to place the young man. 'We met at the Slade, sir, when you came to the graduation ceremony.'

Agnew still looked puzzled until he said, 'Ah yes, now I remember. You're Jessica's brother.'

Sebastian felt a complete fool as he sat back down and once again buried his head in his hands. She walked across and placed a hand on his shoulder.

'Jessica was one of the loveliest people I've ever met,' she said. 'I'm so sorry.'

'And I'm sorry to be making such a fool of myself. I only wanted to find out if you had any of her pictures for sale.'

'Everything in this gallery is for sale,' said Agnew, trying to lighten the mood.

'How much are they?'

'All of them?'

'All of them.'

'I haven't actually priced them yet, as we had hoped Jessica would become one of the gallery's regular artists, but sadly . . . I know what they cost me, fifty-eight pounds.'

'And what are they worth?'

'Whatever someone will pay for them,' replied Agnew.

'I would give every penny I have to own them.'

Mr Agnew looked hopeful. 'And how much is every penny, Mr Clifton?'

'I checked my bank balance this morning because I knew I was coming to see you.' They both stared at him. 'I've got forty-six pounds, twelve shillings and sixpence in my current account, but because I work at the bank, I'm not allowed an overdraft.'

'Then forty-six pounds, twelve shillings and sixpence it is, Mr Clifton.'

If there was one person who looked even more surprised than Sebastian, it was the gallery assistant, who'd never known Mr Agnew to sell a picture for less than he'd paid for it.

'But there is one condition.'

Sebastian wondered if he'd changed his mind. 'And what is that, sir?'

'If you ever decide to sell any of your sister's pictures, you must first offer them to me at the same price you paid for them.'

'You have a deal, sir,' said Sebastian as the two men shook hands. 'But I would never sell them,' he added. 'Never.'

'In that case, I'll ask Miss Sullivan to make out an invoice for forty-six pounds, twelve shillings and sixpence.' She gave a slight nod and left the room. 'I have no desire to bring you to tears again, young man, but in my profession, you are lucky if you come across a talent like Jessica's twice, perhaps three times in your life.'

'It's kind of you to say so, sir,' said Sebastian as Miss Sullivan returned, carrying an invoice book.

'Please excuse me,' said Mr Agnew. 'I have a major exhibition opening next week, and I still haven't finished the pricing.'

Sebastian sat down and wrote out a cheque for £46 12s 6d, tore it out and handed it to the assistant.

'If I had forty-six pounds twelve shillings and sixpence,' she said, 'I would have bought them too. Oh, I'm so sorry,' she quickly added as Sebastian bowed his head. 'Will you take them with you, sir, or come back later?'

'I'll come back tomorrow, that is, if you're open on a Saturday.'

'Yes, we are,' she said, 'but I'm having a few days off, so I'll ask Mrs Clark to take care of you.'

'When are you back at work?'

'Thursday.'

'Then I'll come in on Thursday morning.'

She smiled, a different kind of smile, before leading him back upstairs. It was then that he saw the statue for the first time, standing in the far corner of the gallery. '*The Thinker*,' he said. She nodded. 'Some would say it's Rodin's greatest work. Did you know that it was first called *The Poet*?' She looked surprised. 'And if I remember correctly, if it's a lifetime cast, it must be by Alexis Rudier.'

'Now you're showing off.'

'Guilty,' Sebastian admitted, 'but I have good reason to remember this particular piece.'

'Jessica?'

'No, not this time. May I ask the cast number?'

'Five, of nine.'

Sebastian tried to remain calm, as he needed to get the answers to some more questions, but didn't want her to become suspicious. 'Who was the previous owner?' he asked.

'I've no idea. The piece is listed in the catalogue as the property of a gentleman.'

'What does that mean?'

'The gentleman in question doesn't want it to be known that he's disposing of his collection. We get a lot of customers that way: the three Ds, death, divorce and debt. But I must warn you that you won't get Mr Agnew to sell you *The Thinker* for forty-six pounds, twelve shillings and sixpence.'

Sebastian laughed. 'How much is it?' he asked, touching the statue's bent right arm.

'Mr Agnew hasn't quite finished pricing the collection yet, but I can give you a catalogue if you'd like one, and an invitation for the private view on August seventeenth.'

'Thank you,' Sebastian said as she handed him a catalogue. 'I look forward to seeing you again on Thursday.' She smiled. 'Unless . . .' he hesitated, but she didn't help him, 'unless you're free to have supper with me tomorrow evening?'

'Irresistible,' she said, 'but I'd better choose the restaurant.'

'Why?'

'Because I know how much you've got left in your bank account.'

30

'BUT WHY WOULD he want to sell his art collection?' asked Cedric.

'He must need the money.'

'That much is obvious, Seb, but what I can't work out is *why* he needs the money.' Cedric continued to flick through the pages of the catalogue, but was none the wiser by the time he'd reached *A Fair at l'Hermitage near Pontoise* by Camille Pissarro, illustrated on the back page. 'Perhaps the time has come to call in a favour.'

'What do you have in mind?'

'Who, not what,' said Cedric. 'A Mr Stephen Ledbury, the manager of the Midland Bank, St James's.'

'What's so special about him?' asked Sebastian.

'He's Martinez's bank manager.'

'How do you know that?'

'When you've sat next to Major Fisher at board meetings for over five years, it's amazing what you pick up if you're patient and willing to listen to a lonely man.' Cedric buzzed through to his secretary. 'Can you get me Stephen Ledbury at the Midland?' He turned back to Sebastian. 'Ever since I discovered he was Martinez's bank manager I've been tossing Ledbury the odd bone. Perhaps the time has come for him to fetch one back.'

The phone on Cedric's desk rang. 'Mr Ledbury on line one.'

'Thank you,' said Cedric, then waited for the click before pressing the loudspeaker button. 'Good afternoon, Stephen.'

'Good afternoon, Cedric. What can I do for you?'

'I think it's more what I can do for you, old chap.'

'Another good tip?' said Ledbury, sounding hopeful.

'This is more in the helping-to-cover-your-backside category. I hear that one of your less salubrious clients is putting his entire art collection up for sale at Agnew's in Bond Street. As the catalogue describes the collection as "the property of a gentleman", which is a misnomer by any standards, I assume that for some reason he doesn't want you to find out about it.'

'What makes you think this particular gentleman has an account at West End central?'

'I sit next to his representative on the board of Barrington's Shipping.'

There was a long pause before Ledbury said, 'Ah, and you say he's put his entire collection up for sale at Agnew's?'

'From Manet to Rodin. I'm looking at the catalogue now, and I find it hard to believe that there can be anything left on his walls at Eaton Square. Would you like me to send the catalogue round to you?'

'No, don't bother, Cedric. Agnew's is only a couple of hundred yards up the road, so I'll pop over and pick one up myself. It was very good of you to let me know, and it leaves me in your debt once again. If there's anything I can ever do to repay you . . .'

'Well, now you mention it, Stephen, there is one small favour I might ask while I've got you on the line.'

'Just name it.'

'Should your "gentleman" ever decide to dispose of his shares in Barrington's Shipping, I have a customer who just might be interested.'

There followed a long silence before Ledbury asked, 'Might that customer possibly be a member of the Barrington or Clifton families?'

'No, I don't represent either of them. I think you'll find they bank with Barclays in Bristol, whereas my client comes from the north of England.'

Another long silence. 'Where will you be at nine o'clock on Monday the seventeenth of August?'

'At my desk,' said Cedric.

'Good. I might just call you at one minute past nine that morning, and I may be able to repay several of your favours.'

'That's good of you, Stephen, but on to more important matters – how's your golf handicap?'

'It's still eleven, but I have a feeling it will be twelve by the beginning of next season. I'm not getting any younger.'

'None of us are,' said Cedric. 'Have a good round at the weekend and I'll look forward to hearing from you – ' he checked his calendar – 'in ten days' time.' He pressed the button on the side of his phone and looked across the desk at his youngest associate director. 'Tell me what you learnt from that, Seb.'

'That Martinez might well be putting all his Barrington's shares on the market at nine o'clock on August seventeenth.'

'Exactly one week before your mother will be chairing the company's AGM.'

'Oh hell,' said Sebastian.

'I'm glad you've worked out what Martinez is up to. But never forget, Seb, that in any conversation, it's often something that seems quite insignificant at the time that gives you the piece of information you're looking for. Mr Ledbury kindly supplied me with two such little gems.'

'What was the first?'

Cedric looked down at his pad and read out, *'Don't bother, Cedric, Agnew's is only a couple of hundred yards up the road, so I'll pop over and pick one up myself.* What does that tell us?'

'That he didn't realize Martinez's collection was up for sale.'

'Yes, that's for sure, but more importantly, it tells us that for some reason the fact that it's up for sale worries him, otherwise he'd have sent a member of his staff to pick up the catalogue, but no, *I'll pick one up myself.*'

'And the second thing?'

'He asked if the bank represented either the Clifton or the Barrington families.'

'Why is that significant?'

'Because if I'd said yes, the conversation would have ended

there and then. I'm sure Ledbury has received instructions to put the shares up for sale on the seventeenth, but not to a member of the family.'

'And why is that so important?"

'Martinez clearly doesn't want the family to know what he's up to. He's obviously hoping to recoup most of his investment in Barrington's during the run-up to the AGM, by which time he seems to be confident that the share price will have collapsed without him having lost too much of his own money. If he gets his timing right, every stockbroker will be trying to dump their Barrington's shares, which will ensure that the AGM is hijacked by journalists wanting to know if the company is facing bankruptcy. In which case, it won't be the news that the naming of the *Buckingham* will be carried out by the Queen Mother that will make the front pages the following day.'

'Can we do anything to prevent that?' asked Sebastian.

'Yes, but we'll have to make sure our timing is even better than Martinez's.'

'But something isn't quite right. If Martinez is likely to get most of his money back on the sale of the shares, why does he also need to sell his art collection?'

'I agree that is a mystery. And I have a feeling that once we've solved it, everything else will fall neatly into place. It's also just possible that if you ask the young lady who's taking you to supper tomorrow night the right question, we might be able to fit one or two more pieces of the jigsaw into place. But remember what I've just said: an unguarded comment often proves every bit as valuable as a response to a direct question. By the way, what's the young lady's name?'

'I don't know,' said Sebastian.

Susan Fisher sat in the fifth row of a packed audience and listened attentively to what Emma Clifton had to say about her life as the chairman of a major shipping company, when she addressed the annual meeting of the Red Maids' Old Girls' Association. Although Emma was still a fine-looking woman,

Susan saw that little lines had begun to appear around her eyes, and the head of thick black hair that had been the envy of her classmates now needed a little help to retain its natural dark sheen and not reveal the toll grief and stress must surely have taken.

Susan always attended school reunions, and had been particularly looking forward to this one, as she was a great admirer of Emma Barrington, as she remembered her. She had been head girl, had won a place at Oxford and had become the first woman chairman of a public company.

However, one thing puzzled her about Emma's address. Alex's resignation letter suggested that the company had made a series of bad decisions and could be facing bankruptcy, whereas Emma gave the impression that as the first booking period for the *Buckingham* had been an unqualified success, Barrington's could look forward to a bright future. They couldn't both be right, and she wasn't in any doubt who she wanted to believe.

During the reception that was held after the speech, it was impossible to get anywhere near the speaker, who was surrounded by old friends and new admirers. Susan didn't bother to wait in line, but decided to catch up with some of her contemporaries. Whenever the subject arose, she tried to avoid answering any questions about Alex. After an hour, Susan decided to leave as she'd promised to be back at Burnham-on-Sea in time to cook supper for her mother. She was just leaving the school hall when someone behind her said, 'Hello, Susan.' She looked back, surprised to see Emma Clifton walking towards her.

'I wouldn't have been able to make that speech if it hadn't been for you. It was very brave, because I can only imagine what Alex had to say when he got home that afternoon.'

'I didn't wait to find out,' said Susan, 'because I'd already made up my mind to leave him. And now I know how well the company is doing, I'm even more pleased I supported you.'

'We've still got a testing six months ahead of us,' admitted Emma, 'but if we get through that, I'll feel a lot more confident.'

'And I'm sure you will,' said Susan. 'I'm only sorry that Alex is considering resigning at such an important moment in the company's history.'

Emma stopped just as she was about to get into the car and turned back to face her. 'Alex is thinking of resigning?'

'I assumed you knew about it.'

'I had no idea,' said Emma. 'When did he tell you this?'

'He didn't. I just happened to see a letter on his desk tendering his resignation, which surprised me because I know how much he enjoys being on the board. But as the letter was dated August the twenty-first, perhaps he still hasn't made up his mind.'

'I'd better have a word with him.'

'No, please don't,' pleaded Susan. 'I wasn't meant to see the letter.'

'Then I won't say a word. But can you remember the reason he gave?'

'I can't recall his exact words, but there was something about his first duty being to the shareholders and that, as a matter of principle, someone had to let them know that the company could be facing bankruptcy. But now I've heard your speech, that doesn't make sense.'

'When will you be seeing Alex again?'

'I hope never,' said Susan.

'Then can we keep this between ourselves?'

'Yes, please. I wouldn't want him to find out that I'd talked to you about the letter.'

'Neither would I,' said Emma.

◄○►

'Where will you be at nine a.m. on Monday the seventeenth?'

'Where you'll find me at nine o'clock every morning, keeping an eye on the two thousand jars of fish paste as they come off the line every hour. But where would you like me to be?'

'Close to a phone, because I'll be calling to advise you to make a substantial investment in a shipping company.'

'So your little plan is falling into place.'

'Not quite yet,' replied Cedric. 'There's still some fine-tuning to be done, and even then I'll need to get my timing spot on.'

'If you do, will Lady Virginia be angry?'

'She'll be absolutely livid, my darling.'

Bingham laughed. 'Then I'll be standing by the phone at one minute to nine on Monday,' he checked his diary, 'the seventeenth of August.'

—◦—

'Did you pick the cheapest thing on the menu because I'm paying the bill?'

'No, of course not,' said Sebastian. 'Tomato soup and a lettuce leaf have always been my favourites.'

'Then let me try and guess what your second favourites might be,' said Samantha, looking up at the waiter. 'We'll both have the San Daniele with melon followed by two steaks.'

'How would you like your steak, madam?'

'Medium rare, please.'

'And you, sir?'

'How would I like my steak done, madam?' Sebastian mimicked, smiling across at her.

'He's also medium rare.'

'So—'

'How—'

'No, you first,' she said.

'So what brings an American girl to London?'

'My father's in the diplomatic service, and he's recently been posted here, so I thought it would be fun to spend a year in London.'

'And your mother, what does she do, Samantha?'

'Sam, everyone except my mother calls me Sam. My father was hoping for a boy.'

'Well, he failed spectacularly.'

'You're such a flirt.'

'And your mother?' Sebastian repeated.

'She's old-fashioned, just takes care of my father.'

'I'm looking for someone like that.'

'I wish you luck.'

'Why an art gallery?'

'I studied art history at Georgetown, and then decided to take a year off.'

'So what do you plan to do next?'

'I start work on my PhD in September.'

'What's the subject going to be?'

'Rubens: Artist or Diplomat?'

'Wasn't he both?'

'You're going to have to wait a couple of years to find out.'

'Which university?' said Sebastian, hoping she wouldn't be returning to America in a few weeks' time.

'London or Princeton. I've been offered a place at both but haven't made my mind up yet. And you?'

'I haven't been offered a place at either.'

'No, stupid, what do you do?'

'I joined the bank after taking a year off,' he said as the waiter returned and placed two plates of ham and melon in front of them.

'So you didn't go to university?'

'It's a long story,' said Sebastian. 'Another time perhaps,' he added as he waited for her to pick up her knife and fork.

'Ah, so you're confident there'll be another time.'

'Absolutely. I've got to come in to the gallery on Thursday to pick up Jess's paintings, and the following Monday you've invited me to the opening of the unknown gentleman's art collection. Or do we now know who he is?'

'No, only Mr Agnew knows that. All I can tell you is that he's not coming to the opening.'

'He clearly doesn't want anyone to find out who he is.'

'Or where he is,' said Sam. 'We can't even contact him to let him know how the opening went, because he'll be away for a few days, shooting in Scotland.'

'Curiouser and curiouser,' said Sebastian, as their empty plates were whisked away.

'So what does your father do?'

'He's a storyteller.'

'Aren't most men?'

'Yes, but he gets paid for it.'

'Then he must be very successful.'

'Number one on the *New York Times* bestseller list,' said Sebastian proudly.

'Harry Clifton, of course!'

'You've read my father's books?'

'No, I must confess I haven't, but my mother devours them. In fact, I gave her *William Warwick and the Double-edged Sword* for Christmas,' she said as two steaks were placed in front of them. 'Damn,' she added. 'I forgot to order any wine.'

'Water is just fine,' said Sebastian.

Sam ignored him. 'Half a bottle of Fleurie,' she said to the waiter.

'You're so bossy.'

'Why is a woman always described as bossy, when if a man did the same thing he'd be thought of as decisive, commanding, and displaying qualities of leadership?'

'You're a feminist!'

'And why shouldn't I be,' said Samantha, 'after what you lot have been up to for the past thousand years?'

'Have you ever read *The Taming of the Shrew*?' asked Seb with a grin.

'Written by a man four hundred years ago, when a woman wasn't even allowed to play the lead. And if Kate were alive today she'd probably be prime minister.'

Sebastian burst out laughing. 'You should meet my mother, Samantha. She's every bit as bossy, sorry, decisive, as you.'

'I told you, only my mother ever calls me Samantha, and my father when he's cross with me.'

'I already like your mother.'

'And your mother?'

'I adore my mother.'

'No, silly, what does she do?'

'She works for a shipping company.'

'Sounds interesting. What kind of work?'

'She works in the chairman's office,' he said as Samantha tasted the wine.

'Just what he wanted,' she told the waiter, who poured two glasses. She raised hers. 'What do the English say?'

'Cheers,' said Sebastian. 'And the Americans?'

'Here's looking at you, kid.'

'If that was meant to be a Humphrey Bogart impression, it was dreadful.'

'So tell me about Jessica. Was it always obvious how talented she was?'

'No, not really, because to begin with, there wasn't anyone to compare her with. Well, not until she got to the Slade.'

'I don't think that changed even then,' said Sam.

'Have you always been interested in art?'

'I started out wanting to be an artist, but the gods decided otherwise. Did you always want to be a banker?'

'No. I'd planned to go into the diplomatic corps like your father, but it didn't work out.'

The waiter returned to their table. 'Would you care for a dessert, madam?' he asked as he picked up their empty plates.

'No, thank you,' said Sebastian. 'She can't afford it.'

'But I just might like—'

'She just might like the bill,' said Sebastian.

'Yes, sir.'

'Now who's being bossy?' said Samantha.

'Don't you think conversations on first dates are weird?'

'Is this a first date?'

'I hope so,' said Sebastian, wondering if he dared to touch her hand.

Samantha gave him such a warm smile that he felt confident enough to say, 'Can I ask you a personal question?'

'Yes, of course, Seb.'

'Do you have a boyfriend?'

'Yes I do,' she replied, sounding rather serious.

Sebastian couldn't hide his disappointment. 'Tell me about him,' he managed, as the waiter returned with the bill.

'He's coming into the gallery on Thursday to pick up some pictures, and I've invited him to attend the opening of Mr Mystery Man's exhibition the following Monday. By then, I'm rather hoping,' she said as she checked the bill, 'he'll have enough in his bank account to take *me* out to dinner.'

Sebastian blushed as she handed the waiter two pounds and said, 'Keep the change.'

'This is a first for me,' admitted Sebastian.

Samantha smiled, leant across the table and took his hand. 'Me too.'

SEBASTIAN CLIFTON

1964

31

CEDRIC LOOKED around the table, but didn't speak until everyone had settled.

'I'm sorry to drag you all in at such short notice, but Martinez has left me with no choice.' Suddenly everyone was fully alert. 'I have good reason to believe,' he continued, 'that Martinez is planning to offload his entire shareholding in Barrington's when the Stock Exchange opens a week tomorrow. He's hoping to get as much of his original investment back as possible while the shares are riding high, and at the same time to bring the company to its knees. He'll be doing this exactly one week before the AGM, at the very time when we most need the public to have confidence in us. If he were to pull it off, Barrington's could be bankrupt in a matter of days.'

'Is that legal?' asked Harry.

Cedric turned to his son, who was sitting on his right. 'He would only be breaking the law,' said Arnold, 'if he intends to buy the shares back at a lower price, and that clearly isn't his game plan.'

'But could the share price really be hit that badly? After all, it's only one person who's putting his stock on the market.'

'If any shareholder who had a representative on a company's board were to put over a million of its shares on the market without warning or explanation, the City would assume the worst, and there would be a stampede to get out of the stock. The share price could halve in a matter of hours, even minutes.' Cedric waited for the implications of his words to sink in before he added, 'However, we are not beaten yet, because we have one thing going for us.'

'And what might that be?' asked Emma, trying to remain calm.

'We know exactly what he's up to, so we can play him at his own game. But if we are to do that, we'll have to move fast, and we can't hope to succeed unless everyone around this table is willing to accept my recommendations and the risks that go with them.'

'Before you tell us what you have in mind,' said Emma, 'I should warn you, that's not the only thing Martinez has planned for that week.' Cedric sat back. 'Alex Fisher is going to resign as a non-executive director on the Friday, just three days before the AGM.'

'Is that such a bad thing?' asked Giles. 'After all, Fisher has never really supported you or the company.'

'In normal circumstances I'd agree with you, Giles, but in his resignation letter, which I haven't yet received, although I know it's dated the Friday before the AGM, Fisher claims he's been left with no choice but to resign, because he believes the company is facing bankruptcy, and his only responsibility is to protect the interests of the shareholders.'

'That will be a first,' said Giles. 'In any case, it's simply not true, and should be easy to refute.'

'You'd have thought so, Giles,' said Emma. 'But how many of your colleagues in the House of Commons still believe you had a heart attack in Brussels, despite you denying it a thousand times?' Giles didn't respond.

'How do you know Fisher is going to resign if you haven't received the letter?' asked Cedric.

'I can't answer that question, but I can assure you that my source is impeccable.'

'So Martinez plans to hit us on Monday week when he sells his stock,' said Cedric, 'and to follow it up on the following Friday with Fisher's resignation.'

'Which would leave me with no choice,' said Emma, 'but to postpone the naming ceremony with the Queen Mother, not to mention the date of the maiden voyage.'

'Game, set and match Martinez,' said Sebastian.

'What are you advising we should do, Cedric?' asked Emma, ignoring her son.

'Kick him in the balls,' said Giles, 'and preferably when he's not looking.'

'I couldn't have put it better myself,' said Cedric, 'and frankly, that's exactly what I have in mind. Let us assume that Martinez is planning to place all his shares on the market in eight days' time, and then follow it up four days later with Fisher's resignation, which he hopes will be a double-whammy that will both bring the company down and cause Emma to resign. In order to counter this, we must land the first punch, and it has to be a sucker punch delivered when he least expects it. With that in mind, I plan to sell all my own shares, three hundred and eighty thousand of them, this Friday, for whatever price I can get.'

'But how will that help?' asked Giles.

'I'm hoping that I will have caused the shares to collapse by the following Monday, so that when Martinez's stock comes on the market at nine o'clock that morning, he'll stand to lose a fortune. That's when I intend to kick him in the balls, because I already have a buyer lined up for his million shares at the new low price, so they shouldn't be on the market for more than a few minutes.'

'Is this the man none of us knows, but who hates Martinez as much as we do?' asked Harry.

Arnold Hardcastle put a hand on his father's arm and whispered, 'Don't answer that question, Pop.'

'Even if you pull it off,' said Emma, 'I'll still have to explain to the press and the shareholders at the AGM a week later why the share price has collapsed.'

'Not if I return to the market the moment Martinez's shares have been picked up, and start buying aggressively, only stopping when the price has returned to its present level.'

'But you told us that was against the law.'

'When I said "I", what I meant was—'

'Don't say another word, Pop,' said Arnold firmly.

'But if Martinez was to discover what you were up to . . .' began Emma.

'We won't let him,' said Cedric, 'because we're all going to work to his timetable, as Seb will now explain.'

Sebastian rose from his place, and faced the toughest first-night audience in the West End. 'Martinez plans to travel up to Scotland at the weekend for some grouse-shooting, and he won't be returning to London until Tuesday morning.'

'How can you be so sure, Seb?' asked his father.

'Because his entire art collection is coming up for sale at Agnew's on the Monday night, and he's told the proprietor of the gallery that he can't attend, as he won't be back in London by then.'

'I find it strange,' said Emma, 'that he doesn't want to be around on the day he's getting rid of all his shares in the company, and selling his art collection.'

'That's easy to explain,' said Cedric. 'If Barrington's looks as if it's in trouble, he will want to be as far away as possible, preferably somewhere where no one will be able to contact him, leaving you to handle the baying press and the irate shareholders.'

'Do we know where he'll be staying in Scotland?' asked Giles.

'Not at the moment,' said Cedric, 'but I called Ross Buchanan last night. He's a first-class shot himself, and tells me there are only about six hotels and shooting lodges north of the border that Martinez would consider good enough for him to celebrate the glorious twelfth. Ross is going to spend the next couple of days visiting all of them until he discovers which one Martinez is booked into.'

'Is there anything the rest of us can do to help?' asked Harry.

'Just act normally. Especially you, Emma. You must appear to be preparing for the AGM and the launching of the *Buckingham*. Leave Seb and me to fine-tune the rest of the operation.'

'But even if you did manage to pull off the share coup,' said Giles, 'that still wouldn't solve the problem of Fisher's resignation.'

'I've already set a plan in motion for dealing with Fisher.'

Everyone waited expectantly.

'You're not going to tell us what you're up to, are you?' said Emma eventually.

'No,' replied Cedric. 'My lawyer,' he added, touching his son's arm, 'has advised against it.'

32

CEDRIC PICKED UP the phone on his desk, and immediately recognized the slight Scottish burr.

'Martinez is booked into Glenleven Lodge, from Friday the fourteenth of August until Monday the seventeenth.'

'That sounds a long way away.'

'It's in the middle of nowhere.'

'What else did you find out?'

'He and his two sons visit Glenleven twice a year, in March and August. They always book the same three rooms on the second floor, and they eat all their meals in Don Pedro's suite, never in the dining room.'

'Did you find out when they're expected?'

'Aye. They'll be catching the sleeper to Edinburgh next Thursday evening, and will be picked up by the hotel driver around 5.30 the following morning, and driven straight to Glenleven in time for breakfast. Martinez likes kippers, brown toast and English marmalade.'

'I'm impressed. How long did all that take you?'

'Over three hundred miles of driving through the Highlands, and checking several hotels and lodges. After a few drams in the bar at Glenleven, I even knew what his favourite cocktail is.'

'So with a bit of luck I'll have a clear run from the moment they're picked up by the lodge's driver on Friday morning, until they arrive back in London the following Tuesday evening.'

'Unless something unforeseen happens.'

'It always does, and there's no reason to believe it will be any different this time.'

'I'm sure you're right,' said Ross. 'Which is why I'll be at Waverley station on Friday morning, and as soon as the three of them set off for Glenleven, I'll phone you. Then all you'll have to do is wait for the Stock Exchange to open at nine o'clock, when you can start trading.'

'Will you be returning to Glenleven?'

'Yes, I've booked a room at the lodge, but Jean and I won't be checking in until some time on Friday afternoon, for what I hope will be a quiet weekend in the Highlands. I'll only ring you if an emergency arises. Otherwise you won't hear from me again until Tuesday morning, and only then after I've seen the three of them boarding the train back to London.'

'By which time it will be too late for Martinez to do anything about it.'

'Well, that's plan A.'

Wednesday morning

'Let's just, for a moment, consider what could go wrong,' said Diego, looking across at his father.

'What do you have in mind?' asked Don Pedro.

'The other side have somehow worked out what we're up to, and are just waiting for us to be holed up in Scotland so they can take advantage of your absence.'

'But we've always kept everything in the family,' said Luis.

'Ledbury isn't family, and he knows we're selling our shares on Monday morning. Fisher isn't family, and he'll feel no obligation to us once he's handed in his letter of resignation.'

'Are you sure you're not overreacting?' said Don Pedro.

'Possibly. But I'd still prefer to join you in Glenleven a day later. That way I'll know the price of Barrington's shares when the market closes on Friday evening. If they're still above the price we originally paid for them, I'll feel more relaxed about putting more than a million of our shares on the market on Monday morning.'

'You'll miss a day's shooting.'

'That's preferable to two million pounds going missing.'

'Fair enough. I'll have the driver pick you up from Waverley station first thing on Saturday morning.'

'Why don't we cover all our options,' said Diego, 'and make sure no one is double-crossing us?'

'So what do you suggest?'

'Phone the bank and tell Ledbury you've changed your mind, and you won't be selling the shares on Monday after all.'

'But I have no choice if my plan is to have any chance of succeeding.'

'We'll still sell the shares. I'll place the order with another broker just before I leave for Scotland on Friday evening, and only if the shares have maintained their value. That way we can't lose.'

Thursday morning

Tom parked the Daimler outside Agnew's in Bond Street.

Cedric had given Sebastian an hour off to collect Jessica's pictures, and had even allowed him the use of his car so that he could get back to the office quickly. He almost ran into the gallery.

'Good morning, sir.'

'"Good morning, sir"? Aren't you the lady I had supper with on Saturday night?'

'Yes, but it's a gallery rule,' Sam whispered. 'Mr Agnew doesn't approve of the staff being familiar with the customers.'

'Good morning, Miss Sullivan. I've come to collect my pictures,' said Sebastian, trying to sound like a customer.

'Yes, of course, sir. Will you come with me?'

He followed her downstairs, and didn't speak again until she'd unlocked the door to the stock room, where several neatly wrapped packages were propped against the wall. Sam picked up two, while Sebastian managed three. They carried them back upstairs, out of the gallery, and placed them in the boot of the car. As they walked back inside, Mr Agnew came out of his office.

'Good morning, Mr Clifton.'

'Good morning, sir. I've just come to collect my pictures.'

Agnew nodded as Sebastian followed Samantha back down the stairs. By the time he caught up with her, she was already carrying two more packages. There were another two left, but Sebastian only picked up one of them, as he wanted an excuse to come back downstairs with her again. When he reached the ground floor, there was no sign of Mr Agnew.

'Couldn't you manage the last two?' said Sam. 'You are so feeble.'

'No, I left one behind,' said Sebastian with a grin.

'Then I'd better go and fetch it.'

'And I'd better come and help you.'

'How kind of you, sir.'

'My pleasure, Miss Sullivan.'

Once they were back in the stock room, Sebastian closed the door. 'Are you free for dinner tonight?'

'Yes, but you'll have to pick me up here. We still haven't completed the hanging for next Monday's exhibition, so I won't be able to get away much before eight.'

'I'll be standing outside the door at eight,' he said as he put his arm around her waist and leant forward . . .

'Miss Sullivan?'

'Yes, sir,' said Sam. She quickly opened the door and ran back upstairs.

Sebastian followed, trying to look nonchalant, and then remembered neither of them had picked up the last painting. He shot back downstairs, grabbed the picture and quickly returned to find Mr Agnew talking to Sam. She didn't look at him as he strolled past her.

'Perhaps we could go over the list once you've dealt with your customer.'

'Yes, sir.'

Tom was placing the last picture in the boot when Samantha joined Sebastian on the pavement.

'Like the wheels,' she said. 'And a chauffeur to go with them. Not bad for a guy who can't afford to take a shop girl out to dinner.'

Tom grinned and gave her a mock salute before getting back into the car.

'Neither of them is mine, unfortunately,' said Sebastian. 'The car belongs to my boss, and he only said I could borrow it when I told him I had an assignation with a beautiful young woman.'

'Not much of an assignation,' she said.

'I'll try a little harder tonight.'

'I'll look forward to that, sir.'

'I only wish it could have been sooner, but this week . . .' he said without explanation as he closed the boot of the car. 'Thank you for your help, Miss Sullivan.'

'My pleasure, sir. I do hope we'll see you again.'

Thursday afternoon

'Cedric, it's Stephen Ledbury from the Midland.'

'Good morning, Stephen.'

'I've just had a call from the gentleman in question to say that he's changed his mind. He won't be selling his Barrington's shares after all.'

'Did he give a reason?' asked Cedric.

'He told me he now believes in the long-term future of the company, and would prefer to hold on to the stock.'

'Thank you, Stephen. Please let me know if anything changes.'

'I most certainly will, because I still haven't cleared my debt with you.'

'Oh yes, you have,' said Cedric without explanation. He put down the phone and wrote down the three words that told him everything he needed to know.

Thursday evening

Sebastian arrived at King's Cross station just after seven. He walked up the steps to the first level and stood in the shadow of the large four-sided clock which allowed him an uninterrupted view of *The Night Scotsman* standing at platform five waiting to transport 130 overnight passengers to Edinburgh.

Cedric had told him he needed to be certain that all three of them had boarded the train before he could risk releasing his own shares on to the market. Sebastian watched as Don Pedro Martinez, with all the swaggering confidence of a Middle Eastern potentate, and his son Luis strode on to the platform just minutes before the train was due to depart. They made their way to the far end of the train and stepped into a first-class carriage. Why wasn't Diego with them?

A few minutes later, the guard blew his whistle twice and waved his green flag with a flourish, and *The Night Scotsman* set off on its journey north with only two Martinezes on board. Once Sebastian could no longer see the plume of white smoke coming from the train's funnel, he ran to the nearest telephone box and phoned Mr Hardcastle on his private line.

'Diego didn't get on the train.'

'His second mistake,' Cedric said. 'I need you to come back to the office immediately. Something else has come up.'

Sebastian would have liked to tell Cedric that he had a date with a beautiful young woman, but this was not the time to suggest he might have a private life. He dialled the gallery, put four pennies into the box, pressed button A and waited until he heard the unmistakable voice of Mr Agnew on the other end of the line.

'Can I speak to Miss Sullivan?'

'Miss Sullivan no longer works here.'

Thursday evening

Sebastian had only one thought on his mind as Tom drove him back to the bank. What could Mr Agnew have meant by 'Miss Sullivan no longer works here'? Why would Sam give up a job she enjoyed so much? Surely she couldn't have been sacked? Perhaps she was ill, but she'd been there that morning. He still hadn't solved the mystery by the time Tom parked outside the front entrance of Farthings. And worse, he had no way of contacting her.

Sebastian took the lift to the top floor and went straight to the chairman's office. He knocked on the door and walked in, to find a meeting in progress.

'Sorry, I'll—'

'No, come in, Seb,' said Cedric. 'You remember my son,' he added as Arnold Hardcastle walked purposefully towards him.

As they shook hands, Arnold whispered, 'Only answer the questions that are put to you, don't volunteer anything.' Sebastian looked at the two other men in the room. He'd never seen either of them before. They didn't offer to shake his hand.

'Arnold is here to represent you,' said Cedric. 'I have already told the detective inspector that I am sure there must be a simple explanation.'

Sebastian had no idea what Cedric was talking about.

The older of the two strangers took a pace forward. 'My name is Detective Inspector Rossindale. I'm stationed at Savile Row police station, and I have a few questions to ask you, Mr Clifton.'

Sebastian knew from his father's novels that detective inspectors didn't get involved in minor crimes. He nodded, but followed Arnold's instructions and didn't say anything.

'Did you visit Agnew's Gallery in Bond Street earlier today?'

'Yes, I did.'

'And what was the purpose of that visit?'

'To pick up some pictures I bought last week.'

'And were you assisted by a Miss Sullivan?'

'Yes.'

'And where are those pictures now?'

'They're in the boot of Mr Hardcastle's car. I was intending to take them back to my flat later this evening.'

'Were you? And where is that car now?'

'Parked outside the front of the bank.'

The detective inspector turned his attention to Cedric Hardcastle. 'May I borrow your car keys, sir?'

Cedric glanced at Arnold, who nodded. Cedric said, 'My

chauffeur has them. He'll be downstairs waiting to take me home.'

'With your permission, sir, I'll go and check if the paintings are where Mr Clifton claims they are.'

'We have no objection to that,' said Arnold.

'Sergeant Webber, you will remain here,' said Rossindale, 'and make sure Mr Clifton does not leave this room.' The young officer nodded.

'What the hell is going on?' asked Sebastian after the detective inspector had left the room.

'You're doing just fine,' said Arnold. 'But I think it might be wise, given the circumstances, if you don't say anything more,' he added looking directly at the young policeman.

'However,' said Cedric, standing between the policeman and Sebastian, 'I'd like to ask the master criminal to confirm that only two people boarded the train.'

'Yes, Don Pedro and Luis. There was no sign of Diego.'

'They're playing right into our hands,' said Cedric as DI Rossindale reappeared holding three packages. He was followed a moment later by a sergeant and a constable who were carrying the other six between them. They propped them all against the wall.

'Are these the nine packages you took from the gallery with the assistance of Miss Sullivan?' asked the detective inspector.

'Yes,' said Sebastian without hesitation.

'Do I have your permission to unwrap them?'

'Yes, of course.'

The three policemen set about removing the brown paper that covered the pictures. Suddenly Sebastian gasped, and pointing at one of the paintings said, 'My sister didn't paint that.'

'It's quite magnificent,' said Arnold.

'I wouldn't know about that, sir,' said Rossindale, 'but I can confirm,' he added, looking at the label on the back, 'that it wasn't painted by Jessica Clifton, but by someone called Raphael, and is, according to Mr Agnew, worth at least one hundred thousand pounds.' Sebastian looked confused, but didn't say anything. 'And we have reason to believe,' Rossindale continued, looking directly at Sebastian, 'that you, in collaboration with Miss Sullivan, used the pretext of collecting your sister's paintings to steal this valuable work of art.'

'But that doesn't make any sense,' said Arnold, before Sebastian had a chance to respond.

'I beg your pardon, sir?'

'Think about it, detective inspector. If, as you suggest, my client, with Miss Sullivan's assistance, stole the Raphael from Agnew's, would you expect to find it in the boot of his employer's car several hours later? Or are you suggesting that the chairman's chauffeur was also in on it, or perhaps even the chairman himself?'

'Mr Clifton,' said Rossindale, checking his notebook, 'did admit that he intended to take the pictures back to his flat later this evening.'

'Isn't it just possible that a Raphael might look a little out of place in a bachelor flat in Fulham?'

'This is not a laughing matter, sir. Mr Agnew, who reported the theft, is a highly respected West End art dealer, and—'

'It's not a theft, detective inspector, unless you can prove that it was taken with intent to deprive. And as you haven't even asked my client for his side of the story, I can't see how you can possibly come to that conclusion.'

The officer turned to Sebastian, who was counting the pictures.

'I'm guilty,' said Sebastian. The detective smiled. 'Not of theft, but infatuation.'

'Perhaps you'd care to explain yourself.'

'There were nine pictures by my sister, Jessica Clifton, at the Slade's graduation exhibition, and there are only eight of them here. So if the other one is still at the gallery, then, mea culpa, I picked up the wrong one, and I apologize for what is no more than a simple mistake.'

'A one hundred thousand pound mistake,' said Rossindale.

'May I suggest, detective inspector,' said Arnold, 'without wishing to be accused of levity, that it is not usual for a master criminal to leave evidence at the scene of the crime that points directly to him.'

'We don't know that to be the case, Mr Hardcastle.'

'Then I recommend we all go to the gallery and see if the missing Jessica Clifton, the property of my client, is still there.'

'I'll need more than that to convince me of his innocence,' said Rossindale. He took Sebastian firmly by the arm, led him out of the room, and didn't let go until he was in the back of the police car with a burly constable seated on either side of him.

Sebastian's only thought was of what Samantha must be going through. On the way to the gallery he asked the detective inspector if she would be there.

'Miss Sullivan is presently at Savile Row police station being interviewed by one of my officers.'

'But she's innocent,' said Sebastian. 'If anyone's to blame, it has to be me.'

'I must remind you, sir, that a one hundred thousand pound painting went missing from the gallery at which she was an assistant, and has now been recovered from the boot of the car in which you placed it.'

Sebastian recalled Arnold's advice, and said nothing more. Twenty minutes later the police car drew up outside Agnew's. The chairman's car was not too far behind, with Cedric and Arnold seated in the back.

The detective inspector climbed out of the car, clinging on to the Raphael, while another officer rang the doorbell. Mr Agnew quickly appeared, unlocked the door and stared lovingly at the masterpiece as if he was being reunited with a lost child.

When Sebastian explained what must have happened, Agnew said, 'That shouldn't be too difficult to prove one way or the other.' Without another word, he led them all downstairs to the basement and unlocked the door to the stock room, where there were several wrapped pictures waiting to be delivered.

Sebastian held his breath as Mr Agnew studied each label carefully until he came across one marked Jessica Clifton.

'Would you be kind enough to unwrap it,' said Rossindale.

'Certainly,' said Mr Agnew. He painstakingly removed the wrapping paper, to reveal a drawing of Sebastian.

Arnold couldn't stop laughing. 'Entitled *Portrait of a Master Criminal*, no doubt.'

Even the detective inspector allowed himself a wry smile, but he reminded Arnold, 'We mustn't forget that Mr Agnew has filed charges.'

'And of course I shall withdraw them, as I can now see that there was no intention to steal. Indeed,' he said, turning to Sebastian, 'I owe you and Sam an apology.'

'Does that mean she'll get her job back?'

'Certainly not,' said Agnew firmly. 'I accept that she was not involved in a criminal act, but she was still guilty of either gross negligence or stupidity, and we both know, Mr Clifton, that she isn't stupid.'

'But it was me who picked up the wrong picture.'

'And it was she who allowed you to take it off the premises.'

Sebastian frowned. 'Mr Rossindale, can I come back to the police station with you? I'm meant to be taking Samantha out to dinner this evening.'

'I can't see any reason why you shouldn't.'

'Thank you for your help, Arnold,' said Sebastian, shaking the QC by the hand. Turning to Cedric, he added, 'I'm sorry to have caused you so much trouble, sir.'

'Just be sure that you're back in the office by seven tomorrow morning, as you'll remember it's a rather important day for all of us. And I must say, Seb, you could have picked a better week to steal a Raphael.'

Everyone laughed except Mr Agnew, who was still clutching the masterpiece. He placed it back in the stock room, double-locked the door and led them all upstairs. 'My thanks, detective inspector,' he said as Rossindale was leaving the gallery.

'My pleasure, sir. I'm glad this one worked out for the best.'

When Sebastian climbed into the back of the police car, Detective Inspector Rossindale said, 'I'll tell you why I was so convinced you'd stolen the painting, young man. Your girlfriend took the blame, which usually means they're protecting someone.'

'I'm not sure she'll be my girlfriend any longer after what I've put her through.'

'I'll get her released as quickly as possible,' said Rossindale. 'Just the usual paperwork,' he added with a sigh as the car drew up outside Savile Row station. Sebastian followed the policemen into the building.

'Take Mr Clifton down to the cells while I deal with the paperwork.'

The young sergeant led Sebastian down a flight of steps, unlocked a cell door and stood aside to allow him to go in. Samantha was hunched up on the end of a thin mattress, her knees tucked under her chin.

'Seb! Have they arrested you as well?'

'No,' he said, taking her in his arms for the first time. 'I don't think they'd allow us to be in the same cell if they thought we were London's answer to Bonnie and Clyde. Once Mr Agnew found Jessica's painting in the stock room, he accepted that I'd just picked up the wrong package and dropped all the charges. But I'm afraid you've lost your job, and it was my fault.'

'I can't blame him,' said Samantha. 'I should have been concentrating, not flirting. But I'm beginning to wonder just how far you'll go to avoid taking me to dinner.' Sebastian released her, looked into her eyes and then gently kissed her.

'They say a girl always remembers the first kiss with a man she's fallen in love with, and I must admit it's going to be quite difficult to forget this one,' she said as the cell door swung open.

'You're free to go now, miss,' said the young sergeant. 'Sorry about the misunderstanding.'

'Not your fault,' said Samantha. The sergeant led them upstairs and held the front door of the station open.

Sebastian walked out on to the street and took Samantha's hand, just as a dark blue Cadillac came to a halt in front of the building.

'Oh hell,' said Samantha. 'I forgot. The police allowed me to make one call and I phoned the embassy. They told me my parents were at the opera, but that they'd get them out in the interval. Oh hell,' she repeated as Mr and Mrs Sullivan stepped out of the car.

'So what's all this about, Samantha?' said Mr Sullivan after he'd kissed her on the cheek. 'Your mother and I have been desperately worried.'

'I'm sorry,' said Sam, 'it's all been a dreadful misunderstanding.'

'That's a relief,' said her mother and, looking across at the man who was holding her daughter's hand, asked, 'And who is this?'

'Oh, this is Sebastian Clifton. He's the man I'm going to marry.'

33

'You were right. Diego will be taking the sleeper from King's Cross this evening, and joining his father and Luis at Glenleven Lodge tomorrow morning.'

'How can you be so sure?'

'The receptionist told my wife that a car would be picking him up in the morning and bringing him straight to the lodge in time for breakfast. I could drive to Edinburgh tomorrow morning and double-check.'

'No need. Seb is off to King's Cross again this evening to make sure he gets on the train. That's assuming he's not arrested for stealing a Raphael.'

'Did I hear you correctly?' asked Ross.

'Another time, because I'm still trying to work out what Plan B is.'

'Well, you can't risk selling any of your own shares while Diego's still in London, because if the price were suddenly to collapse, Don Pedro would work out what you're up to, and wouldn't place his shares on the market.'

'Then I'm beaten, because there's no point in buying Martinez's shares at full price. He'd like nothing better.'

'We're not beaten yet. I've come up with a couple of ideas for you to consider – that is, if you're still willing to take one hell of a risk?'

'I'm listening,' said Cedric, picking up a pen and opening his notepad.

'At eight o'clock on Monday morning, an hour before the market opens, you could contact all the leading brokers in the City and let them know that you're a buyer of Barrington's stock. When Martinez's million-odd shares come on the market at nine, the first person they'll call will be you, because the commission on a sale of that size will be enormous.'

'But if the shares are still at their high point, the only person who will gain from that will be Martinez.'

'I did say I had a couple of ideas,' said Ross.

'Sorry,' said Cedric.

'Just because the Stock Exchange closes for business at four on Friday afternoon, it doesn't mean you can't go on trading. New York will still be open for another five hours, and LA for eight. And if you haven't disposed of all your shares by then, Sydney opens for business at midnight on Sunday. And if, after all that, you still have a few shares left, Hong Kong will happily assist you to get rid of them. So by the time the Stock Exchange opens in London at nine o'clock on Monday morning, my bet is that Barrington's shares will be trading at around half the price they were at close of business today.'

'Brilliant,' said Cedric. 'Except I don't know any brokers in New York, Los Angeles, Sydney or Hong Kong.'

'You only need one,' said Ross. 'Abe Cohen of Cohen, Cohen and Yablon. Like Sinatra, he only works at night. Just tell him you have three hundred and eighty thousand Barrington's shares that you want off your hands by Monday morning London time, and believe me, he'll stay up all weekend earning his commission. Mind you, if Martinez finds out what you're up to and doesn't put his million-plus shares on the market on Monday morning, you'll stand to lose a small fortune, and he'll chalk up another victory.'

'I know he's going to put them on the market on Monday,' said Cedric, 'because he told Stephen Ledbury that the reason he no longer wanted to sell them was because he now believed in the "long-term future" of the company, and that's the one thing I know for certain he doesn't believe in.'

'It's not a risk any self-respecting Scotsman would take.'

'But it is a risk a cautious, dull, boring Yorkshireman has decided to take.'

Friday night

Sebastian couldn't even be sure if he'd recognize him. After all, it had been over seven years since he'd last come across Diego in Buenos Aires. He remembered that he was at least a couple of inches taller than Bruno, and certainly slimmer than Luis whom he'd seen more recently. Diego was a snappy dresser: double-breasted suits from Savile Row, wide colourful silk ties and black Brylcreemed hair.

Seb turned up at King's Cross an hour before the train was due to depart, and once again took up his position in the shadow of the large, four-sided clock.

The Night Scotsman was standing at the platform waiting for its overnight passengers to board. Some had already arrived, barely a trickle, the kind of traveller who'd prefer having time to spare rather than risk being late. Diego, Sebastian suspected, was the type who left it to the last moment, not wanting to waste any time hanging about.

As he waited, his mind turned to Sam, and what had been the happiest week of his life. How could he have got so lucky? He found himself smiling whenever he thought about her. They had gone to dinner that evening, and once again he hadn't paid; a swanky restaurant in Mayfair called Scott's, where the guests' menus don't show the prices. But then, Mr and Mrs Sullivan had clearly wanted to get to know the man their daughter had told them she was going to marry, even if she was only teasing.

Sebastian had been nervous to begin with. After all, in less than a week he had caused Samantha to be arrested and sacked. However, by the time the pudding was served – and on this occasion he did have some pudding – the whole 'misunderstanding', as it was now being called, had moved from high melodrama to low farce.

Sebastian had begun to relax once Mrs Sullivan told him how much she was hoping to visit Bristol, so she could get to know the city where Detective Sergeant William Warwick worked. He promised to introduce her to 'The Warwick Walk', and by the time the evening came to an end, he wasn't in any doubt that Mrs Sullivan was far more familiar with his father's work than he was. After saying goodnight to Sam's parents, they had strolled back to her flat in Pimlico together, the way two lovers do when they don't want an evening to end.

Sebastian remained in the shadow of the clock, which began to strike the hour.

'The train on platform three is the twenty-two thirty-five non-stop service to Edinburgh,' announced a strangulated voice that sounded as if he was auditioning to read the news for the BBC. 'First class is at the front of the train, third class at the rear, with the dining car in the centre of the train.' Sebastian wasn't in any doubt which class Diego would be in.

He tried to put Sam out of his mind and focus; not that easy. Five minutes, ten minutes, fifteen minutes passed, and although a steady stream of passengers was now arriving on platform three, there was still no sign of Diego. Sebastian knew that Cedric was at his desk, impatiently waiting for the phone to ring with confirmation that Diego had boarded the sleeper. Not until then could he give Abe Cohen the go-ahead.

If Diego failed to turn up, Cedric had already decided that the game wouldn't be worth the candle, to quote Mr Sherlock Holmes. He couldn't risk placing all his shares on the market while Diego remained in London, because if he did, it would be Martinez who would end up blowing the candle out.

Twenty minutes, and although the platform was now crowded with latecomers, porters by their sides wheeling heavy bags, there was still no sign of Señor Diego Martinez. Sebastian began to despair when he saw the guard step out of the rear carriage, green flag in one hand, whistle in the other. Seb looked up at the vast black minute hand on the clock that bounced forward every sixty seconds. 10.22. Was all the work Cedric had put in going to be for nothing? He'd once told Sebastian that when you set out on a project, always be willing to accept that a one-in-five success rate is par for the course. Was this going to fall into the 'four out of five' category? His thoughts turned to Ross Buchanan; was he waiting at Glenleven Lodge for someone who wasn't going to turn up? He then thought about his mother, who had more to lose than any of them.

And then a man appeared on the platform who caught his eye. He was carrying a suitcase, but Sebastian couldn't be sure if it was Diego, because the stylish brown trilby and upturned velvet collar of his long black coat hid his face. The man walked straight past third class and towards the front of the train, which gave Sebastian a little more hope.

A porter was walking down the platform towards him, slamming the first-class carriage doors shut one by one: bang, bang, bang. When he spotted the approaching man, he stopped and held a door open for him. Sebastian stepped out of the shadow of the clock and tried to get a better look at his quarry. The man with the suitcase was just about to step on to the train when he turned and looked up at the clock. He hesitated. Sebastian froze, and then the man stepped on board. The porter slammed the door closed.

Diego had been among the last passengers to board the train, and Sebastian didn't move as he watched *The Night Scotsman* make its way out of the station, slowly gathering speed as it set out on the long journey to Edinburgh.

He shivered as he experienced a moment of apprehension. Of course Diego couldn't have seen him at that distance, and, in any case, Sebastian was looking for him, not the other way round. He walked slowly across to the phone booths on the far side of the concourse, coins ready. He dialled a number that went straight through to the chairman's desk. After only one ring, a familiar gruff voice came on the line.

'He almost missed the train, turned up at the very last moment. But he's now on his way to Edinburgh.' Sebastian heard a pent-up sigh being released.

'Have a good weekend, my boy,' said Cedric. 'You've earned it. But make sure you're in the office by eight on Monday morning, because I have a particular job for you. And do try to steer clear of any art galleries over the weekend.'

Sebastian laughed, put the phone down and allowed his thoughts to return to Sam.

As soon as he had hung up on Sebastian, Cedric dialled the number Ross Buchanan had given him. A voice on the other end of the line said, 'Cohen.'

'The sale is on. What was the closing price in London?'

'Two pounds and eight shillings,' said Cohen. 'Up a shilling on the day.'

'Good, then I'll be placing all three hundred and eighty thousand shares on the market, and I want you to sell them at the best possible price, remembering that I need to be rid of them by the time the London Stock Exchange opens on Monday morning.'

'Understood, Mr Hardcastle. How often would you like me to report to you over the weekend?'

'Eight o'clock on Saturday morning and at the same time on Monday morning.'

'It's lucky I'm not an Orthodox Jew,' said Cohen.

34

IT WAS TO BE a night of firsts.

Sebastian took Sam to a Chinese restaurant in Soho, and paid the bill. After dinner they walked down to Leicester Square and joined a queue for the cinema. Samantha loved the film Sebastian had chosen, and as they left the Odeon, she confessed that until she came to England, she'd never heard of Ian Fleming, Sean Connery or even James Bond.

'Where have you been all your life?' mocked Sebastian.

'In America, with Katharine Hepburn, Jimmy Stewart, and a young actor who's taking Hollywood by storm, called Steve McQueen.'

'Never heard of him,' said Sebastian as he took her hand. 'Do we have anything in common?'

'Jessica,' she said gently.

Sebastian smiled as they walked back to her Pimlico flat hand in hand, chatting.

'Have you heard of The Beatles?'

'Yes, of course. John, Paul, George and Ringo.'

'The Goons?'

'No.'

'So you've never come across Bluebottle or Moriarty?'

'I thought Moriarty was Sherlock Holmes's nemesis?'

'No, he's Bluebottle's foil.'

'But have you heard of Little Richard?' she asked.

'No, but I've heard of Cliff Richard.'

Occasionally they stopped to share a kiss, and when they eventually arrived outside Sam's apartment block, she took out her key and kissed him gently again; a goodnight kiss.

Sebastian would have liked to be invited in for a coffee, but all she said was, 'See you tomorrow.' For the first time in his life, Seb wasn't in a hurry.

◄○►

Don Pedro and Luis were out on the moor shooting by the time Diego arrived at Glenleven Lodge. He didn't notice an elderly gentleman in a kilt seated in a high-back leather chair reading *The Scotsman* and looking as if he might have been part of the furniture.

An hour later, after he'd unpacked, taken a bath and changed, Diego came back downstairs dressed in plus-fours, brown leather boots and a deerstalker, clearly trying to look more English than the English. A Land Rover was waiting to whisk him up into the hills so he could join his father and his brother for the day's shoot. As he left the lodge, Ross was still sitting in the high-backed chair. If Diego had been a little more observant, he would have noticed that he was still reading the same page of the same newspaper.

'What was the price of Barrington's when the Stock Exchange closed?' was the first thing Don Pedro asked as his son stepped out of the car to join them.

'Two pounds and eight shillings.'

'Up a shilling. So you could have come up yesterday after all.'

'Shares don't usually rise on a Friday,' was all Diego said before his loader handed him a gun.

◄○►

Emma spent most of Saturday morning writing the first draft of a speech she still hoped to deliver at the AGM in nine days' time. She had to leave several blank spaces that could only be filled in as the week progressed, and in one or two cases just hours before the meeting was called to order.

She was grateful for everything Cedric was doing, but she didn't enjoy not being able to play a more hands-on role in the drama that was unfolding in London and Scotland.

Harry was out plotting that morning. While other men spent their Saturdays watching football in the winter and cricket in the summer, he went for long walks around the estate and plotted, so that by Monday morning, when he picked up his pen again, he would have worked out just how William Warwick could solve the crime. Harry and Emma had supper at the Manor House that evening, and went to bed soon after watching *Dr Finlay's Casebook*. Emma was still rehearsing her speech when she finally fell asleep.

Giles conducted his weekly surgery on Saturday morning, and listened to the complaints of eighteen of his constituents, which included matters ranging from the council's failure to empty a dustbin, to the question of how an Old Etonian toff like Sir Alec Douglas-Home could possibly begin to understand the problems of the working man.

After the last constituent had departed, Giles's agent took him to the Nova Scotia, this week's pub, to share a pint of ale and a Cornish pasty, and to be seen by the voters. At least another twenty constituents felt it their bounden duty to air their views to the local member on a myriad different issues, before he and Griff were allowed to depart for Ashton Gate to watch a pre-season friendly between Bristol City and Bristol Rovers, which ended in a nil–nil draw, and wasn't all that friendly.

Over six thousand supporters watched the match, and when the referee blew the final whistle, those leaving the ground weren't in any doubt which team Sir Giles supported, as he was wearing his red-and-white striped woollen scarf for all to see, but then, Griff regularly reminded him that 90 per cent of his constituents supported Bristol City.

As they headed out of the ground, more opinions, not always complimentary, were shouted at him, before Griff said, 'See you later.'

Giles drove back to Barrington Hall and joined Gwyneth, who was now heavily pregnant, for supper. Neither of them discussed politics. Giles didn't want to leave her, but just after nine, he heard a car coming down the drive. He kissed her, and went to the front door to find his agent standing on the doorstep.

Griff whisked him off to the dockers' club, where he played a couple of frames of snooker – one-all – and a round of darts, which he lost. He stood the lads several rounds of drinks, but as the date of the next general election had not yet been announced he couldn't be accused of bribery.

When Griff finally drove the member back to Barrington Hall that night, he reminded him that he had three church services to attend the following morning, at which he would sit among constituents who hadn't attended the morning surgery, watched the local derby or been at the dockers' club. He climbed into bed just before midnight, to find Gwyneth was fast asleep.

Grace spent her Saturday reading essays written by undergraduates, some of whom had finally woken up to the fact that they would be facing the examiners in less than a year. One of her brightest students, Emily Gallier, who'd done just about enough to get by, was now panicking. She was hoping to cover the three-year syllabus in three terms. Grace had no sympathy for her. She moved on to an essay by Elizabeth Rutledge, another clever girl, who hadn't stopped working from the day she'd arrived at Cambridge. Elizabeth was also in a panic, because she was anxious that she wouldn't get the first-class honours degree that everyone expected. Grace had a great deal of sympathy for her. After all, she'd had the same misgivings during her final year.

Grace climbed into bed soon after one, having marked the last essay. She slept soundly.

—◦—

Cedric had been at his desk for over an hour when the phone rang. He picked it up, not surprised to find Abe Cohen on the other end of the line, as clocks all around the City began to chime eight times.

'I managed to offload 186,000 shares in New York and Los

Angeles, and the price has fallen from two pounds and eight shillings to one pound and eighteen shillings.'

'Not a bad start, Mr Cohen.'

'Two down and two to go, Mr Hardcastle. I'll give you a call around eight on Monday morning to let you know how many the Australians picked up.'

Cedric left his office just after midnight, and when he arrived home, he didn't even make his nightly call to Beryl as she would already be asleep. She had accepted long ago that her husband's only mistress was Miss Farthings Bank. He lay awake tossing and turning as he thought about the next thirty-six hours, and realized why, for the previous forty years, he'd never taken risks.

＜◦＞

Ross and Jean Buchanan went on a long walk in the Highlands after lunch.

They returned around five, when Ross once again reported for 'guard duty'. The only difference being that this time he was reading an old copy of *Country Life*. He didn't move from his spot until he'd seen Don Pedro and his two sons return. Two of them looked rather pleased with themselves, but Diego appeared to be brooding. They all went up to their father's suite, and were not seen again that evening.

Ross and Jean had supper in the dining room, before climbing the one flight of stairs to their bedroom at around 9.40 p.m., when, as they always did, they both read for half an hour: she, Georgette Heyer, he, Alistair MacLean. When he finally turned out the light with the usual, 'Goodnight, my dear,' Ross fell into a deep sleep. After all, he had nothing more to do than make sure that the Martinez family didn't leave for London before Monday morning.

＜◦＞

When Don Pedro and his sons sat down for dinner in their suite that evening, Diego was singularly uncommunicative.

'Are you sulking because you shot fewer birds than I did?' taunted his father.

'Something's wrong,' he said, 'but I can't put my finger on it.'

'Well, let's hope you've worked it out by the morning, so we can all enjoy a good day's shooting.'

Once dinner had been cleared away just after nine thirty, Diego left them, and retired to his room. He lay on the bed, and tried to replay his arrival at King's Cross, frame by frame as if it was a black-and-white film. But he was so exhausted that he soon fell into a deep sleep.

He woke with a start at 6.25 a.m., a single frame in his mind.

35

WHEN ROSS returned from his walk with Jean on Sunday afternoon, he was looking forward to a hot bath, a cup of tea and a shortbread biscuit, before he went back on guard duty.

As they strolled up the drive towards Glenleven, he was not surprised to see the lodge's driver placing a suitcase in the boot of the car. After all, several guests would be checking out after a weekend's shooting. Ross was only interested in one particular guest, and as he wouldn't be leaving until Tuesday, he didn't give it a second thought.

They were climbing the staircase to their room on the first floor, when Diego Martinez came bounding past them, two steps at a time as if he was late for a meeting.

'Oh, I've left my newspaper on the hall table,' said Ross. 'You go on up, Jean, and I'll join you in a moment.'

Ross turned and walked back down the stairs, and tried not to stare as Diego chatted to the receptionist. He was heading slowly towards the tea room when Diego marched out of the lodge and climbed into the back seat of the waiting car. Ross changed direction and speed as he swung round and headed straight for the front door, and was just in time to see them disappearing down the drive. He ran back inside and went straight to the reception desk. The young girl gave him a warm smile.

'Good afternoon, Mr Buchanan, can I help you?'

This was not a time for small talk. 'I've just seen Mr Diego

Martinez leaving. I was thinking of inviting him to join my wife and me for supper this evening. Are you expecting him back later?'

'No, sir. Bruce is driving him into Edinburgh to catch the overnight sleeper to London. But Don Pedro and Mr Luis Martinez will be staying with us until Tuesday, so if you'd like to have dinner with them . . .'

'I need to make an urgent phone call.'

'I'm afraid the line's down, Mr Buchanan, and as I explained to Mr Martinez, it probably won't be back in service before tomorrow—'

Ross, normally a courteous man, turned and bolted for the front door without another word. He ran out of the lodge, jumped into his car and set out on an unscheduled journey. He made no attempt to catch up with Diego as he didn't want him to realize that he was being followed.

His mind moved into top gear. First, he considered the practical problems. Should he stop and phone Cedric to let him know what had happened? He decided against the idea; after all, his top priority was to make sure he didn't miss the train to London. If he had time when he reached Waverley, that's when he'd call Cedric to warn him that Diego was returning to London a day early.

His next thought was to take advantage of being on the board of British Railways, and get the booking office to refuse to issue Diego with a ticket. But that wouldn't serve any purpose, because he would then book into a hotel in Edinburgh and phone his broker before the market opened in the morning, when he'd discover that Barrington's share price had plummeted over the weekend, giving him more than enough time to cancel any plans to place his father's shares on the market. No, better to let him get on the train and then work out what to do next, not that he had the slightest idea what that might be.

Once he was on the main road to Edinburgh, Ross kept the speedometer at a steady sixty. There should be no problem getting a sleeping compartment on the train, as there was always one reserved for BR directors. He only hoped that none of his fellow board members were travelling down to London that night.

He cursed as he took the long route around the Firth of Forth Road Bridge, which wouldn't be open for another week. By the time he reached the outskirts of the city, he was no nearer to solving the problem of how to deal with Diego once they were on the train. He wished Harry Clifton was sitting next to him. By now he would have come up with a dozen scenarios. Mind you, if this was a novel, he would simply bump Diego off.

His reverie was rudely interrupted when he felt the engine shudder. He glanced at the petrol gauge to see a red light flashing. He cursed, banged the steering wheel, and began looking around for a petrol station. About a mile later, the shudder turned into a splutter and the car began to slow down, finally freewheeling to a halt by the side of the road. Ross checked his watch. There was still another forty minutes until the train was due to depart for London. He jumped out of the car and began running until he came to an out-of-breath halt by the side of a signpost that read, *City Centre 3 miles*. His days of running three miles in under forty minutes had long gone.

He stood by the side of the road and tried to thumb a lift. He must have cut an unlikely figure, dressed in his lovat green tweed jacket, a Buchanan clan kilt and long green stockings, doing something he hadn't done since he was at St Andrews University, and he hadn't been much good at it back then.

He changed tactics, and went in search of a taxi. This turned out to be another thankless task on a Sunday evening in that part of the city. And then he spotted his saviour, a red bus heading towards him, boldly proclaiming **CITY CENTRE** on the front. As it trundled past him, Ross turned and ran towards the bus stop as he'd never run before, hoping, praying that the driver would take pity on him and wait. His prayers were answered, and he climbed aboard and collapsed on to the front seat.

'Which stop?' asked the conductor.

'Waverley station,' puffed Ross.

'That'll be sixpence.'

Ross took out his wallet and handed him a ten-shilling note.

'Nae change for that.'

Ross searched in his pockets for any loose change, but he'd left it all in his bedroom at Glenleven Lodge. That wasn't the only thing he'd left there.

'Keep the change,' he said.

The astonished conductor pocketed the ten-bob note, and didn't wait for the passenger to change his mind. After all, Christmas doesn't usually come in August.

The bus had only travelled a few hundred yards before Ross spotted a petrol station, Macphersons, open twenty-four hours. He cursed again. He cursed a third time because he'd forgotten that buses make regular stops and don't just take you straight to where you want to go. He glanced at his watch whenever they came to a stop and again at every red light, but his watch didn't slow down and the bus didn't speed up. When the station finally came into sight, he had eight minutes to spare. Not enough time to ring Cedric. As he stepped off the bus, the conductor stood to attention and saluted him as if he was a visiting general.

Ross walked quickly into the station and headed for a train he had travelled on many times before. In fact, he had made the journey so often he could now have dinner, enjoy a leisurely drink and then sleep soundly throughout the entire 330 miles of clattering-over-points journey. But he had a feeling he wouldn't be sleeping tonight.

He received another, even smarter salute when he reached the barrier. Waverley ticket collectors pride themselves on recognizing every one of the company's directors at thirty paces.

'Good evening, Mr Buchanan,' the ticket collector said. 'I didn't realize you were travelling with us tonight.' I hadn't planned to, he wanted to say, but instead he simply returned the man's salutation, walked to the far end of the platform and climbed on board the train, with only minutes to spare.

As he headed down the corridor towards the directors' compartment, he saw the chief steward coming towards him. 'Good evening, Angus.'

'Good evening, Mr Buchanan. I didn't see your name on the first-class guest list.'

'No,' said Ross. 'It was a last-minute decision.'

'I'm afraid the director's compartment –' Ross's heart sank '– has not been made up, but if you'd like to have a drink in the dining car, I'll have it prepared immediately.'

'Thank you, Angus, I'll do just that.'

The first person Ross saw as he entered the dining car was an attractive young woman seated at the bar. She looked vaguely familiar. He ordered a whisky and soda and climbed on to the stool beside her. He thought about Jean, and felt guilty about abandoning her. Now he had no way of letting her know where he was until tomorrow morning. Then he remembered something else he'd abandoned. Worse, he hadn't made a note of the street where he'd left his car.

'Good evening, Mr Buchanan,' said the woman, to Ross's surprise. He gave her a second look, but still didn't recognize her. 'My name's Kitty,' she said, offering a gloved hand. 'I see you regularly on this train, but then, you are a director of British Railways.'

Ross smiled and took a sip of his drink. 'So what do you do that takes you to London and back so regularly?'

'I'm self-employed,' said Kitty.

'And what kind of business are you in?' asked Ross as the steward appeared by his side.

'Your compartment is ready, sir, if you'd like to follow me.'

Ross downed his drink. 'Nice to meet you, Kitty.'

'You too, Mr Buchanan.'

'What a charming young lady, Angus,' said Ross as he followed the steward to his compartment. 'She was about to tell me why she travels so frequently on this train.'

'I'm sure I don't know, sir.'

'I'm sure you do, Angus, because there's nothing you don't know about *The Night Scotsman*.'

'Well, let's just say she's very popular with some of our regulars.'

'Are you suggesting . . . ?'

'Aye, sir. She travels up and down two or three times a week. Very discreet and—'

'Angus! We're running *The Night Scotsman*, not a nightclub.'

'We've all got to make a living, sir, and if things go well for Kitty, everybody benefits.'

Ross burst out laughing. 'Do any of the other directors know about Kitty?'

'One or two. She gives them a special rate.'

'Behave yourself, Angus.'

'Sorry, sir.'

'Now, back to your day job. I want to see the bookings for all the first-class passengers. There may be someone on the train I'd like to have dinner with.'

'Of course, sir.' Angus removed a sheet of paper from his clipboard and handed it to Buchanan. 'I've kept your usual table free for dinner.'

Ross ran his finger down the list, to discover that Mr D. Martinez was in coach no.4. 'I'd like to have a word with Kitty,' he said as he passed the list back to Angus. 'And without anyone else finding out.'

'Discretion is my middle name,' said Angus, suppressing a smile.

'It's not what you think it is.'

'It never is, sir.'

'And I want you to allocate my table in the dining car to Mr Martinez, who has a compartment in coach four.'

'Aye, sir,' said Angus, now completely baffled.

'I'll keep your little secret, Angus, if you keep mine.'

'I would, sir, if I had any idea what yours was.'

'You will by the time we reach London.'

'I'll go and fetch Kitty, sir.'

Ross tried to marshal his thoughts as he waited for Kitty to join him. What he had in mind was nothing more than a stalling tactic, but it might just give him enough time to come up with something more effective. The door of his compartment slid open, and Kitty slipped in.

'How nice to see you again, Mr Buchanan,' she said as she took the seat opposite him and crossed her legs to reveal the top of her stockings. 'Can I be of service?'

'I hope so,' said Ross. 'How much do you charge?'

'Rather depends on what you're looking for.' Ross told her exactly what he was looking for.

'That'll be five pounds, sir, all in.'

Ross took out his wallet, extracted a five-pound note and handed it across to her.

'I'll do my best,' Kitty promised as she lifted her skirt and slipped the note into the top of a stocking, before disappearing as discreetly as she'd arrived.

Ross pressed the red button by the door and the steward reappeared moments later.

'Have you reserved my table for Mr Martinez?'

'Aye, and found you a place at the other end of the dining car.'

'Thank you, Angus. Now Kitty is to be seated opposite Mr Martinez, and anything she eats or drinks is to be charged to me.'

'Very good, sir. But what about Mr Martinez?'

'He will pay for his meal, but he's to be given the finest wines and liqueurs, and it's to be made clear to him that they are on the house.'

'Are they also to be charged to you, sir?'

'Yes. But he's not to know, because I'm rather hoping Mr Martinez will sleep soundly tonight.'

'I think I'm beginning to understand, sir.'

After the steward had left, Ross wondered if Kitty could pull it off. If she could get Martinez so drunk that he remained in his compartment until nine the next morning, she would have done her job, and Ross would happily have parted with another fiver. He particularly liked her idea of handcuffing him to the four corners of the bed and then hanging the *Do not disturb* sign on the door. No one would be suspicious, because you didn't have to leave the train until 9.30, and many passengers appreciated a lie-in before enjoying a late breakfast of Arbroath Smokies.

Ross left his compartment just after eight, made his way to the dining room and walked straight past Kitty, who was sitting opposite Diego Martinez. As he passed, he overheard the chief sommelier taking them through the wine list.

Angus had placed Ross at the far end of the carriage, with his back to Martinez, and although he was tempted more than once to look round, unlike Lot's wife he resisted. After he'd finished his coffee, having rejected his usual balloon of brandy, he signed the bill and made his way back to his compartment. As he passed his usual table, he was delighted to see that it was no longer occupied. Feeling quite pleased with himself, he almost strutted back to his carriage.

The feeling of triumph evaporated the moment he opened his compartment door and saw Kitty sitting there.

'What are you doing here? I thought—'

'I couldn't arouse any interest, Mr Buchanan,' she said. 'And don't think I didn't try everything from bondage to gymslips. To start with, he doesn't drink. Some religious thing. And long before the main course, it became clear that it's not women that turn him on. I'm sorry, sir, but thank you for dinner.'

'Thank you, Kitty. I'm most grateful,' he said as he sank into the seat opposite her.

Kitty lifted her skirt, took the five-pound note from the top of her stocking and handed it back to him.

'Certainly not,' he said firmly. 'You earned it.'

'I could always . . .' she said, placing a hand under his kilt, her fingers moving slowly up his thigh.

'No, thank you, Kitty,' he said, raising his eyes to the heavens in mock horror. That was when the second idea came to him. He handed the five-pound note back to Kitty.

'You're not one of those weird ones, are you, Mr Buchanan?'

'I must admit, Kitty, what I'm about to propose is pretty weird.'

She listened carefully to what service she was expected to perform. 'What time do you want me to do that?'

'Around three, three thirty.'

'Where?'

'I'd suggest the lavatory.'

'And how many times?'

'I would think once would be enough.'

'And I won't get into trouble, will I, Mr Buchanan? Because

this is a steady earner, and most of the gentlemen in first class are not very demanding.'

'You have my word, Kitty. This is a one-off, and no one need ever know you were involved.'

'You're a gent, Mr Buchanan,' she said and gave him a kiss on the cheek before slipping out of the compartment.

Ross wasn't sure what might have happened if she'd stayed a minute or two longer. He pressed the steward's bell and waited for Angus to appear.

'I hope that was satisfactory, sir?'

'I can't be sure yet.'

'Anything else I can do for you, sir?'

'Yes, Angus. I need a copy of the railway's regulations and statutes.'

'I'll see if I can find one, sir,' said Angus, looking mystified.

When he returned twenty minutes later, he was carrying a massive red tome that looked as if its pages hadn't been turned very often. Ross settled down for some bedtime reading. First he scanned the index, identifying the three sections he needed to study most carefully, as if he was back at St Andrews preparing for an exam. By three a.m. he'd read and marked up all the relevant passages. He spent the next thirty minutes trying to commit them to memory.

At 3.30 a.m. he closed the thick volume, sat back and waited. It had never crossed his mind that Kitty would let him down. 3.30, 3.35, 3.40. Suddenly there was a massive jolt that almost threw him out of his seat. It was followed by a loud screeching of wheels as the train slowed rapidly, and finally came to a halt. Ross stepped out into the corridor, to see the chief steward running towards him.

'Problem, Angus?'

'Some fucker, excuse my French, sir, has pulled the communication cord.'

'Keep me briefed.'

'Aye, sir.'

Ross checked his watch every few minutes, willing the time to pass. A number of passengers were now milling around in the corridor, trying to find out what was going on, but it was another fourteen minutes before the chief steward returned.

'Someone pulled the communication cord in the lavatory, Mr Buchanan. No doubt mistook it for the chain. But no harm done, sir, as long as we're on the move again in twenty minutes.'

'Why twenty minutes?' asked Ross innocently.

'If we hang about for any longer, *The Newcastle Flyer* will overtake us, and then we'd be stymied.'

'Why's that?'

'We'd have to fall in behind it, and then we'd be bound to be late because it stops at eight stations between here and London. Happened a couple of years back when a wee bairn pulled the cord, and by the time we arrived at King's Cross, we were over an hour behind schedule.'

'Only an hour?'

'Aye, we didnae get into London until just after eight forty. Now we wouldn't want that, would we, sir? So with your permission, I'll get us on the move again.'

'One moment, Angus. Have you identified the person who pulled the cord?'

'No, sir. Must have bolted the moment they realized their mistake.'

'Well, I'm sorry to point out, Angus, that regulation 43b in the railway's statutes requires you to find out who was responsible for pulling the cord, and why they did so, before the train can proceed.'

'But that could take for ever, sir, and I doubt we'd be any the wiser by the end of it.'

'If there was no good reason for the cord being pulled, the culprit will be fined five pounds and reported to the authorities,' said Ross, continuing to recite the railway's statutes.

'Let me guess, sir.'

'Regulation 47c.'

'May I say how much I admire your foresight, sir, having asked for the railway's statutes and regulations only hours before the communication cord was pulled.'

'Yes, wasn't that fortunate? Still, I'm sure the board would expect us to abide by the regulations, however inconvenient that might prove to be.'

'If you say so, sir.'

'I say so.'

Ross kept looking anxiously out of the window, and didn't smile until *The Newcastle Flyer* shot past twenty minutes later, giving them two prolonged peeps of its whistle. Even so, he realized that if they arrived at King's Cross at around 8.40, as Angus had predicted, Diego would still have more than enough time to reach a phone box on the station, call his broker and withdraw the proposed sale of his father's shares before the market opened at nine.

'All done, sir,' said Angus. 'Can I tell the driver to get a move on, because one of our passengers is threatening to sue British Railways if the train doesn't get to London before nine.'

Ross didn't need to ask which passenger was making the threat. 'Carry on, Angus,' he said reluctantly before closing the door of his compartment, not sure what more he could do to hold the train up for at least another twenty minutes.

The Night Scotsman made several more unscheduled stops as *The Newcastle Flyer* pulled in to disgorge and pick up passengers at Durham, Darlington, York and Doncaster.

There was a knock on the door and the steward entered.

'What's the latest, Angus?'

'The man who's been making all the fuss about getting to London on time is asking if he can leave the train when the *Flyer* stops at Peterborough.'

'No, he cannot,' said Ross, 'because this train isn't scheduled to stop at Peterborough, and in any case, we'll be standing some way outside the station, and therefore putting his life at risk.'

'Regulation 49c?'

'So if he attempts to leave the train, it's your duty to forcefully restrain him. Regulation 49f. After all,' added Ross, 'we wouldn't want the poor man to be killed.'

'Wouldn't we, sir?'

'And how many more stops are there after Peterborough?'

'None, sir.'

'What time do you estimate we'll arrive at King's Cross?'

'Around eight forty. Eight forty-five latest.'

Ross sighed deeply. 'So near and yet so far,' he murmured to himself.

'Forgive me for asking, sir,' said Angus, 'but what time would you *like* this train to arrive in London?'

Ross suppressed a smile. 'A few minutes after nine would be just perfect.'

'I'll see what I can do, sir,' said the chief steward before leaving the carriage.

The train kept a steady speed for the rest of the journey, but then suddenly, without warning, it stuttered to a halt just a few hundred yards outside King's Cross station.

'This is the steward speaking,' said a voice over the intercom. 'We apologize for the late arrival of *The Night Scotsman*, but this was due to circumstances beyond our control. We hope to disembark all passengers in a few minutes' time.'

Ross could only wonder how Angus had managed to add another thirty minutes to the journey. He walked out into the corridor to find him trying to calm a group of angry passengers.

'How did you fix it, Angus?' he whispered.

'It seems that another train is waiting on our platform, and as it isn't due to leave for Durham until five past nine, I'm afraid we won't be able to disembark passengers much before nine fifteen. I am sorry for the inconvenience, sir,' he said in a louder voice.

'Many thanks, Angus.'

'My pleasure, sir. Och no,' said Angus, rushing across to the window. 'It's him.'

Ross looked out of the window to see Diego Martinez running flat out along the track towards the station. He checked his watch: 8.53 a.m.

Monday morning

Cedric had walked into his office just before seven that morning, and immediately began to pace up and down the room while he waited for the phone to ring. But no one called until eight. It was Abe Cohen.

'I managed to get rid of the lot, Mr Hardcastle,' said Cohen, 'The last few flew in Hong Kong. Frankly, no one can fathom why the price is so low.'

'What was the final price?' asked Cedric.

'One pound and eight shillings.'

'Couldn't be better, Abe. Ross was right, you're simply the best.'

'Thank you, sir. I only hope there was some purpose in you losing all that money.' And before Cedric could reply, added, 'I'm off to get some sleep.'

Cedric checked his watch. The stock market would open for business in forty-five minutes. There was a quiet knock on the door, and Sebastian walked in carrying a tray of coffee and biscuits. He sat down on the other side of the chairman's desk.

'How did you get on?' asked Cedric.

'I've rung fourteen of the leading stock brokers to let them know that if any Barrington's shares come on the market, we're buyers.'

'Good,' said Cedric, looking at his watch once again. 'As Ross hasn't rung, we must still be in with a chance.' He took a sip of coffee, glancing at his watch every few moments.

When nine began to strike on a hundred different clocks throughout the Square Mile, Cedric rose and acknowledged the City's anthem. Sebastian remained seated, staring at the phone, willing it to ring. At three minutes past nine, someone obeyed his command. Cedric grabbed the receiver, juggled with it and nearly dropped it on the floor.

'It's Capels on the line, sir,' said his secretary. 'Shall I put them through?'

'Immediately.'

'Good morning, Mr Hardcastle. It's David Alexander of Capels. I know we're not your usual broker, but the grapevine has it that you're looking to buy Barrington's, so I thought I'd let you know that we have a large sale order with instructions from our client to sell at spot price when the market opened this morning. I wondered if you were still interested.'

'I could be,' said Cedric, hoping he sounded calm.

'However, there is a caveat attached to the sale of these shares,' said Alexander.

'And what might that be?' asked Cedric, knowing only too well what it was.

'We are not authorized to sell to anyone who represents either the Barrington or the Clifton family.'

'My client is from Lincolnshire, and I can assure you, he has no past or present connection with either of those families.'

'Then I am happy to make a trade, sir.'

Cedric felt like a teenager trying to close his first deal. 'And what is the spot price, Mr Alexander?' he asked, relieved that the broker from Capels couldn't see the sweat pouring down his forehead.

'One pound and nine shillings. They're a shilling up since the market opened.'

'How many shares are you offering?'

'We have one million two hundred thousand on our books, sir.'

'I'll take the lot.'

'Did I hear you correctly, sir?'

'You most certainly did.'

'Then that is a buy order for one million two hundred thousand Barrington's Shipping shares at one pound and nine shillings. Do you accept the transaction, sir?'

'Yes I do,' said the chairman of Farthings Bank, trying to sound pompous.

'The deal has been closed, sir. Those shares are now held in the name of Farthings Bank. I'll send the paperwork round for your signature later this morning.' The line went dead.

Cedric jumped up and punched the air as if Huddersfield Town had just won the FA Cup. Sebastian would have joined him, but the phone rang again.

He grabbed the receiver, listened for a moment, then quickly passed it to Cedric.

'It's David Alexander. Says it's urgent.'

DIEGO MARTINEZ

1964

36

DIEGO MARTINEZ checked his watch. He couldn't afford to
wait any longer. He looked up and down the crowded corridor
to make sure there was no sign of the steward, then pulled down
the window, reached outside for the handle and opened the
door. He jumped off the train and landed on the tracks.

Someone shouted, 'You can't do that!'

He didn't waste his time pointing out that he already had.

He began running towards the well-lit station, and he must
have covered a couple of hundred yards before the platform
loomed up in front of him. He couldn't see the astonished looks
on the faces of the passengers staring out of the carriage windows as he shot past them.

'It must be a matter of life or death,' one of them suggested.

Diego kept on running until he reached the far end of the
platform. He took out his wallet on the move, and had extracted
his ticket long before he reached the barrier. The ticket collector looked up at him and said, 'I was told *The Night Scotsman*
wouldn't be arriving for at least another fifteen minutes.'

'Where's the nearest phone box?' Diego shouted.

'Just over there,' the ticket collector said, pointing to a row
of red boxes. 'You can't miss them.'

Diego dashed across the crowded concourse, trying to grab
a handful of coins from a trouser pocket on the run. He came
to a halt outside the six phone boxes; three were occupied. He

pulled open a door and checked his change, but he didn't have four pennies; one short.

'Read all about it!'

He swung round, spotted the paperboy and began running towards him. He went straight to the front of a long queue, handed the lad half a crown and said, 'I need a penny.'

'Sure thing, guv,' said the paperboy, who assumed he was desperate to go to the lavatory, and quickly gave him a penny.

Diego dashed back to the phone boxes and didn't hear him say, 'Don't forget your change, sir,' and 'What about your newspaper?' He opened a door to be greeted with the words, *Out of Order.* He barged into the next box just as a startled woman was opening the door. He picked up the phone, pressed four pennies into the black box and dialled CITY 416. Moments later he heard a ringing tone.

'Pick it up, pick it up, pick it up!' he shouted. A voice finally came on the line.

'Capel and Company. How may I help you?'

Diego pressed button A and heard the coins drop into the box. 'Put me through to Mr Alexander.'

'Which Mr Alexander, A., D. or W.?'

'Hold on,' said Diego. He placed the receiver on top of the box, took out his wallet, extracted Mr Alexander's card and quickly picked up the phone again. 'Are you still there?'

'Yes, sir.'

'David Alexander.'

'He's not available at the moment. Can I put you through to another broker?'

'No, put me through to David Alexander immediately,' demanded Diego.

'But he's on the line to another client.'

'Then get him off the line. This is an emergency.'

'I'm not allowed to interrupt a call, sir.'

'You can and you will interrupt him, you stupid girl, if you still hope to have your job tomorrow morning.'

'Who shall I say is calling?' asked a trembling voice.

'Just put me through!' shouted Diego. He heard a click.

'Are you still there, Mr Hardcastle?'

'No, he's not. This is Diego Martinez, Mr Alexander.'

'Ah, good morning, Mr Martinez. Your timing couldn't be better.'

'Tell me you haven't sold my father's Barrington's shares.'

'But I have, in fact, just before you came on the line. I'm sure you'll be delighted to hear that one customer took all one million two hundred thousand of them – in normal circumstances it might have taken two, possibly even three weeks to offload them all. And I even got a shilling more than the opening price.'

'How much did you sell them for?'

'One pound and nine shillings. I have the sale order in front of me.'

'But they were two pounds and eight shillings when the market closed on Friday afternoon.'

'That's correct, but there seems to have been a great deal of activity in this stock over the weekend. I assumed you'd be aware of that, and it was one of the reasons I was so delighted to get them all off the books so quickly.'

'Why didn't you try to contact my father to warn him that the shares had collapsed?' shouted Diego.

'Your father made it clear that he would not be available over the weekend, and wouldn't be returning to London until tomorrow morning.'

'But when you saw the share price had collapsed, why didn't you use your common sense and wait until you'd spoken to him?'

'I have your father's written instructions in front of me, Mr Martinez. They could not be clearer. His entire holding of Barrington's stock was to be placed on the market when the Exchange opened this morning.'

'Now listen to me, Alexander, and listen carefully. I'm ordering you to cancel that sale and get his shares back.'

'I'm afraid I can't do that, sir. Once a transaction has been agreed, there is no way of reversing it.'

'Has the paperwork been completed?'

'No, sir, but it will have been before the close of business this evening.'

'Then don't complete it. Tell whoever bought the shares there's been a mistake.'

'The City doesn't work like that, Mr Martinez. Once a transaction has been agreed, there's no going back, otherwise the market would be in perpetual turmoil.'

'I'm telling you, Alexander, you will reverse that sale, or I will sue your company for negligence.'

'And I'm telling you, Mr Martinez, that if I did, I would be up in front of the Stock Exchange council, and would lose my licence to trade.'

Diego changed tack. 'Were those shares purchased by a member of the Barrington or Clifton families?'

'No, they were not, sir. We carried out your father's instructions to the letter.'

'So who did buy them?'

'The chairman of an established Yorkshire bank, on behalf of one of his clients.'

Diego decided the time had come to try another approach, one that had never failed him in the past. 'If you were to mislay that order, Mr Alexander, I will give you one hundred thousand pounds.'

'If I did that, Mr Martinez, I would not only lose my licence, but end up in jail.'

'But it would be cash, so no one would be any the wiser.'

'I am the wiser,' said Alexander, 'and I shall be reporting this conversation to my father and brother at the next partners' meeting. I must make my position clear, Mr Martinez. This firm will not be doing business with you, or any member of your family, in the future. Good day, sir.'

The line went dead.

─◦─

'Do you want the good news or the bad news first?'

'I'm an optimist, so give me the good news.'

'We pulled it off. You're now the proud owner of one million two hundred thousand shares in the Barrington Shipping Company.'

'And the bad news?'

'I need a cheque for £1,740,000, but you'll be pleased to hear that the shares have gone up four shillings since you bought them, so you've already made a handsome profit.'

'I'm grateful, Cedric. And as we agreed, I'll cover any losses you made over the weekend. That's only fair. So what happens next?'

'I'll be sending one of our associate directors, Sebastian Clifton, up to Grimsby tomorrow with all the paperwork for you to sign. With such a large sum involved, I'd prefer not to entrust it to the vagaries of the postal service.'

'If that's Jessica's brother, I can't wait to meet him.'

'It most certainly is. He should be with you around noon tomorrow, and once you've signed all the certificates, he'll bring them back to London.'

'Tell him that, like you, he's about to have a gourmet experience, the finest fish and chips in the world, eaten out of yesterday's *Grimsby Evening Telegraph*. I certainly won't be taking him to some fancy restaurant with a tablecloth and plates.'

'If it was good enough for me, it'll be good enough for him,' said Cedric. 'I look forward to seeing you next Monday at the AGM.'

'We've still got several other problems,' said Sebastian after Cedric had put the phone down.

'And what might they be?'

'Although Barrington's share price has already begun to bounce back, we mustn't forget that Fisher's letter of resignation will be released to the press on Friday. The suggestion from a board member that the company is facing bankruptcy could send the stock tumbling again.'

'That's one of the reasons you're going to Grimsby tomorrow,' said Cedric. 'Fisher is coming in to see me at twelve, by which time you'll be enjoying the best fish and chips in the land with a side order of mushy peas.'

'And what's the other reason?' asked Sebastian.

'I need you to be out of the way when I see Fisher. Your presence would only remind him where my true allegiance lies.'

'He won't be a pushover,' warned Seb, 'as my uncle Giles discovered on more than one occasion.'

'I don't intend to push him over,' said Cedric. 'On the contrary. I plan to prop him up. Any other problems?'

'Three actually: Don Pedro Martinez, Diego Martinez and, to a lesser extent, Luis Martinez.'

'I am reliably informed that those three are all finished. Don Pedro is facing bankruptcy, Diego could be arrested at any moment for attempted bribery, and Luis can't even blow his nose unless his father hands him the handkerchief. No, I think it won't be too long before those three gentlemen are taking a one-way trip back to Argentina.'

'I still have a feeling that Don Pedro will try to exact the last possible ounce of revenge before he departs.'

'I don't think he'd dare to go anywhere near the Barrington or Clifton families at the moment.'

'I wasn't thinking about my family.'

'You don't have to worry about me,' said Cedric. 'I can take care of myself.'

'Or even you.'

'Then who?'

'Samantha Sullivan.'

'I don't think that's a risk even he'd be willing to take.'

'Martinez doesn't think like you . . .'

Monday evening

Don Pedro was so angry it was some time before he could speak. 'How did they get away with it?' he demanded.

'Once the market closed on Friday and I'd left for Scotland,' said Diego, 'someone began to sell a large number of Barrington's shares in New York and Los Angeles, and then more of them when the market opened in Sydney this morning, finally getting rid of the last few in Hong Kong, while we were all asleep.'

'In every sense of the word,' said Don Pedro. Another long pause followed, and again no one considered interrupting. 'So how much did I lose?' he eventually said.

'Over a million pounds.'

'Did you find out who was selling those shares?' spat out Don Pedro, 'because I'd be willing to bet it's the same person who picked mine up this morning at half the price.'

'I think it must be someone called Hardcastle, who was on the line when I interrupted David Alexander.'

'Cedric Hardcastle,' said Don Pedro. 'He's a Yorkshire banker who sits on the board of Barrington's and always backs the chairman. He's going to regret this.'

'Father, this isn't Argentina. You've lost almost everything, and we already know the authorities are looking for any excuse to deport you. Perhaps the time has come to drop this vendetta.'

Diego saw the open palm coming, but he didn't flinch.

'You don't tell your father what he can and cannot do. I'll leave when it suits me, and not before. Is that understood?' Diego nodded. 'Anything else?'

'I can't be absolutely certain, but I think I spotted Sebastian Clifton at King's Cross when I got on the train, although he was some distance away.'

'Why didn't you check?'

'Because the train was about to leave, and—'

'They'd even worked out that they couldn't go ahead with their plan if you didn't get on *The Night Scotsman*. Clever,' said Don Pedro. 'So they must also have had someone at Glenleven watching our every move, otherwise how could they have known you were on your way back to London?'

'I'm certain that no one followed me when I left the hotel. I checked several times.'

'But someone must have known you were on that train. It's too much of a coincidence that the very evening *you* travel on *The Night Scotsman*, it's an hour and a half late for the first time in years. Can you remember anything unusual happening during the journey?'

'A whore called Kitty tried to pick me up, and then the communication cord was pulled—'

'Too many coincidences.'

'Later I saw her whispering to the chief steward, and he smiled and walked away.'

'A prostitute and a steward couldn't hold up *The Night Scotsman* for an hour and a half on their own. No, someone with real authority must have been on that train pulling the strings.' Another long pause. 'I think they saw us coming, but I'm going to make damn sure they don't see us coming back. To do that, we'll have to be as well organized as they are.'

Diego didn't offer an opinion in this one-sided conversation.

'How much cash have I got left?'

'Around three hundred thousand when I last checked,' said Karl.

'And my art collection went on sale in Bond Street last night. Agnew assured me it ought to fetch over a million. So I've still got more than enough resources to take them on. Never forget, it doesn't matter how many minor skirmishes you lose, as long as you win the final battle.'

Diego felt this was not the right moment to remind his father which of the two generals had voiced that opinion at Waterloo.

Don Pedro closed his eyes, leaned back in his chair and said nothing. Once again, no one attempted to interrupt his thoughts. Suddenly his eyes opened and he sat bolt upright.

'Now listen carefully,' he said, turning his gaze on his younger son. 'Luis, you will be responsible for bringing the Sebastian Clifton file up to date.'

'Father,' Diego began, 'we've been warned—'

'Shut up. If you don't want to be part of my team you can leave now.' Diego didn't move, but he felt the insult more than he had the slap. Don Pedro turned his attention back to Luis. 'I want to know where he lives, where he works, and who his friends are. Do you think you can manage that?'

'Yes, Father,' said Luis.

Diego didn't doubt that if his brother had a tail, it would be wagging.

'Diego,' Don Pedro said, looking back at his older son. 'You'll go down to Bristol and visit Fisher. Don't let him know you're coming, better to take him by surprise. It's now even more important that he hands in his resignation letter to Mrs Clifton on Friday morning, and then releases it to the press. I want the business editor of every national newspaper to get a copy, and I expect Fisher to be available to any journalist who wants to interview him. Take a thousand pounds with you. Nothing concentrates Fisher's mind better than the sight of cash.'

'Perhaps they've got to him as well,' suggested Diego.

'Then take two thousand. And Karl,' he said, turning to his most trusted ally, 'I've saved the best for you. Book yourself on the sleeper for Edinburgh and find that whore. And when you do, be sure to give her a night she'll never forget. I don't care how you find out, but I want to know who was responsible for that train being held up for an hour and a half. We'll all meet again tomorrow evening. By then I'll have had a chance to visit Agnew's and find out how the sale is going.' Don Pedro was silent for some time before he added, 'I have a feeling we're going to need a large amount of cash for what I have in mind.'

37

'I'VE GOT A PRESENT for you.'

'Let me guess.'

'No, you'll have to wait and see.'

'Ah, it's a wait-and-see present.'

'Yes, I admit that I haven't actually got it yet but . . .'

'But now that you've had your way with me, it will be more *wait* than see?'

'You're catching on. But in my defence, I'm hoping to pick it up today from—'

'Tiffany's?'

'Well, no, not—'

'Asprey's?'

'Not exactly.'

'Cartier?'

'My second choice.'

'And your first choice?'

'Bingham's.'

'Bingham's of Bond Street?'

'No, Bingham's of Grimsby.'

'And what is Bingham's famous for? Diamonds? Furs? Perfume?' she asked hopefully.

'Fish paste.'

'One or two jars?'

'One to start with, as I still need to see how this relationship develops.'

'I suppose that's about as much as an out-of-work shop girl can hope for,' said Samantha, as she climbed out of bed. 'And to think I dreamt of being a kept woman.'

'That comes later when I become chairman of the bank,' Sebastian said, following her into the bathroom.

'I may not be willing to wait that long,' said Samantha as she stepped into the shower. She was about to draw the curtain when Sebastian joined her.

'There isn't enough room in here for both of us,' she said.

'Have you ever made love in a shower?'

'Wait and see.'

—o—

'Major, it was good of you to find the time to come and see me.'

'Not at all, Hardcastle. I was in London on business, so it's worked out rather well.'

'Can I get you some coffee, old fellow?'

'Black, no sugar, thank you,' Fisher said as he took a seat on the other side of the chairman's desk.

Cedric pressed a button on his phone. 'Miss Clough, two black coffees, no sugar, and perhaps some biscuits. Exciting times, don't you think, Fisher?'

'What in particular did you have in mind?'

'The naming of the *Buckingham* by the Queen Mother next month, of course, and a maiden voyage which should take the company into a whole new era.'

'Let's hope so,' said Fisher. 'Although there are still several hurdles to cross before I'll be totally convinced.'

'Which is precisely why I wanted to have a word with you, old fellow.'

There was a quiet tap on the door, and Miss Clough entered carrying a tray with two cups of coffee. She placed one in front of the major, the other next to the chairman, and a plate of fat rascals between them.

'Let me say straight away how sorry I was that Mr Martinez decided to sell his entire shareholding in Barrington's. I wondered if you were able to throw some light on what was behind the decision.'

Fisher dropped his cup back in its saucer, spilling a few drops. 'I had no idea,' he mumbled.

'I'm so sorry, Alex, I rather assumed he would have briefed you before he took such an irreversible decision.'

'When did this happen?'

'Yesterday morning, moments after the Stock Exchange opened, which is why I gave you a buzz.' Fisher looked like a startled fox caught in the headlights of an oncoming car. 'You see, there's something I'd like to discuss with you.' Fisher remained speechless, which allowed Cedric to prolong his agony a little longer. 'I'll be sixty-five in October, and although I have no plans to retire as chairman of the bank, I do intend to shed a few of my outside interests, among them my directorship of Barrington's.' Fisher forgot about his coffee and listened intently to Cedric's every word. 'With that in mind, I've decided to resign from the board, and make way for a younger man.'

'I'm sorry to hear that,' said Fisher. 'I've always thought that you brought wisdom and gravitas to our discussions.'

'It's kind of you to say so, and indeed that's why I wanted to see you.' Fisher smiled, wondering if it was just possible . . . 'I have watched you carefully over the past five years, Alex, and what has impressed me most has been your loyal support for our chairman, especially remembering that when you stood against her, she only defeated you because of the outgoing chairman's casting vote.'

'One must never allow one's personal feelings to get in the way of what is best for the company.'

'I couldn't have put it better myself, Alex, which is why I was hoping I might be able to persuade you to take my place on the board now that you will no longer be representing Mr Martinez's interests.'

'That's a very generous offer, Cedric.'

'No, it's quite selfish really, because if you felt able to do so, it would help to guarantee stability and continuity both for Barrington's and for Farthings Bank.'

'Yes, I can see that.'

'In addition to the thousand pounds a year you currently receive as a director, Farthings would pay you a further thousand to represent the bank's interests. After all, I'll need to be fully briefed after every board meeting, which would require you to come up to London and stay overnight. Any expenses would of course be covered by the bank.'

'That's most generous of you, Cedric, but I'll need a little time to think about it,' said the major, clearly wrestling with a problem.

'Of course, you will,' said Cedric, knowing only too well what that problem was.

'When do you need to know my decision?'

'By the end of the week. I'd like to have the matter settled before the AGM next Monday. I had originally planned to ask my son Arnold to replace me, but that was before I realized you might be available.'

'I'll let you know by Friday.'

'That's good of you, Alex. I'll write a letter confirming the offer immediately, and put it in the post tonight.'

'Thank you, Cedric. I'll certainly give it my full consideration.'

'Excellent. Now, I won't detain you any longer, because, if I recall, you said you have a meeting in Westminster.'

'Indeed I do,' said Fisher, rising slowly from his place and shaking hands with Cedric, who accompanied him to the door.

Cedric returned to his desk, sat down and began writing his letter to the major, wondering if his offer would be more tempting than the one Martinez was clearly about to make him.

◄○►

The red Rolls-Royce drew up outside Agnew's gallery. Don Pedro stepped out on to the pavement and looked in the window to see a full-length portrait of Mrs Kathleen Newton, Tissot's beautiful mistress. He smiled when he saw the red dot.

An even bigger smile appeared on his face after he had entered the gallery. It was not the sight of so many magnificent paintings and sculptures that caused him to smile, but the plethora of red dots by the side of them.

'Can I help you, sir?' asked a middle-aged woman.

Don Pedro wondered what had happened to the beautiful young woman who'd met him the last time he'd visited the gallery.

'I want to speak to Mr Agnew.'

'I'm not sure if he's available at the moment. Perhaps I might be able to assist you.'

'He'll be available for me,' said Don Pedro. 'After all, this is my show,' he added, raising his arms aloft as if he were blessing a congregation.

She quickly backed off, and without another word knocked on the door of Mr Agnew's office and disappeared inside. Moments later the owner appeared.

'Good afternoon, Mr Martinez,' he said a little stiffly, which Don Pedro dismissed as English reserve.

'I can see how well the sale is going, but how much have you taken so far?'

'I wonder if we might go into my office, where it's a little more private.'

Don Pedro followed him across the gallery, counting the red dots, but waited until the office door was closed before repeating his question.

'How much have you taken so far?'

'A little over £170,000 on the opening night, and this morning a gentleman called to reserve two more pieces, the Bonnard and an Utrillo, which will take us comfortably over £200,000. We've also had an enquiry from the National Gallery about the Raphael.'

'Good, because I need a hundred thousand right now.'

'I'm afraid that will not be possible, Mr Martinez.'

'Why not? It's my money.'

'I've been trying to get in touch with you for several days, but you've been away shooting in Scotland.'

'Why can't I have my money?' demanded Martinez, his tone now menacing.

'Last Friday we had a visit from a Mr Ledbury of the Midland Bank, St James's. He was accompanied by their lawyer, who instructed us to pay any monies raised from this sale directly to the bank.'

'He doesn't have the authority to do that. This collection belongs to me.'

'They produced legal documents to show that you had signed over the entire collection, with every piece listed individually, as security against an agreed loan.'

'But I repaid that loan yesterday.'

'The lawyer returned just before the opening yesterday evening with a court order restraining me from transferring the money to anyone other than the bank. I feel I must point out to you, Mr Martinez, that this is not the way we like to conduct business at Agnew's.'

'I'll get a letter of release immediately. When I return, I expect you to have a cheque for one hundred thousand pounds waiting for me.'

'I look forward to seeing you later, Mr Martinez.'

Don Pedro left the gallery without shaking hands or uttering another word. He walked briskly in the direction of St James's, with his Rolls-Royce following a few yards behind. When he reached the bank, he strode in and headed straight for the manager's office before anyone had the opportunity to ask him who he was, or who he wanted to see. When he reached the end of the corridor, he didn't knock on the door, but barged straight in, to find Mr Ledbury seated behind his desk dictating to a secretary.

'Good afternoon, Mr Martinez,' Ledbury said, almost as if he'd been expecting him.

'Get out,' Don Pedro said, pointing at the secretary, who quickly left the room without even glancing at the manager.

'What game do you think you're playing, Ledbury? I've just come from Agnew's. They're refusing to hand over any money from the sale of my personal art collection, and say you're to blame.'

'I'm afraid it's no longer your collection,' said Ledbury, 'and it hasn't been for some considerable time. You've clearly forgotten that you assigned it to the bank after we extended your overdraft facilities yet again.' He unlocked the top drawer of a small green cabinet and took out a file.

'But what about the money from my sale of the Barrington's shares? That netted over three million.'

'Which still leaves you with an overdraft –' he flicked through a few pages of the file – 'of £772,450 at close of business last night. In order not to put you through this embarrassment again, let me remind you that you also recently signed a personal guarantee, which includes your home in the country and no. 44 Eaton Square. And I must advise you that, should the sale of your art collection fail to cover your current overdraft, we shall be asking you which of those properties you wish to dispose of first.'

'You can't do that.'

'I can, Mr Martinez, and if necessary, I will. And the next time you want to see me,' said Ledbury as he walked across to the door, 'perhaps you'd be kind enough to make an appointment through my secretary. Let me remind you, this is a bank, not a casino.' He opened the door. 'Good day, sir.'

Martinez slunk out of the manager's office, down the corridor, across the banking hall and back on to the street, to find his Rolls-Royce parked outside waiting for him. He even wondered if he still owned that.

'Take me home,' he said.

When they reached the top of St James's, the Rolls-Royce turned left, drove down Piccadilly and on past Green Park station, from which a stream of people was emerging. Among them was a young man who crossed the road, turned left and headed towards Albemarle Street.

When Sebastian entered Agnew's gallery for the third time in less than a week, he only intended to stay for a few moments to collect Jessica's picture. He could have taken it when the police had accompanied him back to the gallery, but he'd been too distracted by the thought of Sam locked up in a cell.

This time he was distracted again, not by the thought of

rescuing a damsel in distress, but by the quality of the works of art on display. He stopped to admire Raphael's *La Madonna de Bogotá*, which had been in his possession for a few hours, and tried to imagine what it must be like to write out a cheque for £100,000 and know it wouldn't bounce.

It amused him to see that Rodin's *The Thinker* had been priced at £150,000. He remembered only too well when Don Pedro had purchased it at Sotheby's for £120,000, a record for a Rodin at the time. But then, Don Pedro had been under the illusion that the statue contained eight million pounds in counterfeit five-pound notes. That had been the beginning of Sebastian's troubles.

'Welcome back, Mr Clifton.'

'My fault again, I'm afraid. I forgot to pick up my sister's picture.'

'Indeed. I've just asked my assistant to fetch it.'

'Thank you, sir,' Sebastian said as Sam's replacement appeared carrying a bulky package which she handed to Mr Agnew. He took his time checking the label, before passing it to Sebastian.

'Let's hope it's not a Rembrandt this time,' said Sebastian, unable to resist a smirk. Neither Mr Agnew nor his assistant rewarded him with a smile. In fact, all Agnew said was, 'And don't forget our deal.'

'If I don't sell a picture, but give it to someone as a gift, have I broken our agreement?'

'Who were you thinking of giving it to?'

'Sam. My way of saying sorry.'

'I have no objection to that,' said Agnew. 'Like you, I feel sure Miss Sullivan would never consider selling it.'

'Thank you, sir,' replied Sebastian. Then, looking at the Raphael, he said, 'I'll own that picture one day.'

'I hope so,' said Agnew, 'because that's the way we make our money.'

When Sebastian left the gallery, it was such a pleasant evening that he decided to walk to Pimlico so he could give Sam her 'wait and see' present. As he strolled through St James's Park he thought about his visit to Grimsby earlier that day. He liked

Mr Bingham. He liked his factory. He liked the workers. What Cedric called real people doing real jobs.

It had taken Mr Bingham about five minutes to sign all the share transfer certificates, and another thirty minutes for them to devour two portions of the finest fish and chips in the universe, eaten out of yesterday's copy of the *Grimsby Evening Telegraph*. Just before he left, Mr Bingham had presented him with a jar of fish paste and an invitation to spend the night at Mablethorpe Hall.

'That's kind of you, sir, but Mr Hardcastle is expecting me to have these certificates back on his desk by close of business this evening.'

'Fair enough, but I have a feeling we'll be seeing more of each other now that I'm joining the board of Barrington's.'

'You're joining the board, sir?'

'It's a long story. I'll tell you all about it when I know you better.'

That was the moment Sebastian realized that Bob Bingham was the mystery man who could not be mentioned until the deal had been closed.

He couldn't wait to give Sam her present. When he arrived outside her block of flats, he opened the front door with the key she'd given him that morning.

A man hiding in the shadows on the other side of the road made a note of the address. Because Clifton had let himself in with his own key, he assumed that this must be where Clifton lived. Over dinner, he would tell his father who had purchased the Barrington's shares, the name of the Yorkshire bank that had handled the transaction, and where Sebastian Clifton lived. Even what he'd eaten for lunch. He hailed a taxi, and asked to be taken to Eaton Square.

'Stop!' Luis shouted when he spotted the placard. He jumped out of the taxi, ran across to the paperboy and grabbed a copy of the *London Evening News*. He read the headline *Woman in coma after jumping from Night Scotsman* and smiled before getting back in the cab. Clearly someone else had carried out his father's orders, too.

38

THE CABINET SECRETARY had considered all the permutations, and felt he'd finally come up with the perfect way to deal with all four of them in one masterful stroke.

Sir Alan Redmayne believed in the rule of law. It was, after all, the basis of any democracy. Whenever asked, Sir Alan agreed with Churchill that, as a form of government, democracy had its disadvantages, but, on balance, it remained the best on offer. But given a free hand, he would have opted for a benevolent dictatorship. The problem was that dictators, by their very nature, were not benevolent. It simply didn't fit their job description. In his opinion, the nearest thing Great Britain had to a benevolent dictator was the cabinet secretary.

If this had been Argentina, Sir Alan would simply have ordered Colonel Scott-Hopkins to kill Don Pedro Martinez, Diego Martinez, Luis Martinez and certainly Karl Lunsdorf, and then he could have closed their files. But like so many cabinet secretaries before him, he would have to compromise and be satisfied with one kidnapping, two deportations and a bankrupt who would be left with no choice but to return to his native land and never consider coming back.

In normal circumstances, Sir Alan would have waited for the due process of law to take its course. But unfortunately his hand had been forced by no less a figure than the Queen Mother.

He had read in the court circular that morning that Her

Majesty had graciously accepted an invitation from the chairman of Barrington Shipping, Mrs Harry Clifton, to name the MV *Buckingham* at noon on Monday 21st September, leaving him only a few weeks to carry out his plan, as he wasn't in any doubt that Don Pedro Martinez would have something other than a naming ceremony in mind on that particular day.

His first move, in what was going to be a busy few days, was to ensure that Karl Lunsdorf was eliminated from the equation altogether. His latest unforgivable crime, on *The Night Scotsman*, was despicable, even by his vile standards. Diego and Luis Martinez could wait their turn as he already had more than enough evidence to have them both arrested. And he was confident that once the two sons were released on bail, pending their trial, they would flee the country within days. The police would be instructed not to detain them when they turned up at the airport, as they would be well aware they could never return to Britain unless they were willing to face a long prison sentence.

They could wait. However, Karl Otto Lunsdorf, to give him the full name on his birth certificate, could not.

Although it was clear from the description given by the chief steward on *The Night Scotsman* that Lunsdorf had been responsible for throwing – he turned a page of his file – Miss Kitty Parsons, a well-known prostitute, out of the train in the middle of the night, there wasn't a fighting chance of getting a beyond-reasonable-doubt verdict against the former SS officer while the poor woman remained in a coma. Despite this, the wheels of justice were about to be set in motion.

Sir Alan didn't much care for cocktail parties and although he received a dozen invitations a day to attend everything from the Queen's garden party to the Royal Box at Wimbledon, nine times out of ten, he penned the word *No* in the top right-hand corner of the invitation and left his secretary to come up with a convincing excuse. However, when he received an invitation from the Foreign Office to a drinks party to welcome the new Israeli Ambassador, Sir Alan had written 'Yes, if free' in the top right-hand corner.

The cabinet secretary had no particular desire to meet the

new ambassador, whom he'd come across as a member of several delegations in the past. However, there would be one guest at the party with whom he did want to have a private word.

Sir Alan left his office in Downing Street just after six and strolled across to the FCO. After offering his congratulations to the new ambassador, and exchanging pleasantries with several others who wished to pay him court, he moved deftly around the crowded room, glass in hand, until his prey was in sight.

Simon Wiesenthal was chatting to the chief rabbi when Sir Alan joined them. He waited patiently for Sir Israel Brodie to begin a conversation with the ambassador's wife, before he turned his back on the chattering crowd, to make it clear that he did not want to be interrupted.

'Dr Wiesenthal, can I say how much I admire your campaign to hunt down those Nazis who were involved in the Holocaust.' Wiesenthal gave a slight bow. 'I wonder,' said the cabinet secretary, lowering his voice, 'if the name Karl Otto Lunsdorf means anything to you?'

'Lieutenant Lunsdorf was one of Himmler's closest aides,' said Wiesenthal. 'He worked as an SS interrogation officer on his private staff. I have countless files devoted to him, Sir Alan, but I fear he escaped from Germany a few days before the Allies entered Berlin. The last I heard he was living in Buenos Aires.'

'I think you'll find he's a little closer to home,' whispered Sir Alan. Wiesenthal edged nearer, bowed his head and listened intently.

'Thank you, Sir Alan,' said Wiesenthal after the cabinet secretary had passed on the relevant information. 'I'll get to work on it immediately.'

'If there's anything I can do to help, unofficially of course, you know where to find me,' he said as the chairman of the Friends of Israel joined them.

Sir Alan placed his empty glass on a passing tray, rejected the offer of a sausage on a stick, said goodnight to the new ambassador, and made his way back to Number 10. He settled down to go over his outline plan once again, making sure that every 'i' was dotted and every 't' crossed, aware that his biggest problem would be timing, especially if he hoped to have both of them arrested on the day after Lunsdorf disappeared.

When he finally crossed the last 't' just after midnight, the cabinet secretary decided that, on balance, he still would have preferred a benevolent dictatorship.

◄◦►

Major Alex Fisher placed the two letters on his desk, side by side: his letter of resignation from the board of Barrington's, next to a letter from Cedric Hardcastle that had arrived that morning, offering him the chance to continue his role as a board member. A smooth transition, as Hardcastle described it, with long-term prospects.

Alex remained torn as he tried to weigh up the pros and cons of the two alternatives. Should he accept Cedric's generous offer and keep his place on the board, with an income of £2,000 a year plus expenses, and every opportunity to pursue other interests?

If he resigned from the board, however, Don Pedro had promised him £5,000 in cash. On balance, Hardcastle's offer was the more attractive alternative. But then there was the question of the revenge Don Pedro would exact if he backed out of his agreement at the last minute, as Miss Kitty Parsons had recently discovered.

There was a knock on the door, which came as a surprise to Alex, because he wasn't expecting anyone. He was even more surprised when he opened it to find Diego Martinez standing there.

'Good morning,' said Alex as if he'd been expecting him. 'Come in,' he added, not sure what else to say. He led Diego through to the kitchen, not wanting him to see the two letters on his study desk. 'What brings you to Bristol?' he asked and, remembering Diego didn't drink, filled a kettle with water and put it on to boil.

'My father asked me to give you this,' said Diego, placing a thick envelope on the kitchen table. 'You won't need to count it. That's the two thousand you requested in advance. You can collect the rest on Monday, after you've handed in your letter of resignation.'

Alex made a decision; fear outweighed greed. He picked up the envelope and placed it in an inside pocket, but didn't say thank you.

'My father asked me to remind you that after you've tendered your resignation on Friday morning, he expects you to be available to talk to the press.'

'Of course,' said Fisher. 'Once I've handed the letter to Mrs Clifton' – he still found it difficult to call her the chairman – 'I'll send out the telegrams as we agreed, return home and be sitting at my desk waiting to answer any calls.'

'Good,' said Diego as the kettle boiled. 'So we'll see you on Monday afternoon in Eaton Square, and if the press coverage for the AGM has been favourable, or should I say unfavourable' – he smiled – 'you'll get the other three thousand.'

'You won't have a cup of coffee?'

'No. I've delivered the money, and my father's message. He just wanted to make sure you hadn't changed your mind.'

'What could possibly have made him think I might do that?'

'I can't imagine,' said Diego. 'But remember,' he added, looking down at a photograph of Miss Kitty Parsons on the front page of the *Telegraph*, 'that if anything does go wrong, it won't be me who's on the next train to Bristol.'

After Diego had left, Alex returned to his study, tore up Cedric Hardcastle's letter, and dropped the pieces into the wastepaper basket. No need to reply. Hardcastle would get the message on Saturday, when he read his resignation letter in the national press.

He treated himself to lunch at Carwardine's, and spent the rest of the afternoon settling several small debts with various local tradesmen, some of which were long overdue. When he returned home, he checked the envelope to find he still had £1,265 in crisp five-pound notes, with another £3,000 to come on Monday if the press showed sufficient interest in his story. He lay awake rehearsing some statements that he hoped would have the journalists licking their lips. *I fear the* Buckingham *will have sunk even before it's set out on its maiden voyage. Appointing a woman as chairman was a reckless gamble, and I do not believe the company will ever recover from it. Of course I've sold all my shares, I'd rather take a small loss now than a bath later.*

The following morning, after a sleepless night, Alex rang the chairman's office and made an appointment to see her at ten o'clock on Friday morning. He spent the rest of the day wondering if he'd made the right decision, but he knew that if he turned back now, having taken the pirate's penny, the next person who would be knocking on his door would be Karl, and he wouldn't have come down to Bristol to hand over the other three thousand.

Despite this, Alex was beginning to think he might just have made the biggest mistake of his life. He should have thought the whole thing through. Once his letter was published in any newspaper, his chances of ever being asked to join another board were non-existent.

He wondered if it was too late to change his mind. If he told Hardcastle everything, would he give him a thousand pounds in advance, so he could pay Martinez back in full? He would call him first thing in the morning. He put the kettle on and switched on the radio. He wasn't paying much attention, until he heard the name Kitty Parsons. He turned the volume up to hear the newsreader say, 'A spokesman for British Railways confirmed that Miss Parsons died during the night, not having woken from her coma.'

39

ALL FOUR OF THEM realized they couldn't go ahead with the operation unless it was raining. They also knew that there was no need to follow him, as Thursday was his day for shopping at Harrods, and his routine never varied.

If it was raining on a Thursday, he would leave his raincoat and umbrella in the store's cloakroom on the ground floor. He would then visit two departments, the tobacconist's, where he would collect a box of Don Pedro's favourite Montecristo cigars, and the food hall, where he would stock up with provisions for the weekend. Even though they had done their research thoroughly, everything still had to work to the split second. However, they did have one advantage: you can always rely on a German to keep to a timetable.

Lunsdorf came out of 44 Eaton Square just after 10 a.m. He was wearing a long black raincoat and carrying an umbrella. He looked up at the sky and put up his umbrella, then strode purposefully in the direction of Knightsbridge. This was not a day for window-shopping. In fact, Lunsdorf had already decided that, once he'd purchased everything he needed, if it was still raining he would take a taxi back to Eaton Square. They were even prepared for this.

Once he stepped inside Harrods he went straight to the cloakroom, where he handed his umbrella and raincoat to a woman behind the counter who gave him a small numbered disc in exchange. He then made his way past perfume and jewellery before stopping at the tobacco counter. No one followed him. After he'd picked up his usual box of cigars, he moved on to the food hall where he spent forty minutes filling several shopping bags. He returned to the cloakroom just after eleven and, peering through the window, saw that it was what the British call raining cats and dogs. He wondered if the doorman would be able to flag down a taxi. He put all the bags down and handed the brass disc to the woman behind the cloakroom counter. She disappeared into a back room and returned a moment later carrying a lady's pink umbrella.

'That's not mine,' said Lunsdorf.

'I'm so sorry, sir,' said the assistant, who appeared flustered, and quickly returned to the back room. When she eventually reappeared, she was carrying a fox wrap.

'Does that look like mine?' demanded Lunsdorf.

She went back inside, and it was some time before she reappeared, this time with a bright yellow sou'wester.

'Are you bone stupid?' Lunsdorf shouted. The attendant's cheeks flushed and she remained rooted to the spot, as if paralysed. An older woman took her place.

'I do apologize, sir. Perhaps you'd like to come through and show me which are your coat and umbrella,' she said, lifting the counter top that divided the customers from the staff. He should have spotted her mistake.

Lunsdorf followed her into the back room, and it only took him a few moments to spot his raincoat hanging halfway along the rack. He was just bending down to retrieve his umbrella when he felt a blow to the back of the head. His knees buckled, and as he sank to the floor three men jumped out from behind the coat rack. Corporal Crann grabbed Lunsdorf's arms and quickly tied them behind his back, while Sergeant Roberts shoved a gag in his mouth and Captain Hartley tied his ankles together.

A moment later, Colonel Scott-Hopkins appeared wearing a green linen jacket and pushing a large wicker laundry basket. He held its top open while the other three bundled Lunsdorf inside.

Even with him bent double, it was a tight fit. Captain Hartley threw in the raincoat and umbrella, then Crann slammed down the lid and fastened the leather buckles tightly.

'Thank you, Rachel,' said the colonel, as the cloakroom assistant held up the counter top to allow him to wheel the basket out on to the shop floor.

Corporal Crann went out on to the Brompton Road ahead of them, with Roberts only a yard behind. The colonel didn't stop as he wheeled the basket towards a Harrods van that was parked outside the entrance, with its back doors open. Hartley and Roberts lifted the basket, which was heavier than they'd anticipated, and slid it into the van. The colonel joined Crann in the front, while Hartley and Roberts jumped in the back and pulled the doors closed.

'Let's get moving,' said the colonel.

Crann eased the van into the centre lane and joined the morning traffic moving slowly down the Brompton Road towards the A4. He knew exactly where he was going because he'd carried out a dry run the day before, something the colonel always insisted on.

Forty minutes later, Crann flashed his headlights twice as he approached the perimeter fence of a deserted airfield. He barely had to slow down before the gate swung open, allowing him to drive on to the runway where a cargo plane with its familiar blue-and-white insignia awaited them, its ramp down.

Hartley and Roberts had opened the van's back doors and jumped out on to the tarmac even before the corporal had switched off the ignition. The laundry basket was yanked out of the van, pushed up the ramp and dumped in the belly of the aircraft. Hartley and Roberts walked calmly out of the plane, jumped back into the van and quickly pulled the doors closed behind them.

The colonel had kept a watchful eye on everything that was going on and, thanks to the cabinet secretary, he wouldn't need to explain to a vigilant customs officer what was in the basket or where it was destined. He returned to his seat in the front of the van. The engine was still running, and Crann quickly accelerated away as the door closed.

The van reached the open perimeter gate just as the plane's ramp began to rise, and was back on the main road by the time it started to taxi down the runway. They did not see it take off as they were going east and the plane was heading south. Forty minutes later, the Harrods van was back in its place outside the store. The whole operation had taken just over an hour and a half. The regular delivery man was waiting on the pavement for his van to be returned. He was running late, but he would make up the lost time during the afternoon shift, without his boss being any the wiser.

Crann stepped down on to the pavement and handed him the keys. 'Thank you, Joseph,' he said, shaking hands with his former SAS colleague.

Hartley, Crann and Roberts all took different routes back to Chelsea Barracks, while Colonel Scott-Hopkins went back into Harrods and headed straight for the cloakroom. The two cloakroom assistants were still standing behind the counter.

'Thank you, Rachel,' he said as he took off the Harrods jacket, folded it neatly and placed it on the counter.

'My pleasure, colonel,' replied the senior cloakroom attendant.

'And may I ask what you've done with the gentleman's shopping?'

'Rebecca handed all his bags into lost property, which is company policy when we don't know if a customer will be returning. But we saved these for you,' she said, taking a package from under the counter.

'That's very considerate of you, Rachel,' he said, as she gave him a box of Montecristo cigars.

<o>

When the plane landed it was met by a reception committee who waited patiently for the ramp to be lowered.

Four young soldiers marched into the aircraft, wheeled the laundry basket unceremoniously down the ramp and dumped it in front of the chairman of the reception committee. An officer stepped forward, unbuckled the leather straps and lifted the lid, to reveal a battered and bruised figure, bound hand and foot.

'Remove the gag and untie him,' said a man who had waited almost twenty years for this moment. He didn't speak again until the man had recovered sufficiently to climb out of the basket and on to the tarmac. 'We've never met before, Lieutenant Lunsdorf,' said Simon Wiesenthal, 'but let me be the first to welcome you to Israel.'

They didn't shake hands.

40

DON PEDRO was still in a daze. So much had happened in such a short time.

He'd been woken at five o'clock by a loud, persistent banging on the front door, and was puzzled why Karl didn't answer it. He assumed that one of the boys must have come home late and forgotten his key again. He got out of bed, put on a dressing gown and went downstairs, intending to tell Diego or Luis just what he thought about being woken at that hour in the morning.

The moment he opened the door half a dozen policemen burst into the house, ran upstairs and arrested Diego and Luis, who were both asleep in their beds. Once they had been allowed to dress, they were bundled off in a Black Maria. Why wasn't Karl there to assist him? Or had they arrested him as well?

Don Pedro ran back upstairs and threw open the door to Karl's room, only to find his bed hadn't been slept in. He walked slowly back down to the study and rang his lawyer on his home number, cursing and banging his fist repeatedly on the desk while he waited for someone to pick up the phone.

A sleepy voice eventually answered, and listened carefully as his client incoherently described what had just taken place. Mr Everard was now awake, with one foot on the floor. 'I'll get back to you the moment I know where they've taken them,' he said, 'and what they've been charged with. Don't say a word about this to anyone until you've heard back from me.'

Don Pedro continued to bang his fist on the desk and to shout obscenities at the top of his voice, but nobody was listening.

The first call came from the *Evening Standard*.

'No comment!' bellowed Don Pedro, and slammed the phone down. He continued to follow his lawyer's advice, giving the same curt reply to the *Daily Mail*, the *Mirror*, the *Express* and *The Times*. He wouldn't even have answered the phone if he hadn't been desperate to hear back from Everard. The lawyer eventually called just after eight to tell him where Diego and Luis were being held, and then spent the next few minutes stressing how serious the charges were. 'I'm going to apply for bail for both of them,' he said, 'although I'm not all that optimistic.'

'And what about Karl?' demanded Don Pedro. 'Have they told you where he is and what he's been charged with?'

'They deny all knowledge of him.'

'Keep looking,' demanded Don Pedro. 'Someone must know where he is.'

‹o›

At nine o'clock Alex Fisher put on a pinstriped, double-breasted suit, regimental tie and a brand new pair of black shoes. He went downstairs to his study and read through his resignation letter one more time before sealing the envelope and addressing it to Mrs Harry Clifton, The Barrington Shipping Company, Bristol.

He thought about what he needed to do over the next couple of days if he was going to fulfil his agreement with Don Pedro and make sure of receiving the other three thousand pounds. First, he had to be at the office of Barrington's Shipping at ten o'clock to hand the letter to Mrs Clifton. Next, he would visit the two local newspapers, the *Bristol Evening Post* and the *Bristol Evening World*, and give their editors copies of the letter. It wouldn't be the first time a letter of his had made the front page.

His next stop would be the post office, where he would send telegrams to the editors of all the national newspapers, with the simple message, 'Major Alex Fisher resigns from the board of

Barrington Shipping and calls for the chairman's resignation, as he fears the company is facing bankruptcy.' He would then return home and wait by the phone, answers to all the likely questions already prepared.

Alex left his flat just after 9.30 a.m. and drove down to the docks, making his way slowly through the rush-hour traffic. He wasn't looking forward to handing the letter to Mrs Clifton, but like a runner who had to deliver divorce papers, he would be non-committal and leave quickly.

He'd already decided to be a few minutes late, and keep her waiting. As he drove through the gates of the yard, he suddenly realized how much he was going to miss the place. He turned on the Home Service of the BBC to catch the news headlines. The police had arrested thirty-seven mods and rockers in Brighton and charged them with disturbing the peace, Nelson Mandela had begun serving a life sentence in a South African prison, and two men had been arrested at 44 Eaton . . . He turned the radio off as he reached his parking space— 44 Eaton . . . ? He flicked it quickly back on again, but the item had passed, and he had to listen to more details about the running battles that had taken place on Brighton beach between the mods and the rockers. Alex blamed the government for abolishing national service. 'Nelson Mandela, the ANC leader, has begun a life sentence for sabotage and conspiracy to overthrow the government of South Africa.'

'That's the last we'll hear of that bastard,' said Alex with conviction.

'The Metropolitan police raided a house in Eaton Square in the early hours of this morning, and arrested two men with Argentinian passports. They are due to appear at Chelsea Magistrates Court later today . . .'

—◇—

When Don Pedro left 44 Eaton Square just after 9.30, he was greeted by a volley of flashbulbs that half blinded him as he sought the relative anonymity of a taxi.

Fifteen minutes later, when the cab arrived at Chelsea Magistrates Court, he was met by even more cameras. He barged through a scrum of reporters to court number 4, not stopping to answer any of their questions.

When he entered the courtroom, Mr Everard walked quickly across to join him, and began to explain the procedure that was about to take place. He then went over the charges in detail, admitting that he wasn't at all confident that either of the boys would be granted bail.

'Any news about Karl?'

'No,' whispered Everard. 'No one has seen or heard from him since he left for Harrods yesterday morning.'

Don Pedro frowned and took a seat in the front row, while Everard returned to defence counsel's bench. At the other end of the bench sat a callow youth dressed in a short black gown who was checking through some papers. If that was the best the prosecution could do, Don Pedro felt a little more confident.

Nervous and exhausted, he looked around the near-empty courtroom. To one side were perched half a dozen journalists, pads open, pens poised, like a pack of hounds waiting to feast on a wounded fox. Behind him, at the back of the court, sat four men, all of whom he knew by sight. He suspected they all knew exactly where Karl was.

Don Pedro turned his gaze back to the front of the court as some minor officials bustled around making sure that everything was in place before the one person who could open proceedings made an entrance. As the clock struck ten, a tall, thin man wearing a long black gown entered the courtroom. The two lawyers rose immediately from their places on the bench and bowed respectfully. The magistrate returned the compliment before taking his seat at the centre of the raised dais.

Once he was settled, he took his time looking around the courtroom. If he was surprised by the unusual amount of press interest in this morning's proceedings, he didn't show it. He nodded to the clerk of the court, settled back in his chair and waited. Moments later, the first defendant appeared from below the courtroom and took his place in the dock. Don Pedro stared at Luis, having already decided what would need to be done if the boy was granted bail.

'Read out the charge,' said the magistrate, looking down at the clerk of the court.

The clerk bowed, turned to face the defendant and said in a stentorian voice, 'The charge is that you, Luis Martinez, did break into and enter a private dwelling place, namely flat 4, 12 Glebe Place, London SW3, on the night of June sixth 1964, when you destroyed several items of property belonging to a Miss Jessica Clifton. How do you plead, guilty or not guilty?'

'Not guilty,' mumbled the defendant.

The magistrate scribbled the two words on his pad as defence counsel rose from his place.

'Yes, Mr Everard,' said the magistrate.

'Your honour, my client is a man of unblemished character and reputation, and as this is a first offence, and as he has no previous convictions, we would naturally request bail.'

'Mr Duffield,' said the magistrate, turning his attention to the young man at the other end of the bench. 'Do you have any objections to this request by defence counsel?'

'No objection, your honour,' responded the prosecuting counsel, barely rising from his place.

'Then I'll set bail at a thousand pounds, Mr Everard.' The magistrate made another note on his pad. 'Your client will return to the court to face charges on October twenty-second at ten o'clock. Is that clear, Mr Everard?'

'Yes, your honour, and I am obliged,' said the lawyer, giving a slight bow.

Luis stepped down from the dock, clearly unsure what to do next. Everard nodded in the direction of his father, and Luis went and sat next to him in the front row. Neither of them spoke. A moment later, Diego appeared from below, accompanied by a policeman. He took his place in the dock and waited for the charge to be read out.

'The charge is that you, Diego Martinez, attempted to bribe a City stock broker and, in so doing, to pervert the course of justice. How do you plead, guilty or not guilty?'

'Not guilty,' said Diego firmly.

Mr Everard was quickly back on his feet. 'This, your honour, is another case of a first offence, with no prior criminal record, so once again, I have no hesitation in requesting bail.'

Mr Duffield rose from the other end of the bench and even before the magistrate could enquire, announced, 'The Crown has no objections to bail on this occasion.'

Everard was puzzled. Why wasn't the Crown putting up a fight? It was all too easy – or had he missed something?

'Then I shall set bail at two thousand pounds,' said the magistrate, 'and will be transferring this case to be heard in the High Court. A date will be fixed for the trial when a suitable time can be found in the court's calendar.'

'I am obliged, your honour,' said Everard. Diego stepped out of the dock and walked across to join his father and brother. Without a word passing between the three of them, they quickly left the courtroom.

Don Pedro and his sons pushed through the horde of photographers as they made their way out on to the street, none of them answering any of the journalists' persistent questions. Diego hailed a passing cab, and they remained silent as they climbed into the back seat. Not one of them spoke until Don Pedro had closed the front door of 44 Eaton Square and they had retreated to the study.

They spent the next couple of hours discussing what choices they'd been left with. It was just after midday when they settled on a course of action, and agreed to act on it immediately.

◄◦►

Alex leapt out of his car and almost ran into Barrington House. He took the lift to the top floor and quickly made his way to the chairman's office. A secretary, who had clearly been waiting for him, took him straight through.

'I'm so sorry to be late, chairman,' said a slightly out-of-breath Alex.

'Good morning, major,' said Emma, not getting up from her chair. 'All my secretary told me after you rang yesterday was that you wanted to see me to discuss a personal matter of some importance. Naturally I wondered what it could possibly be.'

'It's nothing for you to worry about,' said Alex. 'I just felt I had to let you know that although we've had our differences in the past, the board couldn't have had a better chairman during these difficult times, and I am proud to have served under you.'

Emma didn't reply immediately. She was trying to work out why he'd changed his mind.

'Indeed, we have had our differences in the past, major,' said Emma, still not offering him a seat, 'so I fear in future the board will somehow have to rub along without you.'

'Perhaps not,' said Alex, giving her a warm smile. 'Clearly you haven't heard the news.'

'And what news might that be?'

'Cedric Hardcastle has asked me to take his place on the board, so nothing has really changed.'

'Then it's you who clearly hasn't heard the news.' She picked up a letter from her desk. 'Cedric recently sold all his shares in the company and has resigned as a director, so he's no longer entitled to a place on the board.'

Alex spluttered, 'But he told me—'

'I have sadly accepted his resignation, and will be writing to let him know how much I appreciate the loyal and unstinting service he has given the company, and how difficult it will be to replace him on the board. I shall add a postscript, saying I hope he'll be able to attend the naming ceremony of the *Buckingham*, as well as joining us for the maiden voyage to New York.'

'But—' Alex tried again.

'Whereas in your case, Major Fisher,' said Emma, 'as Mr Martinez has also sold all his shares in the company, you too have no choice but to resign as a director, and, unlike Cedric's, I am only too happy to accept your resignation. Your contribution to the company over the years has been vindictive, meddlesome and harmful, and I might add that I have no desire to see you at the naming ceremony and you will certainly not be invited to join us on the maiden voyage. Frankly the company will be far better off without you.'

'But I—'

'And if your letter of resignation is not on my desk by five o'clock this afternoon, I will be left with no choice but to issue a statement making it only too clear why you are no longer a member of the board.'

Don Pedro walked across the room to a safe that was no longer concealed behind a painting, entered a six-figure code, swivelled the dial and pulled the heavy door open. He took out two passports that had never been stamped and a thick wad of pristine five-pound notes, which he divided equally between his two sons. Just after five o'clock, Diego and Luis left the house separately and headed in different directions, knowing that the next time they met would either be behind bars or in Buenos Aires.

Don Pedro sat alone in his study, considering the options that had been left open to him. At six o'clock, he turned on the early evening news, expecting to suffer the humiliation of seeing himself and his sons running out of the court surrounded by baying journalists. But the lead story didn't come from Chelsea, but from Tel Aviv, and it didn't feature Diego and Luis, but SS Lieutenant Karl Lunsdorf, who was being paraded in front of the television cameras dressed in a prison uniform, a number hanging around his neck. Don Pedro shouted at the screen, 'I'm not beaten yet, you bastards!' His cries were interrupted by a loud banging on the front door. He checked his watch. The boys had been gone for less than an hour. Had one of them already been arrested? If so, he knew which one it was more likely to be. He left his study, walked across the hall and tentatively opened the front door.

'You should have taken my advice, Mr Martinez,' said Colonel Scott-Hopkins. 'But you didn't, and now Lieutenant Lunsdorf will be facing trial as a war criminal. So Tel Aviv is not a city I would recommend you visit, although you'd make an interesting defence witness. Your sons are on their way back to Buenos Aires, and for their own sake, I hope they never set foot in this country again because, if they were foolish enough to do so, you can be sure that we will not turn a blind eye a second time. As for you, Mr Martinez, frankly you've outstayed your welcome, and I suggest that it's also time for you to go home. Let's say twenty-eight days, shall we? Should you fail to take my advice a second time . . . well, let's just hope we don't meet again,' added the colonel, before he turned and disappeared into the dusk.

Don Pedro slammed the door and returned to his study. He sat at his desk for over an hour, before picking up the phone and dialling a number that he had not been allowed to write down, and had been warned that he could call only once.

When the phone was picked up on the third ring, he was not surprised that no one spoke. All Don Pedro said was, 'I need a chauffeur.'

HARRY AND EMMA

1964

41

'LAST NIGHT I read the speech that Joshua Barrington delivered at the first AGM of his newly formed company in 1849. Queen Victoria was on the throne, and the sun never set on the British Empire. He told the thirty-seven people present at the Temperance Hall in Bristol that the turnover of Barrington's Shipping in its first year was £420 10s 4d, and that he was able to declare a profit of £33 4s 2d. He promised the shareholders he would do better next year.

'Today, I rise to address over a thousand Barrington's shareholders at the one hundred and twenty-fifth AGM in Colston Hall. This year our turnover was £21,422,760 and we declared a profit of £691,472. Queen Elizabeth II is on the throne, and although we may no longer rule half the world, Barrington's is still sailing the high seas. But, like Sir Joshua, I intend to do better next year.

'The company still earns its living by carrying passengers and goods to all parts of the globe. We continue trading from the east to the west. We've weathered two world wars, and are finding our place in the new world order. We should, of course, look back with pride on our colonial empire, but be willing at the same time to grasp the nettles of opportunity.'

Harry, seated in the front row, was amused to see Giles jotting down his sister's words, and wondered how long it would be before they were repeated in the House of Commons.

'One of those opportunities was grasped six years ago by my predecessor, Ross Buchanan, when, with the support of the board, he made the decision that Barrington's should commission the building of a new luxury liner, the MV *Buckingham*, that would be the first vessel of a fleet to be known as the Palace Line. Despite having had to surmount several obstacles along the way, we are now only a few weeks from naming this magnificent vessel.'

She turned to face a large screen behind her and, seconds later, a picture of the *Buckingham* appeared, to be greeted first with a gasp, followed by prolonged applause. Emma relaxed for the first time, and glanced back down at her speech as the applause died away.

'I am delighted to announce that Her Majesty, Queen Elizabeth the Queen Mother, has agreed to name the *Buckingham* when she visits Avonmouth on September twenty-first. Now, if you look under your seats, you will find a brochure containing all the details about this remarkable vessel. Perhaps you will allow me to select a few highlights for you to consider.

'The board chose Harland and Wolff to build the *Buckingham* under the direction of the distinguished naval architect Rupert Cameron, working alongside marine engineers Sir John Biles and Co., in collaboration with the Danish company Burmeister and Wain. The result was the world's first diesel propulsion ship.

'The *Buckingham* is a twin-engined vessel, 600 feet long with a beam of 78 feet, and can reach a speed of 32 knots. It is able to accommodate one hundred and two first-class passengers, two hundred and forty-two in cabin class, and three hundred and sixty in tourist class. There will be considerable hold space available for passengers' vehicles as well as for commercial cargo, depending on the ship's destination. The crew of five hundred and seventy-seven, along with the ship's cat, Perseus, will be under the command of Captain Nicholas Turnbull RN.

'Let me now draw your attention to a unique innovation that can only be enjoyed by passengers travelling on the *Buckingham*, and that will surely be the envy of our rivals. The *Buckingham* will not have, as all other liners do, hot weather open decks. For us, that's a thing of the past, because we have built the first sun deck with a swimming pool and a choice of two restaurants.' The slide that came up on the large screen was greeted with a further round of applause.

'Now, I can't pretend,' continued Emma, 'that building a liner of this quality has not been expensive. In fact, the final bill will be just over eighteen million pounds which, as you know from my report last year, has eaten heavily into our reserves. However, thanks to the foresight of Ross Buchanan, a second contract was drawn up with Harland and Wolff to build a sister ship, the SS *Balmoral*, for seventeen million pounds, provided the project is confirmed within twelve months of the *Buckingham* obtaining its certificate of seaworthiness.

'We took delivery of the *Buckingham* two weeks ago, which leaves us with fifty weeks before we decide whether or not to take up that option. By then, we must make up our minds if this is a one-off, or the first of the Palace fleet. Frankly that decision will not be made by the board or even the shareholders but, as in all commercial ventures, by the public. They alone will decide the future of the Palace Line.

'And so to my next announcement: at midday today, Thomas Cook will open the second booking period for the *Buckingham*'s maiden voyage.' Emma paused and looked up at the audience. 'But not for the general public. For the past three years, you, the shareholders, have not received the dividends you have been accustomed to in the past, so I've decided to take this opportunity to thank you for your continued loyalty and support. Anyone who has held shares for over a year will not only be given priority booking for the maiden voyage, which I know many of you have already taken advantage of, but will also receive a ten per cent discount on any trip they make on a Barrington ship in the future.'

The sustained applause that followed allowed Emma to check her notes once again.

'Thomas Cook has warned me not to get too excited about the large number of passengers who have already booked places on the maiden voyage. They tell me that every cabin will have been sold long before the ship sets sail, but that just as every opening night at the Old Vic is always sold out, like the theatre we will have to rely on regular customers and repeat orders over a long period of time. The facts are simple. We cannot afford to fall below a sixty per cent cabin occupancy, and even that figure will mean we only break even year on year. Seventy per cent occupancy will guarantee us a small profit, while we will need eighty-six per cent if we are to repay our capital outlay within ten years, as Ross Buchanan always planned. And by that time, I suspect there will be a sun deck on all of our competitors' ships, and we will be looking for new and innovative ideas to attract an ever more demanding and sophisticated public.

'So the next twelve months will decide the future of Barrington's. Do we make history, or become history? Be assured that your directors will work tirelessly on behalf of the shareholders who have placed their trust in us, to deliver a service that will be the benchmark in the world of luxury shipping. Let me end as I began. Like my great-grandfather, I intend to do better next year, and the year after, and the year after.'

Emma sat down and the audience rose to their feet as if it were a first night. She closed her eyes and thought of her grandfather's words, *If you're good enough to be the chairman, being a woman won't make any difference*. Admiral Summers leant across and whispered, 'Congratulations,' and then added, 'Questions?'

Emma jumped back up. 'Sorry, I quite forgot. Of course, I'll be delighted to take questions.'

A smartly dressed man in the second row was quickly on his feet. 'You mentioned that the share price recently touched an all-time high, but can you explain why in the past couple of weeks there have been such peaks and troughs, which, to a layman like myself, seem inexplicable, not to say worrying?'

'I cannot fully explain that myself,' admitted Emma. 'But I can tell you that a former shareholder dumped twenty-two and a half per cent of the company's stock on the market without having the courtesy to inform me, despite that shareholder having a representative on the board. Fortunately for Barrington's, the broker concerned was shrewd enough to offer those shares to one of our former directors, Mr Cedric Hardcastle, who is himself a banker. Mr Hardcastle was able to place the entire holding with a leading businessman from the north of England, who has wanted for some time to purchase a substantial stake in the company. This meant that the shares were only on the market for a few minutes, causing minimum disruption, and indeed within days the price returned to its former high.'

Emma saw her rise from her place in the middle of the fourth row, wearing a wide-brimmed yellow hat that would have been more appropriate at Ascot, but Emma still ignored the woman, pointing instead to a man a few rows behind her.

'Will the *Buckingham* only be sailing on the transatlantic route, or does the company have plans for her to visit other destinations in the future?'

'Good question,' Giles had taught Emma to say, particularly when it wasn't. 'It wouldn't be possible for the *Buckingham* to make a profit if we restricted her voyages to the east coast of the States, not least because our rivals, particularly the Americans, have dominated that route for almost a century. No, we must identify a new generation of passengers who do not consider the sole purpose of travel as simply to get from A to B. The *Buckingham* must be like a floating luxury hotel, on which her passengers sleep each night, while during the day they visit countries they never thought they'd see in their lifetime. With that in mind, the *Buckingham* will make regular trips to the Caribbean and the Bahamas, and during the summer she'll cruise the Mediterranean and sail along the Italian coast. And who can say what other parts of the world will open up in the next twenty years?'

Once again the woman was on her feet, and once again Emma avoided her, pointing to another man near the front.

'Are you worried about the number of passengers who are choosing to travel by aeroplane rather than ocean liners? BOAC, for example, are claiming that they can get you to New York in less than eight hours, whereas the *Buckingham* will take at least four days.'

'You're quite right, sir,' responded Emma, 'which is why our advertising concentrates on a different vision for our passengers, offering them an experience that they could never hope to have on an aeroplane. What aeroplane can offer a theatre, shops, a cinema, a library and restaurants that provide the finest cuisine, not to mention a sun deck and a swimming pool? The truth is, if you're in a hurry, don't book a cabin on the *Buckingham*, because she's a floating palace that you'll want to return to again and again. And there's something else I can promise: when you arrive home, you won't be suffering from jet lag.'

The woman in the fourth row was on her feet again, waving. 'Are you trying to avoid me, chairman?' she shouted.

Giles thought he recognized the voice and looked round to have his worst fears confirmed.

'Not at all, madam, but as you're neither a shareholder nor a journalist, I didn't give you priority. But please, do ask your question.'

'Is it true that one of your directors sold his vast shareholding over the weekend, in an attempt to bring the company down?'

'No, Lady Virginia, that is not the case. You're probably thinking of the twenty-two and a half per cent Don Pedro Martinez put on the market without informing the board, but luckily, to use a modern expression, we saw him coming.'

Laughter broke out in the hall, but Virginia wasn't deterred. 'If one of your directors was involved in such an exercise, shouldn't he resign from the board?'

'If you're referring to Major Fisher, I asked him to resign last Friday when he came to visit me in my office, as I'm sure you already know, Lady Virginia.'

'What are you insinuating?'

'That on two separate occasions when Major Fisher represented *you* on the board, you allowed him to sell all your shares over a weekend, and then, after you'd made a handsome profit, you bought them back during the three-week trading period. When the share price recovered and reached a new high, you carried out the same exercise a second time, making an even larger profit. If it was your intention to bring the company down,

Lady Virginia, then, like Mr Martinez, you have failed, and failed lamentably, because you were defeated by decent ordinary people who want this company to be a success.'

Spontaneous applause broke out throughout the hall as Lady Virginia pushed her way along the crowded row, not caring whose toes she trod on. When she reached the aisle, she looked back up at the stage and shouted, 'You'll be hearing from my solicitor.'

'I do hope so,' said Emma, 'because then Major Fisher will be able to tell a jury who he was representing when he bought and sold your shares.'

This knockout blow received the loudest ovation of the day. Emma even had time to glance down at the front row and wink at Cedric Hardcastle.

She spent the next hour dealing with a myriad questions from shareholders, City analysts and journalists alike, with a confidence and authority Harry had rarely witnessed. After she'd answered the last question, she closed the meeting with the words, 'I hope that many of you will join me on the maiden voyage to New York in a couple of months' time, as I'm confident it will be an experience you will never forget.'

'I think we can guarantee that,' whispered a man with a cultured Irish lilt who'd been sitting at the back of the hall. He slipped out while Emma enjoyed a standing ovation.

42

'GOOD MORNING. Thomas Cook and Son. How can I assist you?'

'It's Lord Glenarthur. I was hoping you'd be able to help me with a personal matter.'

'I'll do my best, sir.'

'I'm a family friend of the Barringtons and the Cliftons, and I told Harry Clifton that sadly I wouldn't be able to join them on the *Buckingham*'s maiden voyage to New York due to business commitments. Those commitments have now fallen through, and I thought it would be rather fun not to tell them I'd be on board. A sort of surprise, if you get my drift.'

'I certainly do, my lord.'

'So I was calling to find out if it might be possible to book a cabin somewhere near the family.'

'I'll see what I can do, if you'd be kind enough to hold the line for a moment.' The man on the other end of the line took a sip of Jameson's and waited. 'My lord, there are still two first-class cabins available on the upper deck, numbers three and five.'

'I'd like to be as close to the family as possible.'

'Well, Sir Giles Barrington is in cabin number two.'

'And Emma?'

'Emma?'

'I do apologize. Mrs Clifton.'

'She's in cabin number one.'

'Then I'll take cabin number three. I'm most grateful for your assistance.'

'My pleasure, sir. I hope you have a pleasant trip. May I ask where we should send the tickets?'

'No, don't bother yourself. I'll get my chauffeur to collect them.'

—◦—

Don Pedro unlocked the safe in his study and removed what was left of his money. He placed bundles of five-pound notes in neat stacks of ten thousand, until they took up every inch of his desk. He returned £23,645 to the safe and locked it, then double-checked the remaining £250,000 before placing the money in the rucksack they had provided. He sat down at his desk, picked up the morning paper and waited.

Ten days had passed before the chauffeur returned his call, to say the operation had been sanctioned, but only if he was willing to pay £500,000. When he'd queried the amount, it was pointed out to him that considerable risks were involved, because if any of the lads were caught, they would probably spend the rest of their days in Crumlin Road, or even worse.

He didn't bother to bargain. After all, he had no intention of paying the second instalment, as he doubted that there were many IRA sympathizers in Buenos Aires.

—◦—

'Good morning, Thomas Cook and Son.'

'I'd like to book a first-class cabin for the *Buckingham's* maiden voyage to New York.'

'Yes, of course, madam, I'll put you through.'

'First-class reservations, how can I help you?'

'It's Lady Virginia Fenwick. I'd like to book a cabin for the maiden voyage.'

'Could you repeat your name please?'

'Lady Virginia Fenwick,' she said slowly, as if addressing a foreigner.

A long silence followed, which Virginia assumed meant the booking clerk was checking availability.

'I'm so sorry, Lady Virginia, but unfortunately first class is completely sold out. Shall I put you through to cabin class?'

'Certainly not. Don't you realize who I am?'

The clerk would have liked to say yes, I know exactly who you are, because your name has been pinned to the bulletin board for the past month with clear instructions to all sales clerks what to do if that particular lady phoned to make a booking, but instead he said, sticking to his script, 'I am sorry, my lady, but there is nothing I can do.'

'But I am a personal friend of the chairman of Barrington's Shipping,' said Virginia. 'Surely that makes a difference?'

'It most certainly does,' replied the booking clerk. 'We do have one first-class cabin still available, but it can only be released on the express order of the chairman. So if you'd be kind enough to give Mrs Clifton a call, I'll hold the cabin in your name, and release it immediately I hear back from her.'

They never heard back from her.

◄○►

When Don Pedro heard the sound of a car horn, he folded his newspaper, placed it on the desk, picked up the rucksack and made his way out of the house.

The chauffeur touched his cap and said, 'Good morning, sir,' before placing the rucksack in the boot of the Mercedes.

Don Pedro got into the back seat, closed the door and waited. When the chauffeur climbed behind the wheel, he didn't ask where Don Pedro wanted to go because he'd already selected the route. They turned left out of Eaton Square and headed towards Hyde Park Corner.

'I'm assuming the agreed amount is in the rucksack,' said the chauffeur as they passed the hospital on the corner of Hyde Park.

'Two hundred and fifty thousand pounds in cash,' said Don Pedro.

'And we will expect the other half to be paid in full within twenty-four hours of carrying out our part of the agreement.'

'That is what I agreed,' said Don Pedro, as he thought about the £23,645 left in the safe in his office; all the money he possessed. Even the house was no longer in his name.

'You do realize the consequences if you don't pay the second instalment?'

'You've reminded me often enough,' Don Pedro said as the car proceeded up Park Lane, not exceeding the forty mile an hour speed limit.

'In normal circumstances, should you fail to pay on time, we would have killed one of your sons, but as they are both now safely back in Buenos Aires, and Herr Lunsdorf is no longer among us, that only leaves you,' said the chauffeur as he drove around Marble Arch.

Don Pedro remained silent as they proceeded down the other side of Park Lane, then stopped at a set of traffic lights. 'But what if you don't carry out your side of the bargain?' he demanded.

'Then you won't have to pay the other two hundred and fifty thousand, will you?' said the chauffeur as he drew up outside the Dorchester.

A doorman dressed in a long green coat rushed up to the car and opened the back door to allow Don Pedro to step out.

'I need a taxi,' said Don Pedro as the chauffeur drove off to rejoin the morning traffic on Park Lane.

'Yes, sir,' said the doorman, raising an arm and letting out a piercing whistle.

When Don Pedro climbed into the back of the taxi and said, 'Forty-four Eaton Square,' the doorman was puzzled. Why would the gentleman need a taxi when he already had a chauffeur?

◄o►

'Thomas Cook and Son, how may I help you?'

'I'd like to book four cabins on the *Buckingham* for its maiden voyage to New York.'

'First class or cabin, sir?'

'Cabin.'

'I'll put you through.'

'Good morning, cabin-class reservations for the *Buckingham*.'

'I'd like to book four single cabins for the voyage to New York on October the twenty-ninth.'

'May I take the names of the passengers?' Colonel Scott-Hopkins gave his name and those of his three colleagues. 'The tickets will be thirty-two pounds each. Where shall I send the invoice, sir?'

SAS headquarters, Chelsea Barracks, King's Road, London, he could have said, as they were paying the bill, but instead he gave the booking clerk his home address.

43

'I WOULD LIKE to begin today's meeting by welcoming Mr Bob Bingham as a member of the board,' said Emma. 'Bob is chairman of Bingham's Fish Paste, and as he has recently acquired twenty-two point five per cent of Barrington's stock, he doesn't have to convince anyone of his belief in the company's future. We have also received resignations from two other board members, Mr Cedric Hardcastle, whose shrewd and wise advice will be sadly missed, and Major Fisher, who will not be quite so sadly missed.'

Admiral Summers allowed himself a wry smile.

'As there are only ten days to go before the official naming of the *Buckingham*, perhaps I should begin by bringing you up to date with the preparations for the ceremony.' Emma opened the red folder in front of her and checked the schedule carefully. 'The Queen Mother will arrive at Temple Meads on the royal train at 9.35 on the morning of September twenty-first. She will be met on the platform by the Lord Lieutenant of the County and City of Bristol and the Lord Mayor of Bristol. Her Majesty will then be driven to Bristol Grammar School, where she will be met by the headmaster, who will escort her to the school's new science laboratories, which she will open at 10.10. She will meet a selected group of pupils and staff, before leaving the school at eleven o'clock. She will then be driven to Avonmouth, arriving at the shipyard at 11.17.' Emma looked up. 'My life would be so much simpler if I always knew the exact minute I would be arriving anywhere. I will meet Her Majesty when she arrives at Avonmouth,' she continued, looking back down at the schedule, 'and welcome her on behalf of the company, before introducing her to the board. At 11.29 I will accompany her to the north dock, where she will meet the ship's architect, our marine engineer and the chairman of Harland and Wolff.

'At three minutes to twelve, I will officially welcome our guest of honour. My speech will last for three minutes, and on the first stroke of twelve, Her Majesty will name the *Buckingham* with the traditional breaking of a magnum of champagne on the hull.'

'And what happens if the bottle doesn't break?' asked Clive Anscott, laughing.

No one else laughed.

'There's nothing in my file about that,' said Emma. 'At twelve thirty, Her Majesty will leave for the Royal West of England Academy, where she will join the staff for lunch, before opening its new art gallery at three. At four, she will be driven back to Temple Meads, accompanied by the lord lieutenant, and will board the royal train, which will depart for Paddington ten minutes after she has boarded.'

Emma closed the file, let out a sigh, and received a mock round of applause from her fellow directors. 'As a child,' she added, 'I always wanted to be a princess, but after that, I have to tell you I've changed my mind.' This time the applause was genuine.

'How will we know where we're expected to be at any particular moment?' asked Andy Dobbs.

'Every member of the board will be issued with a copy of the official timetable, and heaven help the person who isn't in the right place at the right time. I'll now move on to the equally important matter of the *Buckingham*'s maiden voyage, which as you all know will start on October the twenty-ninth. The board will be pleased to learn that every cabin has been taken and, even more pleasing, the return voyage is also sold out.'

'Sold out is an interesting description,' said Bob Bingham. 'How many are paying passengers and how many are guests?'

'Guests?' repeated the admiral.

'Passengers who will not be paying for their tickets.'

'Well, there are several people who are entitled—'

'—to a free trip. Don't let them get used to it would be my advice.'

'Would you count the board members and their families in that category, Mr Bingham?' asked Emma.

'Not on the maiden voyage, but in the future certainly, as a matter of principle. A floating palace is very attractive when you don't have to pay for your cabin, not to mention your food or your drink.'

'Do tell me, Mr Bingham, do you always pay for your own fish paste?'

'Always, admiral. That way my staff don't feel they're entitled to free samples for their families and friends.'

'Then on any future voyage,' said Emma, 'I will always pay for my cabin, and I will never travel free while I am chairman of this company.'

One or two members of the board shifted uneasily in their chairs.

'I do hope,' said David Dixon, 'that won't stop the Barringtons and the Cliftons being well represented on this historic voyage.'

'Most of my family will be joining me on the trip,' said Emma, 'with the exception of my sister Grace who will only be able to attend the naming ceremony, as it's the first week of term and she will have to return to Cambridge immediately afterwards.'

'And Sir Giles?' asked Anscott.

'That will depend on whether the prime minister decides to call a general election. However, my son Sebastian will definitely be coming with his girlfriend Samantha, but they will be in cabin class. And before you ask, Mr Bingham, I did pay for their tickets.'

'If he's the lad who came up to my factory a couple of weeks back, I'd keep my eyes open, chairman, because I have a feeling he's after your job.'

'But he's only twenty-four,' said Emma.

'That won't worry him. I was chairman of Bingham's at twenty-seven.'

'So I've got another three years.'

'You and Cedric,' said Bob, 'depending on which of you he decides to replace.'

'I don't think Bingham's joking, chairman,' said the admiral. 'Can't wait to meet the boy.'

'Have any former directors been invited to join us on the voyage to New York?' asked Andy Dobbs. 'I have Ross Buchanan in mind.'

'Yes,' said Emma, 'I must admit that I have invited Ross and Jean to join us as guests of the company. That's assuming Mr Bingham approves.'

'I wouldn't be on this board if it wasn't for Ross Buchanan, and after what Cedric Hardcastle told me about what he got up to on *The Night Scotsman*, I think he's more than earned his passage.'

'Couldn't agree more,' said Jim Knowles. 'But that begs the question of what we do about Fisher and Hardcastle?'

'I hadn't thought of inviting Major Fisher,' said Emma, 'and Cedric Hardcastle has already told me that he feels it might not be wise for him to attend the naming ceremony, following Lady Virginia's veiled attack on him at the AGM.'

'Has that woman been stupid enough to issue her threatened writ?' asked Dobbs.

'Yes,' said Emma, 'claiming both defamation and slander.'

'Slander I understand,' said Dobbs, 'but how can she claim defamation?'

'Because I insisted that every word of our exchange was recorded in the minutes of the AGM.'

'Then let's hope she's stupid enough to take you to the High Court.'

'Stupid she is not,' said Bingham, 'but she is arrogant enough, though I have a feeling that while Fisher is still around to give evidence, she won't risk it.'

'Can we get back to the business in hand?' asked the admiral. 'I could be dead by the time the case reaches the courts.'

Emma laughed. 'Was there anything in particular you wanted to raise, admiral?'

'How long is the voyage to New York scheduled to take?'

'Just over four days, which compares favourably with any of our rivals.'

'But the *Buckingham* is equipped with the first twin-engined diesel motor, so surely there's a possibility of capturing the Blue Riband for the fastest ever crossing?'

'If the weather conditions were perfect, and they are usually pretty good at this time of the year, we'd have an outside chance, but you've only got to mention the words Blue Riband and the first thing people think about is the *Titanic*. So we mustn't even suggest the possibility until the Statue of Liberty can be seen on the horizon.'

'Chairman, how many people are we expecting to attend the naming ceremony?'

'The chief constable tells me it could be three, or perhaps even four, thousand.'

'And who's in charge of security?'

'The police are responsible for crowd control and public safety.'

'While we pick up the bill.'

'Just like a football match,' said Knowles.

'Let's hope not,' said Emma. 'If there are no more questions, I'd like to propose that we hold our next board meeting in the Walter Barrington suite of the *Buckingham* on the return voyage from New York. Until then, I look forward to seeing all of you here at precisely ten o'clock on the twenty-first.'

'But that's over an hour before the dear lady is due to arrive,' said Bob Bingham.

'You'll find we rise early in the West Country, Mr Bingham. That's how we birds catch the worm.'

44

'YOUR MAJESTY, may I present Mrs Clifton, the chairman of Barrington's Shipping,' said the lord lieutenant.

Emma curtsied, and waited for the Queen Mother to say something, as the briefing notes had made it clear that you must not speak until spoken to, and you should never ask a question.

'How Sir Walter would have enjoyed today, Mrs Clifton.'

Emma remained speechless, because she knew her grandfather had only met the Queen Mother once and, although he often referred to the occasion, and even had a photograph in his office to remind everyone of it, she hadn't expected HM to remember it as well.

'May I present Admiral Summers,' said Emma, taking over from the lord lieutenant, 'who has served on the board of Barrington's for over twenty years.'

'The last time we met, admiral, you kindly showed me over your destroyer, HMS *Chevron*.'

'I think you'll find, ma'am, that it was the King's destroyer. I was only in temporary command.'

'A nice distinction, admiral,' said the Queen Mother as Emma continued to introduce her fellow directors, and could only wonder what Her Majesty would make of their latest recruit to the board.

'Mr Bingham, you have been banned from the palace.' Bob Bingham's mouth opened, but no words came out. 'To be fair, not you personally, but your fish paste.'

'But why, ma'am?' asked Bob, ignoring his briefing notes.

'Because my grandson, Prince Andrew, keeps putting his finger in the jar, mimicking the little boy on your label.'

Bob didn't say another word as the Queen Mother moved on to meet the ship's architect.

'When we last met . . .'

Emma checked her watch as the Queen Mother chatted to the chairman of Harland and Wolff.

'And what is your next project, Mr Baillie?'

'It's all very hush-hush at the moment, ma'am. All I can tell you is that the letters "HMS" will precede the name on the side of the vessel, and it will spend an awful lot of time under the water.'

The Queen Mother smiled as the lord lieutenant guided her towards a comfortable chair just behind the rostrum.

Emma waited for her to be seated, before she made her way to the rostrum herself to deliver a speech that didn't require notes, because she knew it by heart. She gripped the sides of the lectern, took a deep breath as Giles had advised her to do, and looked down at the vast crowd, far more than the four thousand the police had predicted, which had fallen silent in anticipation.

'Your Majesty, this is your third visit to Barrington's shipyard. You first came here as our Queen in 1939, when the company celebrated its centenary and my grandfather was chairman. You then visited again in 1942, to see for yourself the damage caused by the bombing raids during the war, and today you make a welcome return to launch a liner named after the home you have lived in for the past sixteen years. By the way, ma'am, should you ever need a room for the night' – Emma's words were greeted with warm laughter – 'we've got two hundred and ninety-two, though I feel I ought to point out that you've missed your chance of joining us on the maiden voyage, because we're sold out.'

The crowd's laughter and applause helped Emma relax and feel more confident.

'And can I add, ma'am, that your presence here today has made this an hysterical occasion—'

There was a gasp that turned into an embarrassed silence. Emma wished the ground would open up and swallow her, until the Queen Mother burst out laughing, and the whole crowd began to cheer and throw their caps into the air. Emma could feel her cheeks burning, and it was some time before she recovered sufficiently to say, 'It is my privilege, ma'am, to invite you to name the MV *Buckingham*.'

Emma took a step back to allow the Queen Mother to take her place. This was the moment she had been dreading most. Ross Buchanan had once told her about a notorious occasion when everything had gone wrong and the ship had not only suffered a public humiliation, but crew and public alike had refused to sail on her, convinced that she was cursed.

The crowd fell silent once more, and waited nervously, the same fear passing through the minds of every worker in the yard as they looked up at the royal visitor. Several of the more superstitious of them, including Emma, crossed their fingers as the first chime of twelve rang out on the shipyard clock, and the lord lieutenant handed the bottle of champagne to the Queen Mother.

'I name this ship, the *Buckingham*,' she declared, 'and may she bring joy and happiness to all who sail on her, and enjoy a long and prosperous life on the high seas.'

The Queen Mother raised the magnum of champagne, paused for a moment, and then let go. Emma wanted to close her eyes as the bottle descended in a wide arc towards the ship. When it hit the hull, the bottle shattered into a hundred pieces, and champagne bubbles ran down the side of the ship as the crowd produced the loudest cheer of the day.

◄o►

'I don't see how that could have gone much better,' said Giles as the Queen Mother's car drove out of the shipyard and disappeared.

'I could have done without the hysterical occasion,' said Emma.

'I don't agree,' said Harry. 'The Queen Mother clearly enjoyed your little faux pas, the workers will tell their grandchildren about it, and for once you proved to be fallible.'

'That's kind of you,' said Emma, 'but we've still got a lot of work to do before the maiden voyage, and I can't afford to have another hysterical moment,' she added as they were joined by her sister.

'I'm so glad I didn't miss that,' said Grace. 'But would it be possible for you not to choose term-time when you launch your next ship? And if I have a further piece of advice for my big sister: make sure you treat the maiden voyage as a celebration, a holiday, and not just another week at the office.' She kissed her brother and sister on both cheeks. 'By the way,' she added, 'I loved the hysterical moment.'

'She's right,' said Giles as they watched Grace walk off towards the nearest bus stop, 'you should enjoy every moment, because I can tell you I intend to.'

'You may not be able to.'

'Why not?'

'You could be a minister by then.'

'I've got to hold on to my seat, and the party's got to win the election, before I can be a minister.'

'And when do you think the election will be?'

'If I had to guess, some time in October fairly soon after the party conferences. So you're going to see a lot of me in Bristol over the next few weeks.'

'And Gwyneth, I hope.'

'You bet, although I'm rather hoping the baby will be born during the campaign. Worth a thousand votes, Griff tells me.'

'You're a charlatan, Giles Barrington.'

'No, I'm a politician fighting a marginal seat, and if I win it, I think I just might make the Cabinet.'

'Be careful what you wish for.'

45

GILES WAS pleasantly surprised by how civilized the general election campaign turned out to be, not least because Jeremy Fordyce, his Conservative opponent, an intelligent young man from Central Office, never gave the impression that he really believed he could win the seat, and certainly didn't involve himself in the sort of underhand practices Alex Fisher had engaged in when he was the candidate.

Reginald Ellsworthy, the perennial Liberal candidate, had only one aim, to increase his vote, and even Lady Virginia failed to land a blow, above or below the belt, possibly because she was still recovering from the knockout punch Emma had landed at the Barrington's AGM.

So when the city clerk announced, 'I, the returning officer for the constituency of Bristol Docklands, declare the total number of votes cast for each candidate to be as follows:

Sir Giles Barrington	21,114
Mr Reginald Ellsworthy	4,109
Mr Jeremy Fordyce	17,346.

'I therefore declare Sir Giles Barrington to be the duly elected Member of Parliament for the constituency of Bristol Docklands,' no one seemed surprised.

Although the vote in the constituency may not have been close, the decision as to who should govern the country was, to quote the BBC's grand inquisitor, Robin Day, looking as if it would go to the wire. In fact, it wasn't until the final result had been declared in Mulgelrie at 3.34 p.m. on the day after the election that the nation began to prepare itself for the first Labour government since Clement Attlee's thirteen years before.

Giles travelled up to London the following day, but not before he, Gwyneth and five-week-old Walter Barrington had carried out a tour of the constituency to thank the party workers for achieving the biggest majority Giles had ever secured.

'Good luck for Monday,' was a sentence that was repeated again and again as he travelled around the constituency, because everyone knew that was the day the new prime minister would decide who would join him around the Cabinet table.

Giles spent the weekend listening to colleagues' opinions on the phone, and reading the columns of leading political correspondents, but the truth was, only one man knew who would get the nod, the rest was mere speculation.

On Monday morning, Giles watched on television as Harold Wilson was driven to the palace to be asked by the Queen if he could form a government. Forty minutes later he emerged as prime minister, and was driven to Downing Street so he could invite twenty-two of his colleagues to join him as members of the Cabinet.

Giles sat at the breakfast table pretending to read the morning papers, when he wasn't staring at the phone, willing it to ring. It rang several times, but each time it was either a member of his family or one of his friends calling to congratulate him on his increased majority, or to wish him luck on being invited to join the government. Get off the line, he wanted to say. How can the PM call me if the phone is always engaged? And then the call came.

'This is the Number Ten switchboard, Sir Giles. The prime minister wondered if it would be possible for you to join him at Number Ten at three thirty this afternoon.'

I might just be able to fit him in, Giles wanted to say. 'Yes, of course,' he said, and put the phone down. Where in the pecking order was 3.30 p.m.?

Ten o'clock and you knew you were either Chancellor of the

Exchequer, Foreign Secretary or Home Secretary. Those posts had already been filled, by Jim Callaghan, Patrick Gordon Walker and Frank Soskice. Noon: Education, Michael Stewart and Employment, Barbara Castle. Three thirty was on the cusp. Was he in the Cabinet, or would he be expected to serve a probationary period as a minister of state?

Giles would have made himself some lunch if the phone had stopped ringing every other minute. Colleagues calling to tell him what job they'd got, colleagues calling to say the PM hadn't phoned them yet, and colleagues wanting to know what time the PM had asked to see him. None of them seemed sure what 3.30 p.m. meant.

As the sun was shining on a Labour victory, Giles decided to walk to Number 10. He left his Smith Square flat just after 3 p.m., strolled across to the Embankment and past the Lords and Commons on his way to Whitehall. He crossed the road as Big Ben struck a quarter past, and continued past the Foreign and Commonwealth Office, before turning into Downing Street. He was greeted by a raucous pack of pit bull terriers, hemmed in behind makeshift barriers.

'What job are you expecting to get?' shouted one of them.

I only wish I knew, Giles wanted to say, while being almost blinded by the endless flashbulbs.

'Are you hoping to be in the Cabinet, Sir Giles?' demanded another.

Of course I am, you idiot. But his lips didn't move.

'How long do you think the government can survive with such a small majority?'

Not very long, he didn't want to admit.

The questions continued to be thrown at him as he made his way up Downing Street, despite the fact that every journalist knew he had no hope of getting an answer on the way in, and not much more than a wave and perhaps a smile on the way out.

Giles was about three paces from the front door when it opened, and, for the first time in his life, he entered Number 10 Downing Street.

'Good morning, Sir Giles,' said the cabinet secretary, as if they had never met before. 'The prime minister is with one of your colleagues at the moment, so perhaps you could wait in the anteroom until he's free.'

Giles realized that Sir Alan already knew which post he was about to be offered, but not even the twitch of an eyebrow came from the inscrutable mandarin before he went on his way.

Giles took a seat in the small anteroom where Wellington and Nelson had reputedly sat waiting to see William Pitt the Younger, neither realizing who the other was. He rubbed his hands on the sides of his trousers, although he knew he would not be shaking hands with the PM, as, traditionally, Parliamentary colleagues never do. Only the clock on the mantelpiece was beating louder than his heart. Eventually the door opened and Sir Alan reappeared. All he said was, 'The prime minister will see you now.'

Giles stood up and began what is known as the long walk to the gallows.

When he entered the Cabinet Room, Harold Wilson was sitting halfway down a long oval table surrounded by twenty-two empty chairs. The moment he saw Giles, he rose from his seat below a portrait of Robert Peel, and said, 'Great result in Bristol Docklands, Giles, well done.'

'Thank you, prime minister,' said Giles, reverting to the tradition of no longer calling him by his first name.

'Come and have a seat,' Wilson said as he filled his pipe.

Giles was about to sit down next to the PM when he said, 'No, not there. That's George's place; perhaps one day, but not today. Why don't you sit over there –' he said, pointing to a green leather-backed chair on the far side of the table. 'After all, that's where the Secretary of State for European Affairs will be sitting every Thursday when the Cabinet meets.'

46

'JUST THINK how many things can go wrong,' said Emma as she paced up and down the bedroom.

'Why not focus on how many things will go right,' said Harry, 'and take Grace's advice, try to relax and treat the whole experience as a holiday.'

'I'm only sorry she won't be joining us on the voyage.'

'Grace was never going to take two weeks off during an eight-week term.'

'Giles seems able to manage it.'

'Only one week,' Harry reminded her, 'and he's been fairly cunning, because he plans to visit the UN while he's in New York, and then go on to Washington to meet his opposite number.'

'Leaving Gwyneth and the baby at home.'

'A wise decision given the circumstances. It wouldn't have been much of a holiday for either of them with young Walter bawling his head off night and day.'

'Are you packed and ready?' asked Emma.

'Yes I am, chairman. Have been for some time.'

Emma laughed and threw her arms around him. 'Sometimes I forget to say thank you.'

'Don't get sentimental on me. You've still got a job to do, so why don't we get going?'

Emma seemed impatient to leave, even though it meant they would be hanging about on board for hours before the captain gave the order to cast off and set sail for New York. Harry accepted that it would have been even worse if they'd stayed at home.

'Just look at her,' said Emma with pride as the car drove on to the quayside, and the *Buckingham* loomed up ahead of them.

'Yes, a truly hysterical sight.'

'Oh help,' said Emma. 'Am I ever going to live that down?'

'I do hope not,' said Harry.

—◄◦►—

'It's so exciting,' said Sam as Sebastian turned off the A4 and followed the signs for the docks. 'I've never been on an ocean liner before.'

'And it's no ordinary liner,' said Sebastian. 'It's got a sun deck, a cinema, two restaurants and a swimming pool. It's more like a floating city.'

'It seems strange having a swimming pool when you're surrounded by water.'

'Water, water everywhere.'

'Another of your minor English poets?' said Sam.

'Do you have any major American poets?'

'One who wrote a poem you could learn something from: *The heights by great men reached and kept were not attained by sudden flight, but they, while their companions slept, were toiling upward in the night.*'

'Who wrote that?' asked Sebastian.

—◄◦►—

'How many of our people are already on board?' asked Lord Glenarthur, trying to remain in character as the car drove out of Bristol and headed for the port.

'Three porters and a couple of waiters, one in the grill room, one in cabin class, and a messenger boy.'

'Can they be relied on to keep their mouths shut if they were interrogated or put under real pressure?'

'Two of the porters and one of the waiters were hand-picked. The messenger boy will only be on board for a few minutes, and once he's delivered the flowers, he'll hot-foot it back to Belfast.'

'After we've checked in, Liam, come to my cabin at nine o'clock. By then most of the first-class passengers will be having dinner, which will give you more than enough time to set up the equipment.'

'Setting it up won't be the problem,' said Liam. 'It's getting that large trunk on board without anyone becoming suspicious that I'm worried about.'

'Two of the porters know the number plate of this car,' said the chauffeur, 'and they'll be looking out for us.'

'How's my accent holding up?' asked Glenarthur.

'You'd have fooled me, but I'm not an English gentleman. And we'll have to hope no one on board has actually met Lord Glenarthur.'

'Unlikely. He's over eighty, and he hasn't been seen in public since his wife died ten years ago.'

'Isn't he a distant relation of the Barringtons?' asked Liam.

'That's why I chose him. If the SAS has anyone on board, they'll check *Who's Who*, and assume I'm family.'

'But what if you bump into a member of the family?'

'I'm not going to bump *into* any of them. I'm going to bump them all off.' The chauffeur chuckled. 'Now, tell me, how do I get to my other cabin after I've pressed the button?'

'I'll give you the key at nine o'clock. Can you remember where the public toilet on deck six is? Because that's where you'll have to change once you've left your cabin for the last time.'

'It's on the far side of the first-class lounge. And by the way, old chap, it's a lavatory not a toilet,' said Lord Glenarthur. 'That's the sort of simple mistake that could get me caught out. Don't forget, this ship is typical of English society. The upper classes don't mix with cabin, and the cabin classes wouldn't consider speaking to those in tourist. So it might not be that easy for us to get in touch with each other.'

'But I read this is the first liner with a telephone in every room,' Liam said, 'so if there's an emergency, just dial 712. If I don't pick up, our waiter in the grill room is called Jimmy, and he . . .'

Colonel Scott-Hopkins wasn't looking in the direction of the *Buckingham*. He and his colleagues were scanning the crowd on the quay for any sign of an Irish presence. So far he hadn't seen anyone he recognized. Captain Hartley and Sergeant Roberts, who had both served in Northern Ireland with the SAS, had also drawn blanks. It was Corporal Crann who spotted him.

'Four o'clock, standing on his own at the back of the crowd. He's not looking at the ship, just the passengers.'

'What the hell's he doing here?'

'Perhaps the same as us, looking for someone. But who?'

'I don't know,' said Scott-Hopkins, 'but, Crann, don't let him out of your sight, and if he speaks to anyone or attempts to go on board, I want to know immediately.'

'Yes, sir,' said Crann, who began to weave his way through the crowd towards the target.

'Six o'clock,' said Captain Hartley.

The colonel switched his attention. 'Oh God, that's all we need . . .'

<hr />

'Once I get out of the car, Liam, make yourself scarce and assume there are people in the crowd looking for you,' said Lord Glenarthur. 'And be sure you're in my cabin by nine.'

'I've just spotted Cormac and Declan,' said the chauffeur. He flashed his lights once and they hurried across, ignoring several other passengers who needed assistance.

'Don't get out of the car,' said Glenarthur to the chauffeur. It took both of the porters to lift the heavy trunk out of the boot and place it on a trolley as gently as if they were handling a new-born baby. After one of them had slammed the boot shut, Glenarthur said, 'When you get back to London, Kevin, keep an eye on forty-four Eaton Square. Now that Martinez has sold his Rolls-Royce, I have a feeling he might do a runner.' He turned back to Liam. 'See you at nine,' he added, then got out of the car and melted into the crowd.

'When should I deliver the lilies?' whispered a young man who had appeared by Lord Glenarthur's side.

'About thirty minutes before the ship is due to cast off. Then make sure we don't see you again, unless it's in Belfast.'

—◦—

Don Pedro stood at the back of the crowd and watched as a car he recognized came to a halt some distance from the ship.

He wasn't surprised to see that this particular chauffeur didn't get out when a couple of porters appeared from nowhere, opened the boot and unloaded a large trunk on to a trolley, and began to wheel it slowly towards the ship. Two men, one elderly and one in his thirties, stepped out of the back of the car. The older man, whom Don Pedro had never seen before, supervised the unloading of the luggage, while chatting to the porters. Don Pedro looked round for the other man, but he had already disappeared into the crowd.

Moments later the car swung round and drove away. Chauffeurs usually open the back door for their passengers, assist with the unloading of luggage, then await further instructions. Not this one, who clearly didn't want to hang around long enough to be recognized, especially with such a large police presence on the quayside.

Don Pedro felt sure that whatever the IRA had planned, it was more likely to take place during the voyage than before the *Buckingham* had set sail. Once the car had disappeared, Don Pedro joined a long queue and waited for a taxi. He no longer had a driver or car. He was still smarting at the price he'd been paid for the Rolls-Royce after insisting on cash.

Eventually he reached the front of the queue and asked the cabbie to take him to Temple Meads station. On the train back to Paddington, he mulled over what he'd planned for the next day. He had no intention of paying the second instalment of £250,000, not least because he didn't have the money. He still had just over £23,000 in the safe, and another four thousand from the sale of the Rolls. He thought that if he could get out of London before the IRA had fulfilled their part of the bargain, they weren't likely to follow him to Buenos Aires.

—◦—

'Was it him?' asked the colonel.

'Might have been, but I can't be sure,' Hartley replied. 'There are a lot of chauffeurs in peaked caps and dark glasses today, and by the time I got close enough to have a good look, he was already heading back towards the gate.'

'Did you see who he was dropping off?'

'Look around, sir, it could be any one of the hundreds of passengers boarding the ship,' said Hartley, as someone brushed past the colonel.

'I'm so sorry,' said Lord Glenarthur, raising his hat and giving the colonel a smile before he walked up the passenger ramp and boarded the ship.

—◇—

'Great cabin,' said Sam as she came out of the shower wrapped in a towel. 'They've thought of everything a girl needs.'

'That's because my mother will have inspected every room.'

'Every one?' said Sam in disbelief.

'You'd better believe it. It's just a pity she hasn't thought about everything a boy needs.'

'What else could you possibly want?'

'A double bed, to start with. Don't you think it's a bit early in our relationship to be sleeping in separate beds?'

'Stop being so feeble, Seb, just push them together.'

'I wish it was that easy, but they're bolted to the floor.'

'Then why don't you take the mattresses off,' she said, speaking very slowly, 'put them next to each other, and we'll sleep on the floor.'

'I've already tried that, and there's barely enough room to fit one on the floor, let alone two.'

'If only you earned enough for us to have a first-class cabin, it wouldn't be a problem,' she said with an exaggerated sigh.

'By the time I can afford that, we probably will be sleeping in separate beds.'

'Not a chance,' said Sam as her towel fell to the floor.

—◇—

'Good evening, my lord, my name is Braithwaite, and I'm the senior steward on this deck. Can I say what a pleasure it is to have you on board. If there's anything you need, night or day, just pick up the phone and dial one hundred, and someone will come immediately.'

'Thank you, Braithwaite.'

'Would you like me to unpack your suitcases while you're at dinner, my lord?'

'No, that's very kind of you, but I've had a rather tiring journey down from Scotland, so I think I'll rest and probably skip dinner.'

'As you wish, my lord.'

'In fact,' said Lord Glenarthur, extracting a five-pound note from his wallet, 'can you make sure I'm not disturbed before seven tomorrow morning, when I'd like a cup of tea and some toast and marmalade?'

'Brown or white, my lord?'

'Brown will be just fine, Braithwaite.'

'I'll put the *Do not disturb* sign on your door and leave you to rest. Good night, my lord.'

◄○►

The four of them met in the ship's chapel soon after they'd checked into their cabins.

'I don't imagine we'll be getting a lot of sleep for the next few days,' said Scott-Hopkins. 'After spotting that car, we have to assume there's an IRA cell on board.'

'Why would the IRA be interested in the *Buckingham*, when they've got enough troubles of their own at home?' asked Corporal Crann.

'Because if they could pull off a coup like sinking the *Buckingham*, it would take everyone's minds off those troubles at home.'

'Surely you don't think—' began Hartley.

'Always best to expect the worst-case scenario, and assume that's what they have in mind.'

'Where would they get the money to fund an operation like that?'

'From the man you spotted standing on the dockside.'

'But he didn't come on board, and took the train straight back to London,' said Roberts.

'Would you come on board if you knew what they had planned?'

'If he's only interested in the Barrington and Clifton families, that at least narrows down the target, because they're all on the same deck.'

'Not true,' said Roberts. 'Sebastian Clifton and his girlfriend are in cabin 728. They could also be a target.'

'I don't think so,' said the colonel. 'If the IRA were to kill the daughter of an American diplomat, you can be sure that any funds coming out of the States would dry up overnight. I think we should concentrate on those first-class cabins on deck one, because if they managed to kill Mrs Clifton along with one or two other members of her family, the *Buckingham* would not only be making its maiden voyage, but its final voyage. With that in mind,' continued the colonel, 'for the remainder of the trip we'll carry out a four-hour shift patrol. Hartley, you cover the first-class cabins until two a.m. I'll take over from you then, and wake you just before six. Crann and Roberts can cover the same watches in cabin class, because that's where I think we'll find the cell is located.'

'How many are we looking for?' asked Crann.

'They'll have at least three or four operatives on board, posing as either passengers or crew members. So if you spot anyone you've ever seen on the streets of Northern Ireland, it won't be a coincidence. And make sure I'm briefed immediately. Which reminds me, did you find out the names of the passengers who booked the last two first-class cabins on number-one deck?'

'Yes, sir,' said Hartley. 'Mr and Mrs Asprey, cabin five.'

'The shop I won't allow my wife to enter, unless it's with another man.'

'And Lord Glenarthur is in cabin three. I looked him up in *Who's Who*. He's eighty-four, and was married to the sister of Lord Harvey, so must be the chairman's great-uncle.'

'Why has he got a *Do not disturb* sign on his door?' asked the colonel.

'He told the steward he was exhausted after the long journey from Scotland.'

'Did he now?' said the colonel. 'Still, we'd better keep an eye on him, although I can't imagine what use the IRA would have for an eighty-four-year-old.'

The door opened, and they all looked around to see the chaplain enter. He smiled warmly at the four men, who were on their knees holding prayer books.

'Can I be of any assistance?' he asked as he walked up the aisle towards them.

'No, thank you, padre,' said the colonel. 'We were just leaving.'

47

'AM I EXPECTED to wear a dinner jacket tonight?' asked Harry after he'd finished unpacking.

'No. The dress code is always informal on the first and last nights.'

'And what does that mean, because it seems to change with each generation.'

'For you, a suit and tie.'

'Will anyone be joining us for dinner?' asked Harry as he took his only suit out of the wardrobe.

'Giles, Seb and Sam, so it's just family.'

'So is Sam now considered family?'

'Seb seems to think so.'

'Then he's a lucky boy. Although I must confess I'm looking forward to getting to know Bob Bingham better. I hope we'll have dinner with him and his wife one evening. What's her name?'

'Priscilla. But be warned, they couldn't be more different.'

'What do you mean?'

'I won't say anything until you've met her, and then you can judge for yourself.'

'Sounds intriguing, although "be warned" has to be a clue. In any case, I've already decided that Bob is going to fill several pages of my next book.'

'As a hero or a villain?'

'Haven't decided yet.'

'What's the theme?' asked Emma as she opened the wardrobe.

'William Warwick and his wife are on holiday aboard a luxury liner.'

'And who murders who?'

'The poor downtrodden husband of the chairman of the shipping line murders his wife, and runs off with the ship's cook.'

'But William Warwick would solve the crime long before they reached port, and the wicked husband would spend the rest of his life in jail.'

'No he wouldn't,' said Harry as he selected which of his two ties he would wear for dinner. 'Warwick has no authority to arrest him on board ship, so the husband gets away with it.'

'But if it was an English vessel, her husband would be subject to English law.'

'Ah, there's the twist. For tax reasons the ship sails under a flag of convenience, Liberia in this case, so all he has to do is bribe the local police chief and the case never gets to court.'

'Brilliant,' said Emma. 'Why didn't I think of that? It would solve all my problems.'

'You think that if I murdered you, it would solve all your problems?'

'No, you idiot. But not having to pay any tax might. I think I'll put you on the board.'

'If you did that, I would murder you,' said Harry, taking her in his arms.

'A flag of convenience,' repeated Emma. 'I wonder how the board would react to that idea?' She took two dresses out of the cupboard and held them up. 'Which one, the red or the black?'

'I thought you said it was casual tonight.'

'For the chairman, it's never casual,' she said as they heard a knock.

'Of course it isn't,' said Harry. He walked across to open the door and was greeted by the senior steward.

'Good evening, sir. Her Majesty Queen Elizabeth the Queen Mother has sent flowers for the chairman,' said Braithwaite, as if it happened every day.

'Lilies no doubt,' said Harry.

'How did you know that?' asked Emma as a heavily built young man entered the room carrying a large vase of lilies.

'The first flowers the Duke of York gave her, long before she became Queen.'

'Would you put them on the table in the centre of the cabin,' Emma said to the young man as she looked at the card that had come with the flowers. She was about to thank him, but he'd already left.

'What does the card say?' asked Harry.

'Thank you for a memorable day in Bristol. I do hope my second home has a successful maiden voyage.'

'What an old pro,' said Harry.

'Very thoughtful of her,' said Emma. 'I don't suppose the flowers will last much beyond New York, Braithwaite, but I'd like to keep the vase. A sort of keepsake.'

'I could replace the lilies while you're ashore in New York, chairman.'

'That's very thoughtful of you, Braithwaite. Thank you.'

◄○►

'Emma tells me you want to be the next chairman of the board,' said Giles, taking a seat at the bar.

'Which board did she have in mind?' asked Sebastian.

'I presumed Barrington's.'

'No, I think Mother still has a few gallons left in the tank. But if she asked me, I might consider joining the board.'

'That's most considerate of you,' said Giles as the barman placed a whisky and soda in front of him.

'No, I'm more interested in Farthings.'

'Don't you think twenty-four is perhaps a little young to be chairman of a bank?'

'You're probably right, which is why I'm trying to persuade Mr Hardcastle not to retire before he's seventy.'

'But you'd still only be twenty-nine.'

'That's four years older than you were when you first entered Parliament.'

'True, but I didn't become a minister until I was forty-four.'

'Only because you joined the wrong party.'

Giles laughed. 'Perhaps you'll end up in the House one day, Seb?'

'If I do, Uncle Giles, you'll have to look across the floor if you hope to see me, because I'll be sitting on the benches opposite. And in any case, I intend to make my fortune before I consider climbing that particular greasy pole.'

'And who is this beautiful creature?' asked Giles, climbing off his stool as Sam joined them.

'This is my girlfriend, Sam,' said Sebastian, unable to mask his pride.

'You could have done better,' Giles said, smiling at her.

'I know,' said Sam, 'but a poor immigrant girl can't be too fussy.'

'You're American,' said Giles.

'Yes. I think you know my father, Patrick Sullivan.'

'I do indeed know Pat, and I hold him in the highest regard. In fact, I've always thought that London is nothing more than a stepping stone in his already glittering career.'

'That's exactly how I feel about Sebastian,' said Sam, taking his hand. Giles laughed as Emma and Harry walked into the grill room.

'What's the joke?' asked Emma.

'Sam has just put your son properly in his place. *I could marry this wench for this device*,' said Giles, giving Sam a bow.

'Oh, I don't think Sebastian is at all like Sir Toby Belch,' said Sam. 'Come to think of it, he's like Sebastian.'

'*So too could I*,' said Emma.

'No,' said Harry. '*So could I too. And ask no other dowry with her, but such another jest.*'

'I'm lost,' said Sebastian.

'As I said, Sam, you could have done better. But I'm sure you'll explain it to Seb later. By the way, Emma,' said Giles, 'knockout dress. Red suits you.'

'Thank you, Giles. I'll be wearing blue tomorrow, when you'll have to think of another line.'

'Can I get you a drink, chairman?' teased Harry, who was desperate for a gin and tonic.

'No thank you, darling. I'm famished, so why don't we go and sit down.'

Giles winked at Harry. 'I did warn you when we were twelve to avoid the women, but you chose to ignore my advice.'

As they made their way to a table in the centre of the room, Emma stopped to chat to Ross and Jean Buchanan. 'I see you got your wife back, Ross, but what about your car?'

'By the time I went back to Edinburgh a few days later,' said Ross, rising from his place, 'it was locked up in a police pound. It cost me a fortune to retrieve it.'

'Not as much as these,' said Jean, touching a string of pearls.

'A get-me-off-the-hook present,' explained Ross.

'And you got the company off the hook at the same time,' said Emma, 'for which we'll always be grateful.'

'Don't thank me,' said Ross, 'thank Cedric.'

'I wish he'd felt able to come on the voyage,' said Emma.

'Were you hoping for a boy or a girl?' asked Sam as the head waiter pulled back a chair for her.

'I didn't give Gwyneth a choice,' said Giles. 'Told her it had to be a boy.'

'Why?'

'For purely practical reasons. A girl can't inherit the family title. In England, everything has to pass through the male line.'

'How archaic,' said Sam. 'And I always thought of the British as being such a civilized race.'

'Not when it comes to primogeniture,' said Giles. The three men rose from their seats as Emma arrived at the table.

'But Mrs Clifton is chairman of the board of Barrington's.'

'And we have a queen on the throne. But don't worry, Sam, we'll defeat those old reactionaries in the end.'

'Not if my party gets back into power,' said Sebastian.

'When the dinosaurs will be on the roam again,' said Giles, looking at him.

'Who said that?' asked Sam.

'The man who defeated me.'

—◦—

Liam didn't knock on the door, just turned the handle and slipped inside, looking back as he did so to be sure no one had seen him. He didn't want to have to explain what a young man from cabin class was doing in an elderly peer's room at that time of night. Not that anyone would have commented.

'Are we likely to be interrupted?' asked Liam, once he had closed the door.

'No one will disturb us before seven tomorrow morning, and by then there will be nothing left to disturb.'

'Good,' said Liam. He dropped on his knees, unlocked the large trunk, pulled open its lid and studied the complex piece of machinery that had taken him over a month to construct. He spent the next half hour checking that there were no loose wires, that every dial was at its correct setting, and that the clock started at the flick of a switch. Not until he was satisfied that everything was in perfect working order did he get back off his knees.

'It's all ready,' he said. 'When do you want it activated?'

'Three a.m. And I'll need thirty minutes to remove all this,' Glenarthur added, touching his double chin, 'and still have enough time to get to my other cabin.'

Liam returned to the trunk and set the timer for three o'clock. 'All you have to do is flick the switch just before you leave, and double-check that the second hand is moving.'

'So what can go wrong?'

'If the lilies are still in her cabin, nothing. No one on this corridor, and probably no one on the deck below can hope to survive. There's six pounds of dynamite embedded in the earth beneath those flowers, far more than we need, but that way we can be sure of collecting our money.'

'Have you got my key?'

'Yes,' said Liam. 'Cabin 706. You'll find your new passport and ticket under the pillow.'

'Anything else I ought to be worrying about?'

'No. Just make sure the second hand is moving before you leave.'

Glenarthur smiled. 'See you back in Belfast. And if we should end up in the same lifeboat, ignore me.'

Liam nodded, walked across to the door and opened it slowly. He peered out into the corridor. No sign of anyone returning to their cabins from dinner. He walked quickly to the end of the corridor and pushed open a door marked *Only to be used in an emergency*. He closed the door quietly behind him and walked down the noisy metal steps. He didn't pass anyone on the staircase. In about five hours' time, those steps would be crammed with panicking people wondering if the ship had hit an iceberg.

When he reached deck seven, he pushed the emergency door open and checked again. Still no one in sight. He made his way along the narrow corridor and back to his cabin. A few people were returning to their rooms after dinner, but no one showed the slightest interest in him. Over the years, Liam had turned anonymity into an art form. He unlocked the door of his cabin, and once he was inside collapsed on to the bed, job done. He checked his watch: 9.50 p.m. It was going to be a long wait.

◄o►

'Someone slipped into Lord Glenarthur's cabin just after nine,' said Haskins, 'but I haven't seen him come out yet.'

'It could have been the steward.'

'Unlikely, colonel, because there was a *Do not disturb* sign on the door, and anyway, whoever it was didn't knock. In fact, he went in as if it was his own cabin.'

'Then you'd better keep an eye on that door, and if anyone comes out, make sure you don't lose sight of them. I'm going to check on Crann down in cabin class and see if he's got anything to report. If not, I'm going to try and catch a few hours' shut-eye. I'll take over from you at two. If anything happens that you're not sure about, don't hesitate to wake me.'

◄o►

'So what have you got planned for us when we get to New York?' asked Sebastian.

'We'll only be in the Big Apple for thirty-six hours,' replied Sam, 'so we can't afford to waste a moment. In the morning we'll visit the Metropolitan Museum, followed by a brisk walk around Central Park, and then lunch at Sardi's. In the afternoon we'll go on to the Frick, and in the evening Dad's got us a couple of tickets for *Hello, Dolly!* with Carol Channing.'

'So, no time to shop?'

'I'll allow you to walk up and down Fifth Avenue, but only to window-shop. You couldn't even afford a Tiffany's box, let alone what I'd expect you to put in it. But if you want a memento of your visit, we'll head across to Macy's at West Thirty-fourth Street, where you can choose from a thousand items at less than a dollar.'

'Sounds about my expenditure level. By the way, what's the Frick?'

'Your sister's favourite art gallery.'

'But Jessica never visited New York.'

'That wouldn't have stopped her knowing every picture in every room. You'll see her all-time favourite there.'

'Vermeer, *Girl Interrupted At Her Music*.'

'Not bad,' said Sam.

'One more question before I switch the light off. Who is Sebastian?'

'He's not Viola.'

◄○►

'Sam's quite something, isn't she?' said Emma as she and Harry left the grill room and walked back up the grand staircase to their cabin on the premier deck.

'And Seb can thank Jessica for that,' said Harry as he took her hand.

'I wish she was with us on this trip. By now she would have drawn everyone, from the captain on the bridge, to Braithwaite serving afternoon tea, and even Perseus.'

Harry frowned as they walked silently down the corridor

together. Not a day went by when he didn't reproach himself for not having told Jessica the truth about who her father was.

'Have you come across the gentleman in cabin three?' asked Emma, breaking into his thoughts.

'Lord Glenarthur? No, but I saw his name on the passenger list.'

'Could he be the same Lord Glenarthur who was married to my great-aunt Isobel?'

'Possibly. We met him once when we stayed at your grandfather's castle in Scotland. Such a gentle man. He must be well over eighty by now.'

'I wonder why he decided to come on the maiden voyage and not let us know?'

'He probably didn't want to bother you. Let's invite him to dinner tomorrow night. After all, he's the last link with that generation.'

'Nice idea, my darling,' said Emma. 'I'll write him a note and slip it under his door first thing in the morning.' Harry unlocked the cabin door and stood aside to let her in.

'I'm exhausted,' said Emma, bending down to smell the lilies. 'I don't know how the Queen Mother manages it day in and day out.'

'It's what she does, and she's good at it, but I bet she'd be exhausted if she tried a few days of being chairman of Barrington's.'

'I'd still rather have my job than hers,' said Emma as she stepped out of her dress, and hung it up in the wardrobe before disappearing into the bathroom.

Harry read the card from HRH the Queen Mother once again. Such a personal message. Emma had already decided to put the vase in her office when they got back to Bristol, and to fill it with lilies every Monday morning. Harry smiled. And why not?

When Emma came out of the bathroom, Harry took her place and closed the door behind him. She slipped off her dressing gown and climbed into bed, far too tired even to consider reading a few pages of *The Spy Who Came In From The Cold*, by a new author Harry had recommended. She switched off the light by the side of her bed and said, 'Goodnight, darling,' even though she knew Harry couldn't hear her.

By the time Harry came out of the bathroom, she was sound asleep. He tucked her in as if she were a child, kissed her on the forehead and whispered, 'Goodnight, my darling,' then climbed into his bed, amused by her gentle purr. He would never have dreamed of suggesting that she snored.

He lay awake, so proud of her. The launch couldn't have gone better. He turned on his side, assuming he'd drift off within moments but, although his eyes were leaden and he felt exhausted, he couldn't get to sleep. Something wasn't right.

48

DON PEDRO rose just after two, and not because he couldn't sleep.

Once he'd dressed, he packed an overnight bag and went downstairs to his study. He opened the safe, took out the remaining £23,645 and put it in the bag. The bank now owned the house and all its contents, as well as the fixtures and fittings. If they hoped he was going to repay the rest of the overdraft, Mr Ledbury was welcome to make a trip to Buenos Aires where he would receive a two-word response.

He listened to the early morning news on the radio, and there was no mention of the *Buckingham* in the headlines. He was confident that he could slip out of the country long before they realized he'd gone. He glanced out of the window, and cursed when he saw the relentless rain bouncing off the pavement, fearing that it might be some time before he was able to find a taxi.

He switched off the lights, stepped outside and closed the door of number 44 Eaton Square for the last time. He looked up and down the road, not at all optimistic, and was delighted when he saw a taxi that had just switched on its *For Hire* sign, heading towards him. Don Pedro raised an arm, ran out into the rain and jumped into the back of the cab. As he pulled the door closed he heard a click.

'London Airport,' said Don Pedro, sinking into the back seat.
'I don't think so,' said the chauffeur.

—◦—

Another man, just two cabins along from Harry, was also wide awake, but then, he wasn't trying to get to sleep. He was just about to go to work.

He climbed off his bed at 2.59 a.m., fully rested, fully alert, walked over to the large trunk in the middle of the cabin and lifted its lid. He hesitated for only a moment, then as instructed he flicked the switch, setting in motion a process from which there could be no turning back. After making sure that the large black second hand was moving, 29:59, 29:58, he pressed a button on the side of his watch and lowered the lid of the trunk. He then picked up the small carrier bag by his bed that contained everything he needed, turned off the light, opened the cabin door slowly and stared out into the dimly lit corridor. He waited for a moment until his eyes were focused. When he was certain there was no one around, he stepped into the corridor and quietly closed the door.

He placed a foot gingerly on to the thick, royal blue carpet and padded silently down the corridor, ears attuned for the slightest unfamiliar sound. But he heard nothing other than the gentle rhythm of the engine as the ship ploughed steadily through still waters. He stopped when he came to the top of the grand staircase. The light was a little brighter on the stairs, but there was still no one to be seen. He knew the first-class lounge was one deck below, and in its far corner was a discreet sign: *Gentlemen.*

No one passed him as he made his way down the grand staircase, but when he entered the lounge he immediately saw a heavily built man slumped in a comfortable chair, legs askew, looking as if he had taken full advantage of the free alcohol on offer to first-class passengers on the first night of the maiden voyage.

He crept past the dormant passenger, who was snoring contentedly, but didn't stir, and continued towards the sign on the far side of the room. As he walked into the lavatory – he was even beginning to think like them – a light came on, which took him by surprise. He hesitated for a moment, then remembered it was just another of the ship's proud innovations that he'd read about in the glossy brochure. He crossed to the washbasins and placed his carrier bag on the marble top, unzipped it, and began to take out the various lotions, potions and accessories that would remove his alter-ego: a bottle of oil, a cut-throat razor, a pair of scissors, a comb and a pot of Pond's face cream would all contribute to bringing down the curtain on his opening-night performance.

He checked his watch. He still had twenty-seven minutes and three seconds before another curtain would rise, and, by then, he would just be part of a panicking crowd. He unscrewed the top of the bottle of oil and dabbed it on his face, neck and forehead. After a few moments he felt the burning sensation that the make-up artist had warned him about. He slowly removed the grey balding hairpiece and placed it on the side of the wash-basin, pausing to look at himself in the mirror, pleased to be reunited with his thick, red, wavy hair. Next he peeled off the wine-flushed cheeks, as if he was removing a plaster from a wound that had recently healed, and finally, with the help of the scissors, he cut into the double chin that the make-up artist had been so proud of.

He filled the basin with warm water and scrubbed his face, removing any signs of scar tissue, glue or colouring that remained obstinately in place. After he'd dried his face, the skin still felt a little rough in places, so he applied a layer of Pond's cold cream to complete the transformation.

Liam Doherty looked at himself in the mirror to see that he had shed fifty years in less than twenty minutes; every woman's dream. He picked up his comb, restored his red quiff and then placed what was left of Lord Glenarthur's visage into the bag and set about removing his lordship's apparel.

He began by unfastening the stud on the stiff Van Heusen white collar, which had left a thin red line around his neck, yanked off the Old Etonian tie and dropped them into the bag. He replaced the white silk shirt with a grey cotton one and a thin string tie that all the lads on the Falls Road were now wearing. He slipped off his yellow braces, allowing the baggy grey trousers to fall in a heap on the floor, along with his stomach – a cushion – then bent down and untied the laces on Glenarthur's black leather brogues, kicked them off and put them in the bag. He took out a pair of the latest slim-fitting drainpipe trousers and couldn't help smiling as he pulled them on; no braces, just a thin leather belt he'd picked up in Carnaby Street when he was in London on another job. Finally he slipped his feet into a pair of brown suede loafers that would never have trodden a first-class carpet. He looked in the mirror, and saw himself.

Doherty checked his watch. He had eleven minutes and forty-one seconds left before he had to reach the safe haven of his new cabin. No time to waste, because if the bomb went off while he was still in first class, there would only be one suspect.

He stuffed all of the lotions and potions back into his bag, zipped it up and hurried across to the door, opened it cautiously and peered out into the lounge. No one to be seen in either direction. Even the drunken man had disappeared. He strode quickly past the empty chair where only the deep imprint of a body remained to suggest that someone had recently been there.

Doherty hurried across the lounge to the grand staircase; a second-class passenger in first-class surroundings. He didn't stop until he reached the third deck landing, the demarcation zone. When he climbed over the red chain that divided the officers from the other ranks, he relaxed for the first time; not yet safe, but certainly out of the combat zone. He stepped on to a green cord carpet and jogged down a narrower staircase for four more flights, until he reached the deck where his other cabin awaited him.

He went in search of cabin 706. He had just passed 726 and 724 when he spotted an early morning reveller trying to place a key in a lock without much success. Was it even the man's own cabin? Doherty turned his head away as he walked past him, not that the reveller would have been able to identify him or anyone else when the alarm went off.

When he reached cabin 706 he unlocked the door and stepped inside. He checked his watch: seven minutes and forty-three seconds before everyone would be woken, however deeply they were sleeping. He walked across to his bunk and lifted the pillow to find an unused passport and a new ticket that trans-formed him from Lord Glenarthur to Dave Roscoe, 47 Napier Drive, Watford. Occupation: painter and decorator.

He collapsed on to the bunk and glanced at his watch: six minutes and nineteen seconds, eighteen, seventeen; more than enough time. Three of his mates would also be wide awake wait-ing, but they wouldn't speak to each other again until they all met up at the Volunteer on the Falls Road to enjoy several pints of Guinness. They would never talk in public about tonight, because their absence from their usual haunts in west Belfast would have been noted and make them suspects for months, probably years to come. He heard a loud thump on a door further down the corridor, and assumed the reveller had finally given in.

Six minutes and twenty-one seconds . . .

Always the same anxieties whenever you have to wait. Had you left any clues that would lead straight to you? Had you made any mistakes that would cause the operation to end in failure and make you a laughing stock back home? He wouldn't relax until he was on a lifeboat and, better still, on another ship heading towards another port.

Five minutes and fourteen seconds . . .

He knew his compatriots, soldiers in the same cause, would be just as nervous as he was. The waiting was always the worst part, out of your control, no longer anything you could do.

Four minutes and eleven seconds . . .

Worse than a football match when you're one–nil up but you know the other side are stronger and well capable of scoring in injury time. He recalled his area commander's instructions: when the alarm goes off, be sure you're among the first on deck, and the first in the lifeboats, because by this time tomorrow, they'll be searching for anyone under the age of thirty-five with an Irish accent, so keep your mouths shut, boys.

Three minutes and forty seconds . . . thirty-nine . . .

He stared at the cabin door and imagined the worst that could possibly happen. The bomb wouldn't go off, the door would burst open and a dozen police thugs, possibly more, would come charging in, batons flailing in every direction, not caring how many times they hit you. But all he could hear was the rhythmical pounding of the engine as the *Buckingham* continued its sedate passage across the Atlantic on its way to New York. A city it would never reach.

Two minutes and thirty-four seconds . . . thirty-three . . .

He began to imagine what it would be like once he was back on the Falls Road. Young lads in short trousers would look up in awe as he passed them on the street, their only ambition to be like him when they grew up. The hero who had blown up the *Buckingham* only a few weeks after it had been named by the Queen Mother. No mention of innocent lives lost; there are no innocent lives when you believe in a cause. In fact, he'd never meet any of the passengers in the cabins on the upper decks. He would read all about them in tomorrow's papers, and if he'd done his job properly there would be no mention of his name.

One minute and twenty-two seconds . . . twenty-one . . .

What could possibly go wrong now? Would the device, constructed in an upstairs bedroom on the Dungannon estate, let him down at the last minute? Was he about to suffer the silence of failure?

Sixty seconds . . .

He began to whisper each number.

'Fifty-nine, fifty-eight, fifty-seven, fifty-six . . .'

Had the drunken man slumped in the chair in the lounge been waiting for him all the time? Were they now on the way to his cabin?

'Forty-nine, forty-eight, forty-seven, forty-six . . .'

Had the lilies been replaced, thrown out, taken away? Perhaps Mrs Clifton was allergic to pollen?

'Thirty-nine, thirty-eight, thirty-seven, thirty-six . . .'

Had they unlocked Lord Glenarthur's room and found the open trunk?

'Twenty-nine, twenty-eight, twenty-seven, twenty-six . . .'

Were they already searching the ship for the man who'd slipped out of the toilet in the first-class lounge?

'Nineteen, eighteen, seventeen, sixteen . . .'

Had they . . . he clung to the edge of the bunk, closed his eyes and began counting out loud.

'Nine, eight, seven, six, five, four, three, two, one . . .'

He stopped counting and opened his eyes. Nothing. Just the eerie silence that always follows failure. He bowed his head and prayed to a God he did not believe in, and immediately there followed an explosion of such ferocity that he was thrown against the cabin wall like a leaf in a storm. He staggered to his feet and smiled when he heard the screaming. He could only wonder how many passengers on the upper deck could possibly have survived.